THE RUN

Jim Reay

The Rams Skull Press

Published by The Rams Skull Press, Esk, Queensland in 2016

Disclaimer
All characters and events in this publication, other than those clearly in the public domain, are fictitious and any resemblance to real persons, living or dead, is purely coincidental.

National Library of Australia Cataloguing-in-Publication entry:

Creator	Reay, Jim E. – author
Title	The Run / by Jim E. Reay
ISBN	9781875872916 (paperback)
Subjects	Espionage – Fiction
	Suspense fiction
	Spy stories

Dewey No. A823.4

Edited by Patrice Shaw (www.psediting.com.au)
Typesetting and cover design by Kirsty Ogden
(www.epiphanyediting.com.au)

Printed in Australia by SOS Print + Media, Sydney, Australia

Published and distributed in Australia by The Rams Skull Press
PO Box 5206, Brassall, Queensland, 4305
Website: http://ramsskullpress.com

Solitudinem faciunt, pacem appellant

Roughly translated as

They (the Romans) make a wasteland and call it peace.

Roman Historian, Tacitus, in
De vita et moribus Iulii Agricolae AD 98

Europe and the Middle East

Acknowledgements

I would like to thank many people who have helped to bring this story to publication stage.

The Queensland Writers' Centre gave me the initial courses, master classes and encouragement to develop the craft of the writer.

My editor, Patrice Shaw, has the happy knack of asking the right questions about my intent in the story, with her perceptive structural and copy editing.

Kirsty Ogden has produced the eye-catching cover design and the page-layout so that the story presents clearly.

Over the years, I have had many friends in writing groups who have read and commented on my stories.

Thanks to Deb and Dave Edwards from Rams Skull Press. They gave me my start in publication and have stayed loyally with me ever since. They are good people who are keen to support Australian writers. I am honoured to be one of them.

My brother, Lewis, reads all my stories in draft form. He has many insights – as brothers often do – and a marvellous eye for breaches of continuity and logical anomalies.

My wife, Brenda, and my extended family have been very generous in giving me the time and space to get my stories down onto the page.

Finally to you, the readers and those who access my website, I really appreciate your support, that you read the books and give me such positive feedback. To all of you, please accept my thanks.

www.jimreaywriter.net

Chapter 1

He isn't big.

The kerosene glow of the shaded hurricane lamp glistens off his waders and the open oilskin coat. It floods upwards from the smooth beach stones to highlight his face. With his back to the darkness of the land, he looks young for his years ... and for the power he wields.

'I hope,' his lilting voice breathes the words out slowly, almost cheekily, 'that I am not too much of a disappointment to you.' Beneath his mop of curly locks, he watches the woman – newly-arrived on the shore – and waits with a quizzical gaze for her response.

She gulps ... as if her throat is too dry to speak and flicks a glance at the sound of a gull, suddenly shrieking through the night sky. It soars ghost-like into the inky void, heading towards the dull shapes of the dunes to the north.

Time seems to have slowed.

With her goosebumps prickling, the woman senses the cold Atlantic waves beating their gentle rhythm behind her. She listens, detached, to the latest surge of water swooshing off the rocks and rattling up the shingle beach ... appearing to reach out for her ... only to recoil, as if frightened by the scene just glimpsed so briefly.

A seaweed tang fills her nostrils. She adjusts her beret absently over her long auburn hair, and stares at the Irishman, giving her pulse a chance to settle.

1

'Padraic Hennessy, I presume?'

His men scuffle and humph past them, up the loose pebble shore, then over the rocks onto the low mossy pads above the tide line. They carry one after another of the heavy crates brought by the inflatable, from which she has just landed.

The muted navigation lights of the mother fishing boat flicker over the wavelets as it rolls at anchor, forty metres or more out in the bay. Onshore, pencil torch beams show the path of the men, through the gloom, away from the scrunching shingle of the beach and as far as what looks like marram grass hummocks beyond.

The Irishman's cheeks have just started to puff into a grin at her query when a female voice screams – once, only the once – from behind him in the darkened beachhead; followed by the loud crack of a single gunshot slicing through the sleepy night.

Its echo seems to freeze all life into an eerie silence.

Then, as if nothing has happened, the indifferent tramp of steel-tacked waders break the spell, resuming their weary plod up the loose gravel.

Any hint of a smile has dissolved from Hennessy's face. He speaks in barely a whisper. 'These are hard times, Maeve's daughter. Don't be a judge now … until you understand.'

Chapter 2

June, 2013. Rotterdam, The Netherlands

'He'd be well into his seventies today – indeed, nudging eighty. That's if he's still alive.' Sven Gulbrandson strokes his chin, between speaking his doubts. 'And that's a tall order, given the life he's led.'

'True. Very true.' Arthur Blair acknowledges Gulbrandson's point with a tilt of his jaw. 'But Padraic Hennessy was always a survivor and this business has the mark of *The Cat*. The Provisional Irish Republican Army days might be gone but the Hennessys of this world always find a new mudhole to play in. Whoever is doing this is trained in those cold, callous methods. Our initial clues point towards the Mediterranean … and to that particular old Irishman, bizarre as it seems.'

Gulbrandson frowns, giving an unconvinced shake of his head. 'Arthur, I'm wary. You should be too. This brief is so vague – potentially too open-ended, exposing us to public glare. We've always operated on the quiet – behind and beyond the formal rules of national governments; focused on establishing specific valid evidence. You understand that better than any of us. It's been our mantra.'

With a sigh, Blair brushes the back of his fingernails through his greying hair. Facing the picture window which overlooks the roofs and river docks of Rotterdam, he takes in the late afternoon view from their Maasboulevard headquarters. He always likes the muted tones of grey, mauve, blue and red; especially when they are refreshed and glistening after the recent rain.

'Doesn't that burst of fading sunlight just fair lift the colours?' Blair's arm swings across the scene, changing the focus of their talk.

The Swede gives a tolerant grin. His colleague's Scottish dialect still amuses him, even after all the years of working together. Sven is a former Swedish counter-espionage operative. He and Arthur founded IIB – the International Investigations Bureau – in 2004 as an adjunct to the International Courts of Justice, only a few kilometres away in The Hague. Arthur still retains a substantial public reputation there, from his days as a senior prosecutor of *crimes against humanity*.

Blair turns dramatically, with a lawyer's pleading persuasion. 'Sven, it feels so like the *Mediterranean Run* back in the seventies with Bill Maclean and Maureen Jazy.' Gulbrandson gives a shrug as if trying to dismiss names which he knows are important to his partner, Blair, from the past. 'Hennessy was part of that too, latterly,' Blair continues. 'Maclean only died in 2005. We come from the same stock, the same background. I had many chats with him over in London about his espionage days, long before we formed IIB. We covered those *behind the scenes* agendas. There's a synergy, on several levels. Believe me, this is how it worked back then, and it still is now, for those who have enough ice in their veins to bluff and bully at that high level.'

Gulbrandson meets Blair's eyes, patiently acknowledging their shared understanding. Indeed, in this specialist field of international justice, they learned early about the challenges of high-level manipulation. They are only too well aware of the difficulties in collecting court-admissible evidence against criminals who work across international borders using the restrictive rules of legal ethics to their advantage. It was why they had created IIB in the first place.

Sven's eyebrows lift slowly over his cynical smile. 'I have a vague recollection of reading the files about that British spook and his Mediterranean business.'

Blair grins in mock disbelief. 'C'mon. You've always read everything. I know that. Your famed Viking prescience is not some psychic power ... it comes from you scanning every intelligence brief and listening to all the agents' reports for patterns, coincidences ...'

'My point exactly,' Gulbrandson interrupts. 'We are researchers, Arthur, and listeners, first and foremost – establishing initial irrefutable proof to let the national police response teams take over the more public arrests. The chatter we are hearing at the moment is certainly real, but it doesn't give us grounds to move our agents against a geriatric Irishman; that is, if he is still even alive.'

The Scotsman shrugs, as if he has made his point anyway.

The Swede lowers his head into new contemplation.

Eventually, Gulbrandson's expression indicates that he has sorted through more of his mental records. 'Hennessy's mob of vigilantes ... they had a notoriety in their time. Even we, in Sweden's counter-espionage section, had heard of them; a watching brief, of course – just in case they linked with our underworld. But, Arthur, they were just one of many Irish gangs, on both sides, who used all that Ulster pseudo-politics-cum-religion as an excuse to run wild.' He scratches his head as if to jolt a final fact from his memory. 'Didn't they call Padraic, *The Cougar*, back then?'

'They did, Sven. Well remembered. You're good.' Arthur gives an appreciative smile. 'But it was actually a corruption of his Irish Gaelic code name, *An Cogar*, which really means *the whisperer*. He always spoke very quietly – pure danger in a velvet glove; killed with no compunction, for *The Cause*. And now he may be orchestrating his disciples to do the same for current causes.'

Sven stares at the floor again, pondering Arthur's words. 'Perhaps – although I think, perhaps not. I accept your instinct but it's still a hunch, unless we get more to go on.' He lifts his head. 'We have our agents in place: Sam Hall is in Cyprus at this moment checking things out and we have a couple of teams ready to move, if and when needed. As we speak, Emma Jazy is bringing her father, Jacques, from Switzerland to Rotterdam to give us some background insights into the thinking of her late stepsister,

Maureen. The intel from the usual areas of Israel, Palestine and Lebanon shows their accustomed readiness for a fight. Egypt and Libya are still engrossed in their own problems. Syria and Turkey are the hot spots at the moment.'

The Scot interjects, with a throw-away flick of his hand. 'Bloody Arab Spring – social media inciting the mob into a frenzy at past grievances. You can respect their rebellions but there needs to be some thought into what happens after the dust settles. And Egypt could blow again too.'

'Sure. There's tension … more than enough sensation to confuse the world press. But I take it that you think they're all missing a much more dangerous agenda.'

'I do, Sven. Indeed, I do. The sense I have is that Hennessy's main game – if he *is* behind this – is not about feeding the world's media with images of riots. This is much more about the quiet fear that numbs people into compliant silence. Given the phone call to Emma Jazy's father from Hennessy back in 2011 and the *modus operandi* so far, now added to the background gossip about *The Cat*, it smells of the Irish experience. I know he has made no headlines in decades – that is how he works – but he was involved with Gaddafi and he was there in the Yugoslav conflicts. He knows most of the key resistance leaders in the Middle East. I wouldn't be surprised if he has been quietly stoking fires in Pakistan, Iraq and some of these new revolutionary movements throughout the Arab lands.'

Sven Gulbrandson demurs respectfully again. 'But you're working on intuition, Arthur … and that Emma is one of our agents. It's too close. We need accurate independent evidence before we make such leaps into action. Sam is already checking out your hypothesis on the ground. I've no problem with having our agents discreetly in place before any others – happy to foster the illusion of prescience for prospective government customers.' He chortles briefly at their reputation. 'That's why our Bureau is in demand. I'm all for the speculating *but* … we need to separate the espionage noise from the genuine threats, before the firming up of our plan.'

He glances across at his canny partner for a sign of agreement … and sees an almost imperceptible patient nod, before he continues, 'So, I'm across the current dramas in the Mediterranean. Cyprus has been flagged but it's more than that – farther north too, if the chatter is right. Give me some context on this Hennessy character then. What did Maclean tell you about him?'

'Okay.' Arthur gives a conceding nod. 'I'll take you through Maclean's perspective. To do that, I'll need to go back to how Bill and Maureen Jazy met in Lebanon in 1973. But …' he considers for a few seconds '… this business is really niggling me, Sven. I agree with you … it's mainly intuition. But … my gut instinct is that something really big is worrying the European agencies, something much bigger than gangs of thugs.

'I feel it's about Israel, largely because of Hennessy's phone call and Maclean's background. There's *noise* in the Adriatic too, and up through Switzerland; even farther north. It's a sense – an Arctic wind moving over the continent, invisible, but there. That's what the chill felt like during the Irish *Troubles*. I remember it well.'

He sighs in frustration, refocusing his attention. 'Alright. Let me give you the feel for Maclean's world of the early seventies. He was, as you know, a British agent trying to get a handle on the spate of terrorist groups in the Middle East …'

The Swede's phone vibrates. 'Just hold on for a second.' He glances at the small screen. 'Cyprus. I need to check this. Don't lose your thoughts. I'll be back. This might bring some clarity.'

He gives Arthur an encouraging grin as he leaves the room, but the Scotsman is already at the computer screen, face screwed in concentration at the challenge – the bloodhound on a scent, searching for tangible leads around some ethereal threat. Such is the world of IIB.

Chapter 3

June, 2013. Ypsonas, Cyprus

While Sven and Arthur have been discussing his task in Cyprus, Sam Hall has been moving silently through the orange plantation just south of the red-roofed old town of Ypsonas, near the port of Limassol.

The air on the Mediterranean island of Cyprus is dry and warm, even in the early twilight hours. Sam's 185 centimetres is bent over in the stoop of a farm worker. His normally blond hair is dyed brown and the artificial tan merges with rough woollen clothes and cap to produce little more than a shadow under the dark foliage of the sprouting citrus.

He carries no mobile phone, nor identification of his true purpose. This is to be a verbal briefing from a very skittish local network leader speaking to a contact with links to The Hague.

The meeting place is an innocuous break in the fourth line of trees – the irrigation line must have failed at some point and two trees had died. Without the nourishment from the Kouris Dam, none of the lemons, grapefruit, oranges or table grapes would flow from this area to grace the tables of Sweden or the Czech Republic. Water is everything. It has been so, in Cyprus, since the earliest times – tapping wells into the aquifers. Now, in the modern era, a host of dams irrigate the plantations and recharge the summer water courses downstream, as well as catering for the domestic use of expanding cities.

Sam is early. His large frame merges into the shade and he waits, eyes scanning the tree rows, mind floating between an appreciation of the priorities of this ancient island and the word that a man called Nikkos might have information about *The Cat*.

For two days, he has been slipping stealthily through both the Greek and Turkish parts of Cyprus, trying to pick up scant whispered intelligence from nervous informants. He wants confirmation of rumours – some detail to pursue. Certain sources are keen to enlist a perceived association with the International Courts of Justice, but like so many of the other contacts, there has been nothing tangible, until perhaps now. Now, he has the name of Nikkos, who would only meet him in this lonely location.

The word, both in Cyprus and from the analysts in Maasboulevard, is that something big is about to happen in the eastern Mediterranean.

That, in itself, is scarcely surprising. Such has been the history of the area for millennia. The early twentieth century had exacerbated the situation as the colonial powers of the Ottoman Turks, Britain and France played their power games, using the local tribes as foils between the armies of empires. After World War II, the creation of the State of Israel had resulted in the displacement of the resident Arab peoples into the remnants of Palestine and neighbouring countries. Terrorist and military activities had escalated to new levels.

A quiet mewing interrupts Sam's thoughts. Perhaps one of the many roaming wild cats – or maybe something else. He replies with a similar call.

A shape moves to the edge of the break in the orange-tree line. Sam steps out slowly too, so that he can be seen.

Almost as a cough, he growls, '*Echates.*' Cats, in English.

The reply comes, '*Poulia.*' Birds.

'Nikkos?'

'*Nai.*' Yes. 'Sam?'

Sam moves over to the break in the line. The light is fading fast, just enough to see a smaller nuggety man, unshaven, cap, loose jacket – but with careful darting eyes.

'I can speak English. Easier for you. No misunderstanding.'

'Thank you, Nikkos. Please start.'

'My word is that there was a man who came to Nicosia about two months ago – an old man. May still even be here, on the island. We can't confirm. He has met with leaders over a period – men who were brought to see him one at a time; beys, chiefs, sheiks, resistance group leaders. Our watchers didn't understand what they saw – to join the dots, as you say. But, these are very important men, from across the region. All came in quietly … with only their own bodyguards. None together.'

'To talk about?'

Nikkos juggles his hands to convey his doubts. 'Finance. Alliances. Weapons. Attack?'

'Mmm. Against whom?'

'Israel would be one obvious target. But that has not been said – or at least heard, by any of our people. There is great unrest in many Arab lands. No agreement anywhere. The only common enemy has been America, but maybe some European countries too. And there is more. An Arab man, Bashir Dorda, has been found bleeding in a Nicosia street, in the Turkish section, with his tongue cut out and his hands severed. Whoever did it tied tourniquets round his wrists. They intended him to be found in agony but unable to communicate. He died not long after. The word is that he was a spy – an agent, telling tales on the gang. This is retribution … and a message.'

'Where was the Arab man from?'

'Libya, I'm told. If so, probably, he was a gun runner – been happening out of there for decades. He would be part of some new underground movement on our island – from the Turkish side though.' He spits at the ground. 'Not usually seen but very active, by reputation.'

'You say he was an agent. For whom?'

'I can't confirm anything yet – and it seems odd for an Arab – but they say he was being paid by the *Mossad*.'

'An Arab? Working for Israeli Intelligence?'

'People do many things for money, Sam. They would need sources of information like anyone else. Perhaps it was *Mossad* who finished him off. Who could know?'

'Agents are spying and dying all the time. What's so new about this one?'

'The terror. It is new, Sam. There is a fear in so many people. Dorda was not the first, just the worst so far. All very recent. Since the old man arrived, it seems. Bashings, knifings … of innocents. Threatened for information and obedience – not killing, but viciously cruel. It is not just rumour. It is real.' His quick eyes look behind him as if searching for danger. His hands shake involuntarily for a couple of seconds. 'Whoever is planning this has everyone too scared to *not* be in it … and too scared to speak, when they *are* in it.'

'We've had terror before, Nikkos. All these splinter resistance groups have been brutal with informants.'

'Yes, yes. I know. I *live* here.' He gives a sad patient smile, before continuing with urgency … to make the man from Holland understand. 'But this feels different because no-one knows why it happens … or who is doing these terrible things. Not local, or I would know who they are. Not Cypriot, you understand me? And bad news.'

'Worse than the drug cartels?'

'That is my sense.'

'The police?'

'They try, but this is bigger than local police. International. Spies. Agents. And quiet fear, like a blanket of dust over the people.'

Sam nods his acceptance of the information. 'Then you are a brave man for being here. When will it start? And where?'

'It is strange, what we hear. Is to be in many places. Not just an attack on one country or one group. And when? Soon, I think. Weeks, at most.'

'What sort of attack? Infrastructure? Iconic buildings? Planes? People?'

'No word on detail. Only that it will be … big.'

'And why?'

'Why is it always? Payback. Anger. A cause greater than human life. Who knows why? But, in many countries.'

'Why here in Cyprus?'

The Cypriot shrugs.

'Who is the old man, Nikkos?'

'No name. *Cat* is a codename we have heard.'

'*Cat*? That is all? Is he Arab?'

'No. I'm told … European. Could be from anywhere. Even Chechyen and Russians are considered Europe here.'

'The money. From where? Al Qaeda?'

'I hear it is many sources. South America. Lots of cash for causes there and an ongoing market for their drugs. Arab funds too, certainly. Many raise money on the web. All hidden behind disguises.'

'Okay.' Sam slowly absorbs the significance. 'Okay. That is all?' At the Cypriot's nod, he hands over a bundle of notes and a Dutch call-centre contact number for later. '*Efcharisto*. Thank you, Nikkos. Stay low. I will be in touch.'

'You too, Sam. We need the help of The Hague. This very dangerous, I think. I feel it.' He rubs his stubbled chin, gives a semblance of a parting wave and disappears amongst the shadows of the tree line.

* * * *

The scrambled secure line is relayed through a dummy call-centre in Amsterdam to Maasboulevard in Rotterdam.

On it, Sam passes the information from a Cypriot contact. 'Nikkos is worried, Sven, and he's a tough little man. *In many countries,* he is saying. But no detail, just that Bashir Dorda murder. Well beyond the abilities of the local police, he thinks.'

'Mmm. The most concerning aspect for me is that this nameless old man was meeting them, one at a time. Why? What's his game? Is he playing one off against another? If it was for security, wouldn't he just meet them in different cities? Nicosia doesn't even have an international airport anymore, after the UN partition from nearly forty years ago.'

'No answers for that yet but we are here in Cyprus because of the chatter. If Israel is a target, it could be a launching pad for an offensive.'

'But the Israelis would know that too, Sam. They'd pick up any attack in minutes and blow it out of the water or the air.'

'I agree, but that's all we have here at present.'

'Sam, the mention of *The Cat* is intriguing me … and Arthur too. They have nothing more? *The Cat*?'

'So it seems.'

'Okay. Leave it with us. Get back here to Maasboulevard as soon as you can. We have planning to do. That tortured man escalates things.' He pauses, apparently thinking through something. 'Y'know, Arthur might just be onto something with his theory of the old Irish modus operandi revisited.'

'But Nikkos said it would be big, Sven. Not just in *one* place.'

'You're too young to remember the IRA. They hit Britain and all over Europe. Listen for a man called Hennessy.'

Chapter 4

September, 1973. Donegal, Republic of Ireland

At the head of the shingle beach, Maeve's daughter slows almost to a stop as Hennessy guides her by the arm over the rough ground.

As she looks into the wash of light from the hurricane lamp, her hand goes to her mouth in horror.

Two men are progressively shovelling dirt and shingle onto a shallow grave at the start of the marram grass ... but the bare feet and lower legs of a woman still protrude, her shoes tossed aimlessly on top.

Hennessy's voice comes in a whisper. 'At this very moment in Kinnagoe Bay, just up the north Donegal coast from Derry, a couple of hours drive cross-country from here, there are two truckloads of the *Garda* – the Irish police – silently watching the waters, expecting *your* boat to come ashore and for *us* to be meeting with you. This woman passed the story on. If that was where we had been, we would all now be in jail or dead. But we had fed her the line and she sucked on the hook.

'I told her straight,' the matter-of-fact murmured tones continue, 'as we sat in the dunes here waiting for you, facing the *west* Atlantic, not the north. See, we are honest with people. I told her that if the *Garda* arrived at Kinnagoe Bay this evening, then she would be executed as a traitor. And that is exactly what has happened, when the call came through from our spotters ... after a bit of interrogation about her associates, mind you, throughout the afternoon.'

The woman Hennessy is calling *Maeve's daughter*, draws her hand down from her mouth, deliberately looking away from the grave, and she shakes her head slowly. Peering at Hennessy in the darkness, she tries to mouth some words but no sound comes out.

So Hennessy's whisper carries on, as he steers her up towards the dark green van on the dirt road. A truck is just pulling out, loaded with the crates from the inflatable. Two other cars and a farm vehicle are just visible in the gloom.

'You have done well, Maureen. This delivery will make a huge difference to the fight.'

She stops at the car door, her face just inches away from the Irishman. At last, the words spew out, with a pent-up passion in their tone. 'But you will die in this fight, Padraic Hennessy. That is the tragedy of all this. Do you think the British are going to leave? Do you think all of Ulster will up and off to the mainland after four hundred years of settlement?'

His stare lasers through her, as if some terrible heresy has been uttered. There is no smile on his face but the cockiness remains … just in the lifted left brow and the assured twinkle in the eye.

He pauses for several seconds before, 'Now, if I were to agree with you, then we'd both be wrong. Wouldn't we?' His jaw juts with a confident, defiant dare as he continues, but still in the same breathy muttering. 'Yes, I think that the British will go. The soldiers don't strut through Derry and Belfast now like they did before. They scurry around in their armoured tanks. And we pick them off a few at a time. But, even if we don't defeat them in the battle and the politicians have to come up with a solution, we will be negotiating from strength. It will be the hard, brutal edge of breakaway groups like ours that will win the day. The English public don't have the stomach for the body bags coming home. And the Irish Republican Party, *Fainna Fail*, will one day rule all Ireland on the back of our struggle.'

She gazes at him wide-eyed.

He watches her, squinting, checking to see if he has been understood. Still appearing unsure of how to interpret her look, he

15

confronts her, 'You don't believe me, Maeve's daughter? Then I'll walk with you in a couple of days through the Bogside, around the streets of Derry, to see for yourself … into Divis and Ballymurphy in Belfast … you'll see how those *Praatestant baastards* treat us. Like it has been for generations, we have been just dogshit on their shoes.'

'It's not about religion, Padraic. Don't give me that. You all believe in the same God.'

He laughs. 'Yar right, it's not about God. There *is* no God. But it *is* about belief … about marginalising one group and the way they have been treated. Others have used *their* religion to squeeze *us*; because we are not *chosen*, like them.' He pauses and stares at the woman. 'You're sounding awful like an apologist for the other side, Maureen. Hard to believe I'm hearing that from Maeve Gallaher's daughter. She was one of Letterkenny's best … and a lovely woman at that. You are descended from generations of proud tough Republican fighters.'

'Maeve is dead. And I'm here for her … respecting her beliefs, and honouring her ancestry. She was my mother and the cancer took her – six years ago it was. In Switzerland. But you, Padraic Hennessy – you know all of that – and I didn't see *you* coming to visit her when she was sick. Not once, not a peep from you. Not even to her funeral, when I was looking out for you. And you … *you*, my natural father, even though I haven't met you in person until this night. And what a place and a night to meet you it has been.'

'Well, you are feisty at least. Speaks your mind, you do.' Hennessy touches his nose and speaks even quieter. 'Fine, when it is just us together, Maureen; we have things to work through, for all the lost years. But you'd want to be real careful how you speak around others. They'd take you the wrong way.' And he nods back to where the men are returning with shovels from the grave.

Chapter 5

June, 2013. Rotterdam, The Netherlands

'Sam Hall is on his way back from Cyprus now, Arthur,' Sven Gulbrandson says, as he returns to Blair's office-cum-meeting room. 'He'll be here in an hour or so. Our jet has been on standby at the Akrotiri RAF Base. He has some information – maybe the start of something tangible. I think this could be a long night ahead.' He pauses to ensure that he has Arthur Blair's full attention. 'Now, this story about Maureen Jazy and your British spook, Maclean? You'd better give me a bit more than the bare bones. I need to get my own feel for what's missing. Sam's Cyprus contacts are talking of something really big, in *many* countries, and a link to a *cat*. It might just be a bit like *your* gut feeling.'

Arthur Blair gives a mystical smile and a confirming nod. He glances back through the picture window to the early evening dockland lights, which are starting to twinkle at the dusk. 'Well, first of all, Maureen Jazy was actually Maureen Gallaher before her mother, Maeve, married a French-Swiss and they left to live in Montreux. And second of all, Maeve Gallaher was descended from the Letterkenny Gallahers of Donegal, renowned Republican activists. And third of all, when she was seventeen, Maeve fell pregnant to an eighteen-year-old firebrand from Derry called ... Padraic Hennessy. That was 1953. The child was born – but not in Ireland – in Paris.'

Gulbrandson lets out a low whistle as Arthur continues. 'Now there was apparently friction between the families. Maeve headed, or was sent, to Europe; living with distant Gallaher relatives, initially in Paris. They protected her from the shame of an illegitimate birth and gave her space to start a new life as a *young widow*. Parisians are very accepting of such matters. Maureen never took up Hennessy's name and, according to Maclean, she'd never even met him nor spoken to him until she was dropped off in Donegal in 1973 during *The Run* from the Mediterranean.

'Meanwhile, Hennessy had moved up through the ranks of the Republican resistance and by the time *The Troubles* started in Derry with the civil rights march in 1968 and the battle of the Bogside in August 1969, he was a company commander in a fighting group that later morphed into the Provisional IRA. He was well-known for his emotionless ability to maim and kill enemies of his cause. He was especially feared because he never raised his voice – just a quiet whisper and a cold cruelty that scared even much-older activists. By the early seventies, he'd gone freelance; leading his loyal private group. Non-Gaelic speakers heard him being referred to as *An Cogar*, which as you know they interpreted as *Cougar*, and so the group became known to the Royal Ulster Constabulary and the British as *The PIRA Cat Pack*, with Hennessy being branded disrespectfully by them as *That Cat*.'

Sven rises and paces slowly around the office. 'Okay. I get the Irish connection better now. Give me more about Maclean.'

Arthur stretches back in his reclining chair, squeezes his brow as if to extract his memory, and starts on Bill Maclean. 'He was an embassy attaché – a linguist-cum-agent, able to understand Russian, Spanish, Arabic and smatterings of other tongues, but he was born a Scot.' He grins as if claiming some ancestral fame by association. 'He was thirty-four in 1972 when he went to Beirut, really just to listen to the chatter. The rumblings of civil war could be heard in cafes and hotels and, as we all know now, it broke into fifteen years of horrendous killing in 1975.

'Maclean's cover was as a reporter for a London news agency. He filed stories on tourist attractions and social occasions; positive stories – the antithesis of what he was listening for. And in 1973, he bumped into a twenty-year-old Swiss investigative journalist who, despite their differences in age and life experiences, just swept him off his feet.

'She was Maureen Jazy, the illegitimate daughter of Maeve Gallaher and Padraic Hennessy.

'William Maclean was always known as Bill when I was talking to him in the late 1990s and he was still quite emotional about those days back in 73 and 74.'

Gulbrandson continues slowly pacing the office – attentive, poised to find a clue or an error – while Blair rises to collect a digital player and a disc-case from a drawer.

He fiddles a disc into the machine. 'Bill told me his story on tape in a select London club but I've transferred the tapes to digital. Listen to some of it. You'll feel him reliving the times, in his soft Angus accent.'

'Lebanon is slowly recovering from being smashed to ruins in the civil war of 1975 to 1990 and there are still lots of on-going tensions, particularly with Israel, in the years since. But when I was there in 72 to 74, it wasn't like that at all.

'Beirut was still the jewel of the Mediterranean. Its history goes back to Phoenician times when its name meant *the wells*. The Romans took over the area, followed by the Arabs, the Crusaders and then the Turkish Ottoman Empire, which brought us up to World War I. All that diversity of its history is there in the architecture. Such a spectacular city with its views to the west over the blue Mediterranean; picturesque Mount Lebanon overlooking the city; a place of olives, date palms, cedars and bougainvillea blossoms – and it was beautiful for its mix of peoples too: Muslims, Maronites, Phalangists, and the Arab Druze who follow old Egyptian beliefs; and the Palestinian refugees. We had all the major resistance groups too, particularly after 1970 when Jordan expelled the Palestine Liberation Organisation.

'Beirut had every nationality you could imagine. It was thriving, cosmopolitan and a relatively tolerant place – a real-life example of the clichéd melting-pot of peoples; and a centre of learning and intellectual debate from the nineteenth century. Do you get the feel? It was some place. I felt comfortable to move in the cafes, restaurants and hotel foyers, listening to the gossip. I interviewed the occasional person for a report on civic functions or social events. It was a relaxing time. Then, Maureen Jazy came into my life.

'She was a captivating young woman, not tall, with auburn hair and green eyes with a most attractive honey-fleck through them. Hypnotic eyes. But more than her physical charm was her happy interest in me; our ability to have robust debates and still remain friends, soul-mates even. You see, I'd been to lots of countries – places that she wanted to visit, some day. So she laughed and gently seduced me for my opinions, observations and perspectives on my travels.

'For her part, she was a wealth of competing ideologies, but with the emotional ability to accept, analyse and move positions as she absorbed new frames of reference. And, really, she was still a kid, only twenty. But thanks to her very different upbringing, she had a maturity ... a confidence about her. She'd lived at an intellectual level and intensity far greater than most who were decades older.

'I met her in the foyer of the Cavalier Hotel on 22nd February, 1973. I'd been chasing some background on the Israelis shooting down a Libyan airliner over the Sinai Desert on the day before and she was working for the Reuters' agency, out of Zurich. She asked me about how to contact certain Lebanese officials and we got into a discussion of Palestinian refugees and their resistance movements. She was feisty. I liked that.

She usually wore a beret over her long hair – she could have been a Chc Guevara poster girl. And yet, if I started to agree with her arguments about the underprivileged in the camps – and there was a philosophical rigour to her reasoning – she would suddenly start arguing for the Israeli cause. I loved it – the cerebral stimulation.

'And I loved her – so vivacious, energetic, keen to learn – but also with a pain behind her ready laughter – a pain that was hard to understand at that time.

'I'd been in Beirut since 1972 so I offered my local knowledge to show her around. I lived in the Hamra district and so did she, eventually. We went to many news events together and argued about perspectives well into the evening.

'She really swept me off my feet, Arthur, and, although it might've appeared silly for a man of my age at the time, I seemed to be having the same effect on her.

'Maureen was Swiss, from the town of Montreux on Lake Geneva. Her step-father, Jacques Jazy, was a French-Swiss, who ran a small publishing business. He was … is … an avid researcher for social justice causes, particularly trying to challenge what he saw as the super-power agencies vying for control of nations and the minds of the people. That was how Maureen had acquired her encyclopaedic awareness of what she saw as resistance to global manipulation, anywhere in the world. Yet, for all her stepfather's passion for justice, when I eventually met him he was a very serene person – a radical intellectual, to my way of thinking.

'Her mother, Maeve, must have been the fiery one. She was only seventeen years older than Maureen and sadly died from leukaemia back in 67, so we never got the chance to meet. She was Irish, from Eire. From what I gathered from Maureen, she was a strikingly good-looking woman – and was from staunch

Republican stock in Donegal, not the Ulster plantation which she never ever acknowledged as being Irish.

'But, she'd had Maureen as an illegitimate child at seventeen, in a religious family. It was 1953 and attitudes were much stricter then. The family had sent her to relatives in Paris to bring up her child and she immersed herself in the Republican cause from afar, helping with its publications while she lived there. That was where she met the smoothly-handsome thinker, Jacques Jazy, who was trying to make his way as an independent publisher of provocative opinion pieces.

'Anyway, back to Beirut. Maureen had seen me looking intently at the fluster of activities in the foyer of the Cavalier. Clearly, I was a reporter of some sort and she started the conversation. The rest was history. Despite my background in espionage, I only ever presented myself as a journalist for an agency. Somehow we clicked. We laughed and joked, toured through all parts of the city; and then went off to Sidon to Baalbek to Damascus to Jerusalem.

'I fed her a sanitised version of some of my travels round the world and of my upbringing in Dundee – always cautious, despite the joy in my soul. Maureen seemed to accept what I was telling her. At least, I thought so at the time but, perhaps in retrospect … who knows?

'She talked to me often about the conflicting struggles in the Middle East. There was a real dislike for the British ingrained in her psyche. And yet she obviously knew I was Scottish. Figure that. Like I said, she had the ability to imagine being in other people's shoes. But, she spoke passionately about the deception of the Balfour Declaration after World War I, and the selling out of Lawrence of Arabia after he had promised the Arab tribes that they were fighting for their independence if they helped defeat the Turks. All that historical scheming – or at least that perspective of it – seemed to have been internalised in this twenty-year-old woman's thought processes. What an amazingly intelligent person, irrespective of her years. That was an aphrodisiac as much as her looks and laughs.

'Arthur, early 1973 was a blissful time for me … and then I got drawn into *The Run*.'

Sven indicates to pause the recording as he resumes his seat. He taps his nose towards Arthur Blair. 'Mmm. I'm thinking *honey trap*. Wouldn't Maclean be thinking exactly the same?'

'Probably,' agrees Arthur. 'Definitely, in fact. Though my senses tell me he was really smitten with this lady – even till the day he died. But, yes, his training would have been cutting in, urging caution. He wasn't naïve; just caught up in something bigger than himself. As you know and I know, these espionage exploits are never as clean and clear as in the movies and Bill Maclean was a capable agent. But, even he …'

The buzz of the internal phone interrupts their conversation.

As Arthur replaces the receiver, he announces, 'Emma has arrived with her father. This should be interesting.'

Chapter 6

June, 2013. Rotterdam, The Netherlands

The seventy-eight-year-old Jacques Jazy walks slowly, but admirably erect, into the meeting room on Maasboulevard, accompanied by a smiling dark-haired female IIB agent in her late twenties. He supports himself with a black walking stick in his left hand while he extends his right hand towards Blair.

'*Bonjour.* Good to see you again, Arthur. Lovely evening view,' as he takes in the window scene. 'I like these summer solstices. Well, this Hennessy business seems to be developing after all, doesn't it?'

'Indeed. Thank you for coming, Jacques, especially at this unfashionable hour. Much appreciated. Let me introduce you to Sven Gulbrandson, my partner in this Bureau. And,' looking across to the smiling agent, 'thank you, Emma, for bringing your father to Rotterdam.'

As the four settle around the oval walnut table, 'Tea, Jacques?'

'*Merci.* No milk or sugar.'

As tea is poured for each and the Swiss declines the offer of biscuits or fruit, Arthur returns to Jacques Jazy's earlier question, 'Yes, Jacques. I think it could be hotting up now. Sven has some background to this matter, but I think it would be good if you could fill us in from your perspective. Perhaps, start with the phone call in 2011.'

Emma smiles encouragement to the old man and pats the back of his hand.

He nods and speaks quietly with a gentle French intonation. 'The phone call was a surprise. I live in Montreux on Lake Geneva, Sven,' he glances at his new acquaintance, 'as you would be aware. My elder son, Martin, looks after me since my wife, Simone, passed away. She was Emma's mother – and Martin's and William's too – she was my second wife. I was nearly fifty when Emma was born.' He grins discreetly at a recollection. 'You see, I married a lady from Ireland back in 1955. Her name was Maeve Gallaher and she had a daughter, then two years old, called Maureen. They have both passed, years ago. But Maureen's natural father was an Irishman by the name of Padraic Hennessy. I have never met him and have spoken to him only twice on the phone, with the last time being nearly two years ago.

'A man called Michael McSweeney rang our house and said that he was Donnie McSweeney's son, as if that might mean something to us. I had heard the name years before from Maeve so I did know that Donnie McSweeney had been Padraic Hennessy's right-hand man in the late sixties and when he led a breakaway IRA gang during *The Troubles* in the 1970s.

'Anyway, it appeared that Hennessy wanted to speak with me. I assumed that Michael might have been looking after Padraic much as Martin looks after me. We are the same age, you see.

'I said I would speak with him and I listened to the husky whispering voice that had been so much a part of the world of two treasured women in my life. Hennessy said he had been thinking a lot about the past – the fifties and right through to the seventies. He talked of wanting to right some wrongs he had committed. It brought an ironic smile to my face, at the time. He is alleged to have been a multiple murderer and terrorist, but all that has apparently been resolved in the eyes of the world since the Good Friday Peace Agreement of 1998. *D'accord*? You are both following me?'

Sven nods. 'Very clearly, Jacques. *Merci*. Please continue.'

Jacques looks across at his daughter and then resumes. 'It was a surprise because Maeve Gallaher had to leave Letterkenny in Donegal back in 1953 when Hennessy would take no responsibility for the child he had helped to conceive. And, while he might have spoken to Maeve a few times over the years on the phone, his disinterest was a source of real anger for me, early on. Then, when Maureen finally met her father in 1973, I believe she would have had long discussions with him in their months together in Ireland. That would have been interesting because she could fire up for a young one. He wouldn't be left guessing as to her opinions.

'Anyway, back to 2011. I asked him how he might think he could right the wrongs and he spoke about Maureen's passion for resolving the tensions around Palestine, Israel and Lebanon from back in the early seventies. Maeve had always been a staunch advocate for the Irish Republican cause and the Middle East struggles too. Maureen was brought up having discussions over the kitchen table about Ireland, as well as the Middle East – you know, about President Nasser, Egypt, the Suez Canal, Israel, Syria, the French and British, Palestine, refugees and the issues going right back into colonial times. That was actually why Maureen ended up as a reporter in Lebanon – she believed she was carrying on one of her mother's fights.

'So then Hennessy said the strangest thing. *If we could solve the problems of the Middle East, Jacques, would you forgive me for deserting Maeve and Maureen in their time of need?* I was sure he must have been drinking but his whispering voice seemed steady enough.'

Sven's eyebrows rose in surprise. 'How did you answer that one?'

'I told him that he needed to seek forgiveness from his God, not from me. And he replied, *There is no God but you are the last link to that time to ease my conscience.*'

'Ah ha,' interjects Arthur. 'He *did* have a conscience. It comes to them all in time – no matter how cold they seem. That's the justice that *we* can't impose but *they* can't escape.'

Jacques tilts his head in acknowledgement before continuing. 'So I told him just to enjoy his last few years. He owed nothing to me. I had got rid of my anger towards him, years ago.'

'Did that satisfy him?' Sven asks.

'He said he would be in touch.' He gives a wry smile. 'I am still waiting. But Emma, here, who now works with you at the Bureau, has spent much of her adult life doing a lot of what Maureen started out to do.' He turns to defer to his daughter's achievements. 'After studying in Qatar and Jordan, she has used her Arabic to work in many countries; and now she does the same for you.' The proud father indicates with his hand that his daughter should carry on the explanation.

Emma hasn't said a word, out of respect, so far and she takes her cue. 'It was early 2011 when we first heard that two of Gaddafi's female guard platoon had signed up with a mysterious group, potentially terrorist in nature. The rumour was circulating in Jordan and it seemed like a joke at the time … that strong-willed women would just walk out on the self-styled hero of masculinity, with no apparent consequences.'

Sven chortles. 'Maybe they could see the writing on the wall.'

Emma shrugs with a smile. 'Perhaps. But insurrections had been tried and failed badly against Gaddafi before. Anyway, we laughed too, at the time. Then word came about some women from the Gaza Strip of Palestine being signed up to a group calling themselves, *Akhawat*. And a link to cats, which at the time we thought was some female gang allusion to the ancient Egyptian cult of feline worship. But now it appears it may have some connection with Dad's phone call from Hennessy, *The Cat* from back in Ireland. It came through at roughly the same time – as if the two matters could be related. We just wanted to ignore Hennessy's call back then as the ravings of a deranged old man, didn't we, Dad?' She glances at her father. 'A connection just seemed too fanciful for credibility.'

'Back then, it probably would have seemed bizarre,' Arthur agrees. 'But at least, Emma, you did pass the intel through to us, for the record. That was good precautionary procedural work. Well done! That's part of why you are such a good agent. You are smart, perceptive, as well as being action capable. Because, now, they may well indeed turn out to both be linked.'

Emma quietly acknowledges the compliment from the director with a slight nod and smile, as Arthur continues with scarcely a pause.

'Sam Hall has been picking up similar cat rumours in Cyprus, as well as a connection to an old man meeting up with Arab tribal leaders. Sam will be landing back here soon, hopefully within the hour. Do either of you have any idea what the old man might be up to, if it is Hennessy?'

Jacques shrugs as he answers. 'No-one has managed to get even close to solving the Middle East tensions in millennia.' He shrugs while Emma just shakes her head.

'Interesting. Maybe …?' The Swede makes to speak and then …

Jacques taps his stomach. 'May we have a short break, *s'il vous plait*? Not as young as you … and the travelling.'

Emma leads him out to the amenities.

Chapter 7

'Well, I'd never have thought that Maeve's daughter, at twenty years old, would be running guns into the Lebanon.'

Padraic Hennessy's dark eyes stare at the daughter he had fathered but never met. The large peat fire glows in the grate, sending flickers of golden warmth around the white-washed stone kitchen walls. They face each other over the sanded wooden table, nursing enamel mugs of tea and thick fresh-baked slices of bread with cheese.

'So, how *did* you get into that business, Maureen?'

She has scarcely said a word; not as they left the beach – nor on the drive through hedged country roads to the farmhouse, in the dark. And she is not rushing to speak in response to Padraic's quiet questioning. She can hear the sounds of men moving around outside, carrying the crates and muttering in thick accents to each other.

Someone knocks a coded rhythm on the door before a raw-boned hard-faced man in a cap and tweed jacket looks in to tell Padraic that the perimeter is secure and everything is sweet.

'This is Donnie McSweeney, Maureen. My right-hand man.' And then, to the stone-faced man. 'Meet Maeve Gallaher's daughter, Donnie. Fine Letterkenny stock she is from, and there's no doubting it.'

'Hi,' she says quietly as she watches him.

'Hi,' he replies and, with a nod to Padraic. 'I'll be getting on then. Leave you both to it.'

'Not a man of many words is our Donnie,' after the man left, 'but he's the bloke you'd want covering your back. He's keeping us safe from British and *Praatestant* kill squads.'

Maureen shudders, nods and sips her tea.

'So,' repeats Hennessy. 'How come you were smuggling arms to the Palestinians?'

'It's just the way it happened. I'm me mother's daughter ...' an accent remembered from her childhood is infiltrating her speech. '... always willing to support a good cause.'

'Alright. But how did you get on *this Run*? It was a surprise when I was told you were on board.'

'Not as surprised as I was when I heard who we'd be meeting on the beach. They only told me a few metres from landing.'

'So, how *did* you get on this *Run*?'

'The man I'm with was on it. And I am carrying out a promise to Maeve. It is just that it has turned out to be more than I expected.'

'You're not telling me you're disappointed now, are you?'

'No. Not in meeting you. I'm glad for that chance. I had hoped for it ... in time. Still a bit shocked at the murder on the beach.'

'Like I said, don't judge till you understand the facts. No doubt there are those in Lebanon who have to do similar.'

'True, Padraic. No doubt, as you say. But I'm a reporter. Hearing the stories is not quite the same as standing by an open grave with the body still warm.'

Hennessy nods. 'So you are here to support *the cause*, then?'

'That I am. And to see the land of my ancestors.' She pauses as her eyes wander round the kitchen, taking in the old grate and the blackened pots.

She shakes her head as if to clear some thoughts before focusing back onto the quietly-spoken man who is peering patiently at her.

'Heard so much ... but that's not the same as being here. Don't know that I need to see some of those that rejected my mother all those years ago. But yes, I'm here to see what it's all about.'

'This man you were with on the boat. What's he to you?'

'I love him, I think. He's good to be with. He has lived, has views. My Dad likes him.'

Hennessy rails back at the last comment. It is not lost on Maureen.

'Shit, Padraic.' She fires the words out. 'Jacques Jazy looked after Mum and me when you were nowhere to be seen. He's a good man.' She points a fierce finger at him as the next words flow. 'Maeve and I have never faltered from supporting *the cause* – even from overseas. But he is the only Dad I've ever known, *in person*.'

Hennessy's head bows as he gulps loudly and then looks at his fiery-eyed daughter. 'Maureen, I have regretted what happened to Maeve and you, ever since it happened. No excuses. But we were just kids when me and Maeve met. I was just turned eighteen and pedalled my bike to Letterkenny, that's twenty miles each way, just to see her. Maeve Gallaher was the most beautiful girl in the world. We were madly in love … and one thing led to the next. You can know for sure that you were conceived in love.' He gives a wry grin which produces a pursed lip shudder in his daughter. 'Maeve loved me too. We made each other laugh. I thought our lives would be together, forever, back then.'

His eyes pull back from some memory and the expression hardens.

'But sadly, I was a Derry scruff from the Bogside. A Gallaher girl was up the duff. And the daughter of the great Republican patriot, Seamus Gallaher, at that. Ah, the politics of families. Their moral masks came down like a fucken portcullis. I was cut out of all the decisions and Maeve was sent to some distant relatives in Paris. That's why you were born French. Me, I was threatened with hanging, a real hanging from a tree; my family too if I so much as … well, you know.

'Maeve and I spoke a couple of times after, by phone, but by then she had met her Frenchman – and he had all the stability and breeding that I didn't. So I accepted that was the way life was – and had to be. We were nice to each other, even then. We had some quiet contacts after that. Careful like. Always nice. I loved her. Still do.' He winces and pauses to look at his daughter's eyes before continuing. 'I got on with working my way up with the Republicans – not the Letterkenny ones though, I grant you. Although I always showed respect for them, their history, their generations of patriotism – and for them being the family of Maeve. But no, I found my own pathway. That's how it happened. And I'm truly sorry that I was not a real father for you.' He smiles ruefully. 'Mind you, you have turned into a fine woman – and a real stunner, like your mother.'

Maureen Jazy sits, nodding slowly, even managing a slight grin at the compliment as she takes in the story. 'Maeve always spoke well of you to me, Padraic, in private. She talked often about *the cause* but, out of respect for Jacques, your name wasn't raised often in the family – and always about a time gone past, not what you might be doing in the present. I never heard her speak a bad word of you. She probably understood what you have just told me – that you had no say in how it had to pan out. When she raised *Ireland for the Irish*, your presence was always implied, to me. And Jacques was ever the protestor too – but not a fist fighter, more a writer of challenges, a denouncer of injustices – so *your* cause, and many like it, have been part of my very breathing; all my life.'

They sip their tea some more.

'So back to this man you love. He'd be near as old as me, wouldn't he?'

'Yes, he's thirty-five. I've no problem with that. This is a different world from the fifties when you were young. I can't abide most air-headed people my age. That's not the world I grew up in. Mum died when I was fourteen, but we had been discussing the problems of the world – serious discussions – from as young as I could remember. Jacques likes to debate issues too. I had that all through my teens, after Maeve passed, following on with *her* ideas as well as his own. That's a bit different from going out and getting smashed at a party. No, Bill and I get on far better than anyone else I've been with.'

'Ah, Bill ...' Hennessy rubs his stubbly chin for a second or two and then gets up to stoke the peat coals with a poker. As he turns, he asks in his whispery voice, 'And you know he's a British agent?'

'I do.'

He stands motionless, poker still in hand. 'So what are you, a Letterkenny Republican, doing with a fucken British agent?'

'I have brought you the arms that you needed for the fight, have I not?'

'You have. That's true. But at what price?'

'Padraic, I know you see the world as *us* against *them*. Maybe that's the way it is for you here in the Ulster battles. But I don't see people with only white hats and black hats. The world of the Middle East where I live at the moment is nothing like that simple. It's not just Arab against Jew. It's much more complicated and the British, French and Turks were all the main part of creating the mess from their colonial days. *They* were the ones who drew arbitrary lines on the map, just like the six counties here. That was the way of their world back then. *They* made deals and lied and cheated like all people with too much power and too few brains. They presumed to know what was best for the people they had conquered; like it was their birthright to play God.

'But, Padraic, it wasn't Bill Maclean that drew up those boundaries. That was a product of an earlier time – just as the settlement of the Protestants in Ulster was a decision made over four hundred years ago. You can't hold the present people responsible for ancient decisions. None of us can choose when they were born or to whom or even where. Given what you have just told me, you should understand that better than most.'

He grins. 'Passionate words.' His face becomes serious. 'But if the current ones continue to be our enemies, we will hold them to account for bloody sure. And that includes your Bill, if he gets in our path. Just so that there are no misunderstandings down the track.' He says with a nod and touch to his brow. 'He didn't come ashore, your Bill. Why was that?'

'He was only ever in it for *the Run*.' She silently thanks her mother for her quick mind. 'We've done many like this together in the Med, but he understood my need to see this land. He was giving me space to come ashore, without any baggage from his background. I'm able to be here just as me. Like I say, he is a good man.'

Hennessy watches his daughter for a few seconds and then he suddenly relaxes visibly. 'I believe you. It would take a fair bit of courage not to follow you ashore. That's some trust in you ... and care for your welfare.' His head nods slowly. 'Yes, indeed. Especially for a Brit agent. And it seems he hasn't given this *Run* away to his own side. Our spotters would have picked up any movement towards us. The threat is in Kinnagoe Bay, not here.' His eyes stare into the distance for a few reflective seconds. 'So tell me how your Lebanon and Palestine have got so fucked up. The Munich Olympics shone a torch on it, last year. We share with Hamas, Fatah ... all types of Palestinian liberation groups. Are you sure they aren't just fighting to get the Jews out of Israel because they've all been pushed into refugee camps? Isn't their fight just like ours? They've been getting treated like shit.'

Maureen picks up the knife she has been using to cut her cheese and points for emphasis. 'Like I said, life is seldom that simple. I'll talk to you about it, if you are really prepared to listen. But, for me, this is more than an intellectual exercise. There are ways to fix the mistakes of past generations. It's just those who would be the mediators are the very people the Arabs hate – America, Britain, France – none of those colonial power-players is trusted. And it's America and Britain that supported the State of Israel's formation in 1948. How are they ever going to be able to walk in the shoes of people in the Gaza Strip? Solzhenitzen said, *A man who is warm can never understand a man who is cold.* That is a major part of the problem. There is another way.'

'Okay.' His face is serious and attentive. 'So tell me. I'll listen. How can it be done? I'm so proud that you have turned out to be such a savvy, gutsy woman. Who would have thought it?'

34

He is on his feet again, moving over to the fireplace. He watches her quietly for a few seconds, dark eyes thoughtful, as he picks up the dusty poker.

'I can't retrieve the lost years, Maureen, but maybe I can start to make up for it. Tell me your story. We have all night. I'll stoke the fire up a bit more. Are you warm enough?'

Chapter 8

June, 2013. Rotterdam, The Netherlands

'Hi all!' Sam Hall breezes into Arthur Blair's office, taking in the three expectant males faces as he arrives. 'Nikkos has just reported in from Cyprus. I just received his midnight message through the call-centre as I came in.' The owners of the three faces do not speak – their expressions merely change to tolerant smiles. So, Sam continues. 'The person generating all the fear in the network probably has the name, Macan.'

Arthur gazes in amazement at his agent, just returned from RAF Base Akrotiri in Cyprus, still with the dyed hair and deep tan. 'Well, welcome back, Sam, O bearer of news. You've made good time. I'm so pleased that you stopped to draw breath during that.'

With a cheeky expression, Sven Gulbrandson adds, 'I'm just getting used to your new rural look. So, you have a possible name for us? Is that your report?'

Ignoring the jibe, the agent replies, 'The Bureau jet makes a difference. Very fast. Thanks for organising it. No! There's more. The report, I mean. Good of Nikkos to call in so quickly. It's only a few hours since I left him.'

The other man at the oval conference table is Nils Houweling, head of operations at IIB, a forty-year-old systems man from Maastricht, who manages the deployment of agents and researchers as well as overseeing the process for the constant in-flow of intelligence. He smiles a welcome at Sam but says nothing.

Arthur says, 'Emma and her father, Jacques, have arrived here at the Bureau. But he is a bit unwell – needing a night's rest; the travelling. So tell us what you have for us, while we wait.'

Hall continues his information download. 'Nikkos had just got back to his base to hear that Ari, one of his Nicosia team, has got a basic ID for this man. Macan is in his early twenties and is possibly Croatian. Even has a description: dark hair, just under 183 tall, very strong and fit, *no tan* … that stands out in the Mediterranean, cold eyes. An angry man. How's that for an up-to-the-minute report for you all?'

'So? Macan?' Arthur queries, slowly, to calm the energy in his agent's voice. 'That's his first name, surname or a nickname?'

'It's the first name, I believe. Other names are not known yet. But if he is the right person then he is allegedly a torturer, a knife man, and a murderer. According to Nikkos's sources; he has been scaring most people into silence. No details of who has been killed or injured; beyond Bashir Dorda, recently. You've been told about him?' Sam looks at Gulbrandson to verify.

'How do they know he's Croatian?' Arthur quizzes calmly.

'He's been overheard, this Macan. He speaks some English words apparently but very haltingly. He reverts most of the time to what the listeners believe is Croatian.'

'Overheard? By Cypriots? They are *linguists* now?'

Sven adds distractedly, 'Non-British Europeans can follow many languages, Arthur. They are not so insular as some … even on an island.'

Sam shrugs patiently at the banter, before adding, 'They even refine the accent to coastal Croatian. Chew on that detail, as well. I believe that the word, Dubrovnik, has been picked up and relayed on. But then he might just have visited the place or have mentioned it in passing.'

Arthur Blair looks in question at Sam, over to Sven Gulbrandson and Nils Houweling, then back to Sam, before a resigned, 'Okay. We'll take it as a possible line of inquiry – for the moment. Coastal Croatian, then, eh? Interesting. And in his twenties? How does he communicate in Cyprus with their Greek and Turkish communities? And maybe with the north Africans in his gang, if that's where *they* are from?'

'Only needs a translator.' The Swede's distracted tone suggests that his mind is thinking elsewhere.

Nils adds, 'English would be understood by many in Cyprus. It's a former British colony.'

Gulbrandson lifts his eyes and comments with a dismissive shrug. 'I repeat. Don't devalue the ability of islanders to understand multiple languages, my Scottish friend. I wouldn't be at all surprised if Croatian has been heard there on the island, too. Perhaps they might actually even *know* what dialect they're hearing – they are not stupid. They had sophisticated trading civilisations long before any of us. Any leads are possibles at this stage.' He grins pointedly, to defuse any affront.

'Fear is a great communicator too,' Sam Hall adds quickly.

'Indeed,' Arthur agrees with a chastened frown and turns to his operations manager. 'Nils, what is your pragmatic rebuttal?'

Houweling's eyes show his usual patient cynicism. 'Croatian is a very definitive description. Too much so, without more corroboration; for me, at least. How different is Croatian from Serbian or Bosnian? As I understand it, the differences would be subtle rather than major. Accent and dialect – otherwise similar. Old Yugoslavian Balkan, to untrained ears. They wouldn't just be adding Dubrovnik to a roughly Balkan language and coming up with coastal Croatian as the solution, would they? Two and two making five. Like you, Arthur, I would question if they are all linguists in Cyprus.'

Arthur smiles at the support.

'It only takes the one who is listening,' Sven derides gently, again.

'Mmm. Alright,' Blair responds. 'Let's take it as it has been given. He is *Croatian*, until we disprove it. What other news have *you*, Nils?'

'Our Irish sources have no evidence that Padraic Hennessy is dead, so we would assume he's still with us on the planet. I'll keep digging away.'

Sven adopts his nose-rub position as Arthur reaches for his phone and taps away, seemingly in frustration.

'So,' asks the Swede, of the others, 'was Padraic the old man in Nicosia, speaking with the clan chiefs? Could it really have been Hennessy, based on what we know or surmise, so far?' He glances at Sam.

'I have no more information,' the agent says. 'After your suggestion, I'd jumped to the supposition that it was Padraic Hennessy.'

'Well, I'll be,' interrupts Arthur, looking up from searching on his smart phone. 'I thought so. The name Macan in Croatian means *cat*. More than that, actually. It means tomcat or boss cat.'

Nils Houweling gives a hands-in-the-air sigh. 'Another distracter? The link to Padraic Hennessy is looking pretty lame now, isn't it? The Croat could be the cat reference for the women's network, if indeed there is any realistic link between them and cats; and Nikkos suggests that this young man is the one creating the fear anyway. The only vague tie-in with Hennessy now is the story of an old man in Nicosia.'

'Ah,' adds Sven. 'Don't discount the phone call to Jacques Jazy.'

'Offering to solve the Middle East problems?' Nils laughs. 'A bit of a stretch for an old IRA gangster. No?'

Arthur muses for a couple of seconds while the others wait, watching. 'Maybe. There could be another connection linking Hennessy in. I was involved in sorting the evidence for the trials with the International Criminal Tribunal for the former Yugoslavia, from back in the nineties. The Croatians were fighting for their independence from 1991 to 1995 effectively, against the Serbs mainly. But Croatia had hardly any weapons at the start. They were up against the Serb army and a stack of paramilitaries, like the White Eagles, Serbian Guard and Dušan Silni's disciples. So, hundreds of mercenaries came in there from Western Europe to fight for Croatia and there were gun runners bringing in weapons, as well. Hennessy was reputed to have been one of those. I saw documentation on him for that conflict, way back. So, let's not just rule him out quite yet.'

Nils seems to enjoy being the Devil's Advocate. 'Was there any religion involved in the Yugoslav conflict?'

'There was, to an extent – picking on Muslims, for example,' Arthur responds. 'But terrorists and revolutionaries are not necessarily fanatics believing in religion …'

'Or even an obvious *cause*, in some cases,' interrupts Sven.

'Yes, indeed, Sven,' Arthur says – and for Nils' benefit. 'Often they are just people alienated from society – who want to make a statement, to hurt something or someone, to be thugs and bullies, to feel important in their own terms, a sense of belonging in a gang, to go out in a blaze of their own glory – which alienates them even further from society.'

'But,' persists Nils, 'Hennessy had a *cause* – the *Irish* cause. That's what he was fighting for. Isn't that what I'm hearing Maeve and Maureen Gallaher/Jazy were passionate about too?'

'Certainly. That would appear to be Padraic's reason for rebelling, for being a freedom fighter.'

'Well, Arthur, we are talking about the 1990s. *The Troubles* were still dragging on in Northern Ireland until the end of that decade … until 1998 officially. Yugoslavia wasn't *his cause*. And, he'd have been in his late fifties then – so are you sure about his Adriatic involvement?'

Blair smiles at the intellectual joust. 'But, is there any evidence that Hennessy was still fighting those old Ulster battles? The Croatian war was twenty years on from when Maureen Jazy landed in Donegal. Perhaps, Padraic was less involved in the day-to-day fighting and was away on the fundraising tours to Irish communities in the States or Australia. He was an organiser. He led The *Cat Pack*. He might even have been much higher up in the Republican cause – secretively. Bill Maclean certainly thought so. Maybe he really was sailing weapons past the blockades into Dubrovnik or Split or Senj, as the informers suggest. Once a revolutionary, always a revolutionary. Well?'

'I'll check out what we can,' Nils replies, deferring to his boss with a head shake.

'So?' Sam asks. 'Which trail do you want *me* following, Arthur?'

'Good question, Sam.' Blair looks across at Gulbrandson who is sitting quietly with his chin supported between his thumb and forefinger. 'Sven, you are deep in thought.'

'I'm thinking that you could be right, Arthur. Unlikely, I know.' He grins again. 'But possible. It might just be worth investigating your Yugoslav angle, for a bit at least. Who is this Macan … the *Cat*? Early twenties. He was born while the War of Independence was happening in Croatia. We need some factual meat on these rumours. Was Hennessy running weapons into Croatia? Was McSweeney with him – either Donnie or Michael – the younger one would have been the age that Padraic was when he was running the PIRA Cat Squad? Lots of questions, don't you think?'

'Yes. But rule out Donnie. He died in 1991, in Ireland. It's in Bill Maclean's tapes. Over to you, Sam.'

'Do we have any contacts in Croatia?' the tanned agent asks.

'As it happens, I do.' Arthur gives a self-satisfied smirk. 'Goran Bikić has worked with me on the war crimes trials. He actually is from Dubrovnik but he's still here in The Hague for half of each year. I'm sure he could give you a start or a contact.

'Now, Sam, we will want to speak again to Jacques Jazy, with Emma, as soon as he is able. Could you join us first thing in the morning – as in *very* early? We will aim for a dawn breakfast, old people rise with the light. Give you a chance to grab an hour or two of well-earned sleep.'

'I'll need it, if I'm to be heading over to the Adriatic next. No rest for the wicked.'

Chapter 9

June, 2013. Rotterdam, The Netherlands

A summer dawn gently revives the night sky as Arthur Blair introduces Sam Hall to Jacques Jazy.

IIB is in action for a new day and the official sunrise is still half-an-hour away. Sven offers a selection from a platter of fruit and *fresh-from-the-bakery* croissants. Emma charges the cups from the coffee pot. Nils looks in the door with a smiling, 'Hi,' and a quick introduction to Jacques, before excusing himself to chase up more information.

To his elderly guest, Arthur says, 'Thank you for being here at this uncivilised start time, Jacques. Hope you are feeling better this morning.'

'Fine, I think. *Merci.*' He shakes his head at the blur of early morning activity. 'Your guest suite is very comfortable. Does IIB ever sleep?'

'When we can, Jacques. These are busy times. If we may?' He pauses for Jazy's polite nod. 'I have been talking to Sven about my discussions with Bill Maclean in the nineties. Perhaps we could visit that time before Maureen headed to Donegal. We might click on something. For our understanding. Emma, if you would listen in – from your special family position – we might glean an even deeper perspective. What do you think?'

As he notes Jazy's second nod and Emma's smile, Arthur turns to the Swede. 'Sven, you had an idea before we broke?'

'I did, and do. But not ready yet for putting into words. Please carry on.'

'Right. Let us start, then. I have the audio recordings Bill agreed I could make at the time. I can still picture him, settled back in those big leather chairs of the retired spies' club in Kensington. His dreamy eyes were back quarter of a century to his times with Maureen. He really wanted me to understand – and you feature in it, Jacques.'

The soft voice of Bill Maclean drifts out from the player, just after Arthur presses the start key:

> By May of 1973, Maureen and I were rarely apart. We were a journalistic team, travelling all over Lebanon and Israel, often into areas thought to be dangerous – where the refugees lived. We were gathering opinions and keeping our antennae up for any big event that my superiors thought was sure to be coming soon.
>
> I sent my stories back to London to help build the intelligence picture. Maureen sent her writings off to Reuters and she had some published world-wide. I chose to be less prominent. I had a deeper agenda.
>
> Then Maureen suggested a holiday – home to see her father, Jacques, in Switzerland. I leapt at it: two weeks away from the tension of the Middle East.
>
> Jacques Jazy ran a printing/publishing business near the centre of Montreux on Lake Geneva. I found him a thoughtful man, very welcoming. From my observations, it was mainly Jacques's influence and the exposure to the world of printing that had encouraged Maureen to embark on a career in journalism.
>
> As I've told you, Maureen's mother, Maeve, had passed away. By all accounts, she'd been quite a personality – from the cathedral town of Letterkenny in County Donegal; and a fervent Irish Republican.

Donegal is now in Eire, the Republic of Ireland, governed from Dublin, but it had been part of Ulster until the partition in 1922. So there was history in her upbringing. Maeve had relatives just over the border in Londonderry – she had only ever been known to call it Derry; never any reference to Britain's capital.

According to what Maureen told me, Maeve's view was that the minority Catholics were treated as lower class by the police of the majority Protestant rule. She believed that some day all Ireland would be governed as one, by *Fianna Fail*, the major Dublin Republican party of her time; and that the IRA were patriots putting their lives on the line for a just cause. That was definitely the position that Maureen held too.

Jacques' raised hand indicates to pause the recording.

As all eyes turn to him, he explains, 'Maeve was passionate about many issues in life. You need to realise that, latterly, she and Maureen were more like sisters than mother and child. Not many years between them at all. Even before Maureen had reached her teens, she called her mother, *Maeve*, rather than Mum or Mother. She talked like an adult from an early age … and Maeve encouraged that closeness and maturity. Maureen was not a conventional child. Is this helping you understand how it was? I know you are looking for connections. I'm not sure how to help. Maybe play some more, Arthur.'

As Arthur follows Jacques's suggestion with a grateful nod, Maclean's voice floats out again.

In Switzerland, we travelled – the Chateau de Chillon, the alpine resort of Les Diablerets and through the mountain valley of the Rhone, over to the Rhine, into Liechtenstein and on to Zurich. A beautiful land.

Maureen enthused about her mother's teachings and her own dream to live with a view over Lac Leman, that's Lake Geneva in French; and about me being in that vision. I was flattered and happy about it, albeit a wee bit cautious given my background. I wasn't sure how the whole thing could play out but I was enjoying the ride. Anyway, the days we spent round her old haunts just reinforced that we should indeed make plans for a possible future together. It was a fabulous time – a carousel of joy and hope and promise.

I remember looking at the painting of Maeve on the corridor wall and saying, "Your Mum was a good-looking lady, Maureen."

"And I'm not, Bill?" She grinned back at me.

But my *Mo* was just lovely. I told her so … often. She had inherited her mother's good looks and her stepfather's quiet charm.

As I looked at the painting, I remember saying, "Your mother was really fanatical about the IRA?" It was more of a statement than a question, but it induced her response.

She told me, "Yes, she certainly was." And not just for Ireland, it seems. She had a strong sense of justice in her own way. She fired up at the powerful people hassling the less influential, using their laws or denying them fair jobs. For Ulster, she apparently thought the solution was to have one Ireland with one set of rules for all.

But, as I reminded Maureen, the problem is that there were a lot of people who came from Scotland and England some four hundred years before, with a different religion; and they set up their laws quite deliberately to limit the power of the papacy in Ulster.

She agreed. She said that, in many ways, it was not too different from the challenges in Lebanon, Israel and disputed Palestine.

I asked her deliberately, "Is that why you are in the Lebanon? Carrying on your mother's cause?"

"Maybe it is," she agreed with me.

She told me that she had promised her mother on her deathbed to do some things for the Irish cause that Maeve hadn't been able to do in her lifetime. Being in the Lebanon had sharpened her senses around injustice; the way information and rules are manipulated by people in power.

She said to me, "The problems in the Middle East are not insoluble, Bill, just difficult."

I asked her what the solution was but she just said, "Later."

I persisted with asking her what Maeve had asked her to do for the Irish cause.

But she just replied that she would tell me some day and turned her attention back to the magnificent view.

"Wouldn't you like to live here with me, in our chalet looking over the whole valley?" I remember the words as if it were yesterday.

Arthur stops the player. 'Do you know what her Middle East solution was, Jacques?'

He shakes his head. 'I'm afraid not. But let me think about it – something may come to mind.'

Arthur presses play again and Bill's voice continues.

Our funicular train clawed up the steep slope to the ski resort of Les Diablerets. In winter, the place would have been thronging with bronzed skiers in their designer padding – but in May, it was short sleeves, sunscreen and sunglasses. I was taking in the complexity of the integrated transport and the quality accommodation – and imagining the money involved.

Maureen just laughed at me. She was happy to tell me that the *Gnomes of Zurich* were renowned for storing the finances of the world in their impenetrable vaults. She took pleasure in explaining what I already knew about the Swiss and Liechtenstein banks; how they held confidential accounts of billions of dollars in corporate, perhaps criminal funds; how if you knew the password and had the key, you could access the money without anyone even asking your name. I was happy to let her tell me all that in her own way – I'm a listener; that's what I do, and did, for a living. She could always articulate views, like some wise old philosopher. I had another challenge for her to try to explain.

High up in the Alps there, with our view over the skyline, Switzerland looked small. I'd really always puzzled how Switzerland had managed to remain neutral through World War II. Why hadn't Germany just invaded? I had my own thoughts but Maureen surprised me again. For a twenty-year-old, she knew a lot.

She told me that everyone from eighteen to fifty-five is in the army reserve, National Service. It would have needed massive numbers of troops to subdue this country and for what? Mountains? Then the cities actually have large parts built underground because of the snow. They can keep operating effectively if attacked. But most importantly, the Swiss neutrality and confidentiality were, and are, legendary. She smiled as she said she would bet that squillions of German war-time money was, and maybe still is, salted away in Swiss banks. In her view, neutral Switzerland was an advantage to all countries in the war. Other countries could do deals with bankers and diplomats in a safe haven. It was too valuable to all of them to be invaded by anyone.

"And Liechtenstein is in the money business too?" I asked her innocently.

She seemed to have pat answers on the history of her part of the world or maybe she had just internalised what she had heard in her protest arguments – that Liechtenstein has a castle, a business in making stamps and not a lot more, except banks. I remember her saying that *In Switzerland, the bankers don't talk. In Liechtenstein, they don't have tongues.*

She told me that these countries were the preferred banking locations for anyone wanting to hide away money – legitimate business, organised crime or company profits avoiding the taxes; nations squirreling money away for safety in case of a coup – or some revolutionary cause like her mother's IRA.

She was wise beyond her years was Maureen. God, I miss her.

Jacques Jazy raises his hand again for the recording to pause. He coughs, face pointing down and gathers himself.

Allowing the old man time, Arthur takes control gently. 'Yes. We can hear the emotion in Bill's voice, Jacques. Several times he needed a break too. But he wanted me to hear his story; particularly the parts about Maureen, Ireland and *The Run*.'

The Swiss man dabs discreetly at his right eye with a tissue. '*Oui*. Strange to hear his voice again … after all these years. Kind things he said about me. He didn't need to do that. It was a happy time when we were all together. They were, how do you say, *head-over-heels* for each other. It was easy to see. Bill Maclean won me over.' He sips at his coffee cup. 'I had thought the age difference would (and should) be an issue, but I changed my mind when I met him. And then came the *Mediterranean Run* and it all went to *merde*.'

There is a sad fatalism in his tone as he continues. 'She knew the dangers. They both did. But how could you stop such a head-strong young woman. There was a destiny that she felt. It has taken me years to realise that.' He wipes a drying tear from his cheek. 'You see, it was a long time before Maureen came to terms with Maeve's death. Hard, so very hard, losing a mother at a young age – especially when they had been so close. We talked a lot, through her teens – much more than most fathers would with daughters, I think. It helped me too, because *I* was hurting badly as well.'

He smiles sheepishly and carries on. 'In many ways, Maureen's mind and attitudes passed out of childhood early; but that didn't take away her pain – and the absence of her natural father in her life.' His expression hardens. 'You see, after our initial conversations when Maeve and I first met – and they were thorough talks so that I could fully understand her situation – we didn't really discuss Hennessy again after we married; out of respect and for moving on. But, as Maureen grew older and became closer to Maeve, as a friend you understand, I'm sure they would have discussed the *what happened* and *whys*, of leaving Ireland – and her biological father.

'Even in her grieving, Maureen tried to avoid mentioning Hennessy to me. But I knew she took that part harder than she showed. Perhaps, I should have …? But I didn't want to talk of him. I had no respect for such a man. How could a father just wipe a child from all contact?' He shudders in disbelief.

'And I could sense it eating away at Maureen; the wondering, pushing her into risky places, trying to understand – even just to feel wanted. That is the crux of this *violent* revolutionary mentality – the sense of being shunned, being a lesser person, not being part of the favoured group, no way out except by fighting – wanting to hit back at oppressors; and usually through no fault of their own, just an accident of birth.

'It happened in the five-year Russian Civil War, after the revolution; those born of the *kulaks*, *Cossacks* or any trace of the White Russian lineage were always to be persecuted as inferior people in the Red Russian State. Then, African Americans in *the land of the free,* the coloureds of South Africa, the Aboriginal people of Australia, the Indians in the caste system and *the shit of the kings* in the British class structure – the Brits have no higher moral ground, imposing their colonial will across the globe, including their homelands – and all designed to make some feel falsely superior and to ostracise others. No wonder the likes of Hennessy emerged in Ireland. The history of British oppression in that land goes back at least to the sixteenth century, maybe further.

'I never condone violence – nor anyone like Padraic Hennessy. He is a murdering criminal and an insult to the protest movements. I like the Ghandi approach; passive resistance while educating the people, making them think, overcoming the social brainwashing.

I am a publisher of revolutionary arguments – it's a cerebral non-violent approach.

'But the disenfranchised often can't read or are not allowed to read. They are fed one-sided *pap* from whoever is running their communities. Sadly, they gravitate to the gangs where they feel welcomed. They are not necessarily stupid people – some are very clever; and street-wise – but the *violent* ones are almost always dangerously misinformed, misguided and maladjusted. They'll fight under any banner to get their sense of power and belonging – the flags of the meek, or the powerless; or any snake-oil cause, religion and the range of distortions of its interpretation …

'But, Maureen? I tried to be her balanced educator, and her substitute father, as well as the absent mother … but I was neither her natural father nor her mother. I'm sorry. I was just learning too. *Comprenez-vous?* So now, I don't stand in the way of the young. People, like Emma here, choose their paths. It's the parent role to give them guidance, multiple viewpoints – the experience benefit. Yes? But also the space to breathe and grow in their own ways.'

He gives a wan smile to the three others. 'There are more tapes, I imagine?'

'There are. Digitised now.'

'A little later then for me, please. I still don't fully understand what happened in Lebanon in 73.' He taps his stomach again with an apologetic smile.

Chapter 10

June, 2013. Rotterdam, The Netherlands

'Where is Padraic Hennessy at the moment? Isn't that our fundamental question?' Sam Hall asks.

There are four men in Arthur's office on Maasboulevard, overlooking the early morning freshness with the recent sunrise brightening the Maas and Rhine deltas. Emma is caring for her resting father and his jippy stomach, in the guest suite.

Nils now sits at the oval table with a laptop, two smart phones and an old-fashioned notebook.

'Whoa!' he says. 'Aren't we making an illogical leap to implicate Hennessy with any of this? Or do you have some evidence that I haven't seen?'

'What do *you* think we have, Nils?' asks Sven.

'I have the intel that Sam brought back from Cyprus about an old man in Nicosia speaking with leaders of gangs or clans from Mediterranean countries. No name, no nationality … just an old man, maybe European. We have the Arab, Bashir Dorda, murdered brutally in Nicosia … with a suggested link to *Mossad*. And speculation from Nikkos that Dorda probably wasn't the first. General chatter about something about to happen. Then we have Emma Jazy's analysis of a couple of Gaddafi's former female guards signing up for some generalised network involving cats, apparently. And possibly other women have become involved too. Her reports have mentioned Palestine resistance fighters … and a new group, *Akhawat*. I believe that name is Arabic and means *sisters*.

51

'Now, I can advise you that Hennessy is apparently missing from his last known address in Ireland. That is, he's not at the property in Buncrana in County Donegal, where his last passport was sent. Both Hennessy and Michael McSweeney have current passports although they don't need them to travel into most of Europe.'

Arthur held up his hand. 'That last statement is a *yes* and a *no*. UK and Eire didn't join the Schengen passport-free zone of the European Union. They'd still need passports to get into the zone – once in, they'd be fine, presumably. No?'

'Okay,' agreed Nils. 'I take your point. Anyway, to continue. McSweeney is in his late fifties. The house is officially owned by him. But, neither has been at Buncrana for at least eighteen months, maybe longer. The place is rented. An agent manages the property from a working credit union account.

'Then we have the phone call via Michael McSweeney in 2011, where Padraic Hennessy offered to right the problems of the Middle East in return for Jacques wiping the slate clean over Maeve and Maureen. How weird is that?'

He adjusts his spectacles as he gives a final look at his laptop screen before summing up. 'That is hardly compelling evidence to implicate the seventy-eight-year-old Padraic Hennessy in anything. And isn't that all we have, at this stage?'

'Perhaps.' Arthur smiles, ever patient, orchestrating the discussion. 'Sven, what do you think?'

'Sure. Hard evidence is thin on the ground,' Gulbrandson responds. 'That clearly is task number one ... to get something definitive. We have only been hearing whispers for a few weeks – a month really – and not just from Cyprus. There is more. As you have heard, chatter about the Adriatic too – this time from our North African and former Yugoslav sources, and about an old *Arab* man, too. You are aware of all that, Nils?'

Houweling nods his agreement, while the Swede continues.

'So, could we be confusing two old men; this one and the mysterious Cyprus figure? Or could they be one and the same? This Arab one anyway was probably part of the old Gaddafi networks – the runs that smuggled weapons to the states of the former Yugoslavia in the 90s. So, that would probably make him younger than Bill Maclean's era in that part of the world, and Padraic Hennessy's, too.'

Houweling shakes his head. 'But Sven, your case against Hennessy is not getting any stronger. The options about others are just getting larger.'

The Swede pauses to process some thought. 'Patience. This is our business, Nils – to be ahead of the game, to hypothesise and test our theories. No criminal network will be sending out postcards of their intent. So let's see what we else can find out – and what we can surmise – or what we can provoke.'

Nils, pen at the ready. 'Okay. Provocateurs, one step forward.'

Sven's brow furrows fleetingly at the jesting and then deepens, as if trying to resolve a problem in his mind, before continuing with the earlier theme. 'Mind you, Libya has supported most rebel causes … from the Provisional IRA and the Lebanese revolutionaries with Maureen and Bill Maclean, to the Red Brigade in Germany. Perhaps, you'd be aware that Gaddafi actually flew the bodies of the five Black September terrorists, killed during the Fürstenfeldbruck Airbase gun battle after the Munich Olympics massacre, back to Libya for a hero's funeral. That was way back in 1972. So the appearance of old men, from that network, appearing in new criminal scenarios is no great surprise to me at all. Sorry, I shouldn't bore you with my reminiscing.'

'No problem,' Houweling replies. 'It helps me fit events and issues into my historical chronology. You have lived these things. I wasn't even born then.'

Gulbrandson acknowledges the respect with a gentle nod, before continuing. 'But, as yet, Nils, I'd have to admit that your assessment is right. There is a lot of grey around our established facts. In fairness, IIB's brief has been to sound out our suspicions. Our task is to be intuitive, as well as evidence-based. Something is about to happen. That sense is all through the national agencies who have been picking up the waves. They all report it. We agree on that part, surely? That's why Sam was sent into Cyprus to sus out those latest rumours and why Emma has been following the chatter about this possible new network of women.'

Nils gives his usual non-committal grin. This is their normal process of teasing out their strategic thinking in the International Investigations Bureau.

Arthur chimes in. 'We have just been revisiting Bill Maclean's work with Maureen Jazy in Lebanon in 1973. They were both listening out for something big about to happen back at that time too. It was in fact only a few months away, in the end … and it sounds strikingly parallel to what might be happening now, don't you think?'

Sam's newly darkened eyebrows rise, creasing his dyed brow in question. 'As in chatter making no sense … but becoming pretty clear over time?'

'Indeed,' answers Arthur. 'And fear.' He closes his eyes and pauses. *'Don't dismiss the fear.* It is not the usual terrorist type – more like a dust silently infiltrating everyone's psyche. Let's take your question first, Sam,' he continues. 'It's two years since Padraic Hennessy's call to Jacques Jazy. If he is alive, where is he? Ireland? Cyprus? How is he travelling? Still smuggling himself around in fishing boats?'

Nils nods. 'Maybe. I can tell you that the Irish Government has not been particularly co-operative with information. I sense the man has legendary patriot status in some of their community. I'll keep at them.'

Sven has his usual head-bowed, nose-stroking pose as he ponders. 'Michael McSweeney. He's a key. Find him and you find Hennessy. He may be easier. Did you say his father Donnie is still alive?'

'No … died in a car crash in County Fermanagh in the first week of January 1991. Bill Maclean mentioned it and I remember checking those briefing details clearly.'

'Okay. Yes, you did say that. An accident, of course? Snow on the road, eh?'

'You believe what you wish. Either way, he is dead. Okay, questions?'

The pragmatic Nils shakes his head. 'I'll get on with establishing the base data. Oh, and … I repeat that Hennessy might have absolutely nothing to do with this. Yes. One question. Do we have a particular government wishing to sponsor this investigation – to pay the bills, that is? The paperwork hasn't reached me, yet.'

'We have been retained, effectively and very quietly, by the intelligence agency of the USA, on behalf of Britain and France,' advises Arthur. 'By implication, that would include Israel too. But this is all very new, less than two weeks for us.'

'Less than two weeks. A month from the Mediterranean chatter? That is my point.' Nils says. 'And yet Hennessy supposedly made his offer nearly two years ago?'

Sven raises his head again. 'He's an old man now, Nils. They don't think like young men. Maybe he had careful plans to develop that he has to put in place now, before Jacques Jazy might no longer be around to forgive him. No?'

'I'll take your word on that, Sven.' Houweling rises to leave the room, with the comment, 'Perhaps the intelligence agencies have been confused as to who should pay the bill, Arthur?'

'I'll see to it, Nils,' Blair replies testily not needing the reminder.

Sven shrugs at Arthur as Houweling closes the door behind him.

'He is young, relatively speaking,' as Sven smiles at Sam's querulous look. 'Good that he will challenge everything and us. One thing not mentioned is the Iranians. Could they be involved in this new women's group?'

Sam grins. 'I'm young too. *Akhawat* is Arabic, is it not? Farsi-speaking Iranians wouldn't have a stake in the ownership of a women's group, would they? Let alone with an Arabic name.'

'They might, if you acknowledge their stated opposition to the very existence of Israel,' Sven offers. 'They are players in keeping up the tensions. Distracters are always helpful with the mind games. And their nuclear enrichment always just bubbles along. Yes?'

'No.' Arthur is unconvinced. 'That's just another piece of unsubstantiated speculation. And you criticise *my* proposed theory on Hennessy? If the group includes Gazan women and Libyans with maybe Hezbollah and offshoots of the old Palestinian Liberation Organisation, then the membership will be Arabic speakers. Let's flick the Iranians for the moment.'

'Okay. As you wish,' Sven concedes. 'I was just testing the thought. By all means, keep the usual suspects …'

'Point taken.' Arthur's mind seems in no mood for more distractions.

'Fine for now,' Sven agrees, grudgingly. 'But let's not jump unwisely by discarding anything too soon.' The Swede shrugs and then returns to his provoking. 'Now, our pedantic Nils is right, too. Why would an Irishman have any link at all?'

Arthur stands up and moves over to his window, before turning. 'I accept your doubts. However, for me, first, there is the mention of cats. Innocuous, I know, but Hennessy was known as *The Cougar* and his gang was the PIRA *Cat Pack*. Second is the old man connection. He is old. No doubt about that. Third, the phone call to Jacques Jazy expressing his interest in a Middle East solution. Fourth, given his background with arms smuggling through the old *Mediterranean Run* – albeit a long time ago – he probably has strategic and tactical expertise … and some respected status in the international resistance movements. He might just have sufficient credibility in the revolutionary groups to persuade militant leaders to listen to his case – not to mention his record of being able to get insurgent groups to work together. That is reinforced by the old man apparently meeting the leaders individually – to present the case rationally without power plays getting in the way. Finally, intuitively, it sounds like the kind of operation he would be promoting, at least in his younger years.'

'And women being involved?' Sven asks.

'I don't know. Guessing? It could be symbolic in some way? His quest for redemption because of two women.'

'Or,' suggests the quietly thoughtful Sam, 'whatever he is planning might need women to achieve the goal.'

'A good thought, Sam! Hold on to that.'

Arthur's lips purse in agreement. 'This is real enough. The chatter through the networks might be a couple of weeks older, but the Cypriot ones are very recent – as in today, Sam, eh? People being scared has been very intensive in the past few days – and generally, I suppose, the fear has been around for about a month or more in the Med and northern capitals. Nikkos's information supports that. The intelligence agencies are each running their checks and correlation analyses. I would expect that intel will flow quite soon.'

Sven scratches his ear. 'Mmm! Nils is right. What's Hennessy been doing since the peace accord in Ireland? That's fifteen years ago.' He raises his palms in query.

Arthur smiles patiently once more and glances at Sam. 'Isn't this business wonderful? Trying to be prescient is not as easy as it might sound. Sam, let's get the basics established first. Can you work with Nils to get this info captured, as soon as? The Cyprus connection came to us indirectly from the Israelis – *Mossad* to the CIA – and your inquiries have confirmed some of it. I can't see Hennessy at his age flying boldly out of Dublin and landing in Cyprus. Just guessing, but I think he will be near to the action.'

'As in where?' Sam asks.

'Probably the Mediterranean or close to.'

'And the women being trained?'

'Probably not by an old man. There are plenty of activist cells around who could do that. Yemen, Sudan, Somalia, maybe? But I would think it could be in the Mediterranean too, especially if they are all Arab women.'

Sven looks up again. He asks, 'How good is your Irish Gaelic, Sam? I think you could be the tracker on Hennessy's trail, so we better get you up to speed on his past with The Cat Pack, his connections with the Gallaher/Jazy family and their *modus operandi* with arms smuggling, not to mention his fighting against the British and the Protestants. Arthur will give you it all; about William Maclean, his recordings, Maureen Gallaher and Maeve … as well as all our speculation in between. You never know when the detail of the background can be put to good use.'

'And the women?' Sam suggests, hopefully.

Arthur shakes his head and grins. 'A job for Emma initially, I think. Don't you?'

Sven springs to his feet. 'Let me have your discs again, Arthur. I need to understand Lebanon in 1973. Something isn't fitting for me. And yet …'

Chapter 11

May, 1973. Lebanon.

'Something big is coming.' Maureen's eyes betray her sense of excitement. 'The rebels want to be part of it.'

Back from the romance of Switzerland earlier in May, Maureen and Bill find quiet rumours floating around Lebanon … about a build-up of arms in the camps and fighting groups.

The question had seemed so simple, from Maclean's controller in London, 'How are they getting arms into Lebanon undetected?'

It takes only a couple of weeks of quiet investigation amongst their trusted contacts before the term, *Mediterranean Run*, comes to their notice – a system for smuggling arms from North Africa, usually Libya. It hasn't been hard for Bill to co-opt Maureen into this quiet journalistic research – she is as passionate about the rebels as Bill appears to be.

But he is living a lie … and it eats away at him. She doesn't know that he is a British agent. Why would she even suspect it? It has never been even hinted. To all appearances, he is an investigative journalist, willing to find out information for a protest cause and to send it back to a newspaper agency in London.

It has never bothered him before. He has become accustomed to years of living a double life; keeping acquaintances at a casual distance and being superficial to all people. But now he is in a different type of relationship. This has been a whirlwind romance – not even fully three months old but he has the strong sense that this is not like his fleeting affairs of the past. Maureen trusts him. She has taken him to Switzerland to meet her father. She is talking of an immediate future together ... and he isn't averse to that idea. Yet, he is no journalist; and his research is no investigative article for a newspaper.

Just as he ponders the possibility of leaving his employment with the British Foreign Service, London requests him to infiltrate that *Run*, to find out how it works, who is involved and where the money comes from.

Covert work is an implied part of Maclean's role, but that was before meeting Maureen. Their travels in Lebanon are no longer just about work. They feel like a team – a partnership in every sense, seeking out beauty, away from the crowds; up into the remnant cedar forests, the legendary *Cedars of Lebanon*, in the mountains; lush with the pervading scent of sap from the bark. She says that he reminds him of Jacques – reliable, cerebral and caring – quite a compliment, but compounding his deceitful dilemma.

Is he being stupid – carried away by the euphoria of the moment? In the past, he would just have moved on with some lame excuse ... but now?

While they have visited inland Baalbek to savour its classical music concerts, in their Beirut flat, Louis Armstrong's jazz creates the sentimental ambience of their time. His voice is linked with Lac Leman because Jacques played it constantly as background. It isn't hip music in any way for 1973, but Maureen likes it – and Bill can live with it. Indeed, Louis's gravelly voice is growing on him; hitting the notes on the off-beat, taking on a special meaning for them both; music evoking emotional connection.

'Why New Orleans jazz?' he asks her.

'Can't you feel it?' she replies. 'It's the rhythmic identity of protest. It's the music of a challenge ... rebelling against the restraints of tradition, the shackles of society's bondage. It speaks to me of civil rights ... no matter what lyrics are sung. It's a melody with soaring counterpoints of virtuosity that make you sit up and take notice.'

'Wow! Where do these ideas come from? Did you just think them up?'

'These particular words, I have.' She grins. 'But the original theme is Jacques's, from our talks around the kitchen table ... thrashing out the political issues of the world. He can interpret feelings into a well-crafted phrase, in several languages, can Jacques. That's why he's such a good publisher. And all that passion was spurred on by Maeve. She loved that music just as much. Look, it's not the music of my first choice but I feel the spirit of revolution from both of them as I listen to Louis – their vigour, especially my mother's. That's why I play it. Transcendental, Bill. Calming. No need for drugs – just the meaning behind the rhythms.'

'You're quite a remarkable woman, Maureen ... quite remarkable indeed.'

As he looks into her eyes, with all their joint hopes for the days and months ahead, he struggles to work out a way where he can successfully broach the matter of him being employed by the British Government ... and their request for him to infiltrate *The Run* ... or even to confess that has been his past.

* * * *

'Where did this come from?' Anger blazes in Maureen Jazy's eyes.

Her relationship with her journalist partner has just moved from robust debate and dreamy passion to outright ferocious argument, the pain of betrayal. And the catalyst has been his suggestion that he might work for the British Government from time to time ... and that he is going to travel on a gun-running ship in the Mediterranean for a few days.

He has decided to try for honesty being the best approach, to clear the air.

'You've done stunts like this before, haven't you?' Her auburn hair flies up. 'When the fuck were you going to break this to me in our relationship? And the bloody British at that? How *could* you? How long have you been working for them? I'm the daughter of an Irish Republican activist, for Christ's sake.'

* * * *

The several days of frosty antagonism and silent stares seem like years as Maclean watches his tormented partner wrestle with fierce emotions and moral dilemmas. Finally, the silence is broken when, seated facing each other at the kitchen table with sunlight streaming in the window, she finally points her finger directly at Maclean, while the other hand holds a kitchen knife, low over the table.

'Right, Bill. Here's the litmus test for any relationship we could have together from here on. I can handle you pretending to be a smuggler on a ship, running guns into Lebanon. That's a *cause* to help the disadvantaged. I think I can even force myself to live with the fact that you are doing it with the fucking Brits. That's a real hard one for me; but I'll manage if the outcome is to help the refugees … and because of how I think I feel about you.' Her eyes drill through him. 'You should feel pretty important with that, Bill Maclean, because I have never even thought about saying that to anyone else in my life.'

She clears her throat. 'So, here's the rub. *You* go. *I* go too. And before you give me any answer, let me tell you that there's no way I'll be sitting here at home like the little lady worrying if her man will return. Me Mother would be insulted if I hadn't the gonads to run guns to help an oppressed people.

'There's the condition, Bill. You go! I go! I'll make my mother proud of me. My natural father too maybe, if I'd ever known him. They would have been game to fight for a cause. Maureen Gallaher will not step back from the fucking challenge either! Well, Bill? What's it to be?'

The thirty-five-year-old agent sits back at the kitchen table and looks at the jutted jaw on the fiery love of his life. She faces him, knife loosely in hand, giving the ultimatum. She hasn't asked him *not* to be involved. She seems to have rationalised everything in her own way. She got that he hadn't disclosed his true occupation; and he is working for *the enemy*, in a sense; and that there is danger involved. As she said, she is prepared to live with that. She has made the first move. Their relationship is clearly a high priority for her. This is no con job … their love must be as real for her as he has hoped it is.

He watches her, not game to speak too quickly. Her eyes don't flinch; green, the honey fleck paused in her fixed stare. Clearly, no entreaty from him about protecting her from danger will wash. That time has long passed.

He understands that the days of being blinded by candy-coloured dreams, fuelled by lustful delights, will have to be replaced by a more mature appreciation of each other.

Bill Maclean nods deliberately. 'Alright. I go! You go! *We* go. We are a team.'

The knife is released onto the table. Her intent has never been clear. Just a prop for effect, maybe. But it has made a point.

'Right! Right then. We put this bad week behind us. Right?'

'Right, Maureen.'

'And there'll be no patronising protectiveness as we move on. Right? I'm not some little woman dependent on her man. Right?'

'I hope I would never patronise you, Maureen. Never mistake loving care for doubting your capacity to look after yourself.'

'Right!'

* * * *

They set out in early June 1973 on a small fishing boat, with a winch for the drift net at the front and the wheelhouse nearer the rear. The facilities are primitive – hammocks under the wheelhouse; the oil and diesel smells of the engine compartment struggling to compete with the stench of fish oil which pervades the whole vessel; a compact hold into which the fine mesh bags of the net will empty their sparkling catch. Toilet is a bucket and over the side

Maureen doesn't complain. In her purple beret over her deep auburn hair, jacket and jeans, she could pass for a pirate queen. Her whole presence demands respect and she gets it … from the tiny crew as well as the quiet people who load and unload at either end of *The Run*

There is a captain and a deckhand. Bill is onboard as a worker. With a two-day beard, he can pass easily for a Lebanese fisherman. The captain clearly accepts him as being a useful extra pair of hands, endorsed by contacts from the resistance movement in his home port. That is the deal – quiet favours being called in

Maureen is the investigative journalist, ostensibly trying to learn about the difficulties of fishing in waters patrolled ceaselessly by the Israeli Defence Force boats. She is fighting in her own way for the same cause – protecting the embattled – and she has a fierce confidence about her

They sail in daylight for hours without dropping the net … and continue after nightfall. Then, well outside territorial waters, the navigation lights of a large vessel come into view. Radio contact in Arabic passes a coded message

The fishing boat pulls alongside in the gloom. Four boxes are winched across and lowered into the fish hold. Then, the large boat moves quickly away

'Now, we fish!' announces the captain, for Maureen's benefit, as the fine nets are lowered into a wide crescent across the water. The line of corks can just be seen, glistening occasionally in the pale starlight as the boat loops around over the evening sea. Then the winch kicks into life and the wet, salty net is gradually hoisted on board, funnelling the trapped fish back to the fine-meshed bags. The large seething mass of slippery silvery fish is dropped into the fish hold on top of the tarpaulin covering the four boxes from the large ship. With a couple more loads of fish, the boat heads eastward and approaches Lebanese waters.

* * * *

An Israeli patrol boat draws alongside with armed sailors demanding their business. They come with one interpreter who speaks Arabic. The captain invites them onboard. He protests that they are a humble fishing boat taking their catch back to the port of Ouzai at Beirut. The sailors look in the fish hold and apparently don't suspect anything. Bill looks so scruffy and grunts so much that they pay him little attention.

After checking Maureen's reporter credentials and listening to her tale about researching a story on dwindling fish stocks, they let the boat pass, perhaps not wanting to antagonise a foreign journalist. Good press is always important in the battle for international support

The boat comes into the harbour past the glow of spectacular white sea-stacks and the load is quietly taken away in a smelly darkened truck

That is the start of their involvement in the *Mediterranean Run* and, after that first trip, Maureen is happy to leave the bulk of the future trips to Bill, with the *You go, I go* option available for whenever she might choose. She understands that he looks and sounds the part, while she is too memorable to be using her reporter story very often.

* * * *

Throughout June and July, they establish the route and the African contacts. Loads of rifles, explosives and rocket-propelled grenades arrive in small batches on *The Run*. Bill passes the information back to his controller as the build-up continues to something significant that seems to be getting nearer and nearer

If Maureen is battling with her conscience in allowing the British to be aware of gun-running contacts, she keeps it to herself. It is becoming very clear that there are other resistance organisations involved, not just the Palestinians

In late July 1973, Bill's London controller passes on his intel that the same mother ship system which is supplying the runs into Lebanon is also part of a chain, running arms into Ireland – for insurgents battling the British in Ulster.

They want William – the controller always calls him William – to dig deeper into the motherships. Who is behind their other passages to Ireland? Is there Russian involvement?

Then, they request William to join a ship running weapons to Ireland – to follow the distribution line; learning the personalities, drop-off points, suppliers and financiers.

London has a plan. William will replace a crewman who has been the clandestine source of British intel. But that man has been in the danger zone for too long. Conveniently, he is being rushed to hospital for an urgent operation. Bill Maclean will fill the vacancy as part of a significant arms deal with the Irish.

While the revolutionaries in Ireland need the delivery, the cover story for Maclean is that the Lebanese *Run* wants to learn improved techniques to keep ahead of the Israeli monitoring. Maclean comes with the endorsement of respected Palestinian and Libyan contacts. This is a sharing between revolutionary groups

The shipment will be into Donegal and link with a group whose contact man is a Donnie McSweeney.

* * * *

Maclean is riven with doubt. His role is usually as a listener, not a fighting agent. This proposed operation is a whole new level of danger, involving the smuggling of weapons which could be used against British soldiers.

To compound the matter, he has to tell Maureen that he will be away for two months on a trip to Europe.

It is then that Maureen's promise to her dying mother is laid on the table.

Chapter 12

June, 2013. Rotterdam, Netherlands

'Jacques, good to see you on the mend.' Arthur says. 'Emma, thanks for your care.'

Emma has returned with her father to settle in Arthur Blair's comfortable meeting room on Maasboulevard to tease out their background understanding of Padraic Hennessy's strange offer for redemption.

The morning sunlight brightens the whole atmosphere. They, and Sven Gulbrandson, are each seated in black leather chairs with more coffee and healthy nibbles on the low tables beside them.

Jacques appears to be substantially recovered from his earlier ailment. 'I'm sorry, Arthur. The old body is not responding well to changes in my routine. But let's continue, please.'

'Okay. Thanks,' says Arthur. 'Sam and Nils have commitments. They apologise. Let's return to Bill and Maureen. I think we need you to give us a feel for the types of discussion that Maeve would have had with Maureen as she was growing up with you in Montreux. Okay?'

Jacques slowly steeples his fingers and, with a careful nod, begins. 'Maeve was always the activist. Well, we both were. Just that we were different personalities. Our shared passion for causes was the attraction at the start in Paris. We thrashed out world issues, attitudes and ideologies in a world before television or computers. We had libraries and access to revolutionary newsletters, student papers – all sorts of ideas challenging the *status quo*. I published for many small groups. And Maureen was a part of those discussions right from the start. She was arguing about capitalism and Marx's ideas of communism by the time she was eight. She was not your normal child – *comprenez-vous?* She really wanted to understand these complex ideological questions like others of her age might be interested in horses, dolls or playing.'

He stops for a smile at some memory in his mind's eye and takes a sip of his coffee before continuing.

'Maeve really fired up about Northern Ireland and the injustices she had felt as a teenager – how her relatives were treated in Derry; the stories her parents and grandparents told her of past struggles against colonial-style oppression. She always wanted to hit back and was attracted to people who were prepared to stand up, not be passive, you understand. That would be why the young, intense Padraic Hennessy might have caught her attention.

'In the early days of our relationship, as I say, she did speak to me about who he was and his quiet impassioned plans for resistance. She had to get it out of her system, yes? He'd apparently pedal his bicycle all the way over to her home in Letterkenny and they would get off to quiet spots under the trees to talk about teenage views of revolution.

'Clearly, they did more than talk. The aftermath of the pregnancy confirmation was a seminal moment for her. She had effectively been exiled. That made her angry but she was also very tired, trying to bring up a baby with minimal support; and she did it well. She was young. Maureen was only a year old when Maeve and I started our relationship.

'And then I got the chance to have a share in a small publishing house in Montreux. We married a year later, as much to bear acknowledgement to the restricting mores of the time as to confirm our commitment to each other. We understood our responsibilities to each other, as well as to the baby Maureen and …' he smiles '… even revolutionaries have to fly beneath the radar if they are to have subversive success. So, we moved to Switzerland – a fresh start.'

Sven, as usual, has his head lowered in chin-stroking pose, listening intently while referencing and re-referencing what he is hearing, within his encyclopaedic mind. 'Did you discuss Middle East issues, along with the Irish challenges?' he asks.

'*Absolument. Bien sûr.* Of course. The issues behind the partitioning were common discussions. I remember when the movie, *Lawrence of Arabia*, came out we went into Geneva to see it. It was well made and ... striking. Maureen would have been ten, probably. Yes, it brought out all the political deceit and snobbery which was part of all empires – the wheeling and dealing with people's lives and livelihoods. It annoyed both of them.'

Sven has scarcely moved. 'So, particularly, what annoyed them? Can you recall any specific issues that fired them up?'

'Yes. The arrogant attitude of the British establishment at the time, in stark contrast to the way Lawrence had tried to conduct himself. The British army treated him as an insolent upstart, to be tolerated and discarded, as soon as convenient. That was Maeve's view of their ruling attitudes in Northern Ireland, as well.

'Lawrence was the noble patriot to her; but as an ideal, for values – not colonial jingoism. He saw the uniting of the Arab tribes as an aspiration that had validity in itself, as well as providing practical benefits, such as the return of the lands lost to empires. And then, in the end, the British lied. They cheated Lawrence – hung him out to dry, as you say. Maeve never thought his motor-cycle death was an accident, despite the story of him dodging to miss two children. To her, it was a statement that a good man cannot live without the principles of trustworthiness and integrity.

'You see, General Allenby, the British chief, swore blind that they had no designs on Arabia. Yet, after the war, they divided it all up between France and Britain: British Mesopotamia, Iraq really, the British Mandate of Palestine, today's Jordan, Israel and Palestine ... and the British also had Egypt, Yemen, Muscat, Oman, the Trucial States, Qatar and Kuwait. Then the French got the mandate for Syria while provision was made for Independent Turkey, Iran and Saudi Arabia.' The encyclopaedic facts rattle off Jacques's tongue like a message often told. 'The Arabs who fought with Lawrence were left out in the cold. And while all this was going on, Lord Balfour was quietly guaranteeing that Israel could have a homeland around Jerusalem. What pompous deceit – and they tried to renege on that too between the wars.' He pauses. 'Sorry. I still get fired up. It was diplomacy decided on a map with no regard for the people on the ground. And totally messed up. It infuriated Maeve. So, *oui*, we talked about it often. Maureen was certainly an active questioning part of our talks.'

'Jacques, in these discussions did Maeve ever talk about a possible solution to the mess?' Arthur asks quietly.

'I see your point, Arthur. Something that the young Maureen might have heard and processed for later, that she might have told Padraic when they were together in Ireland? Mmm.'

'Exactly!'

'Mmm. *Oui*. The big mistake – yes, we would have talked about this openly. The big mistake of the British was to allow anyone of Jewish faith to see Israel as the homeland; to which they had an automatic right to return. You take my point. Any of the millions of Jews in the world could flood into Israel. It is a tiny state and a dry place at that. Clearly, Israel would have to expand if the newcomers were to be settled. And that meant displacing the people who were already there, mainly Palestinian Arabs. So, all the remembered conflicts of millennia would bubble to the surface. Isn't that just what has happened?'

'Indeed, Jacques. Indeed. Sven, your thoughts?' Arthur invites his partner into the conversation.

'Did Maureen agree with that scenario, Jacques?' the Swede asks.

Jazy laughs. 'I suspect. Yes. We had Jewish friends in Montreux; still do. They have a different world view and ideological perspective. Yes, I tried to explain their viewpoint to Maeve *and* Maureen – playing the opposition, giving the contrary argument – that a fundamental tenet of Zionist ideology is *Aliyah*. As you would know, it means the *ascent*, the return of Jewish peoples to Israel after the *diaspora*, the scattering. Zionists call the leaving of the Promised

Land, the *yerida* or the *descent*. This notion of the right of Jews and their relatives to ascend to the Promised Land is enshrined in present day Israel's *Law of Return*. But I lost that debate with them. It was a hard one to win. You see, the Jewish case defies intuitive logic. You can't fit more in a container than the container can hold, without it overflowing.

'Maeve always spoke vehemently against people who *presumed to know* what was best for people, without ever asking or checking. It was the *born to rule* syndrome with its corollary, *born to be ruled*.'

Sven's head is still down as he persists, 'So the notion in Maureen's mind might be to change the *Law of Return*. Yes? That might be what she could have suggested to Padraic. No?'

'Possibly,' agrees Jazy.

'Then our next challenge is how might he think he could achieve that?'

'And all the time,' Emma chimes in. 'More and more settlements are being built out into the West Bank.'

'Yes, Emma,' Arthur agrees, giving her a small smile, as if to appreciate her patience in being the passive listener rather than her usual role as an active field agent. 'And that is the next point, because when the United Nations finally agreed in 1947 that Israel should have a homeland – largely in response to their suffering and displacement during the World War II Holocaust – the area designated was nothing like the present area.'

'So I've heard. But, how different was it, really?' Emma queries encouragingly, looking at her father for a response.

'Very different.' Jacques Jazy regains his role of explainer. 'In 1947, they were given Jaffa and Tel Aviv plus the Negev Desert from Beersheba down to the Gulf of Aqaba and some of the Jordan River around Lake Tiberias … the Sea of Galilee. *N'est-ce pas?* That was all they were to have. No more. The UN were to control Jerusalem as a protectorate for all religions. The Arabs had a large area of the West Bank and a strip of sea frontage at Gaza. It is hard to remember that was all there was.

'Then, in the 1948 War of Independence, the Israeli army took over the north from Haifa to the Jordan River … and Jerusalem. They left the Arabs with a reduced area of the West Bank and a tiny strip of land at Gaza.

'But more. In 1967, their pre-emptive defence against what they declared as Egyptian and Syrian aggression took over the whole Sinai Desert, the West Bank from Jordan and the Golan Heights. That was the *Six Day War*. And, give or take, that's pretty much the way it still is.'

Sven raises his head at last. 'A good summary, Jacques. But I am left wondering what it might be that Padraic Hennessy, at seventy-eight years old, could possibly think he could do to change a large chunk of history, based on what Maureen might have told him in 1973. A latter day Lawrence of Arabia forging disparate Arab groups into some force to influence Israeli law regarding settlements? Surely not?'

Jacques Jazy lifts his hand, to hold the conversation and to collect his thoughts. 'I haven't physically been to the Middle East but I am well aware of the large number of ethnic groups that have historical connections to the lands from the Caspian to the Persian Gulf, to the Red Sea, to the Mediterranean and into North Africa. It is the history of the conquerors, the conquered, the enslaved and the massacred – back and forward like the tides, any excuse, banner, belief or bandwagon being enough to foster a cause to fight.' He pauses. 'Lawrence united some of the tribal groups against the Turks in World War I – but that is just the tip of a very large patchwork of cultural and religious allegiances, across that whole area.'

'So,' queries Gulbrandson, 'Hennessy might be trying to amalgamate those many disparate groups into agreeing to his proposal, whatever it is?'

'Why not?' The Swiss shrugs. 'It is a massive area, which they all think should be theirs, and not colonised by outsiders. Maybe, he is offering incentives – a competition to be in it, or to miss out. But it is not likely to go back to the old tribal areas. Too many people there now for the space that is available; and too much historical pain. You can't just go back to the traditional ways.'

'I agree; and even less likely is a reversion to the UN partition agreement for Israel,' suggests Arthur.

'*Absolument.* That was foisted on the local Arab populations, without any understanding of cultural histories.'

Blair looks to Emma, who gives an imperceptible nod that she has helped elicit the information the team needs to hear.

'So it leaves us, as a working hypothesis,' Arthur summarises, 'that, at the simple level, Hennessy will do something to induce the Israelis and the Palestinians to the negotiating table, to agree on some kind of peace accord, such as in Ireland.'

Sven shakes his head in doubt, 'You think? Except, as Jacques has said, that the challenges of the Middle East are much more entrenched than that relatively recent history of Northern Ireland. And all to get … what? Forgiveness from Jacques, the stepfather of his daughter? With all respect to you Jacques, it makes no sense.'

'Nor to me,' the Swiss man replies. 'The man's skill is in murdering, kidnapping, bombing; not diplomacy.'

'I don't think I am prescient enough to work out what he might be trying to do.' Sven shakes his head in bewilderment.

Chapter 13

August, 1973. Lebanon

'I promised my mother.'

The vehement words resound around their small Beirut flat. Maureen Jazy stands with hand on hips, jaw jutted and eyes firing. 'On her deathbed, I promised her, Bill, that I would support the IRA in their struggle; to bring fairness into the fight until there was peace again in Ireland. I promised her that I would take whatever opportunities that presented themselves. This is an opportunity – a golden one. This was my promise.'

Bill Maclean stares at her, speechless, as she draws a second breath and then launches into her next salvo. 'You'll be running weapons into Eire. That's precisely what Maeve used to advocate. She'd fire up at the prospect. She wanted to get arms to the resistance fighters – to let them fight with some balance against the oppressive British colonial power.'

They stare at each other across their small kitchen.

'You go, I go!' she reiterates, her voice rising. 'We're a team. I'm the granddaughter of Seamus Gallaher ... and generations of resistance before that. I'd be immediately accepted as a patriot, returning to *the cause*. You know that, Bill. This is destiny!'

His voice is little more than a whisper. 'I'm a British agent, Maureen. You're on the opposite side of the ideological fence on this one. It could never work.'

'No, Bill. I don't buy that. You are a philosopher, not an ideologue; no matter who is employing you. You work out right and

74

wrong based on reason not on colonial dogma. I've seen you and listened to you. You are better than that.' She pauses and smiles before settling into a grim pleading expression. 'You want to know the supply chain. And then what? Report it back to Britain. How'd you propose to do that, then? Surely, you wouldn't be falling into that superior trap of thinking the republicans are just a bunch of ill-informed *Paddies*? They are very smart, as they have already proved many times over in this conflict. Do you think they'll give you a radio or are you just going to phone it through to London?'

Maclean shakes his head slowly; his shoulders stoop in resignation at the argument he doesn't want to have.

'There'll be contacts,' he replies in a flat, soft voice. 'Dead-letter drops. Very quiet. There are procedures in place. But I don't intend to be hanging around terrorist groups. It's more about finding out the systems, the places and the names – as an endorsed representative of resistance groups. And then, like here in Lebanon, I get out fast and let the hard men take over.'

She shakes her head slowly. 'Are you going to doctor the arms you're smuggling? They'll be used against British soldiers. You know that.'

'No. We'll leave them clean. At the end of the chain, the IRA'll be scanning all the crates for tracking devices. Just one firing pin missing or one electronic bug and the repercussions would follow us back down the line to here.'

'You're sending real weapons to be used against your own country's troops? Where's the ethics in that? How can you justify that one to your conscience?'

'I've already had that argument with London. They're after a bigger picture – the key people behind the scenes. They'll save many more lives in the long term. If we don't supply, someone else surely will – and we will miss the intel on who is who in their systems. But, yes … it's a dilemma, for sure.'

'Jeezus, it's a bloody cold attitude your people have.' She bangs the table. 'And that settles it. I *have* to go, Bill. Since we're talking ethics, I want to see the fighting over there finished even more than the Brits do – just as much as I want it to stop here in the eastern Med. It's a dodgy mission, they've given you. You can see that. I don't know how you can reconcile sending live weapons into the fight and still be working for the British. I sure as hell wouldn't be shipping arms to my enemies.'

Bill's voice stays quiet. 'A Palestinian put it well, here in Beirut, when it was first suggested that I get involved in the *Mediterranean Run*. He said that there was more to it than any puritanical view of morality. There's so much suffering happening anyway that we can't get distracted by a very natural handwringing about things that can go wrong. It's not about the present or protecting individuals. This is a war. It's a long-term view and a bigger picture. It's about forcing peace. We will lose some battles along the way, for sure. You and I agree that getting weapons in from Libya could balance the equation here. Yes?'

Maureen doesn't move, so he continues.

'London has the view that, over in Ireland, people dying and killing for a cause will never solve the situation. They have to get to the decision-makers to make a difference, particularly with the paramilitaries. No, I don't think they're stupid. Even though there will be plenty of one-eyed mental pygmies on all sides, the people behind all this are very smart. It's about getting to the money supply, their bankers, and the weapons runners – to cut off their life blood in the long run. If we can do that, we'll save thousands – the innocents, the British soldiers and even the warring Irish gangs. So, it's short-term support of an enemy, to get information against them. That could save everyone in the long term. It is a big-picture strategy. A balance of ethics, if you like. Short-term pain for long-term peace.'

She looks at him with piercing eyes. 'Well then, the British'd pay well for the correct information, wouldn't they?' She waits. 'Wouldn't they? It's worth everything to them, isn't it?' She waits again and then speaks very quietly. 'I've much more chance of finding out what's going on than you ever will. I'm a patriot; daughter and granddaughter of patriots. Without me covering your back, you could be a *dead man walking*. I can get the introductions, if that's what you need. When this is all over, we'll take our money and retire to Lac Leman. I want some peace too … with you ideally, before tackling the *Muddle* East again.'

She smiles at him to see if he gets her humour and her gesture for them both.

But he doesn't. Maclean squeezes his brow and winces. His mind is instinctively back to protecting his partner from impetuosity.

'You're now telling me that you're prepared to be a double-agent … effectively, to betray the promise that you made to your mother. Is that what you're saying?'

She sighs. 'I'm saying that we'll take the arms into Ireland to even up the fight – to bring it to a head, like *you* want, like *I* want – so that they'll sit down and talk. *That's* my promise to my mother. There are long standing issues of social justice to be resolved; been going on for hundreds of years. They won't bloody listen to an enemy unless they're forced to, by fear of not doing it. This is not simple stuff, Bill. Maeve understood that. I'm not betraying her. Getting them talking and listening is not betraying her. That's the key to all these conflicts! The IRA will bring the pig-headed colonists and their lap-dogs to the table. But the Irish will not be the bloody down-trodden, again – they'll be equals in the process.'

She sits down at their *own* table, in their Beirut flat, elbows resting on the cloth-covered top, hands supporting her lowered face as she adds, *sotto voce*, 'But I am very happy with you as well, Bill – most of the time.' She flicks a smile. 'When the sides are even, we stop all the future runs. The only people harmed will be the gun runners and they deserve what they get. This is about justice for an oppressed people, squaring up the contest and taking away the power from those who are just cold to suffering. Yes, I'm saying – two birds with one stone. We balance the ledger and we'll bring out the information to stop the future supply line. Your British can have the smuggling chain – put them out of business. I'll shop them all for an end to the pain, to get them all to negotiate.'

Maclean nods slowly. 'You're quite a woman, Maureen Jazy. Alright. Alright. We're a team. I go, you go. As long as London approves.'

* * * *

To Bill's surprise, London is not averse to Maureen accompanying him. The controller seems to understand their demonstrated skills as a team in the eastern Mediterranean. As he explains it, he supports the idea of embedding a covert reporter into the scenario which they expect could, and would, bring great independent media support to the intelligence work of the British forces – and strength to the anticipated final negotiations.

But the deal has to be that the Irish will know nothing of Maureen's reporting brief – not even a whisper. The cover story has to be watertight. As far as the Republicans are concerned, she is simply the fanatical Maeve Gallaher's daughter coming back to Donegal to work for *the cause*. She will travel on the boat runs as a cook and be offloaded in Eire as a Republican activist. Discreet payment on results will happen into a numbered Swiss bank account by the British agency, after they are both extracted.

As Maclean struggles with his moral dilemma, his mind is tortured on two fronts: the hope that his actions won't add to the cold devaluing of human life in Northern Ireland and that the operational teams of the British will arrest the whole network quickly, without collateral damage.

The second front is his natural protective response toward a twenty-year-old woman – the first he believes he has truly loved at such an intellectual and physical level in his life, albeit only for the past few months. And he trusts her to protect his own role from any disclosure – trusts her, indeed, with his life.

'So what's the arrangement?' she asks.

'*My* credibility is the endorsement of the Lebanese, Libyans and Palestinians from our local work here – revolutionary contacts, street cred. You too. But you have your other credentials as well. The deal with the Irish lads is that we, on behalf of the eastern

Mediterranean Run, want to understand their systems, learning from their experience to help the Palestinian struggle. If there's no letting us in on their fundraising and logistics systems, then there'll be no arms deal. They have accepted that.' He grins. 'In principle, at least, even if it was under a bit of duress. They need the weapons and we are fellow revolutionaries insisting on their support.'

'Right. Okay. How will it work?'

'Out of Libya. One of the big ships that we usually have. Boat alongside, take on cargo-crates of plastic explosives and armaments and head towards Gibraltar. Then transfer to a trawler off Portugal. Somewhere off the Donegal coast, an Irish fishing boat will confirm the exact contact location. Inflatable with the crates will see us onto the beach at night.'

'You already know all that about *The Run*?'

'The Brits have an agent on the Portuguese boat. The skipper has been compromised by them. But, all we know is the general pattern. Our people haven't yet identified the main Libyan contact or the actual ship that will be used. All information gets relayed, just in time, the same as with the Irish. As far as they understand, we are looking at their general processes, their checks and balances; but we actually want to know the *real* identities of people on the ground in Ireland – and the financial sources that are backing them so strongly.'

'It all sounds pretty iffy to me.'

'My tasks are often as vague as that. I'm a listener. What we don't know means we won't compromise ourselves. We are what we appear to be – gun runners from Lebanon learning from fellow revolutionaries. Do you still want to go?'

'You go, I go.' She grins at our mantra. 'But ...' The smile disappears.

Chapter 14

June, 2013. Dubrovnik, Croatia

Ivana Bikić stares out through the Dubrovnik window of her business practice onto the turquoise Adriatic Sea. 'Macan, you say. 183 tall. Dark hair. Strong. Possibly involved in crime?'

She turns to look at Sam Hall, with his still dark hair and bottle-tanned skin.

He adds, 'He may have been in Greece, can speak a bit of English.'

'Most of us can speak some Greek and a fair bit of English, French, Italian and Croatian too. That is the world in this melting pot, especially in the legal business. Phew! My father rarely makes it easy for me. Macan? It's not an uncommon name here.' She gives a full-toothed smile which lightens her eyes into a sparkle. The flick of her long dark hair might have been an accident but Sam is quite prepared to believe otherwise. 'I,' she continues, '*we*, will have to make some enquiries. You have no Croatian language, is that right?'

'I'm happy to be taught.' He grins. 'But no – Latin if there are any ancient Romans around; reasonable Spanish plus a traveller's smattering of spoken Greek, French, Pashto, Arabic and Mandarin. Croatian hasn't been part of my learning as yet, I'm afraid.'

'Then we will have to stay together.' She gives a surprising giggle, as if it might be an enjoyable experience. And the smile remains.

'That suits me,' he replies, mildly confused at her jovial response – this is work-time. 'I would need to be looked after.' He gives a clipped smile. 'So, you're a lawyer like your father?'

'A lawyer, yes. Not like my father. Goran is in The Hague. I am *here* – running the *actual* business. No similarity, at all.' She moves over to her desk, crossing her long black business-trousered legs as she sits and adjusts a light, gold necklace above her understated red-patterned top. Phone in hand, she punches in a speed dial.

'Luka, I need your wisdom.'

Sam watches her, while trying to work out her words and body language. Is he misinterpreting? Is she nervous? Mention of The Hague can sometimes do that to people. Or is this playful innocent flirting?

She pauses to listen to a response on the phone, before saying, 'Do you know a Macan, Luka? Criminal. Stand-over man. Coastal dialect?'

She waits as she listens and then turns to Sam, her hand lightly covering the mouthpiece. 'We have three possibles.'

She turns back to the phone to speak to Luka. 'Dark hair. Just under 183.' She waits. 'Can you check for me please? Then we'll follow your best lead first. Love you, Luka.'

As she turns back to the quizzical, perhaps disappointed, Sam 'He's my cousin. He'll get back to me. Have you been to Dubrovnik before? We could take a quick tour to get your bearings. Luka will get me on the mobile.'

'Thank you. That would be very nice.' Sam graciously stands as his English upbringing has instilled in him. He waves Ivana towards the door, as she flicks her hand in farewell at the pile of papers on her desk.

* * * *

They stroll out past the ancient stone walls and red roofs of the *Stari Grad*, the old town, past the Courthouse and onto the seawall to marvel at the spectacular ancient Fort Lovrjenac, high on its rocky peninsula, glistening grey in the early summer sun.

'Very impressive. What a beautiful place you live in.'

'Yes, it has a lot of history. These walls could tell some stories. A bit cramped and crowded sometimes for the twenty-first century, but we manage.'

'I'm glad I came here.'

She rewards him with another broad smile. 'So you are an investigator, Sam. I can imagine what sort of business, if you are working near Dad.'

'And Luka? Is he an investigator too?'

'In a way. Police. Detective, in fact. So he will be narrowing down the Macans who fit your brief.'

Sam gives an impressed nod and a sweeping wave at the spectacular old town. 'Quite a fortress. You'd be too young to remember the War of Independence?'

She laughs. 'It never works to use reverse-deprecating charm. You could have come straight out with it, Mr Investigator. I'm thirty-two. How old are you?'

'Thirty-eight.'

'You see. You look older. Must be too much sun to give that deep tan.' She laughs cheekily. 'You'd look good with blond hair, don't you think?' He hangs his head. 'You really should think about it.'

She is too smart for him – to see through the dye and fake tan. She just continues to laugh with him, at his discomfort. 'You want to know about our independence. I was at primary school when the war was on, since you ask. It was quite scary at times. We were shelled here in town. Just pig-headedness that started it. You see, after Marshal Tito's time, there was agreement that the position of head of Yugoslavia would be rotated round each of the provinces. In 1991, it was Croatia's turn but the Serbs blocked it in the parliament and it just escalated.'

She seems relaxed as they walk. Noticing Sam's obvious interest, she continues.

'Our country wasn't prepared. We had only crop-dusters for an airforce and a handful of tanks. It was very hard. Much worse close to the Serbian border where the main fighting happened. Dubrovnik got off quite lightly really, by comparison to some places in the former Yugoslavia – but it was bad enough here, believe me. Very scary, when it is all happening to you and you don't know how it is going to end. A lot of foreign fighters came in to help us and many landed in our port. They had boats bringing weapons and ammunition in too, running through the blockades.

'But it's peaceful here now. My father, Goran, knew much more about what was going on than I did, naturally enough, which is why he has been away in the Netherlands working with all the trials, on and off over the years. Mind you, it seems to have been more *on* than *off* there recently. He is leaving me to run the business on my own.'

'You have no partner.'

She grins provocatively. 'I assume you mean in the legal business. No, I don't. The business is small enough to be just manageable and I have plenty of contacts for assistance when needed. And, I have no partner in the rest of my life either …' she laughs at him again '… at the moment.'

Her mobile rings to spare him. 'Yes, Luka. Right. I'll let him know.' She turns to meet his expectant look. 'Of the three Macans, one has blondish hair. That might rule him out … unless he has dyed it.' The cheeky smile again. 'That leaves Macan Horvat who comes from Senj, up the coast, but lives in Dubrovnik now; and Macan Granić who actually comes from here. Both have records with the police, and both roughly fit your description. Luka is checking further. This will cost me in legal favours, you know.'

'So how can I make that up to you?'

She flicks her long dark hair and grins. 'I'll think of something.'

Chapter 15

1973. Heading for Ireland

As the ship approaches the Straits of Gibraltar, Palestinian revolutionaries from *Black September* are seizing the Saudi Embassy in Paris. The headlines flash worldwide and the bridge relays the gist down to all the crew.

Bill Maclean wonders if that is the big event that he has been pre-empting to London. But, surely not … his advice suggested something much bigger than that and aimed against Israel, not fellow Arabs. He has been passing on lots of specifics about weapon caches in Lebanon, troop movements in Syria and guerrilla activities, generally. There has been no mention that the *Black September* dissidents might engage in this type of action. But they are a very secretive group.

Everything remains quiet on board. Apart from the initial excitement, they are in an information vacuum on the ship.

* * * *

Once through the Straits, Bill and Maureen change ships (with their cargo) onto a bona fide deep-sea trawler with a licence to fish the Bay of Biscay and the Atlantic coast of Ireland.

The ship is registered in northern Portugal and has a surly bearded skipper. Perhaps his manner is due to being compromised by the British over criminal activity in the past.

The two newcomers join an unshaven four-person crew. If one of those four is a British agent, he is well disguised. They all speak in Portuguese, with only the captain appearing to converse in reasonable English.

The ship logs its course up the coast of Portugal, out into the Atlantic, to be off the coast of Cork and Kerry in mid-September.

Then, by late September, it plans to be circling its nets off Donegal where it will be met at sea by a vessel near Aran Island. There, the final drop location will be confirmed and the crates offloaded, with Bill and Maureen to be transferred by inflatable at night to a lonely shingle beach.

* * * *

The trip up the coast of Ireland is uneventful. The sturdy trawler groans in the big swell, causing Maureen to be groaning into the *heads*, pale with sea-sickness.

They pass the mountain tips of the MacGillycuddy's Reeks in County Kerry, and on up the coast.

* * * *

It is a moonless night in late September 1973 when the dull shape of Aran Island comes into view. Two lighthouses flicker their protective strobes, welcoming the trawler cautiously to the southern edge of Maghery Bay.

There is just the slightest ambient reflection off the rolling water as the crew pick out the muted navigation lights on the darkened shape of a fishing boat that has moved down the channel, past Arranmore, and out to meet them. The little boat heaves in the steady swell.

The much smaller Irish vessel manoeuvres into a closer position underneath the trawler's loading derrick. Maclean stands with Maureen, near the winch, watching the shapes of the skipper and three men on board the Donegal vessel. The skippers shout something across the rails and the deckhands start the delicate transfer of the boxes on the connecting wire line between two boats several metres apart.

Given the swell in the water, a harness is rigged for transferring Maclean and Maureen Jazy from deck to deck. Jazy is winched over first on the pulley system. Bill watches her being unstrapped from the harness and waving *okay* from the Irish boat.

As the harness is pulled back over to the trawler for him to use, he collapses on the deck, stunned by the force of a cosh, swung by a bearded crew member.

* * * *

With the connecting ropes disengaged, the Arranmore boat turns for the darkness of the land, in the general direction of Dungloe.

As Maclean slowly recovers his senses, he kneels against the gunwale looking at the disappearing boat. His last vision of his Maureen is her pale face mouthing something to him as her boat melts into the darkness.

Behind him, the English voice whispers through his Portuguese fisherman's dark beard, 'Orders from London. Sorry.'

'What orders?'

'You are compromised. They know you are a British agent.'

'How?'

'Don't know that yet. But the shipment is heading for *The Cat Pack* on shore. The leader of that group is one Padraic Hennessy. He would kill you without a qualm.'

'What about Maureen? You stupid bastard! You've let her be carried into that whole business. Aaah!' He winces from the recurring pain of the earlier clubbing.

'Sorry. London thought she was a fair risk.'

'A fuckin fair risk, London thought, did they? She's my partner. She goes, I go. That is the deal.'

'She's a returning patriot. She'll be welcomed.'

'Welcomed,' Maclean shouts. 'Her mother was banished from that bloody land just because she was pregnant. Maureen may be the granddaughter of Seamus Gallaher but she was born in France – an exile. God, you've really fucked this up. How do I get to shore?' He tries to struggle to his feet but is restrained by the strong bearded man.

'You're not going to shore, Mr Maclean. I have instructions to see you safely back to London.'

'With my woman in danger, you've Buckley's chance of doing that. You've off-loaded her to a pack of Irish gangsters. Padraic Hennessy and *Cat Pack*, you say. Even *I* have heard of that mob. She will be gone and I will hold you and London directly responsible.'

'London says she will be safe. Much safer if you're not with her.'

'And how do they figure that?'

'Because Padraic Hennessy is her natural father and he knows she is on that boat – and he knows that you are a British agent. You can't be part of that scene onshore now.'

Chapter 16

September, 1973. London

The green vibrancy of summer foliage has started to wither into autumn browns. It is a time of change in the trees – and in the emotions that Bill Maclean is feeling, having arrived in the capital. Padraic Hennessy is Maureen's natural father. Stunning!

She has never once mentioned his name – or any name – as her natural father. Why not? Not through all their fiery arguments about running weapons. He has just assumed that the identity of the father was unknown – not a notorious republican gang leader. The conversation was always about her mother, the Gallaher connection and stepfather, Jacques Jazy. Assumptions!

With his mind feeling tortured, he stares disinterestedly at couples strolling blissfully through Hyde Park, savouring the last dregs of summer warmth, storing away their memories, squirrel-like, before the briskness turns to the cold of winter.

But, his stride has no bounce as he walks through the parks and streets towards an appointment he doesn't want to keep. Perhaps it is the influence of *the gaoler* accompanying him – as if an agent can't be trusted to return to his head office.

Feeling uncharitably cold of spirit, he is escorted in to meet with his controller. The familiar room seems to stink in a way it never did before – the metaphor of lost glories – an anachronism; the whole building, paintings of past heroes, florid wall paper and polished furniture. It has become an alien world, exuding no warmth to a desolate man.

'You are too emotionally involved, William.' The controller flicks his lank hair from his forehead, throwing the slightest cloud of dandruff onto the dark shoulder material of his regulation suit. 'Of course, you would have tried to save her. And then we would be looking for both your graves.'

Weasel words. But Maclean's sense of patriotic duty – discipline – tempers his language and enables him to contain the strong urge to smash his fist into the condescending face.

'I was the one appointed for this mission, not Maureen. She is not employed to take these risks. This had better not go pear-shaped. Mark my words.'

'It will work well, William. Just be patient.' He nods encouragingly, with a patently false smile.

Maclean shakes his head in thinly-veiled disgust. 'But she doesn't know any of the dead-letter drop sites. She has no way of communicating with you or me. How is the information going to get out?'

'It's the detail about the financing and the people at the Eire end that we need. We can wait till she is extracted. Then, we'll move. We are after the *big picture*. It will take time. Now, I wouldn't be surprised if she doesn't write a note to you at some stage. It might be via her stepfather, Jacques Jazy, in Montreux. Padraic knows about him ... and about you now, obviously. I imagine they'll control what she can write and to whom. Certainly, they will check everything. Maureen will, I hope, play innocent; or she may handle it in her own way. If she does send you messages, irrespective of whatever personal things she might write, we will need to read them for any information included for our eyes.'

Bill Maclean can't hold back the snarl. 'Shit! Is there no end to you people? You have the emotional sensitivity of rocks.'

'This is not a game, William. Individual feelings have to defer to the common good. But likewise, I would add, if you get the chance to reply to whatever postbox she might give you, we will want to read that too, so that no subliminal dangers are transferred to these madmen. They can be very skittish and we don't want to frighten them into any permanent solutions.' A limp smile just fails to form but the thought is clear in his eyes. 'This is about Maureen's safety.'

'Is *that* right? I've had enough of this … and you. Is it alright if I see myself out?'

'Of course, William. Be sensible now. We understand how you must feel.'

Maclean shakes his head in disbelief and leaves.

* * * *

He can do no more in London or Ireland, so he returns to Beirut. He is still a trained British agent, bound by the Official Secrets Act. The talk of something big happening is still the constant chatter on the resistance grapevine. It is all in Arabic, which may have been code enough to keep it undetected. But Maclean passes the information back to London, translated verbatim.

* * * *

On October 6, 1973 – the *Yom Kippur* religious holiday in Israel – Syria and Egypt launch huge simultaneous attacks on Israel.

Israel appears to have been both unsuspecting and unready.

Maclean wonders if his information has even been passed on. Hadn't they believed him? The Brits have little love for the Israelis after their many casualties in the Palestinian policing experience up until 1948. But still, a quarter of a century on, intelligence of this nature wouldn't be withheld? Surely not?

He had reported the quiet accumulation of Syrian tanks, 1,400 of which were at that moment pitted against an apparent 180 Israeli tanks on the Golan Heights. He had flagged several other rumours of the seemingly suspicious build-up of what might potentially be 80,000 Egyptian soldiers now harassing what appears to be only 400 Israeli troops trying to defend along the Suez Canal.

Surely this is the big event he has been flagging? Surely, they have understood – or why else has he been here, sending back regular intelligence warnings? Are the Israelis not part of the

British intelligence loop? Is this another piece of colonial deceit or just plain incompetence?

Lebanon is also allowing Palestinian fighters to shell Israeli border positions from its territory, no doubt using weapons that Bill and Maureen have helped smuggle in on the *Mediterranean Run*. But Maureen, at least, would be pleased that the balance of power appears to have evened up. Perhaps, it will bring all the parties to the negotiating table.

* * * *

After two days in total defence, the Israeli Defence Force regroups and progressively overcomes their aggressors. To their military credit, this is the third time in their short history that the IDF has proved their worth in major battles. The Israeli cost is 2,688 soldiers dead and 7,250 wounded. The cost to the combined Arab side is much much higher – in the many tens of thousands – and they have lost that short war.

Maclean knows that he isn't responsible for the battles but he is in a fragile emotional state. He carries a huge sense of transferred guilt from smuggling arms. It keeps him awake at night, along with his worry over how his Maureen might be faring – and his anger at his employers in London, who presume to know what is best for the woman he wants to spend his immediate future with.

As a salve, he listens to Louis Armstrong's music, particularly where the New Orleans crooner sings with gravelly off-beat compassion in his voice. It keeps him close in spirit to Maureen.

He writes carefully worded letters to her and addresses them – as London advised – through her stepfather in Montreux, in the hope that she will get them, forwarded at some stage by Jacques Jazy, through the agency censor.

London tells him that their observers in the Republic have noted that Maureen is alive, travelling with Hennessy and appearing to be in good health. It is head office's expectation that she will probably be in Ireland for six months.

After a month, he does indeed receive a brief written note from Maureen, relayed through Montreux and doubtless combed over by the censor, where she writes in superficial language about enjoying being with family over there and looking forward to the time when she and Bill will picnic again up amongst the Cedars of Lebanon. Try as he might, he can't deduce any extra meaning but it is reassuring at least to hold the message in his hand.

* * * *

The months pass slowly for Maclean in Lebanon. Even with all the busy work caused by the fighting and the aftermath of the *Yom Kippur* War, Maclean is scanning every report from Ireland for any hint of Maureen's progress. The tiniest bit of news takes on vastly greater importance as he tries to read significance into every story.

In mid-November 1973, eight IRA terrorists are found guilty of a bombing in London.

By the end of the month, the two-hundredth British soldier is killed in Ulster, all since *The Troubles* started.

His conscience tortures him. Are the weapons that he helped smuggle contributing to those deaths?

On into 1974, there seems to be no let up. On 20th April 1974, a Catholic man is shot in Belfast, becoming the thousandth recorded victim of the unrest.

* * * *

He continues to collect information and interview people in Lebanon, trying to find some chink in that particular challenge which might lead to a solution to all the killing.

Hope always seems to spring up in the Middle East and be swatted down again, unceremoniously. The most promising sense of elation had come in November 1973, when the United Nations brokered a cease-fire between Israel and Egypt. However, it only just managed to last through till the end of the month – the result of generations of children on both sides being brought up to hate. And the hatred was directed at a group of people, stereotyped as being the enemy. They might as well be branded as such on the forehead.

Depression has started to sink its insidious claws into William Maclean. He recognises the signs, but cares so little that he draws a perverse pleasure from just wallowing.

* * * *

Then, the London controller advises him that Padraic Hennessy appears to have left Ireland. Oh, joy! The word is that he has gone to Massachusetts on one of his many fundraising trips.

Even the dandruffed controller assesses that as promising information for Maureen being able to return, soon.

Chapter 17

'Macan Horvat is twenty-three, Macan Granić is twenty-one,' Luka Jusić advises. 'They both have dark hair and police records for serious assault, theft and actual bodily harm using weapons.'

The detective sits with his cousin, Ivana, and Sam Hall in her Peugeot 508, in the car park of the grey-block police station in *Vladimira Nazora* Street, Dubrovnik. Luka has a ready smile as he shares his information; a favour for his cousin.

'Horvat is in town at the moment – in custody actually, down-stairs – being held for disorderly behaviour; drunk. He'll be released later when he has calmed down and sobered up. Granić has been away from here for a few weeks, probably over two months, but his mother lives only a few blocks away from here.'

'Thanks, Luka. You are a big help.' Ivana smiles, as she takes the handed note with the last known addresses for the two Macans. 'Sam is working with Goran in The Hague.'

He nods his understanding as he looks at Sam. 'Happy to help my cousin's friend. Be careful. You are not mixing with good people with these Macans.'

'Understood.' Sam looks at the solidly built policeman, perhaps in his early thirties, dressed in a grey suit; but his concentration is on listening to every word, while taking in the accents and the unfamiliar surroundings. 'I'm just following up a vague lead of a name and a connection to Croatia. These fellows may not have any involvement in anything to do with us.' He pauses before venturing, 'Could either of those two Macans have travelled overseas recently? You'd need a Croatian passport still, is that right?'

'Yes, at least until 1 July – not long now – when we are officially accepted into the European Union. Then we can travel through the member countries without paperwork problems.'

'What about going to Cyprus?'

'This month, they would still need passports but thugs like them could be smuggled in on a boat. That's not unlikely. And Macan Granić has been away for a while. It's possible. What is it they might have done?'

'It could be gang related; stand-over stuff, instilling fear. The other lead we have is something to do with cats.'

'Cats?' Luka's eyebrows raised in question. '… as in gangs linked to cats?'

'Perhaps. It's quite vague.'

Luka ponders for a few seconds, as if deciding what to say. 'Cats? Like tigers, maybe?'

'Go on.'

'Have you heard of Željko Ražnatović … sometimes he was known as Arkan? He ran a paramilitary force for the Serbs during the War of Independence. Indicted for war crimes, he was.'

'Yes. I've heard the name. Wasn't he shot in a hotel in Belgrade about a decade ago?'

'That's right. That is the man. His fighters were called Arkan's Tigers. Some of the gangs here use that term – *teegar*, we say it – to make themselves feared.'

'And are these Macans feared?'

'Macan Granić certainly is. He's a knife man. Charged with rape four months ago but the case fell over through lack of evidence. A rabid dog would be a good description; but hard to pin things on him because victims are too frightened to speak up. Dubrovnik has been much quieter with him out of the area. We hassle him, and the others, as much as we can. To not let them settle … so maybe he has gone away for some peace. Macan Horvat is more a thug heavy.

He has no parents down here to be a good influence. They still live up north in Senj. The gangs are his family. There's not much up top,' he taps his forehead, '… but big … and muscles … often too much beer and slivovitz, our powerful plum brandy.'

'So who leads their gangs?'

'They're not really very organised – more just groups of young bullies looking for mischief. We take them off the streets but they are allowed out again. The courts – they need so much evidence. So we pester them. They go; they come back. Frustrating.'

'Granić sounds more like the sort of man I might be seeking.'

'Well, he's not around. Like I say, hasn't been seen for a few weeks.'

'What about his mother? She lives nearby, you said? Can I speak to her?'

Luka smiles and shrugs. 'Perhaps I should go with you … to translate, you understand – cultural protocols. His mother might not make you very welcome.'

'Could you do that? That would be brilliant, Luka.'

Ivana smiles and holds up both her hands. 'If you two are off to speak with suspects, this lawyer has a stockpile of case notes and letters to complete. Can you excuse me from the detective work? Okay?' And to the man from IIB, 'See you later, Sam, back at the office. Don't be too long. I don't want to work all day.'

'Fine, Ivana,' agrees Luka. 'I'll drop Sam back to you in an hour or so.'

* * * *

The Granić flat is in a three-storey block, grey with thick, orange tiles brightening the roof. A string of washing hangs on a pulley clothesline from a top-floor window.

Luka pulls his green, four-door Skoda into the paved yard. He and Sam climb the internal stairs between rough, stone walls and knock on the unpainted wooden door at the top.

A high pitched voice calls out something that sounds to Sam like 'Taw ye taw'.

'She is saying, who is it,' Luka explains then raises his voice to say, '*Policia*.'

Grumbling oaths come from inside. Something bangs, like a chair falling over but the door opens to reveal a tired woman, mid-forties perhaps, shapely in a solid way, wearing an apron, with a cloth band holding back her straggly dark hair. She rubs her red hands dry on the towel she is holding.

'You speak any English, *Gospodja* Granić?' Luka queries, in a commanding tone. 'This man wants to ask some questions.' He flicks his hand towards Sam, as her hostile eyes follow the gesture.

'Some,' she says, in a growl. 'Macan not here.'

'That was question one. Where is he?'

'How would I know? You think he tells his mother?'

'When did you see him last?'

'Months ago. He not here.' She shrugs and drapes the towel over her shoulder.

Sam's quiet voice takes over from Luka's authoritative police-man tones. 'Your English is good, Mrs Granić, *Gospodja* Granić.'

She gives a bewildered look from Sam to the policeman. 'Polite, eh? What he know of Macan or me?'

'Only that you are Macan's mother. He wonders where Macan is?'

'I don't know. Told you. Not here. Not for weeks.'

Sam tries again. 'What about Macan's father? Could he be with *him*?'

A torrent of Croatian abuse pours out of the woman before he picks up the often repeated word, '*Eertsi*'.

'Irish,' Luka explains to Sam's questioning look, with a suppressed grin at the tirade. 'Macan's father was Irish. Over here for the Independence War. She hasn't seen the father since.' With a wry smile, he adds with classic police understatement. 'She doesn't have fond feelings for Macan's father.'

'Macan has his mother's surname,' observes Sam. 'What was the father's name.'

She spits the words out, as she registers his question. 'Sweeney. McSweeney,' followed by another outpouring of vitriol.

Luka shrugs. 'Macan was born in 1992. Back then, there were Irish and British and French and Germans … many nationalities here … fighting … bringing in weapons for the defence. Things happened. Macan's mother hasn't had it easy. But that's when she would have learned her bits of English. Now, useful for tourists. Lots of deals.' He gives a non-commital grin.

At that, the woman lets fly with another cascade of Croatian abuse at the absent father of Macan.

Sam and Luka leave as the angry woman turns back into her room, shouting abuse at the ceiling, the walls and the world for her situation.

'Not a happy lady,' Sam says. 'But an interesting comment about Sweeney or McSweeney. That surname has come up in our conversations in Rotterdam quite recently.'

Luka gives the patient perennial grin of a detective who has seen it all before. 'Do you want to try the other Macan? Just in case?'

* * * *

Back in the Skoda, they head to the police station.

* * * *

In the holding cells, Sam walks with Luka and a guard along the underground corridor, with the pervading smell of disinfectant clearly trying to mask something more offensive.

'Horvat definitely speaks no English. I'll ask questions and translate for you.'

Sam nods his agreement as the guard unlocks a heavy cell door and ushers them in. A large unshaven man sits on the only bunk looking pale, tired and unhappy. He is not old but he has the derelict look of someone sleeping rough – yet with a strong physique.

Clearly, he knows Luka, the detective, because a faint respect shines through the eyes, despite his surly expression. He scratches and shifts uncomfortably as the questions and answers start to flow.

Eventually, Luka turns to Sam to explain in English. 'He claims he hasn't seen Macan Granić for several weeks. Doesn't miss him, he says. Granić is a bully to everyone. He was told he had gone on a fishing boat somewhere.'

'Can you ask him if there is an old man involved with the gangs anywhere?'

The detective's brow creases in question but he relays the message.

Immediately, Horvat's eyes become very sly – peering and darting – but he answers, '*Ne.* No.'

'What about gangs calling themselves *cats*?'

Patiently, Luka relays the question, and clarifies for the puzzled Horvat. Sam hears the sound '*teegar*' in whatever answer is given.

'He says that lots of gangs call themselves tigers, panthers, lions … even leopards.'

'Ask him about cougars.'

As the question is relayed, Horvat's eyes widen, then his head goes down as he mumbles, '*Nema. Nista.*'

Luka gives a wry smile back to Sam. 'He says, *no, nothing,* but you may have struck a nerve.' He looks back at the silent bowed Horvat. 'Perhaps, we leave him just now and go to my office, where you can give me some clue what we are looking for.'

As they leave the cell door, Horvat looks up, dejected, scared, '*Ne, Ne Tsogar, Nista.*'

'He is saying, *No. No cougar. Nothing.* Which is very interesting, very interesting indeed.' Luka gives Sam a querying look. 'You need to tell me what is going on here in my Dubrovnik, I think.'

Chapter 18

May, 1974. Lebanon

Life moves slowly for Bill Maclean. It is the start of May.

Refugees continue to pour into Lebanon. Maclean watches the pressure in the bulging *Shatila* camp, near where he lives in Beirut. The Red Cross struggles to help desperate people or even to maintain sanitary conditions.

Every day seems to increase the danger level on the streets. Sectarian flyers flaunt the horror, in photos, across the Middle East; the mutilating aftermath of bombings and shootings. Beirut, *the jewel of the Mediterranean*, is being progressively defiled.

Israeli troops conduct what they claim to be retaliatory raids into Lebanon while many international calls plead to the United Nations for Israel to return the abducted Lebanese citizens.

Maclean despairs at the language of the world's media. They don't convey the shiver of fear that he senses – the desolation in the slums of the displaced; the numbed shock in the eyes of those just trying to live another day, the hopelessness. The press use antiseptic words: *assassination*, not murder; or *killed in cross-fire, collateral damage* as if the deaths were some anonymous accident – the sanitising analgesic of politics and diplomacy.

But the reporter in him continues to move around the city, asking the people he meets how to stop this tragic horror getting worse. And he hears, almost universally, that the simple cause of the problem is the Israelis pushing them out of their land and not just the territory promised to them by the British after World War I, but all the lands that the Israelis have occupied later by military invasion and by settlement.

In the Arab view, there can be no resolution until their stolen land is returned – until they can return to the houses of their forefathers, to the places which generations of their ancestors have called home, for hundreds and hundreds of years. How can they be displaced at the whim of conquerors? Thrown into exile; just barely existing in the despair of the refugee camps.

Several generations have already grown up displaced, being taught that *the only cause* is the fight to remove the Jews. That is what life is about, daily – survival and *the cause*. In Lebanon, the standard cry from young alienated men is to put both thumbs in the air and cry in Arabic, 'It is everything! We must avenge the murders. We die for *the cause*', with a few automatic religious mantras thrown in for good measure.

Maclean listens impassively to the relayed tales of the terror from 1948 when whole villages in the Galilee area were forced out by violent Jewish gangs. He records the passionate talks in the camps and the lack of sympathy for the Jews when the Israelis speak of their genocide in the Holocaust.

An old woman, sitting in a raggedy shawl to keep the harsh weather from her gnarled features, explains in a tired Arabic voice, 'The 1948 massacres at Deir Yassin by the Stern and the Irgun Gangs were just the continuation of a whole wave of genocide against the Arabs. They were killing us; forcing us to leave our homes; terrifying any who would not go.' She shudders in her memories, dabbing her eyes, as a young activist in her twenties spares the elderly woman more speech but continues to impress on the reporter, 'And it continues today in more subtle forms. Yes, we must fight for *the cause*.'

* * * *

For balance, as an independent reporter, Maclean travels to Jerusalem … anything to take his mind off waiting for Maureen

101

to return from Ireland. There he puts the Arab complaint to any, in hotel bars, who will listen.

Invariably, their replies express their exasperation. 'Arabs being terrorised out of the villages?' they question.

One impassioned older woman gives an ironic laugh. 'Do they tell you about the Kfar Etzion massacre carried out by Arabs in the same year before the Declaration of Independence? No? I didn't think so. They don't say anything about the Arab Legion terrorising our kibbutzim on a daily basis. Would they tell you that all the Jewish defenders of the Kfar Etzion, on the Jerusalem to Hebron road, surrendered to the superior Arab force and were machine-gunned in cold blood, every last one – just one example of many from that decade on. Do they tell you about the machine-gunning of school children in their buses, heading home to their families? Do they tell you about rocket attacks on our peaceful settlements and the bombings in our markets? Still going on – most days, even today.'

And when Maclean throws out his standard question for such occasions to ask what the solution to this fearful impasse might be, the answer is inevitably for the Arabs to stop the violence and to live in peace on the land that they still have. The Israelis say – they believe – that, in time, the Arab and the Jew can live together as they have for lengthy periods in the past. But while violence continues to be rained on the Israeli people then they will retaliate with terrible force.

Even when Maclean tells the view of one Arab resistance fighter he has interviewed, who justifies plane hi-jackings and bombings by saying, 'The world is listening to what we are saying now. For decades, our view was ignored.' The Jewish men simply say, 'See! That is what we are dealing with, every day. Every day.' And they shake their heads in sad despair. 'How can there be a solution with people like that?'

* * * *

Maclean files his reports back to the London agency as he becomes more and more gloomy about the future in the Mediterranean lands that he has grown to care about so deeply. Faced with the entrenched viewpoints of so many, fuelled by the documented memories of the deaths of friends or martyrs to support their fixed views of the world, he can see no hope. A negotiated peace appears to be a long way away.

In Ireland too, the legacy is decades – centuries – of advantage and disadvantage, followed by lawless resistance gangs on both sides killing people in a ruthless spread of terror. How can such intractable enemies ever sit down at a peace table and forget all that has happened.

Is it better to have peace or ... to have justice for all the people wronged? If it is to be the latter, then it will never end. Payback never stops. If your innocent family members have been murdered as collateral damage for *the cause*, how can you not want justice to be served on the culprits?

* * * *

On 10th May, word comes from Maclean's controller in London that Maureen's mission in Ireland is nearly over. He has more information. She has actually only been in Ulster with Padraic Hennessy for part of her time over there. The rest has been in the south, in Eire.

As she had indicated to Bill before they left, she must have used her patriot contacts to get into the Republican networks and she has apparently been learning about the secretive structures, finance and supply chains in the Republic.

He can feel the surge of relief through his system. The *black dog* of the past few months is lifting by the minute. So, she has been away from the steady violence of the North. Despite the occasional censored notes from her, which were about Lebanon or Lac Leman and her dreams for the publishing business, Maclean has never allowed himself to believe that she has been in anything other than a terrible dangerous situation. At last, with this latest news, they will be together again. Their shared dreams can become a reality again.

* * * *

The controller tells him to come to London for a grand reunion on 20th May 1974, a Monday – a new week, a new beginning. Maureen would be back and a couple of the leaders of their agency group will take them to a private room for dinner in an exclusive hotel, off The Strand. There, they will debrief on the mission, of course, while sharing good food and wine. Then he and Maureen will be on well-earned leave.

* * * *

On Friday 17 May, Bill Maclean boards a plane for London – a very happy man. On arrival, he settles into a five-star hotel, on the government's account, and looks forward to a bit of sight-seeing, while he waits for Maureen after the weekend. At last, this very difficult phase in their lives will soon be over.

Chapter 19

June, 2013. Dubrovnik, Croatia

'Nikkos is dead in Cyprus.'

Arthur Blair, from his office on the Maasboulevard, conveys the words to Sam Hall in Dubrovnik, over the phone.

'How?' Sam Hall stands, temporarily stunned in his hotel room, mobile frozen in his hand. He is part way through getting dressed before going out to be entertained for an evening meal at Ivana Bikić's mother's home, with the two women and Ivana's uncle, Danko Jusić.

'Tortured. The network found him in an empty Nicosia house. He was gagged, tied in a chair, with deep knife wounds in each thigh, other stabs had been twisted into the sides of the knees, and into the arms too, biceps slashed. He bled to death, in a lot of pain.'

'Jeezus. He told me people were terrified. What was it that he knew … that the torturer needed to find out?'

'Or perhaps it was a signal to everyone else to be frightened. It does suggest that Nicosia is still part of what might be happening. How's progress in Dubrovnik?'

'Yes? Here?' He shakes his head to refocus his thinking. 'Sorry. Of course, Arthur. Just a bit of a shock – Nikkos's death. Dubrovnik? Yes.' Back in control, he continues. 'Goran Bikić's daughter has been a big help. Thank him for me, please. Her name is Ivana and she's actually a very busy lady running Goran's family law practice while he's over there with you helping the international court build its prosecution cases.

'Her cousin, Luka Jusić, is a detective here. We have spoken to one of the Macans. He's a pretty brutish thug and is hiding something. He was in the cells, drunk and disorderly. But, he is definitely physically here in Croatia, not in Cyprus.

'We spoke to the mother of Macan Granić. He has a history of knives and has not been around for a couple of months or so. He could be the man in Nicosia. And interestingly, his mother told us that the father was an Irishman called Sweeney or McSweeney. It all came out in a torrent of not-very-clear Croatian abuse. She wasn't overly complimentary about him, so not much opportunity to clarify what she was actually saying. I'm guessing that he hasn't been seen since doing the deed. I leave the scenario to your imagination.

'But Luka suggested that McSweeney could have been running arms for the Croatian defence in the War of Independence. That was 1991 to 95, as you indicated. Granić was born in 92.'

Arthur Blair absorbed the information with a thoughtful 'Mmm. Well, it definitely wasn't Donnie McSweeney. He died in Fermanagh in early 1991. But it might have been the son, Michael, I suppose, working with Padraic Hennessy.'

'Very possible. A working hypothesis at least. I agree, Arthur. And something else, the other Macan, Macan Horvat, reacted to the mention of cats – even to denying the name *cougar* for a gang. But apparently, the gangs here sometimes use *big cat* names to look tough, trying to mirror Arkan and his Tigers from the early nineties.'

'Good, good.' Arthur pauses for a few seconds, collecting his thoughts again. 'It is coming together, Sam. Even if it seems to be getting more complex. There are ties now linking the threads. We are nearing the time when we can home in on what might really be happening. It's still pretty vague but, from talking with Jacques Jazy, it seems that whatever Maureen said to Padraic all those years ago might be about getting Israel to change its *Law of Return* – that's the rule which lets any Jewish person, or their immediate relatives, have the right to come back to Israel, even if they had never ever been there before. It's the *Promised Land* notion. But what Hennessy might think he could do to make that happen is beyond us all at the moment.'

'Sounds totally bizarre, Arthur. *Mossad* would have to be across any threat the mad Irishman could think up. Surely?'

'You might choose to think that, Sam, but there is a man in Nicosia who has met his end in a very painful way – presumably for talking to you, amongst others.'

'Yes, Arthur. I'm still a bit shaken by that news. Nikkos seemed like a good and brave man … and he was keen to see us help them. Very sad. What happens with his group now?'

'We'll get someone out to them, as soon as we can – Emma probably. Just be careful as you follow your threads over there, Sam. Talk soon.'

Chapter 20

May, 1974. London

It is Monday 20 May 1974. The Thames River snakes through the city as it always has, under bridges, sparkling in the fading flecks of late afternoon sunlight.

Bill Maclean emerges from the black beetle-shape of a London taxi and walks past the doorman, who is dressed in a gold-trimmed coat and top hat, beside the grandiose hotel entrance … through the marbled atrium, over to the walnut reception desk. He asks for the Wellington Room. Another servant in gold braid and an old-fashioned cap ushers him up the sweeping staircase, over the springy red carpet to an ornate wooden entrance to the private dining room – the Wellington Room.

Inside are two men, standing, goblet in hand, near a large, polished dining table set for four. Maclean addresses one as 'Brigadier' and the other is his dandruffed controller.

Candelabra in the centre give a flickering low sheen over gold cutlery and drinking goblets – not glass, but gold. The settings have a range of cutlery on either side of white and gold plates and Bill Maclean has the look of a man seeing another world for the first time. It appears to him that the powers that be are going out of their way to make his reunion with Maureen particularly special.

He glances around the walls where a series of concealed light bulbs send an ambient glow, making the room seem bright and dark at the same time while not detracting from the luminous warmth of the candles on the table.

A light beam focuses on a large portrait of Lord Wellington, mounted on a horse at some battle. There are other paintings which seem to fit with an early nineteenth century era. In all, the room would have cost a fortune to furnish.

'Maureen? Is she here yet?'

The Brigadier replies, 'We are just waiting for word.'

'A burgundy, perhaps?' asks the controller.

'Thank you,' Bill replies, and a servant in a braided jacket appears as if from nowhere to fill a golden goblet with the dark red wine.

'Let's sit,' suggests the Brigadier. 'We will start. Maureen will join us when I get word.'

Maclean nods – puzzled, but accepting. He is in the care of experienced men who are clearly used to this high-class style of living.

'My parents would be amazed to think that I am dining in a room like this,' Bill says to open some distracting conversation, thinking back to the small flat in the tenement in Dundee where he grew up.

'It is very nice,' says the controller.

Waiters just appear, saying nothing and placing an entrée of an artistically presented salmon cutlet on the plate before them. Golden scales? Was it just the reflection from the gold cutlery? No, these were yellow/red scales, almost golden in this light, and familiar from his youth.

'Sir, do you realise that this salmon has come to you from the River Tay in Scotland?'

'How ever would you know that, William?' asks the Brigadier, with an almost owl-like expression over his half glasses. 'It is indeed from the River Tay.'

'I used to be a salmon fisherman on the Tay. You can tell by the reddish-gold tinge in the scales. This cutlet has come from a *banker salmon*. The scales get tanned from the fish settling in the sunlight over the sand banks in the Tay estuary. At least, that's what the *old hands* told us. I'm not aware that this tanning happens anywhere else.'

'You have an amazing knowledge, William,' the Brigadier acknowledges, as they continue to eat quietly.

Neither of Bill's hosts seem to want to initiate a conversation topic. They appear to be content just to eat quietly, while responding politely to any observations from their guest. Bill avoids asking any more about when Maureen would arrive. It is either a very carefully contrived surprise or she has been delayed and they are rushing to get her there, probably the former. And they have obviously put a lot of preparation into this dinner.

The dishes from the entrée are cleared. The wine goblets are replenished and the main course is delivered on golden serving platters, wheeled in on silent trolleys. They just materialise, pushed over the plush carpet with no sound.

'Pheasant or venison, Sir?' the waiter speaks for the first time. It is indeed a different world. Both pheasant and venison belong to the landed gentry of Britain. No lowly Scot like Bill Maclean would ever have been exposed to these culinary delights, unless by poaching the Laird's stock.

'Pheasant, please.' He manages to get the words out.

'You like pheasant?' asks the Brigadier.

'Brigadier, in a past life, I used to *beat* pheasants on a lord's estate in Fife.'

'You have led such an interesting life, William.' The controller's voice is very quiet; no hint of sarcasm, just polite conversational responses and enquiry. 'How did you come to be *beating* pheasant?'

'It was another seasonal job like salmon fishing. It's a world away from this. I caught the Tay Ferry in the morning from Dundee to Newport. A cattle float picked me up at the jetty along with other local boys and took us out to the estate. It took about an hour to get to the big house and the grounds. I remember it well because they never hosed out the cattle float very well. That rich organic scent stayed with us for the whole day.'

'Fascinating!' The Brigadier smiles his appreciation of the tale. 'I have obviously been pheasant and grouse shooting but I have never really appreciated how the *beating* worked. Do tell!'

As neither of the chiefs seem to want to volunteer any conversation topics, Bill is content to at least educate them in the ways of the support people, the serving class.

'The gamekeeper was in charge of the beating. The whole estate was set up to enable pheasant shooting. They had many fairly large rectangular clumps of trees, surrounded by open fields. In the off-season, the pheasants would breed up and hide in the trees. The gamekeeper would line us up along the side of a bit of woodland and, on his signal, we moved through the fence and into the trees, *beating* the branches. It made a hell of a noise and scared any birds in the wood out the far side where a line of lords and ladies were waiting with their shotguns to shoot the birds as they flew over. Another of the *sports of kings*, I believe.'

'Indeed. How often would you do that in a day?' asks the Brigadier.

'Until the gentry got tired of shooting at the birds. Then the cattle float would take us back to the ferry.'

'You are such a fount of unusual information …' The controller's sentence is interrupted by a tall man in a dark suit who passes him an enveloped note on a silver plate. His expression changes into a worried crease as he passes the note and envelope to the Brigadier.

The Brigadier sighs, draws a deep breath, pauses, reads, coughs and then takes the responsibility to speak.

With a sombre face, he says, 'No easy way to say it, I'm afraid. William, I'm afraid I have bad news. Maureen Jazy has passed away this evening.'

A truck could have hit Bill with less impact. He can feel the colour drain straight out of his face and the room seems to swirl.

The Brigadier continues, as if to counter Bill's shock with explanation. 'As you know Maureen has been working for us since the September incident at Maghery Bay, where you were present. She has managed to provide superb intelligence, through her work in Donegal and latterly further south in Eire. Her task was complete and she was due to fly out on Saturday to be with us all for this dinner.

'On Friday past, the 17th, she went shopping for a present for *you*, I believe, in a Dublin department store. You would have been in the air from the Lebanon at the time. Anyway, there was a bomb alert and the store evacuated all the customers out into the street. It is normal practice. There would have been nearly a hundred people in the street ... when a car bomb exploded.'

Bill slumps, his face in his hands. The controller passes a glass of water and reaches out to comfort him. But Maclean draws back as if burned by the touch.

'Several people were killed in the blast and many others were injured.' The Brigadier's words continue: Maclean's numbed brain can hear but not fully comprehend. 'Maureen was protected to some extent by a lamp post but she was knocked unconscious and injured by the blast. Our people got to her. An ambulance took her to hospital but we decided that her injuries required the best treatment available, not in a hospital overcrowded with casualties. We got her flown out from a private airfield, south of Dublin, and admitted to a private hospital here, in London. Just round the corner from here, in fact.'

He continues, scarcely drawing breath. 'We had hoped that she would pull through – she had rallied somewhat several times – so that we could reunite her with you today. However, her internal injuries and ... were such that she never regained consciousness and she has passed away in the last hour.'

Bill Maclean's whole body feels numb. There is a fury brewing in him but it cannot yet reach his mouth. To his ear, his voice sounds disembodied, so controlled as he carefully and slowly asks, 'Can I see her?'

'I don't think that is advisable, William,' says the controller. 'Her injuries ... she is not the Maureen that you knew.' And just a split second before Maclean's fast-rising clenched fist could have buried itself in his face, he hands over an envelope. 'I have this letter that she wrote to you on the sixteenth. It was in her handbag when the bomb went off.'

The letter is addressed to *William Maclean, Soon to be residing on Lac Leman, Switzerland.* Always the joker. Always trying to make him laugh. There are burn marks on the edge of the paper as if someone has taken a candle and singed the side.

'The effects of the blast,' says the Brigadier, impersonally, as he notices Bill examining the envelope and pages.

The full impact of what has happened to his darling Maureen is sinking in now. If that was the effect on an envelope in a handbag, what had happened to the owner who was carrying the bag? Somewhere, deep in the recesses of his numbed but angry mind, Bill Maclean understands why they don't want him to see Maureen.

'I still want to see her.' The words come out slowly, with a visceral tone.

The Brigadier nods his agreement, solemnly.

'Now! Fuckin now!' Maclean shakes the envelope in front of him as his voice strains to hold back his powerful emotion.

* * * *

The evening sky of Monday 20th May in London is clear. Stars are starting to twinkle and smile. The street lights have kissed the glow of the dusk goodbye. A romantic time for lovers to be together.

A very dazed Bill Maclean leaves the hospital building with a fellow agent and a doctor for company; a dream shattered, a charred letter still in his hand. A limousine takes him back to the five-star hotel where the champagne is still on ice in the bucket.

He is not to be left alone during the night. The doctor gives him a powerful sleeping draught.

* * * *

The funeral is held on the following Friday at the Catholic church in Montreux.

Jacques Jazy, looking gaunt but as dignified as ever, has organised it all. Perhaps there would have been about fifty people there, including the Brigadier and the controller. Bill scans around the mourners. Is Padraic Hennessy there? What does he look like? Maclean has only ever seen hazy shots of a dark-haired man around forty-years-old, usually identified by his quiet voice rather than his nondescript appearance. But no-one seems to fit the description … and sunglasses hide most red eyes.

Bill manages a few wry smiles as the happy celebration of the fun life of his beautiful lady are recounted: childhood pranks, family jokes, her passion for the disadvantaged, the comforting jazz music, her professed joy amongst the Cedars of Lebanon … and her recently declared love for William Maclean. Oh the pain of loss, mellowed only by the torpor of powerful drugs.

Louis Armstrong's *Wonderful World* plays between the eulogies and prayers.

As the coffin is taken to the cemetery, Armstrong's gravelly and shaky voice sings out the last song he ever recorded – and the poignancy is not lost on anyone – *We have all the time in the world.*

The world is floating by … dreamlike. It seems so surreal – that particular song being played as she is taken respectfully to her final rest, until Bill realises that his love will be forever young. She is forever where she wanted to be, overlooking her precious Lac Leman; forever the love of his life, where indeed she would always have … all the time in the world.

It seems alright – the peace of Lac Leman, the timeless voice of Louis Armstrong, her pain is over – as Bill walks away from the cemetery with a sense of surreal peace, the anger spent. He would find solace in a memory of the joyous months that they'd shared.

* * * *

He goes back to Lebanon. Nothing has changed in the old hostilities but Bill Maclean has changed. He requests London to be relocated to another task, and he packs up his and Maureen's memories, to be preserved in a sealed cardboard box.

His last act is to travel up into the mountains of Lebanon where Maureen had loved to sit with him, under the ancient cedar trees, inhaling the aroma from the bark as the clouds of mist swirled around. He sheds a loving tear as he takes out his cassette recorder and plays *Wonderful World*. With that moving song in his head, he leaves Lebanon with a plan to never return.

Chapter 21

November, 1991. London

The *Mediterranean Run* for Bill Maclean ended effectively in 1974 when he was posted away from the Lebanon to new operations.

But the story emerges again in 1991.

His dandruffed controller has died. As a concession to his new peaceful self and being in chilly London at the time anyway, Maclean attends the funeral of his former supervisor.

The old Brigadier from the Wellington Room, seventeen years before, is at the service. Despite the frailty of his age, when he sees Maclean, he asks to talk with him privately.

They retire to a garden seat in the warmth of the fern house under some purple bougainvillea blossoms – a stark contrast to the leaf-less trees outside, which are shivering in the early winter winds. In a way, the flowering creeper reminds Bill of the Lebanon, which is appropriate since that is the era which the Brigadier wants to speak about.

'William, when you get old like me, your conscience plays on you more than it ever did in the excitement of youth. I hold many secrets about which I *should* have a conscience but which I will happily take with me to the grave. But, I thought I might see you here today. There is a matter which I would like to clear up.'

Bill waits patiently – ever the listener – as the old man fiddles with the walking stick resting between his legs. He clasps his hands over the ornate handle and draws a deep breath.

Eventually, with a sigh, he begins, 'You remember the dinner at the Wellington Room?'

'How could I forget it? It is emblazoned in my memory – 20 May, 1974.'

'There was a bigger picture at the time. Your cover was blown on the boat heading to Donegal. It was a leak at our end of the business – not your fault nor your lady's – but, nevertheless, we had to ensure that you didn't get on the last leg into Dungloe. We knew from our insiders that it was actually Padraic Hennessy, in person, who was going to collect the crates. We, well *I* in truth, it was my decision alone – the blame rests entirely with me – I decided to use Maureen Jazy's ancestry and the linkup with her birth father to get the intelligence we vitally needed to break them up. *I* did that. *My* decision. And, that it didn't work out as it should, is a matter of the deepest regret for me. And I apologise to you.'

Maclean gives a wry smile. 'And I was blaming the man whose funeral we are here for.'

The Brigadier speaks softly again. 'I couldn't tell you any more at the time. There were security issues. And I handled that dinner with you about as badly as I have dealt with any interpersonal matter in my life. For that also, I am deeply sorry. You see how conscience plagues the old, eh William? Ah, the mistakes we have made! But there is a better side to my story.'

Maclean waits patiently.

'I can't bring her back to you. I truly wish I could. But you should know that Maureen Gallaher/Jazy achieved some amazing results in getting intelligence out to my section. She had in fact compiled a list of senior officials, most of whose identities were very heavily protected. And she got those who had worked with Hennessy in the supply chain to get armaments to Republican fighters, as well as those who had the contacts around the financing of the arms operations. She got *all* of that, William. Do you understand what I'm saying? That was an absolutely amazing achievement.

'As a result of her information, matched and added to intelligence from many others in the field, the vast majority of key players in the arms network were taken out over a few months, although we have waited some years to get certain major players. Many of them went in accidents or the work of Ulster Protestant groups, if you take my meaning.' He gives a sly grin. 'Donnie McSweeney left this Earth earlier in the year over in County Fermanagh and good riddance to him too. Padraic Hennessy is still eluding us. We're told he is in Yugoslavia running arms to the Croatians. He has Michael McSweeney, Donnie's son, as his offsider now, at least so I'm told. I'm too old to be in the main active loops, these days.'

'Okay.'

'William, your Maureen was a hero. She had to prove her loyalty to the resistance movement – just being the granddaughter of Seamus Gallaher was not enough in itself. You take my point.' He sighs again at some recollection. 'But, in war, lots of terrible things happen – and have to happen. Life is cheap. Soldiers understand that; you understand that too, I trust – I don't need to explain further – although the general public just wring their hands. But it's only when the evil is right in your face, when the terror is looking straight at your eyeballs, that you're glad that we have hard men and women who will do the deeds that others shy away from. Let's say no more about that part.' He stares into the distance for a second or two, before focusing back onto Bill's face.

'So your Maureen's work in those six months in Ireland had the effect of significantly immobilising the effectiveness of nationalist gangs; it might even have forced them into changing their focus away from Ulster and into trying to attack mainland England.'

Bill listens, letting the old man pour out his story as he again stares away into the comfort of the non-judgmental bougainvillea blossoms.

Is this just an old soldier seeking redemption?

'Brigadier,' Bill's voice is slow and precise. 'How did you contact Maureen in Ireland? How did she know to speak to you when she was surrounded by Hennessy's men? I had told her nothing of contacts or dead-letter drop locations.'

'Now.' The Brigadier's head turns to face him. The glazy eyes are moist. 'I met with Maureen while she was over there. It was on a lonely Eire road after Hennessy had gone across to the States. She knew what she was doing – one very brave young woman.'

Maclean persists. 'But how did she know to contact *you*?'

'As I say, after Hennessy went overseas, one of our people – a woman – touched base with her. She was much freer to move about by then; she had already proved herself to the paramilitaries.' He pauses, old head nodding slowly at some recurring memory. 'But, of course, there was always natural suspicion and she feared a set-up. So, another of our people contacted her with information from me that only a controller could know, about your work together in Lebanon, the letters through Montreux, as well as a line from a Louis Armstrong song which her stepfather told us would prove our bona fides. She took a big chance to meet with me on that road – as did I too, but we needed the information. She had been collecting it in her head – bloody good memory work – knowing that somehow she would get it out. And it was for *you*, William, dammit, not for *us*; she actually said that to me, to my face – *for her Bill Maclean*. That's why she did it all. She had some fire in her. She was giving no acknowledgement to Britain.'

Maclean doesn't react to the comment. Rather he maintains his polite persistent expression. 'You had not spoken to her before I was coshed on that trawler?' His eyes bore into the old soldier. 'Is that right?'

'Absolutely not, William. How could you suggest such a thing? It was a leak in our section that required you to be taken out. Hennessy had been told you were our agent. She knew nothing of that … or of us. As I said, it was my decision to proceed as we did. I will die with that decision on my conscience. Goodness, man! You need to know that she spoke to me of fulfilling her promise to *you*, just as much as her pledge to her mother – Maeve, she called her. She told me of your joint Swiss dream, the promise she had made that you were both going to move to Lac Leman. You certainly had an effect on her. And it would all have turned out smelling of roses if she hadn't gone to buy a present for you in that Dublin department store when a fucking loyalist gang chose to explode their bomb.

'We tried everything that we could to save Maureen's life. We did, William. Trust me, we did. I knew it was touch and go. We had an ambulance team waiting to bring her, burn-bandaged and all, into the Wellington Room that Monday evening, if she as much as regained consciousness. Seeing you there might have picked her up – that was my hope; misguided maybe, but I had to try.'

He pauses, staring at Maclean to ensure that his rationale is being received. 'I had a logic of doing it the way I did and not sending you to the hospital. She needed all her strength for the fight. We didn't believe she would die that night. We had a reasonable hope that she would pull through in time. *Give her an hour or so,* the doctors had said, enough so that your presence could help make the necessary difference. We accepted that advice. We meant well. We were trying to look after you – both. But the internal blast injuries, coupled with the burn complications … they got her first. A tragic bloody shame!' He pauses. 'I thought you should know everything. I couldn't tell you all that at the Wellington Room. Wrong time. Security. And I couldn't get my words anyway.' He stops again and gulps. 'You handled yourself better than I did back then. Bloody conscience. Terrible thing. Watch out for it when you get older. Sorry, William, I really am.'

Maclean sits quietly looking at the bowed old man. 'Brigadier, the anger has gone for me now, long ago in fact. I sealed the pain of that part of my life up in the hills of Lebanon, after the funeral. It wasn't meant to be, for any longer than the times we had. But I have kept the love free in my mind. For that, she and I always have had … all the time in the world.'

The old soldier looks up, as if Maclean has lost it – or to check if he is suddenly dressed in Buddhist robes.

'Good then,' he says, eventually. 'Okay. I'm glad you have understood.'

'Oh, what was the line from the Louis Armstrong song that you used?'

'It was, *A kiss to build a dream on*. Apparently, it was a favourite of Maureen's mother. It had a significance that would not be lost on her, or so the stepfather told us.'

Maclean nods, his eyes distant in memory. 'And he would have been right – the music of protest, resistance and hope.' He can visualise her explaining that to him back in their Beirut flat. 'She would have understood instantly. But, sadly, it was all a world of lost dreams and kisses.'

The Brigadier glances at him again, puzzled, but returns to his theme of justification. 'They were hard times and they're not over yet. There's so much guilt floating around. There will never be peace over there in Ulster. A bloody mess. But, at least, there are fewer murderers there now, than there were.'

Maclean pats the old man on his bony shoulder. 'I have more confidence than that, Brigadier. I want to find the way to a resolution – out of respect for the people we have lost – and, I'm pretty sure, that the majority on the other side of *the cause* will be feeling just the same. Apart from the hard-nut criminals, who exist in every society, most people are crying out for peace. And when the old stagers have lost their vitriol or they pass on, a younger generation and the mothers of the newborns will bring this to an end.'

The Brigadier just smiles. 'Thank you, William. I hope you're right.' And then he chirps, with a devilish twinkle, 'Maybe these Croats will top Hennessy over in the Adriatic and that will solve another of the problems.'

Bill Maclean's face is stonily polite. Which of the two of them doesn't get it?

Chapter 22

June, 2013. Rotterdam, The Netherlands

'What is it that needs women rather than men? Why would Gaddafi's female guards choose to join a network to do with cats?'

Sven's question finds no ready answer from Emma or Arthur, as they ponder in the Maasboulevard office.

Jacques's son, Martin, has arrived in Rotterdam to accompany his father back to Switzerland, but the ageing French-Swiss man's discussion and recollections of Maeve and Maureen are still resonating within the group. And Emma Jazy is better placed to take her more accustomed active role in the discussions.

'Perhaps we are trying to read too much into links back to Ireland,' suggests Arthur. 'It is a potential criminal activity, which might not be all female. We're running on pretty scant information – rumours – which could even be totally wrong.'

'I agree,' Emma offers. 'Shouldn't we be trying to establish if the rumour is true and where the women have gone – if they have actually joined some mysterious network?'

'Honey traps?' Sven suggests. 'Why else would they recruit good-looking Arab women? All those Gaddafi guards were lookers.'

'They could have a less sexist or xenophobic role.' Emma grins. 'But if that was to be their function, we would still need to know who the targets might be.'

'Senior Israeli officials?'

'Sorry to debunk the idea so quickly,' Arthur argues, 'but there is no evidence to support that type of premise. We have no historical examples of the Israeli military ever using or endorsing sexual abuse or rape against enemies. Nor is there evidence of their political leaders consorting with Arab women, even in the most discreet ways – indeed, it would be rather the opposite. For whatever reason, their discipline in those matters has always been very tight. So, who could these women get to? Who would have the power and authority to change a fundamental tenet of Zionist thinking? I can't imagine it ... as yet.'

'You may be right, Arthur,' Sven acknowledges, 'but, if not that, then you are reduced to looking for situations where only women can enter.'

'Keeping with teasing out the places for women only, what could be the situation ...' Emma asks. '... where Israeli women and Arab women would meet easily? A social occasion? They wouldn't even use the same schools or childcare or shops. It doesn't fit.'

'Alright.' Sven nods. 'But, let's not lose the idea, just in case. Moving on and taking your idea further logically, Emma, what Hennessy may have is men and women being trained together, for an – as yet – unknown mission. Our questions should now be: where are they being trained? And for what?'

'Sam is in Croatia, following up whatever loose leads he can find,' Arthur volunteers. 'I spoke with him an hour ago to tell him about Nikkos being murdered in Nicosia. He might even have a possible surname for the murderer, Granić; a Macan Granić. A twenty-one-year-old Dubrovnik hard man, known for using knives, a bully – and possibly the son of a McSweeney – maybe even Michael McSweeney.'

'Well, at last. Something that we actually know ... that's a good link.' Emma sighs. 'It draws Padraic Hennessy into the present-day picture at least.' Her jaw juts forward as if to suggest her need to move beyond hypothesising and get into action.

'Don't jump too fast, Emma.' Arthur raises his hand in caution. 'It may not be the same McSweeney. There were lots of foreign nationals in Croatia in 1991 and 92, including Irish. It was the start of their War of Independence. But, there's more. Sam thought he might have picked up a faint connection with the term, *cougar*.'

Sven's head is back into its bowed hand-supported pose as he listens. Eventually, he volunteers, 'We have two theatres of activity at present, if we accept that Ireland is quiet. They are Croatia and Cyprus. Why? What is the connection? Then we have the Irish link back to conversations forty years ago about the Israeli *Law of Return*. Why? Are we just being manipulated to think in this way?'

'And your alternative thought is?' asks Arthur.

'Where could a terrorist team attack Israel? Where is it vulnerable? Why don't we just go down that conventional path to start with? Maybe we are being bluffed into being too clever?'

Arthur sighs. 'You mean power, water, communications, weapon silos? Or are you talking about softer targets like school buses, markets or beach resorts?'

'Both ... and all?'

'I would have thought there would be few places on the planet with as much high-level security and intelligence capture as Israel. *Mossad* would be monitoring all contingencies. The Israeli Defence Force would intercept any attack, even sent over as missiles from other countries.'

'Unless,' suggests Emma. 'Unless it is not an attack on Israel, per se, but something that would influence Israel to change its stance on immigration. No?'

'Like what?'

'I don't have that answer, but perhaps we should have our antennae up in case we hear whispers like that. Could be embassies? Or places where Israelis are attending meetings?'

Sven nods. 'Good point, Emma. Keep the open question out in front of us. The other aspect is that we are assuming that Israel is being painted as the bad guy in all of this. No?' His head is up, eyes wide and palm open in questioning challenge. 'But, the Israelis could quite justifiably argue that (a) the aggression comes from Palestine, and their supporters, who do not even acknowledge that Israel has the right to exist; (b) that they have rockets and bombs aimed at them every day and have done for years; and (c) that they have the right to defend themselves, even very aggressively if and when required.'

Emma shakes her head in surprise. 'So are you suggesting that Padraic Hennessy might be going to attack Arabs ... to get *them* to change *their* stance over Israel?'

The Swede shrugs. 'Why would you rule that out? That would be another way toward the solution that Hennessy has flagged. Open-ended questioning, Emma. We don't know what they are up to. Little of it makes any sense as yet. And Arab women could access Arab people without any problem ... following on from our earlier question.'

'Alright.' Arthur interjects. 'Let's keep the open-ended approach. But, back to the evidence and a safer way forward, what we do know is that Nikkos was brutally murdered in Cyprus, pre-sumably because he was watching, listening and then working with us. So, we are dealing with criminal activity at the very least, as well as a potential philosophical or ideological position. And our poor Greek Cypriot informer may have been forced to divulge informa-tion about Sam and our questions.'

'Have the Cypriot police made any progress?'

'Too early. He was only found overnight. But that is *their* task, not ours.'

'So our brief is still just to find out what is happening ... and report to ...?'

The Swede's quiet voice answers. 'The relevant national agen-cies, who can then decide how much more they want to involve us. We operate behind the scenes to get admissible evidence. That is always our primary contract at IIB.'

'Mmm.' Arthur takes up the conversation. 'My suggestion is to leave Sam in Croatia to follow what leads he can. Emma, perhaps you are the person to go into Cyprus, with your multi-lingual back-ground from Switzerland. They may not be expecting a woman. You might pick up different waves from other agents, particularly about women in a network involving feline creatures. What do you think?'

'Happy to go there. I have a fair bit of Greek … and an understanding of Turkish at a pinch – a hard language for a West European background. And Arabic I have, if that is what the Africans are speaking. I'll talk with the operations team and see what we can set up. I would really like to be at the sharp end of this action, particularly if it is connected to the stepsister that I never had the chance to know.'

'Good,' Sven acknowledges. 'Travel safely, Emma. I have a feeling this may well be much worse than it appears.'

Chapter 23

June, 2013. Dubrovnik, Croatia

Hvala Bikić is an attractive, dark-haired woman around fifty – the smiling older version of her daughter who has just ushered the tall tanned man into the parental home with, 'Mama, meet Sam Hall.'

'Welcome, Sam. My husband, Goran, has mentioned you … and your organisation. Important work. Yes?'

'Nice to meet you, *Gospodja* Bikić. Yes, we think it is important work.'

'Oh, please call me Hvala,' she smiles. 'That name means *Thanks* in Croatian. I like being called *Thanks*.'

She turned to introduce a broad-shouldered, dark-haired man in his late fifties. 'And this is my elder brother, Danko. You have already met Danko's son, Luka. Yes?'

* * * *

The Bikić home is in the Dubrovnik suburb of Ploce, with a veran-dah view high out over the beach, the old town and beyond to the sun setting into the Adriatic.

'The legal profession must do very well in Croatia.' Sam gasps at the sparkling boating lights moving steadily back to port, in contrast to the stationary flickering glows from islands, farther out. 'This is brilliant.'

'A combination of hard work,' Hvala bows at the praise. '… some good luck and living here for generations; not to mention the financial rewards of Goran's special contracts in The Hague.'

'It's a more impressive city than I had imagined.'

'Most visitors say that,' agrees Hvala. 'Especially in the summer with blue skies and sunshine.'

* * * *

They enjoy a pleasant seasonal meal with light conversation about the tourist attractions of the Adriatic, while they sip a *vinum alba*.

'Ivana has walked me through some of your old city, out through the Pile Gate, to a view of the fort. And we have been over to Luka's police station and a few blocks beyond.'

'It is good that you could come,' Danko says. 'Croatia has much to offer. Visitors are welcome. And it gives me chance to practise my English on you. My generation didn't get taught that in school – unless you were going to be lawyer or teacher.'

'You speak it fine,' says Hvala. 'Doesn't he, Sam?'

'Yes, indeed. And it is much better than my Croatian. So you are not a lawyer, Danko?'

'Enough lawyers for the family. I was in police and reserve army. Retired now. What are your plans while you here, Sam? It is not all work?'

'I'm looking forward to getting onto the beach, out to an island and up into these white rocky hills behind the city. It really looks beautiful. And Ivana has offered to show me the sights, I think. Am I right?' He looks at the surprised but grinning lady, who gives a confirming nod to the older generation ... and a cheeky reproachful glance to Sam.

Danko chimes back. 'I have boat. I can get you out to Lokrum Island – that's the nearest one you see out there – but Ivana has licence too, so she can take you yourself.' His eyes are smiling. Indeed, the three seem to be a very contented happy group to Sam – easy banter and gentle embarrassment without offence.

With meal plates cleared away, Ivala asks, 'Would you like to sample one of Croatia's best wines, Sam? A ruby-red *Dingač*. You will taste our Adriatic flowers and scents in it.'

'That would be very pleasant after such a lovely meal. Thank you.'

'And we must have *slivovitz* shot before you leave,' Danko adds. 'Part of our culture.'

'A small one, Danko,' cautions Ivana. 'He is here to work.'

'Ah yes,' her uncle notes. 'Investigating, eh? If it is to do with Goran's prosecutions at The Hague, more power to you.'

'It's not directly related to the war trials – more just that a Croatian might be able to lead us to someone elsewhere.'

'Luka is helping you, Ivana says.' Hvala speaks as she pours the fruity red wine into balloon glasses. 'Is there anything we can help you with? Not chasing villains, of course, but maybe background to this place.'

'It has a lot of history. I can see that. The old town and its fortifications are amazing. And they survived the war in the nineties?'

'Just.' Hvala nods. 'The JNA shelled us for months – sorry, our acronyms, that was the Jugoslav National Army, Serbs mainly – even hitting the old town. You can still see some shell marks in the *Stradun*, the main street through the *Stari Grad*. It was and is World Heritage listed. They made a big mistake attacking that. It brought a wave of world opinion to our support.

'But yes, we were under siege from about October of 1991, from the north and up on Mount Srdj in the east. The sea was blockaded to stop supplies getting in. It continued for six months at least, till the HV – that is the Croatian Army, literally *Hrvatska kopnena vojska* – led by General Bobetko who turned the fighting in our favour and recaptured about a thousand square kilometres around us. But the JNA looted and damaged our city suburbs terribly. I think it was finally in July of the next year, that they were finally driven right out of the area. Operation Tiger. That's what it was called, Danko? Yes? It secured the road behind this house and to the south and into Bosnia-Herzegovina to the east.'

'Yes.' Danko nods. 'Along with the airport and Port of Ploće up to north of here, not to be confused with our suburb here called Ploce, and Konavle with Bay of Kotor further to south. But I wasn't here when that was happening. I was with HV up in north-east of Croatia, near place called Vukovar.'

'I've heard of that place.' Sam sips his red wine. 'I was a teenager in school at that time. They had a few news shots but it was always hard to understand what was happening, probably because so much was going on all over Yugoslavia and with such unpronounceable names. But also because my parents kept turning the TV off to protect us kids. Anyway, the truth usually gets lost in the propaganda. I found that out with my own service, with the British army.'

'You were soldier then?' Danko questions, with a respect in his eyes.

'Yes, second Gulf War and then a bit more with special forces in Afghanistan. Never came here though. Got out a few years ago and signed up with IIB. I'm keen to understand what your War of Independence was all about, from the local perspective.'

Danko draws a deep draught of his wine and glances at the women. 'Generally, yes, okay. I think we could talk about it in general way just now.' He pauses. 'Maybe you and me, old soldiers, later, we could take drive sometime up into hills – beautiful country – and we might speak of things, not suited for dinner table and ladies.'

Sam reaches out and touches Danko's forearm. Nothing is said. An understanding and agreement has been made.

'Ivana was here, though,' Danko adds, 'through the siege – and at school. *You* tell our guest what war was about, at strategic level, legal level. This family has always been lawyers.'

It is her turn to take a huge gulp of wine and a quick look towards Sam. 'Okay.' She collects her thoughts. 'We are in family law usually, Sam, not international justice. But okay, you jump in, Danko, where I get it wrong. This will sound more like a history lesson. I'm suddenly nervous talking to two returned soldiers about what happened in a war. I was just a school student, trying to be a child – a civilian.'

'It was as real for civilians as it was for us in army,' her uncle says, with a gentle respect.

'Alright. Here goes. Brief version. Croatia voted at a referendum to be an independent nation in 1991 – to leave the Republic of

Yugoslavia. But Serbia wanted to create a new Serb state including much of Croatia. That was the crux of the legal problem.

'Relationships deteriorated fast with nasty propaganda, probably on both sides, I would imagine. As I told you earlier in my office, there had been a rotation of presidents in Yugoslavia for the previous decade, each state in its turn. It was Croatia's turn. On 15 May 1991, the Serbs influenced the other states to block that move. And so, on 19 May 1991, Croatia declared independence. We learned those dates well in school.

'Then the Serb militias – and there were lots of them, gangs of thugs really – they started blocking roads near Vukovar, up on the Danube River, on the border with Serbia. Croatia is a strange banana-shaped country from here on the coast, up to Opatija, then inland to Zagreb and Vukovar.

'From July to November 1991, the gangs started to terrorise and kill. The siege of Vukovar was as significant to our war as Stalingrad was in World War II. I learned that in school too. They say that twelve thousand rockets were fired *every day* into Vukovar at this time. Many lives were lost – as in tens of thousands of lives.

'But at the same time, the Serbian JNA was pushing through Bosnia-Herzegovina on our east, in on a wide front, to try for Adriatic access and just to impose their will. They were headed here, to Dubrovnik, to cut us – the coastal area – off from the rest of Croatia.

'Croatia wasn't well prepared for war at the start. We really just had a police force. So it took time to build an army, to bring in weapons and fight back. There were many defeats and retreats early on.

'You see, I told you it would be like a history lesson because I don't want to talk about the shells whistling over – we girls crouching in the bomb shelters; the fear, the not knowing. Terrible stories filtered down from the north, even into school corridors. We were scared but you just had to put it out of your mind and not listen to it all. But there were horrific reports of murders – and a lot more – whole families, whole villages.

'Anyway, General Bobetko beat them back from here. We had United Nations troops in the blue berets and their white tanks from time to time. There were lots of different nationalities who came through here to help our struggle; the official UN soldiers and lots of mercenaries.

'And so gradually the Serbs retreated. *Our* war, in terms of the worst fighting, was over in a year. However, it took four years for the whole of Croatia to be free; for the last skirmishes with militias to end and for all war prisoners to be released from detention camps – and it was even longer for other parts of the old Yugoslavia. For some, it was a decade of fighting and then trying to pick up the pieces of their lives again. Even now, they are still finding mass graves in the other provinces. It's not over for those who lost so much. How's that?'

'Fine,' replies Sam tactfully. 'Thank you. I get the picture. A sad time … and hard to live through, I'm sure. Danko and I may talk about the soldier tactics on another occasion but that's a very good summary, Ivana. One thing though, from something said earlier … Operation Tiger. Why would that operation be named after a cat?'

Chapter 24

June, 2013. Akrotiri, Cyprus

In the darkness, Emma Jazy's plane flies quietly into the RAF Base at Akrotiri. She feels the enveloping warmth in the air as she disembarks under the stars on the peninsula to the south of Limassol.

Escorted away from the plane into a military jeep, she is driven across the runway into a discreet hangar.

The woman, who meets her inside the huge building, has dark hair drawn back into a bunch. Her piercing eyes sparkle with alert intelligence in a tanned face. She stands about 173 cms high and is dressed in a black turtle-neck and pants.

'Emma Jazy, I'm Thea Spyrou, part of Nikkos's network.' The voice is controlled and confident. As Emma accepts the outstretched hand, Thea says, 'Welcome to my Cyprus – always a place of intrigue and never more so than now. Coffee? Tea?'

Emma replies, 'Tea. Black. Thank you,' as they walk together into a private office, nestled at ground level on the inside wall of the hangar. 'I'm very sorry about Nikkos. Bad business.'

'Thank you. He knew the risks.' Thea speaks in a matter-of-fact tone as she pours hot water from a glittering coffee machine onto spooned tea-leaves in a ceramic pot. 'Real tea. There are still some standards left.' It is almost a smile on her serious face before she returns to the business in hand. 'Half a dozen of them came for Nikkos. Late evening. His partner, Galen, was outside in the shed, when he heard the scuffles from the house. No shouts. Really quiet. By the time he got to the back door, Nikkos had already been bundled out the front into one vehicle. He saw three of the remainder as they headed for the second car. It all happened too fast to stop them. A very organised gang. Two looked North African to him, the third was issuing quiet instructions mainly by pointing and grunting. He was paler, dark hair, big shoulders. Definitely not speaking Greek or Turkish. Galen is fluent in both. A foreign gang.'

Emma takes her cup of freshly-made tea and sips as she listens.

Thea continues her briefing, 'Galen warned the network immediately but we didn't find Nikkos until the next day. He was dead by then. Not good.'

'Any clues?'

'The Nicosia police are looking ... but ... you know ... this is a gang ... foreign. They could even be out of the country by now.'

'Sam told me that Nikkos had mentioned the fear in the community a week ago, and the presence of an old man in Nicosia. Anything further on that?'

'Yes, he even thought that there could be *two* old men. He hadn't seen either of them ... but he spoke to me of an Arab man and a European ... both old ... both at the Nicosia meetings. He only found out about the second man on the day before he died.'

Emma purses her lips and asks, 'That discovery could have been the motive for him being abducted. Don't you think?'

'Maybe. Maybe.' She shrugs. 'To the young ones now ... in the gang. Our guess is that the pale-face with the kidnappers is probably the one doing the maiming and killing. Nikkos is not the first – just the nastiest – and the closest to us. He was on their trail. There has been some training of these people going on up in the mountains north of Nicosia, near Karaagac. Nikkos and Galen had tracked them there. They alternated their surveillance for safety – a change of face and not being seen together. But Nikkos had told us that the gang had been rehearsing what looked like digging or boring holes in the earth; but silently. That's how he and Galen both described it. It's rugged country and lonely up there.

'Neither of them could work out what was happening, though. There is nothing to drill for in those mountains. But the man calling the shots in the mountain was certainly not an old man but in his

134

mid-thirties – definitely not the pale-face in his early twenties – and he was a white man; European. He was the trainer, respected clearly, but not the young feared Croatian (if that's where he is from). According to Nikkos's reports, that Croatian man was early twenties; gun holster on one hip, knife sheath on the other – always carried a Kalashnikov in the hills. He could be the one that Ari heard and saw in Kyrenia, on the north coast. But he didn't understand the significance at the time.'

Emma sips again. 'So, was this the same pale man from the kidnapping at the house?'

'Could have been. Galen had that impression. He wasn't sure, though. He didn't really hear or see the people clearly. It all happened very quickly. Blurs of figures in the dark.'

'And he and the others were foreign ... to Cyprus?'

'The ones they saw and heard? Yes. Galen suggested the Balkans as a possibility for the younger pale one – at a guess – but who knows? Voices, accents and shadows are hard at a distance.'

'We had word that Nikkos definitely mentioned Croatia for the killer. Is that right?'

'I heard that was what he'd said. It could be. Nikkos was better with voices than most. Ari understands Adriatic tongues. You will meet him later. But maybe he is also going on what others have suggested. He has heard pale-face's voice at the port and told Nikkos that, if it was the same man with that distinctive appearance, then he was speaking like a coastal Croatian, that he might even have mentioned Dubrovnik. But, who knows, Greek accents I can pick ... but Croatian? Balkan is close enough for me. Maybe it was for Nikkos too, until Ari put the Croatian suggestion forward. It is the pale face that seems to be the stand-out feature on him. They mention it as if it is very unusual.'

'Understood.'

Thea thumps her fist slowly onto the table top. 'He must have been seen. Nikkos. He must have been seen.'

'Or betrayed.'

Thea's eyes flash. 'We do not betray our own.'

The uneasy silence is eventually broken by Emma, 'Why would a gang choose Cyprus to train? Is there something happening here again – with the partition, I mean?'

'Something is always happening in Cyprus. Stirrers. Turks are always agitating. Not so much the island locals, but the mainland ones.'

'Help me understand, Thea.'

'Do you know any of our history? Where are *you* from? You sound French?'

'Switzerland. French-speaking Switzerland. But I have some Greek language and a bit of Turkish to hear – not really to speak.'

Thea gives an impressed nod and changes immediately to speaking in Greek. 'This land has been with Greece for centuries until the Ottomans made it part of their empire, from the sixteenth century to the ninteenth.' She pauses with a look at Emma to check that she is following, and then continues. 'The British took over the island in 1878 as a protectorate from the Turks. It was properly annexed at the start of the First World War and became a crown colony in 1925. Schoolgirl history. Are you still with me?'

Emma replies in Greek that she is – clearly – with another appreciative nod.

Thea continues. 'The British had promised that Cyprus could unite with Greece fully if they helped them in the war … that's the First World War, but it never happened. Nor in the Second World War, either. So, in 1955, EOKA was formed – the National Organisation of Cypriot Fighters – to achieve unification. We call it, *enosis*, you understand … away from Britain and attached to Greece. EOKA attacked locations in Nicosia and Famagusta, and then lots of sabotage attacks. They were trying to get world head-lines. A lot of British troops were killed – ours too, in truth. The start of the modern terror in this island goes back to that time. Cypriot traitors were brutally dealt with. Then the Turks took the opportunity to jump onto the bandwagon. They made up less than twenty per cent of the island's population in 1955 but they started claiming that they had rights from the earlier centuries of Ottoman history; hardly a balanced comparison. Before long, neighbours were fighting neighbours … and over what?'

'So how did it end?'

'It has never ended. But in 1960 they – that is the United Nations – created the Republic of Cyprus. But no *enosis*, no unification with Greece. Instead, the partition. Can you believe that? The Turks were given administrative control over the north – thirty-six percent of the area. Greek-Cypriots had the south and two areas were exempt. Akrotiri, where we are at present, has remained a British sovereign base, as has Dhekelia along the coast to the east, past Larnaca. My family, the Spyrou, have lived in Nicosia for generations. But even the capital was divided in two, as well – a line down the middle.

'In 1964, the Turks tried to invade. That drew the Soviets and the Americans into the stand-off. We pushed them back on our own – not me personally, you understand, I wasn't even born – but our Greek-Cypriot people. And in 1974, we Greeks had a *coup d'état* to try for *enosis*, again; and the Turks responded by landing thirty-thousand troops using the justification of the 1960 agreement. It was very fast, and a huge force.

'My parents remembered it well. It only lasted a few days and 180,000 of our Greek community ended up being evicted from the Turkish area – most down to the south coast near Larnaca.

'Our family did not go. They held their heads high and refused to move. We have lived proudly in Nicosia for generations, even had friendships with Turks going back into history. This is about people, not geo-politics. At least, that's what the people thought at the time. But many hundreds died in that fighting. Old friendships were severely tested. Fifty-thousand Turks were moved onto the island north of the partition – as new settlers.'

Emma smiles sadly. 'It seems like the history of so much of recent civilisation. It follows a pattern – like Palestine, like Northern Ireland.' She pauses. 'And that would be why there is no international airport in Nicosia; why we have to fly into Akrotiri or Larnaca?'

'Oh, the old Nicosia International Airport is still there, lying derelict, gathering dust in the UN Buffer Zone – even with abandoned planes and vehicles still stranded on the taxiing aprons. What a waste. And the Turks have their military airfield at Ercan. That is just eleven kilometres east of Nicosia. Some planes land there, but from Turkey only. Other planes land at Paphos International. It is on the west coast – a Greek-Cypriot airport. It takes scheduled flights from all over Europe and, now that you mention, from Croatia too. But it is nearly a two-hour drive to Nicosia from there. So, yes, the vast majority of commercial flights come in to Larnaca. It is the main airport and only thirty-six kilometres away from the capital. Not far, really.'

'So, if the old man that Nikkos mentioned was flown in, and was in Nicosia, he probably would have come into Larnaca, through that airport? Or Paphos, perhaps, as an outside possibility? The same for beys and sheiks that he might have met with?'

'If they flew into Greek Cyprus – and if he didn't have a special deal with the Turks.' Thea growls the last words. 'But, there are other ways to land on an island – lots of fishing ports, coves and beaches.'

Thea opens a cake tin to reveal small home-cooked biscuits, covered in icing sugar. 'Have a treat,' she offers as she continues her story. 'Invaders and occupiers are not new to this island. It has been going on for millennia in this part of the world. Two thousand years ago, the Romans just dropped their culture, and their settlers, right on top of the Cypriot society that had existed here. And it goes back further, Phoenicians … a very long history.

'But it *is* oppressive now, for us. The Turkish settlements have continued in violation of a series of UN agreements, which Turkey just ignores. There are now a hundred and fifty thousand *new* Turk settlers living in their section. My Nicosia always stretched across each zone – there was even a wall down the centre for many years, although that has gone now, thankfully. Your Greek language is alright, Emma, yes? You are still understanding?'

Emma nods. 'I am. But it is hard work. We might try English again for a change, to give me a break, since we are in a British air force base.' It draws a grin from them both. 'So the Greek-Cypriots were largely pushed out of the north and the UN keeps an uneasy peace?'

Thea shrugs. 'Yes, yes. That is about right.'

'And the gang that took Nikkos? Could they have anything to do with this disputed partitioning of the island?'

'They are African and Balkan, as far as we know. I don't see any connection.'

'But they are training here. Why? Are they criminals or freedom fighters or terrorists or nutcases?'

'Or all of the above? Who knows? Terrorists can train anywhere right across North Africa ... from Chad, Sudan, Somalia to Yemen. Al Qaeda. Al Shabaab.'

'Oh, are they sub-Saharan Africans?'

'Galen though they were Mediterranean Africans. Like Libyan, Egyptian ... Algerian, maybe.'

'Could they be Palestinian?'

'Possibly. They are all Arab peoples. But they are definitely not Turks.'

'Okay. That's three of the gang. So, why are they using Cyprus?'

'If they are terrorists, they are close in distance to Syria. We are a short sea voyage away, if they dodge the navy patrol boats. There are all sorts of revolutionaries in there at the moment with that huge uprising against the government. Tens of thousands. It is all mad around the Mediterranean just now. Egypt, Libya and even Tunisia ... they are not resolved there yet. It is just off the international headlines because the horror of Syria has been all-consuming for nearly two years now – and Turkey has all those refugees on its border.' She grins as if it was poetic justice. 'See how they like it.'

'What about Israel? Could this group in Cyprus be going after Israel?'

'It is close, in distance, but no closer than Syria. No. That doesn't make sense. Israel has too many defences. Only the suicidal brave or the stupid would go after that country. My bet is Syria.'

'And the boring, the drilling?'

'Guess, if you like. I don't know. Oil? Water? Gas? What can you drill for? Whatever it is, it is not like your normal drilling – and I don't really know what Nikkos meant by that. He did say it was silent. How can you drill silently?'

'And the man from the Balkans is the young man they fear but he is not the leader of the training? The training leader is a white man in his thirties? Is that what you are telling me?'

'Yes. Definitely. He is training the Africans. Yes. But he must be a hard man too … to be leading *The Fear*, the pale-faced Croatian. In those gangs, power only comes from being tougher than those you lead. The pale-face definitely obeys the thirty-year-old.'

'What of the old man or men? Are they trainers?'

'Nikkos spoke of an old man or men gathering leaders, Arab leaders, to a cause. That could be about Syria – to overcome the dictatorship.' Thea pauses. 'No, the old men wouldn't be trainers. It will be someone else – the man in his thirties, I am thinking. Our word is that there are others around the training area. It is not all Africans. There are definitely Europeans there too – just that Nikkos and Galen didn't get close enough. They have only just found this camp, only recently. It is on the side of a wooded mountain valley.'

'And, last question, are any of this gang … women?'

'Women? Why would you think that? Only men were reported taking Nikkos. Galen never mentioned women. Nor did Nikkos in his reports.'

'Okay, let's head for Nicosia. I want to get into the hills near Karaagac … to see what is happening.'

'It is dangerous, Emma … very dangerous.'

'Thea … believe me, so am I.'

Chapter 25

June, 2013. Rotterdam, The Netherlands

'I still don't see the connection with Ireland, let alone Padraic Hennessy. Do you think we have been sidetracked?' Nils Houweling asks.

He has been giving his regular early evening update of incoming daily intelligence to his directors, Arthur Blair and Sven Gulbrandson.

'Not admissible evidence connections yet, I grant you, Nils,' Arthur responds, 'but there are lots of casual similarities and signposts. However, I accept that you could still be right. That's why Sam is in Croatia and Emma in Cyprus, each linking up with our contacts over there, seeking a reason to bring in more of our team to establish incontrovertible linkages, if required.' He moves over to his electronic whiteboard to drag the computer-generated images and bubbles into new patterns of sense. The major bubble has Padraic Hennessy's phone call to Jacques Jazy in the centre.

'That was the start of this train of thought. An old revolutionary fighter seeking redemption for some of the bucket of guilt in his past ...' Arthur pauses and points at the screen '... by fulfilling a dream he'd heard relayed by his daughter from his teenage sweetheart, Maeve Gallaher/Jazy, the mother of the child he had abandoned for the first twenty years of her life. That's the start of this challenge. Agreed?'

Sven's head is stooped as it usually is when deep in thought. Only his right eye flicks up under his whitening hair, taking in the smart board, like a whale peering out from breaking waves. But he says nothing.

Nils Houweling is attentive. He scans his two phones, laptop and notebook as he fits his researched information around whatever Arthur Blair would present to him. Nils is the voice of evidence, of logical reason, to challenge the speculative investigations of the two proven prescient leaders of IIB.

Arthur continues, undaunted. 'But we don't know what Maeve's dream was. Probably something to do with supporting the rights of the downtrodden, particularly when it might be peoples being treated badly … like second-class citizens … or refugees from persecution …'

Nils interjects, 'And you, or we now, have hypothesised that Padraic's interpretation of Maeve's wishes have come from Maureen Gallaher/Jazy when she ran guns to Hennessy in Donegal in 1973. Sadly for her and our theorising, she died in London from injuries sustained in Ireland. So, I need to emphasise the point that neither her letters from there, nor the anecdotes spoken to her stepfather or any others, have enlightened us definitively to *the cause*. Nor do we know what solution she might have imparted to Hennessy. No evidence, other than your speculation.'

'Well put, Nils. Again,' agrees Arthur, patiently. 'But we've some whispers through the fog of intelligence chatter that an old man might have gone to Cyprus to form some secretive alliance with Arab revolutionary groups. And we know from Jacques Jazy that the Israel–Palestine situation had been a topic of heated conversation which Maureen Jazy would have heard as a child growing up.'

Nils nods as Arthur drags another electronic bubble across his whiteboard screen, while continuing his narrative.

'And,' adds Sven, as if to prove he hasn't been asleep, 'she was in the Lebanon, researching and reporting on the disquiet there in 1973. That should indicate her priority at the time. No-one would stay in a potential war zone just for the fun of it.'

'Point taken,' agrees Arthur, as he carries on with his catalogue of possibilities. 'Next, we have the story of women security guards from the former Libyan regime signing up for some project to do with cats ... maybe calling themselves *Akhawat*; and a possible Balkan or Croatian thug torturing one of our informers on Cyprus; with the name Macan, which *is* Croat usually, and the coincidence of another Macan in Dubrovnik reacting to a reference to a *cougar*, which just happens to be the nickname for Padraic Hennessy from the seventies.

'And then, that one of the Macans, a knife man, is missing on a fishing boat when Nikkos is murdered ...' He raises his hands in victorious gesture of resting his case '... and that his father was called McSweeney, possibly an associate of Hennessy.'

Nils takes up the story, with a dismissive expression that emphasises the strength of the professional trust held amongst these collegial debaters. 'And you have surmised that McSweeney could well have been in Dubrovnik in 1991 and later, carrying guns for their defence in their War of Independence, giving him time to father the child, Macan Granić. You have also presumed that Hennessy could have been there too, because the Croat scenario was not unlike the Northern Ireland situation. Agreed?'

He waits for Arthur's look of agreement.

'Then, you have made the quantum leap to assume that Hennessy is planning some form of attack against Israel to get them to change their fundamental *Law of Return* ... and none of this, I have to say, has supporting evidence of any credible kind nor, dare I emphasise it, of any linear correlation.'

At that, Sven's head rises slowly. 'There's another type of connection, though – more esoteric perhaps. We have had evidence from a number of countries that have had issues stemming from ethno-centricity – where dominant groups, linked by cultural narratives, were trying to replace the status quo with their own settlements; backed up inevitably by military force. And the predictable reaction has been revolutionary terrorism. Yes?

'It has definitely been happening in the places where we surmise Hennessy has been – Northern Ireland, Croatia, Cyprus and, by extrapolation – to Palestine. I don't believe in coincidences. Our past experiences with IIB have all demonstrated the unlikelihood of coincidence being a significant factor. So we are searching for connections, Nils. That's all. And, I'll be very surprised if they don't surface … and soon. Be patient, my teasing antagonist.'

'And,' Arthur adds, 'we came in to this on a brief from the CIA, British Intelligence and, by implication, *Mossad*. They have been interpreting the security chatter. It is our role to probe beyond the speculation, to get to the truth.'

'Then,' Nils taps his smart phone screen for some information, 'can I suggest that establishing the present location of Padraic Hennessy or Michael McSweeney or Macan Granić would be a huge step forward in proving or denying your hypotheses.'

'Always the pragmatist, Nils.' Arthur sighs. 'And I agree. I am guessing. That's our job. Particularly, I'm theorising that all or some of those players are in Croatia or Cyprus at this moment. We have established that they are unlikely to be in Ireland. That is why we have agents on the ground who, I would absolutely guarantee, are totally immersed in the task as we speak.'

Chapter 26

June, 2013. Dubrovnik, Croatia

Sam Hall flops back spent, on the bed, his right arm still around the bare shoulders of the smiling glowing Ivana Bikić.

The Dubrovnik late evening sky is clearly visible through their uncurtained upper-floor window as they lie in a panting euphoria. She rolls towards him again, her naked right breast caressing his chest. Her expression is a grinning question as he answers her look.

'I'm glad I came to Dubrovnik, Ivana.'

'I'm glad you came too.' She giggles, as she searches his face some more and then snuggles close into him. Laughing, she suddenly lifts her head, 'I suppose you will be telling your bosses in Rotterdam how hard you are working here.'

'My mother always told me to make my work my pleasure and then I'd always be happy. Although, I grant you, she probably didn't have our scenario in mind when she said it.'

'You are such good fun, Sam. You make me laugh.'

'Life is for enjoying. Savour each day. You never know what the future might hold.'

At the comment, Ivana shivers and cuddles in closer to him. 'I wish you hadn't said that, Sam. You are going out with Luka again in the morning. For all the beauty of Dubrovnik and the Adriatic, there is danger here … and I think you move in a dangerous world.'

'That's why we have lawyers to tie up the bad guys in rules. Then good guys like Luka go and catch them. Rogues like me just get to enjoy beautiful company ... and you are a charming, beautiful lady, Ivana Bikić ... your happy personality ... and your gentle care, that sense of justice, of right and wrong ... each a thing of beauty, as much as your stunning looks.'

'Flatterer.' She grins at his words and then turns away before raising her head again and looking long into his eyes, 'Let's sleep, my big man. We will both need our rest for a busy day soon enough.'

* * * *

Macan Horvat still looks as sullen as he had been on the previous day. Sam sits to the side of Luka, who quietly asks questions of his prisoner in Croatian. While usually getting only one word responses, occasionally he sparks an outraged flurry, before the stubbly Horvat sinks back into unresponsiveness again.

Luka turns to Sam, changing from Croat to English. 'Our grumpy friend is still hung over and, by law, we can detain him for another twenty-four hours without charge. He is considering whether or not he should give me more information, and then I might let him go earlier.'

'What has he told you so far?'

'Only that *Cougar* does refer to a group in the area. He has tried to laugh it off with the American use of the word referring to older women preying on younger men.'

'Are there women involved in the group, then? Is that possible?'

Luka asks the question in Croatian and receives a dismissive sneer with a few words. 'He said, *What else does Cougar mean?* There is more to this than he is telling us.'

He speaks again to his Croatian detainee, without a response.

'I'm trying to get him to give me a location for this gang.'

'Ask him about the old man.'

'What old man?'

'No. Give him no clues. Just ask him to tell you about the old man.'

Luka asks the question and Horvat's eyes close to slits. He shakes his head, repeating *Nema, nista*.

'You've struck a nerve there, Sam. He was shaking there for a few seconds. Let's leave him to sweat a bit more. The solitary and the clang of the locked metal doors … it gets to them in time. We can talk in my office.'

Two burly guards arrive to escort Macan Horvat back down to the cells while Sam and Luka head to an upper floor office with a view of blue skies, red roofs and tree tops.

* * * *

'Who is the old man? What is the connection with *Cougar* women?' Luka is unhurried … calm. He seems happy to help his cousin's friend, the associate of his uncle, Goran, who was doing important work for the International Courts of Justice in The Hague. 'Perhaps, *your* investigations will help me clear up some of *my* investigations. How much can you tell me?'

Sam stretches his large frame in the easy chair, his muscles still vibrating pleasantly with the sweet memory of the previous night.

'The old man may be an aged Irish revolutionary, part of the Provisional IRA breakaway groups of the early seventies. Back then, he was a very hard man – softly spoken – who could apparently kill without any conscience. We believe that he might have been here in Croatia, running guns and maybe fighting in your War of Independence, in the 90s. But he's nearing eighty years old now and perhaps his conscience is seeking some form of redemption. In the Irish days, his bodyguard-offsider was a man called Donnie McSweeney.'

Luka's eyes widen as the connection is made with Macan Granić's mother's tirade on the previous day.

Sam continues, shaking his head at Luka's anticipation, 'Not so fast. Donnie was killed in Ireland at the start of 1991, so it wasn't him. But we also know that, from at least two years ago, old Hennessy was being looked after by Donnie's son. He is Michael McSweeney. He'd be in his late fifties now. We don't know much about him except that he comes from a long line of tough men. It is just possible that Michael could have been here with Hennessy in 1991, and just possible again that he could be the same man who fathered Macan Granić.

'The next point is that the old man's nickname in the Irish *Troubles* was *The Cougar* and he ran a militia known as *The Cat Pack*. They were a feared group.

'I'm only working on rumours and guesswork but it seems to fit what you and I are finding here in Dubrovnik. We've heard whispers that some of Gaddafi's female guard might have left Libya to train with a group. Maybe they're here too? And they could be ... the women.'

Chapter 27

June, 2013. Nicosia, Cyprus

'I see what you mean.' Thea Spyrou stares at Emma Jazy who is putting the finishing touches to her preparation. 'You *do* look extremely dangerous.'

Emma's acknowledgement is not a cheery grin; more the grimace of a cobra about to strike. Her 175cm frame is clad in black, with subtle grease-paint smudges on her face to break up the contours. Her purpose-made webbing disguises a variety of grenades, spare ammunition clips, water, scopes, a zoom-lens camera and her radio comms master set. An earpiece is visible beneath her cap in her left ear, with a small dark microphone extending out. And she looks comfortable … not burdened; as if this gear is part of her persona, no encumbrance. Rather, it is the familiar tool-set of a very professional IIB agent.

She watches with distracted amusement as her new team play with their own personalised comms, which she has brought in on the plane to Akrotiri. They seem impressed that they need only whisper to be heard in the earpieces across the entire group of six. But they have declined similar apparel to Emma's, instead choosing their accustomed rural clothing, designed to merge into the community if spotted, while still allowing them the protection of deception in their rough spying activities.

Galen, the surveillance partner of the late Nikkos, is a key member of the team who can lead them to the training site that he observed earlier in the week, in the mountains to the north. Apart from Emma, Galen and Thea, the three others are young fit Greek activists by the names of Cristof, Ari and Jason. Each has experience with the surveillance network which, amongst others, was liaising with Sam Hall. Each is driven by a passion for *enosis* on their Cyprus island. Each is fired with vengeance to find the killers of Nikkos and bring them to their own form of justice.

Ari is the man who can apparently distinguish a coastal Croatian accent. 'I worked for six months in Dubrovnik as a chef.' He smiles. 'I too can use knives.' The smile disappears into a determined flinty focus.

A close team who are united by purpose and, for the present, are content to follow this Swiss agent from IIB. Emma has a Glock strapped to her thigh as well as a sheathed knife on the other leg and carries a light-weight Heckler-Koch automatic rifle. She ponders a fleeting query as she watches these strong-willed Cypriot men being led effectively by two women – and she wonders how often that might have happened in the culture of this part of the world. *Akhawat* flashes through her mind briefly before the task takes over again.

'Are we ready?' she asks, glancing over the preparations of the team. 'Plans fully understood?'

The silent group nods.

'Last check of comms,' she announces and each whispers into the ear pieces while widened eyes and nods acknowledge that everyone is receiving on the selected waveband.

'Remember, we are observers today. There is a much bigger picture than what is happening here. We need photographs and intel to relay back, but no shooting or killing, unless it proves unavoidable – and then only on my call – or, if I am dead, on Thea's call.' The tension is clear on each person's expression as they absorb those words, but Emma continues. 'If Nikkos's killer is there, you will have him for retribution. I guarantee that, but not today. Today, we watch and photograph. Absolutely clear?'

More silent nods on faces steeled for the operation ahead.

'We speak Greek from now on. As few words as possible. We will assume that the enemy will use Arab or Croatian or English. I will understand the Arabic but they won't understand us, if they chance on our wavelength.'

Emma's voice carries an authority well beyond her twenty-nine years. It is a respect not created by any advance reputation of her field experience in the deserts and mountains of conflict zones. It merely comes from her demonstration of extreme competence in organising, providing equipment and planning for their sortie into the mountains near Karaagac.

* * * *

The grey limestone rocks of the rugged Kyrenia Range stretch before them as they head north through the heavy forests of cedar, cypress and oak. Spread out in an arrow shape advance, with metres between them, Galen leads the team with an occasional whisper, through the comms, until the trees start to thin with altitude.

Eventually, he holds up his hand and mutters, 'Close now. Very close.'

Emma moves forward to Galen's shoulder as he points to a rocky crag. 'Nikkos and I, we watched from there. There is a bit of clearing ahead. Still trees but clearer. That's where we saw them boring holes.'

With an affirming nod, she moves forward alone to the vantage point while Thea keeps the group in alert order behind.

As Emma peers carefully round the weathered rock, telescope in hand, she focuses on a bizarre exercise some thirty metres ahead and below. She watches as a team of men, in green fatigues, leopard-crawl through sparse trees in a semi-circle towards a low box-shape in the small clearing.

On arrival, the first three stay on their stomachs while they appear to use a form of hand brace and auger to drill into the ground. As they work, two others crawl towards them with short sections of what appear like a plumber's snake. As the second group join the pieces together methodically, the first group appear to pour

151

water into the drill hole and push the snake down behind. Then they continue to manipulate the boring equipment with the brace.

Emma beckons Thea and the others forward to observe.

Over several minutes, they watch the two teams of crawling men repeat the process at the box-shape, beavering away over the hole in the ground and making minimal sound. At no stage does anything or anybody rise more than a metre above the ground. Indeed, the bodies stay below half that height, all the time.

Emma points in askance to Thea and the others, who look just as perplexed in reply.

Emma takes several quick camera shots through the trees.

As they watch, something moves behind some cypress foliage on the edge of the clearing – a man standing watching; definitely a white man. Emma zooms her scope onto him.

He wears a green canvas hat and the same fatigues as the men, almost invisible against the tree, and he is timing the exercise. As Emma looks on, he clicks a stop watch and gives a low whistle. Then the crawling men dismantle their equipment and start their leopard-wriggle back to the edge of the clearing. While they are doing that, the watching man removes his cap and wipes his brow. He has red hair, pale skin and freckles. At a guess, he is mid-thirties in age and average height.

Immediately, she focuses her zoom camera lens on him and snaps several shots.

Emma looks again in question at Thea, who merely shrugs.

Galen whispers that there is an old stone building up to the right in the trees. 'Maybe fifty metres. Someone was there on our last visit.'

'Take me to it,' says Emma, then whispers to Thea. 'Galen, Cristof and I will circle up to the building to see what is happening. Fifteen minutes tops. You watch here for any changes.'

As they glance back to the clearing, it appears that the green-clad men are about to repeat the crawling exercise.

* * * *

They hear the faint sound, like music and rhythm, before they see the building.

As they crawl low through the trees, an old rough-stone house comes into view – perhaps a goat-herder's place from years ago. But there are glass window panes intact, looking incongruously recent under faded roof tiles and beside an unpainted weathered door.

Yes, it is definitely music coming from within; familiar music to Emma. Like her father's taste, bluesy jazz. *Jazy by name, jazzy by taste,* he used to say.

But yes; it is New Orleans trad jazz in a Kyrenian wilderness.

She signals to Galen that she is moving forward and, with the innate skills of their Cypriot spy group, Galen and Cristof spread out to watching positions.

As she lifts her head to the window ledge and glances carefully inside, she is shocked to see a white-haired old man in a checked shirt and grey trousers bending over a CD player. He wears no glasses and appears at ease as he presses the play button with purpose.

The gravelly tones of Louis Armstrong float out – she could have been back in Montreux watching Jacques Jazy in similar pose – with old Satchmo's voice warbling one of her father's favourite tunes, *That's what the man said.*

The old man jigs stiffly to the beat, as she watches mesmerised.

He turns toward her.

She freezes, but there seems to be no reaction from the swaying old man. He is too engrossed in the music and perhaps is short-sighted anyway.

Quickly, she focuses her camera and takes several silent photographs, including one of the holstered pistol on his hip as he turns fully around.

He starts, as if at a sound, and looks back into the house.

A young man appears – a striking young man. Incongruous. He has an almost alabaster skin but spotted with occasional large brown freckles. Yet his hair is dark and his eyes are hidden by sunglasses, even inside the building. His appearance suggests that the hair should be red or blond. He is well-built, around twenty-years-old, a huge knife in a sheath sits on his left hip and a similarly large pistol on his right hip.

He says something to the old man, which Emma can't catch, and then waves his hands in a rotating motion. White-hair flicks his hand in agreement, followed by an impatient gesture to his music.

From her vantage point, Emma zooms her camera in for a number of quick shots of this new man, before he heads for the door. Almost immediately, Galen's voice in her earpiece warns that the red-head is approaching the building.

She slips away from the window and crawls back to the others. Within minutes, they rejoin Thea and the team – and they head south through the trees to their vehicles.

As she explains what they have seen to Thea – the descendant of generations of the proud Cypriot Spyrou family – she says, 'I want these photographs beamed through to Rotterdam as soon as possible. We may have hit a jackpot of sorts here. Well done to all of you.'

Chapter 28

June, 2013. Dubrovnik, Croatia

Sam Hall examines the coloured police mug-shot of Macan Granić, which Luka has provided from the Dubrovnik records.

'That is a memorable face,' he says. 'I need to get this image through to Rotterdam. Any protocol problems with that?'

Receiving a non-committal shrug, Sam snaps the photograph and beams it immediately through to his head-office relay centre, on the smart phone. 'His skin is the wrong colour for the hair. And the freckles – really large and brown. Strange, isn't it? As if the skin pigment got confused. The eyes seem strange too. What colour are they?'

'Mmm, the eyes? They are pale blue but there's a fleck of lightness in them, which can even look like pink at times. Yes, he *is* different,' agrees Luka. 'And his behaviour is something for a psychiatrist or psychologist to analyse – his physical oddity might play a part in explaining away his gross anti-social development. But I suppose now you can start to understand his mother's reaction to anything about the father. Not only was she left to bring up the child on her own, but he was a very different child, picked on, I'm told, as a young boy because of his looks. Maybe, he should have been albino but he isn't – black hair and the skin of a red head.'

'But he has survived,' Sam notes with a wry nod.

'Yes, yes. He certainly has – the classic body-building case study – with a strike-first attitude to anyone giving him a hard time.

Not only is he very strong physically but, as a teenager, he scared his peers with his viciousness; often with a knife; the sort who pulls the legs off insects and stabs small birds – cruel. He came to police attention before his teens. Neither the school nor his mother could cope. But he is not stupid. He can play the game. He came out of detention centres with all the correct promises of his rehabilitation. And he conned us all.'

'Ah ha. So he gravitated to the gangs.'

'Yes, but adult gangs – and he was accepted by them – even as a young teenager. They taught him to be an enforcer. Now he is scarcely into his twenties and hardened criminals would think twice before tangling with him.'

'And the police?'

'We have pulled him in but we need evidence. No-one will speak against him. They are petrified. And he has cultivated power-ful protectors.'

'And this *Cougar* could be the latest?'

'Perhaps. He is a new player to us. We have nothing on him at all. But Horvat seems to know something. Let's visit him again in his cell. He has been sweating for a while now. We need a lead, a location, something to work with.'

* * * *

The cell door opens to an angry, dishevelled Horvat but his atti-tude collapses quickly as Luka and Sam enter ... and the metal door slams shut again.

Luka stares at his prisoner silently for thirty seconds before he whispers, '*Vi tse terorist.*'

Even Sam can understand that language; the police accus-ing Horvat of terrorism, and the implications that are understood worldwide, in this current era – for long incarceration.

Horvat leaps to his feet in fierce denial. '*Nisam terorist.*'

The detective waves the big man to sit down and he speaks quietly in Croatian. Sam guesses he is explaining how long a person can held in prison on suspicion but all he has to do is to tell these kind detectives where *The Cougar* might be hiding.

Slowly, Horvat's bold façade crumbles. When he replies to the detective, his face is down, never looking at the source of his pain. The conversation continues for ten to fifteen minutes while the unshaven gang member occasionally shivers and stares ahead, with frightened eyes. Finally, his head sinks into his hands, over his knees ... and he weeps.

'Jas am mrtav.'

'Ne. Ne,' Luka replies as he turns to Sam. 'He thinks he is a dead man but I have told him, No.' He speaks again in Croatian to Horvat who simply shakes his bowed head and throws his hands up in a despairing gesture.

'We will leave, Sam.'

And they leave Horvat to wait while they check his information.

* * * *

Back in the airy light of Luka's office, the detective unfolds a map of southern Croatia for Sam's benefit.

'He tells me that there is a house in Cavtat, to the south of here, near the airport, where he knows an old man was, some months ago. We will go and check it out. Macan Granić was there too at the time. But, he thinks they are gone now – away on a fishing boat, he was told.'

'Were women part of this deal too?'

'He says there were. Arab women, and not prostitutes. He says it was nothing like that. They were confident, strong women – like soldiers. He wasn't around that place when the stories were first circulating. He was with another gang which ran protection rackets in north Dubrovnik. But a body had been found floating in the bay at Cavtat ... decomposed.

'He was sent with his people to check out this new mob in the area – a group called *The Cats* and an old man called *Cougar*. And there was another man there, red hair, looking after *Cougar*, presumably. Not a young man. Heavy build. Strong accent. North European, anyway.

'But Horvat's team had walked in on something way more powerful than they were. According to him, there were rumours of *The Cat* connection with a gang up in Zagreb – a burglary mob, as well as stand-overs. We have received notifications at the station, warning us of a Zagreb mob, but they were without any mention of a cat connection – so he is quite possibly telling the truth. We have had burglaries here too, over the past few months, targeting tourists and locals for money, jewellery, passports; light stuff. That seems to be the same pattern as up in the north of the country.

'Anyway, the red-head moved Horvat and his men on; with a language they could easily understand – a silver SIG pistol in their faces. Granić was definitely there too and everyone was well aware what he was capable of. But, Horvat says, Granić was showing amazing respect to the red-head. He was surprised. That was not usual. It was Granić who relayed the red-head's commands to them – although they would have been pretty obvious from the gun.

'They were all forced to their knees and threatened with painful execution – he scared the shit out of them. They are only knuckle men, full of size and bluff, occasional knives but not shooters. Horvat already knew of one corpse in the bay.

'And Horvat described the old man at the back of the room as dark-skinned, bald on top with white hair above the ears and back of the head. He was speaking to the women, maybe in Arabic. He heard him called *Maziq*, not *Cougar*, but he thought he must be *The Cougar* … because it was *The Cougar's* mob.'

'What? What? That has just blown most of my assumptions out of the water. Hennessy sure as hell doesn't have dark skin, nor is he called *Maziq* and I would really doubt that he would speak in Arabic.' Sam shakes his head to clear his thinking. 'But, if it is true, it is very interesting. Another message for Rotterdam. And I wish them luck with it all.' He smiles at his mental picture of Sven trying to make sense of it all.

'Of course,' Luka adds. 'Horvat now says he is a dead man breathing, for telling us.'

* * * *

The house in the picturesque old port of Cavtat is built in the sturdy, large stone, traditional style of the area, with stone pavers for perimeter walkways and the patio. Heavy red roof tiles contrast with a green creeper climbing up the wall. It is just one street back from the sparkling blue bay … and it looks deserted.

It has taken a few hours from the morning meeting in Horvat's cell to this point with Sam and Luka observing the house from a neighbouring yard. They had spent time with senior police in Dubrovnik getting clearances for Sam's role through the state security and intelligence agency in Zagreb, liaising with IIB in Rotterdam.

High-level clearances having been approved, a special police response team is supporting Sam and Luka (who are in business suits) from around the street corner.

Through his earpiece, Luka confirms the team are in place. The adjacent houses have been quietly locked down. Snipers watch windows through telescopic sights.

Giving a discreet thumbs-up, Sam and Luka stroll round the corner, clip-boards in hand, and up to the front door. The bell sounds clearly inside. Their plan is to be the innocent conductors of a survey of behalf of the Land Administration of Croatia.

The bell chimes again … with no response. Sam knocks loudly on the door, while Luka calls out, 'Halo! Bok!'

They move round the stone pathway to the rear. Everything is locked. A peer through the windows shows no signs of life.

A call from Luka through his microphone brings a man in a suit to the front door.

'He is our locksmith,' Luka grins.

And they are quickly inside.

With another call from the hallway to no response, they call one assault team forward to move progressively through the two floors of the house.

Nothing. Clean.

'Cellar?' queries Sam.

It is there that they find it – the solitary clue to where the occupants might have gone … plus a single blank page from a Cypriot passport.

Chapter 29

June, 2013. Rotterdam, The Netherlands

Arthur Blair whistles quietly. Nils Houweling has just produced the folder of photographs. 'Sven. Conclusive? Do you think?'

All three stare at the comparative photos sent by Emma Jazy from Cyprus and the mug-shot of Macan Granić from Sam in Dubrovnik. It confirms identity.

Sven nods. 'It would appear that we have our pale-faced gang member from Nicosia, the alleged killer of Nikkos and probably others.'

'And,' Arthur adds, 'a link between Cyprus and Croatia. Agreed, Nils?'

'Potentially,' the pragmatic operations director says. 'We also have the Cyprus shots of a white-haired man with a pistol on his hip, average height … and a red-haired man, solid build, mid-thirties at a guess, who is training some, possibly North African, guerrillas. I can't make much of the crawling men in green. Emma's report has them wriggling up in a three and a two, then turning a brace into the ground, before pushing what she described as a plumber's snake into the hole … with water added. It makes no sense at all, yet.'

'Alright. That's what we have,' Arthur confirms. 'One identified enemy. Granić. Who are the other two? Could the old man be Padraic Hennessy? He's the right age, size and shape. His hair isn't curly anymore, as the old descriptions used to indicate, but that could just be age. If yes, he's not far from Nicosia, where he might have been talking with Arab tribal leaders a month ago.'

Nils replies, 'We have no recent photographs of Hennessy, as yet. The Irish are displaying singular reluctance to release what we need. But I agree that he fits, roughly, what we could assume he might look like, based on those descriptions from decades ago.'

'Assume, then,' Sven suggests, 'that it is Hennessy. Then that red-head is too young to be Michael McSweeney. This man is in his thirties. McSweeney is closer to sixty.'

'So Macan is the protector?' Nils asks, shaking his head. 'He is a man, as far as we know, who only speaks Croatian fluently. Really? *He* is the protector? Emma's report shows that he was using hand signals to the old man. Where *is* Michael McSweeney?'

'Mmm. Interesting. Very interesting.' Arthur grins at the others. 'We like a challenge, don't we?'

'Do we have any photos of Michael McSweeney?' Sven asks.

'A passport photo only. At least one courtesy we have received from our Irish friends. I have it here on my screen. But as I say, no photo of Hennessy. For some reason, they say, the photo isn't on their system.' He shrugs.

With two taps, they are looking at a red-headed man, freckles, solid face, most likely late fifties, as his passport declares.

'Definitely not the man in Emma's photo,' Arthur says, '... but not unlike him either. Just a lot older.'

'Are you grasping at straws?' Nils Houweling smiles.

'You like being Devil's Advocate, don't you?' Sven is still shaking his head in dismay. 'Assume again that Padraic Hennessy is positioned in Cyprus, with Macan Granić. The as-yet-unidentified red-head is looking after him. Alright.' He pauses. 'I agree with you. Where is Michael McSweeney?'

Arthur Blair steeples his fingers. 'Sam Hall is following a lead in Dubrovnik which appears to link a group to *The Cougar*; perhaps cats, perhaps women, perhaps an old man. He's following a trail which he has from the other Macan – the Horvat fellow.'

Houweling interjects. 'I note in Emma's report that, at the goat-herd's house in the Kyrenia mountains, the old man in Cyprus was playing jazz on a CD. She was specific enough to identify Louis Armstrong's voice and even the song he was singing.'

'How would she know that?' Sven questions. 'Armstrong has been dead for years. Hardly a twenty-year-old's tastes.'

'She's nudging thirty, Sven, and she grew up in the house of Jacques Jazy,' Houweling continues. 'She notes her father listening to Armstrong regularly. The trumpeter was one of Maureen's favourites. Jacques even played Armstrong tracks at his stepdaughter's funeral. Maclean's tapes mention the sounds of *All the time in the world* as she was laid to rest. Isn't that right, Arthur?'

'That is right.'

'What was the tune then that Emma heard?' asks Sven, in a disbelieving tone.

Nils checks his screen. 'She notes it was *That's what the man said*. I don't know it myself but my discography search certainly has him singing it often enough in his career.'

'Well, I'll be ...' Sven drops his head back into thinking pose.

'So,' Arthur queries, 'you are contending that Padraic Hennessy is playing Maureen's favourite jazz artist. What? To bring him closer to his deceased women?'

'No,' Nils replies. 'I'm merely giving you information. It's *your* task to put forward interpretations. For me, he might just like New Orleans jazz, without any ulterior motives.'

Sven slowly raises his chin from his pincer-grip of forefinger and thumb, before offering a speculative suggestion. 'An old man looking for redemption might well do strange and unbelievable things – not least trying to find a solution to the problems of the Middle East. Isn't that what he said to Jacques Jazy two years ago? We are not dealing with a rational man.'

'What is the latest from Sam?' Arthur asks, his eyebrows lifting in frustration.

'He's pursuing a lead in a place called Cavtat,' Nils replies. 'It's about fifteen kilometres south of Dubrovnik, near the airport. But it is in itself an ancient port from Greek and Roman times. A very pretty Adriatic place is the Dalmation coast, you know. Cavtat hosts lots of conventions.'

'Now you're a travel agent for Croatian tourism, Nils?'

'You asked.'

'And Sam's lead is?'

'A potential terrorist link with alleged murders. The Croatian Security and Intelligence Service have been in touch to clear Sam's bona fides. That's all been done. Whatever they're going into has involved the back-up of a special response team from the Dubrovnik police.'

'Okay. We'll wait till that all unfolds. Anything happening elsewhere?'

Nils' phone buzzes with a message.

'Text from Sam,' he advises, as he reads on … and then whistles. 'This will test your theories now.'

Arthur and Sven are peering at him with maximum intensity as they wait for him to speak.

'Sam quotes Macan Horvat as describing the old man who is supposed to be *The Cougar* in the Cavtat house as … dark-skinned, bald on top, white hair round the ears … probably speaking in Arabic to the women in the house … and being called *Maziq*.'

The silence is palpable.

'That's all?' asks Sven, eventually.

'Isn't that enough?' Houweling gasps. 'Sam was heading to Cavtat with the police as I received this.'

The Swede smiles. 'Well, clearly we have two old men. Because the information is concurrent, No?'

'Not necessarily,' the factual Nils returns. 'We don't have a time frame on Horvat's description yet. But, potentially, okay – we have two old men; one in Emma's photo and this one in Cavtat. One with lots of white hair who likes Louis Armstrong, while the other is bald and is called Maziq.'

Sven is persistent. 'Well, this information tallies with the chatter from the Adriatic that I mentioned earlier … that we might be dealing with two old men. And one was possibly an old Libyan

164

gun runner from the 70s. Perhaps now we have a name for him – Maziq. Though, how he fits in is not immediately obvious to me as yet.'

Arthur shrugs. 'Nor to me. Anything happening elsewhere, Nils?'

'There's still chatter about something big about to happen. The Israelis have heightened their advisories. Their embassies are on alert.'

Sven has retreated to his comfortable chair, head in pondering pose. 'Nils, what do we have on the enemy plans? Apart from the personalities. What are they up to?'

Houweling doesn't need to touch his screens. 'In summary as I read it, we have a team of Africans – Arab we believe, but not confirmed – who appear to be practising an exercise of drilling or boring on their stomachs in the Kyrenian range.

'We have stories of Arab women signing up with a group associated with cats, for reasons as yet unknown. They may or may not be in Croatia. We have chatter on terrorist wavelengths about something big about to happen in *many* places – not just one – and most intelligence agencies around Europe are quietly aware.

'And – importantly, for all of us – we haven't received ongoing contracts to pay the *bills* around our investigations. We can't just survive on good will.'

Arthur Blair's Scottish twang is resurrected in his voice. 'What? Not being paid? Indeed, Nils. That *is* serious. Indeed. There will be a particular agency accountant or two getting an earful very soon. We need to be properly recompensed for all this prescient thinking.'

Sven's head lifts. 'Nils, see if you can identify the red-head in Cyprus … and we need a location for Michael McSweeney. Is Emma asking for back-up?'

'She's happy at the moment. They'll be going back into the hills tomorrow to see what else they can discover.'

'And no more contact from Sam?'

Nils glances at his screens, shaking his head as he does so. 'I expect something very soon. They should be in Cavtat now. Let's see where that might take us.'

'Then we await developments …'

Chapter 30

June, 2013. Cavtat, Croatia

'Where are Kuna Konovoska and Snijeznica?' Sam asks Luka, as he glances at the find in his hand.

They are in the cellar of the rented property in Cavtat, searching for evidence of the people who have lived there for several months … and, more importantly, where they might be now. All personal belongings appear to have been removed from the house. The rooms upstairs are spotlessly clean.

'Up in the mountains to the south-east of here. Not very far. Pretty rugged. Hikers love it. Karst country. Limestone. What do you have?' He glances at the glossy papers in Sam's hand.

'As you say, this is a hiking brochure. Fallen off the table and landed behind that cabinet. Missed in the clean-up, eh? Could that be where they are heading? One of the maps has a location circled in red.'

'Show me.'

Sam passes the brochure and Luka checks, before, 'Snijeznica is the name of the mountain. It is very rugged and dry. Lots of hiking trails. Terrible in winter and not too pleasant even now, unless you really like roughing it.' He looks again at the circle on the pamphlet. 'Kuna Konovoska is a village, lower on the slope and this circle has been drawn outside the town – an old house on its own, by the looks. But – who knows – it's worth checking. We have nothing else to go on.'

Luka's phone buzzes. 'The neighbour here is available to be interviewed. She's lived in this street for years.'

'Just before we go, Luka.' Sam hands over the torn blank page of a Turkish-Cypriot passport. 'What do make of that?'

The policeman turns it over. 'There's nothing on it. Where did you find it?'

'It was caught at the back of that cabinet over there, like the brochure.'

Luka nods and bends close to the back wall, working his way methodically along, past a large wooden table … to the cabinet. He opens the doors. The shelves are empty. 'What do you smell, Sam?'

'Some industrial spirit?'

'Put it in your report to Rotterdam. Maybe it will be a part of the jigsaw yet. I think it might be ink,' Luka adds, as he resumes his quick but detailed examination of the table-top.

He drops the page into a paper sample bag. 'Strange. They've been up to something down here. The cleaners haven't been as thorough here as upstairs. I'm betting ink or paint.'

They leave to speak to the lady next door.

* * * *

Gospodja Babić is a widowed long-term resident and Luka speaks gently to her in Croatian.

She replies calmly, pointing occasionally at the neighbouring house and smiling happily when the detective thanks her profusely at the end. No doubt this has been one of the most exciting days in the street for years; even although nothing has actually happened, apart from a sudden police presence.

Luka heads back to the patio of the rented house, with Sam, where he can brief him quietly.

'She tells me that the group has been in this house for several months – five months probably, she believes. Early on, it was very quiet, just an old man with white hair who played jazz music – but never so loud as to annoy Mrs Babić. She likes trad jazz. It reminds her of the old days with her husband. She remembered a strange

168

pale-faced man there too. She saw him doing push-ups out the back. Very fit, she said. Strong.

'Then, after a month, some of the young bully boys from up in Dubrovnik would visit. They were never drunk and – she was keen to say – never more noisy than the presence of a lot twenty-year-old males would make. Maybe she likes distractions. Who knows?

'But she thought they were up to something wrong because one night there was a really loud bang like something very heavy falling out of a window – maybe a table – but then it went quiet again.

'About two weeks after that, several darker-skinned women arrived – olive-skinned, she corrected it to. They kept to themselves. She thought they might have been itinerant workers but they didn't seem to leave the house grounds. She saw them sitting out here on the back patio, just talking quietly. Some foreign tongue. Caused no trouble. Smiled when she looked at them.

'Then another older man was there, darker-skinned too – a deeper dark than olive, she thought, when I questioned her further – with a fringe of white hair. And the first old man wasn't there after that – she thought maybe about three months ago – and the pale-faced young man seemed to have been replaced by an older red-haired man.

'She insisted that they really were no trouble. Then, two days ago, she heard no sound. And now all the police have arrived. She can't understand why the police would be so interested. It really is a very quiet street.'

Luka smiles after his report.

'They sound like a bunch of angels to me too,' replies Sam. 'So what do you think? Do we head for Kuna Konovoska? Are there police up there?

'Maybe only one. We'll follow protocol and inform him. We can't really drag the response team all the way up there, for no pay-off. This false alarm is as much as we can get away with, for the moment. Let's just start with a quiet reconnaissance, eh? I'll get the local man to see if anyone is actually in the house. Maybe he can get a description, even a photograph, if he is careful.'

'Right. I'll take your wise advice. I need to get my report through to Nils at head office – and then what do you suggest?'

'It's summer. Spend some time with my cousin. I think she likes you. We might check on Macan Horvat again. He has given us one piece of correct evidence, and I'm betting he knows more than he has told us. That *Cougar* gang probably has more than one safe house in the area, and they will have bumped into other gangs over the few months they have been around – maybe even bumping some of them *off*, as Horvat suggested. And as *Gospodja* Babić also intimated, when a gunshot sounds like a table falling out of a window, to her. I mean, you've got to love an old dear like that.'

'D'you mean tables don't regularly fall out of windows here in Croatia? I'm stunned.'

'So was the fellow on the pointy end of the bang.' Luka laughs. 'Ended up going for a long, slow swim in the bay.'

Chapter 31

June, 2013. Rotterdam, The Netherlands

'We have a breakthrough at last on the McSweeneys.' Nils Houweling actually looks excited. 'A Sean McSweeney attended University College in Dublin and studied geophysics. We have the photo from his graduation in 2000.' He passes his screen over to the others. 'He would be thirty-four now. He matches the photo of the red-head from Cyprus, don't you think?'

Sven and Arthur nod as they continue staring at his image.

'You have more on this Sean McSweeney?'

'But, of course. He has worked as a surveyor in engineering projects around the world and ... he spent several years working for the Gaddafi regime in the Libyan oil fields – before the collapse of the regime, naturally.'

'Naturally.' Arthur grins at his operations chief. 'Well done, Nils! More information wouldn't be too much more to ask, eh? Is he a relative of other known McSweeneys perhaps?'

'Well, the photos from that time confirm he has red hair.'

'Good,' responds Arthur patiently. 'Anything we don't already know?'

'As it happens, yes,' he replies, as Sven splutters with impatience. 'He has a mother – Michael McSweeney's wife – who just happened to run with the successor to the *Baader-Meinhof* gang in Germany, as it evolved into the *Red Army Faction* in the seventies. She was with them for a few years from 1974.'

171

'Wowee! What a parentage.' Arthur throws his voice to the ceiling. 'Provisional IRA and one of the most infamous German guerrilla revolutionary groups – and both associated with Libya and the Palestinian Liberation Organisation. What a double whamee!'

Sven's quiet tones stabilise the conversation with, 'And now we have a whole new set of variables. Now, it suddenly makes sense why Israeli Embassies in northern Europe have been put on raised alert. Something is frightening the horses. The chill that Nikkos mentioned. The chatter is sensing it too.'

'Indeed,' responds Arthur. 'But how are *they* getting wind of it?'

'Mmm … always the unknowns. And, we should not now be ruling out situations where Arab women would be obvious. Depending on who the contacts of Mrs McSweeney's are, women from other countries could also be involved. This *is* starting to look big … as Nikkos suggested.'

'And,' Arthur rejoins the hypothesising of scenarios, 'if we believe his earlier advice, it's all going to happen *in many places* and *within weeks* – maybe only a couple of weeks. And we are now at the end of June. What major events will occur for Israel or the world, in July?'

'Croatia joins the European Union on Monday, the 1st July.' Nils looks remarkable jolly, despite the seriousness of the situation, as he taps his machines for information. 'That's big for them. It should send a firework or two in the air.' He smiles as he glances back at his phone screen. 'And Israel will host the Maccabiah Games. That *is* a major sporting event – huge in fact – based in Jerusalem but with events all over the country … and tourists galore.'

Nils clicks on his screen again. 'Twenty-five esteemed Israeli authors have signed a petition to halt the proposed live-firing range in the South Hebron Hills. It would remove hundreds of Palestinian goat herders who have lived there for centuries. Other than that, there are lots of conferences all over the world, but nothing as big as Maccabiah.'

'The sporting games is a possibility.'

'But if it is to happen in many places …? Drilling little holes in the ground isn't going to affect the Games, is it? What will they do – make an explosion of some sort?'

'Perhaps? Perhaps not.' Arthur's eyes have a sparkle – the thrill of the chase. 'Let's keep an open mind. On the bright side, if Hennessy *can* actually resolve the dilemmas of the Middle East in a fortnight, maybe we – and the world – should thank him.'

'Depending on the price to be paid,' Sven mutters into his hand. 'More likely, he will compound the problems for another couple of millennia unless we can get to the bottom of this fast.'

'Good news for you, Nils, at least,' Arthur announces. 'Thanks to the facts we've been gathering and my not inconsiderable Scottish sales-pitching abilities, we are now being retained by several government intelligence agencies on significant sums to resolve this, before it hits the fan.'

'Whoopee!' Houweling cheers. 'Wages can be paid.'

'And we will have the money to grease some more paths,' adds Arthur. 'I'm still pondering how the revolutionary chatter has been getting wind of this proposed attack. Indeed, it was *Mossad* indirectly that put us on to it in Cyprus. I would lay you dollars to doughnuts that the unfortunate Bashir Dorda has been the source. And that was how he met his very messy end. We have the suggestion that he might have been their spy … and he would probably have been one of the crawling men in green … or a supervisor, maybe.'

'I'd bet …' Sven doesn't raise his head as he speaks. '… that he shopped what he knew of the operation, early on, to *Mossad* … and Macan Granić was called in to make an example of him. Then *Mossad* has fed the information into the grapevine to flush out what else might be planned. We have been recruited to see what we can discover … and now the dots are being slowly joined.'

'And,' Nils suggests, 'although I am not a speculator by profession, the dots seem indeed to be forming an arrow aimed at Israeli interests. Perhaps, you wiser ones have been right in your hypothesis about Padraic Hennessy's boast. And his life-long areas of expertise.'

'No speculation in that, Nils. We know he made the offer in the phone call to Jacques Jazy.' Arthur pauses. 'See what you can find out about Bashir Dorda. Maybe his background can provide a clue to what else is happening apart from Cyprus ... and the women in Croatia. Just a thought.'

Sven lifts his head, still focused solely on the earlier problem. 'Do we have a name for this mother? Sean McSweeney's mother. Who is she? Where is she?'

'I do have info,' Nils replies. 'Always happy to oblige.' He laughs at Sven's stunned expression. 'She was born in 1955 as Waltraud Muller in Wurzburg, Germany. But more recently she has been known as Val McSweeney, wife of Michael. She was university edu-cated – a BA from Heidelberg in political science. We know they lived in Dublin from 1994 till 2005. Michael was an activist for hire. Val organised resistance seminars for a fee. I imagine they were in demand internationally in their chosen fields of insurrection.'

'And where is she now?' asks Sven. 'Should I take it she is not in either Cyprus or Croatia?'

'No record of her being seen.'

'Then she could be preparing the ground in any of the cities of Europe ... or the States ... for whatever the women and the crawl-ing men are practising.'

'That would be true,' agrees a more subdued Nils. 'I'll go and check the chatter on the system. Suddenly, it has all become super-complicated again.'

To which, Arthur responds, 'On the other hand ...'

Chapter 32

June, 2013. Kyrenia mountains, Cyprus

Emma and her team move slowly, following a similar course to the previous day, climbing up the wooded slope in a spread-out arrow formation. But, on this day, their plan is for the Greek-Cypriots to bring out the pale-face; alive or nearly dead – perhaps the last option being their preferred choice; justice.

And they will make it look like a revenge attack from the local Cypriot network – that foreigners can't come to their island and mess with the proud Greek warriors of Cyprus.

Arthur Blair himself has given the approval, provided that it can be done discreetly, with no suggestion other than that the Cypriots have exacted their revenge on a killer. Arthur believes that Granić is the man who made the example of Bashir Dorda, as well as Nikkos. He would dearly like to know what that captured Croatian could add to IIB's understanding of the bigger picture.

Each of the six carries an HK automatic rifle along with a pistol and knife. The comms are working as smoothly as before … but, apart from Emma, they still look like Cypriot herders, in jackets and caps.

Adrenalin is surging through their veins as they near the limestone rock lookout. Three will cover any reaction from the crawling team while the other three will take care of the old man, the redhead and the pale-face.

They have rehearsed the moves. They could carry them out blindfolded if need be. If the crawling men and the others choose to fight and become collateral damage, so be it. But, the ideal scenario is that Emma, Galen and Cristof will spirit pale-face away unde-tected. To that end, each of them carries a syringe, the contents of which can immobilise their victim in seconds – but it is for the pale-face, him alone.

* * * *

At the limestone rock, Emma scans the clearing. Nothing. Empty. Not even a box in the centre of the rough training patch.

While Thea, Ari and Jason wait – tense, expecting the surprise – Emma Galen and Cristof head for the stone hut ... spread out ... crawling ... listening.

Up to the window. Emma peers in. All is quiet. Front door unlocked. No sign of an enemy waiting in ambush. No CD player in the main room. Clear. The whole house is clear.

* * * *

Back to the clearing – to where the box had been. Thea organises the men into a defensive perimeter as Emma crawls to the centre. There, a filled-in hole is clearly visible, about ten centimetres in diameter. Limestone pebbles stare back at her. It looks like the mark of an over-sized old hole on a golf course putting green.

Nothing.

* * * *

They fan out slowly and silently to scout for tracks. Perhaps there is a base farther into the hills. Or have the group decided that they are well-enough practised ... and have actually set off on their mission?

* * * *

Ari finds a track ... the faintest of trails ... freshly broken twigs ... weathered stones which have been turned by a boot.

Towards a cave in a low limestone cliff.

Again, the tactics of mountain warfare make a defensive perim-eter while Jason and Ari cover each other into the cave mouth.

* * * *

After two minutes, they emerge.

Inside, they have found the detritus of a recent camp fire. Many boot scuffs on the ground. Urine stains against the deep back wall. No more than a day old.

'Maybe more than the eight people we have seen? Many more, perhaps. What do you think, Galen?'

'Could be.' He is looking around. Are their enemies watching? Danger!

* * * *

Their recce procedures are thorough. After an hour of searching the area, there is no-one to be found. Thea leads her disappointed team down from the mountain as they puzzle about this sudden departure.

Cristof is the only one who mutters in Greek that they should have killed the pale-face yesterday when they had the chance. But Thea reassures everyone, 'His time will come. Revenge is best when it is served cold.'

* * * *

That afternoon, Emma beams her report through the secure dummy call-centre to Arthur Blair in Rotterdam … and awaits further instructions.

Chapter 33

June, 2013. Dubrovnik, Croatia

'How was beautiful Cavtat?' Ivana asks, as Sam enters her office.

'Beautiful, but unfortunately our birds had flown.'

'So sad. What now? This is Saturday. I have so much to do. When you get back to The Hague, please send my father home. There is work for him *here*. But Uncle Danko has given us his boat for tomorrow. I'll take you out to the islands. A day of rest … for us both. How does that sound?'

'Very nice.'

'And after, there will be celebrations in the *Stari Grad* because Croatia will join the European Union at midnight. Many will be rejoicing. Me? I think the jury is out on whether we want to be part of that economic crisis. But you and me, Sam … we can party on 1st July for EU Croatia. Okay?'

'Any excuse for a party with you. Terrific! Thank you.'

'Good, good. But that is tomorrow. Today, I really must work. Tonight, come to see me. Oh, and Danko wants to take you for that drive he promised, whenever you are free.' She wags her finger in warning. 'But he just wants to talk about the war. Nobody in the family listens to his stories. We don't understand him and then he is offended. Maybe we don't believe that it all happened like he says or we have heard too much of it before. It was so much worse up in the north-east, on the border. We know that but … you can take only so much. Anyway, you have been warned. You old soldiers can swap tales.'

'It will be fine, Ivana. I'm keen to understand what happened … from someone who was there. I know I'll only get one side of the story but even that is important. How will I contact him?'

She already has the phone in her hand. 'You are free now?' … and she is speaking within seconds.

Sam smiles at her avid phone-listening while he whispers cheekily and annoyingly, 'You really must be busy to be pushing me out the door so fast,'… and she pouts in reply to his cynicism.

'He'll pick you up at your hotel at two. Okay?' Then she pauses as she replaces the phone. 'You don't need to be paying for a hotel. I have a spare room – to drop your bags; not necessarily yourself.' She giggles with a wink, before adopting her serious face and waving him away. 'Be gone. I need to work. Look at this pile of files. I'll see you this evening,' followed by the easy grin. 'Bring your bags with you.'

* * * *

Danko pulls his powerful German Opel Insignia off the Adriatic Road and heads up into the mountains behind Dubrovnik.

'We'll drive up to Bosanka and onto Mount Srgj, up on ridge. It is good to get up into hills, Sam. Beautiful view over town, the islands and Adriatic. You and Ivana are going out on boat tomorrow. You'll have good time. And then there will be fireworks at midnight. We fought so hard to be independent – and here they are now, taking us into an alliance with lots of dodgy European partners. I don't know.'

'That's the job of the politicians, I suppose.'

'*Ne.* I don't trust them. Too many compromises. Too politically correct. It is all re-integration talk today. Maybe, young ones will manage more easily. They won't have lived through it.'

'Did I understand you correctly earlier, Danko? You were at Vukovar?'

'Not in the siege itself. My uncle was. He was there for three months and then marched off into Serbia to a detention camp – murder camp really. I fought with Croatian National Guard, and

179

actually with a paramilitary group before that, in Osijek to Vukovar area. We were like the Partisans from the old war – you might understand that better – fighting Cetniks, but instead we fought against Arkan's Tigers, Dušan Silni, Ninjas from Knin. Just lots of gangs of murdering thugs really – like mobs of football hooligans gone wild, except these ones had weapons and open licence to terrorise.

'We picked at the enemy, disrupting them, sabotage … because, until the foreigners arrived – the mercenaries, the gun runners – with more equipment, we were surviving on wit and good will. The locals – the civilians – had it really bad. We defended them where we could but lots of evil happened there, on both sides, if I tell the truth.'

The car climbs onto the ridge from Bosanka.

'Stunning view, Danko. You are right.'

'Was what we fought for. Ivana has told you how it started – the politics, the Serbs, Arkan's gangsters raiding villages. They just wanted our land – along the border – and they peddled such rubbish stories, lies. I'm trying to think of your English words – *unity through ethnicity*. Does that make sense to you?'

'I understand what the words are meant to mean.'

'Well, it is rubbish. We never thought like that. Serb and Croat lived peacefully together for generations. We intermarried. My aunt was of Serb ancestry and my uncle – an ethnic Croat married to a Serb woman – ended up in Serbian prison camp.

'Anyway, it really started when Serbs killed police at Borovo Selo. They had captured two policemen who had raised the Croatian flag in the village … and they held them – kidnapped – to bargain with. Extra police were sent in to rescue, but it was ambush. Their buses were attacked with automatic weapons. Twelve police died and twenty-two wounded. After that, all killing groups were off leash. Politicians just fuelled tension and refugees fled the area. But Vukovar was progressively cut off.

'The city stands where the Vuka River meets Danube. Thirty-six thousand JNA, Yugoslav Army troops, surrounded it; Serbs, mainly. They bombarded city using planes, tanks and heavy artillery. Eighteen hundred fighters resisted from within – not even an army, just police and ZNG, the national guard … and civilians.

'So, it started throughout April 1991, when Serb paramilitaries barricaded roads and ambushed anyone around. Borovo was in May and vote for independence (also May) was ninety-four per cent in favour of Croatian independence.

'By August, the city was totally cut off. No longer were there any smuggling routes along canals and drains. No food, no supplies of anything could get in. People were hiding in ditches, cellars, anywhere to be safe because, as Ivana told you, 120,000 artillery ordnance on some days were shot into Vukovar, into houses, even into hospital with its red cross clearly showing.

'When city finally fell on 18th November, 700,000 shells plus 2.5 million mortars … or artillery over 20mm … had landed in Vukovar. You are soldier. You understand what I'm saying. The water tower stands today, as memorial, peppered through like cheese. The smell of smashed buildings, mixed with dead bodies and that stink that artillery explosives make … it went through everything.

'Then massacres started … along with all other abuses of women, in particular. Horrible stories filtered out. Terrified whole country … all way down to here in Dubrovnik. We all knew what to expect if we lost the battles.

'Hundreds of starving Vukovar soldiers and civilians were just butchered. Others were deported to detention camps, where random selections for mass-executions happened daily … along with starvation, torture and brutality, just to break spirits.

'My uncle was in one of those, *Sremska Mitrovica*. He survived – just – but he didn't live long after. Starvation, no hygiene, disease and bashing took its toll; and Vukovar town had surrendered under agreement that civilians would go free. No-one went free; until Serb war with us was over, nearly a year later. My uncle was released in August 1992. He had spent months in what was known as Pavilion Three – I don't need to explain that further to a fellow soldier – it was worst. And what was it all for?

181

'Before re-integration a few years ago, school textbooks in Croatia called Vukovar ... *the battle where a Croatian city was destroyed and, with its sacrifice, the whole of Croatia was saved.* That was pretty right. It was most catastrophic siege, they said, since Stalingrad. Yet, Serb and Croat had lived there for generations ... good friends ... neighbours ... together, in same city. Bloody politicians and their fanatical causes.

'That battle broke the Serb army. Cost in resources and support was huge for us, but it was beginning of end for them. They moved away from Croatia – all too hard for them – and we had built a strong army over months. Their own conscripts left their country rather than serve Serbia and do what they were ordered.

'Vukovar was the first but not the last. *Culturocide* is what I've heard it called; another term is *ethnic cleansing.* I hate those words. Mostar and Sarajevo followed in Bosnia ... and Srebrenica – terrible, just terrible – but world opinion eventually starved ability of aggressors to keep fighting. And then it was over.

'Now we have to re-integrate – so they tell us – as if none of that horror actually happened. I'm not so forgiving. I was there. I saw with my own eyes what was going on. Thankfully, people like Goran – Ivana's father – are in The Hague helping compile cases to bring those evil ones to some form of international justice – to not let them sleep in peace; to make sure that this land never repeats that terror. Are these the people in The Hague that you work for too, Sam?'

'Yes, Danko, in a way. My job is to investigate, to collect evidence – in current cases – to prevent them happening in the first place, as much as possible. Our group works in conjunction with the International Courts of Justice. We deal in crimes against humanity, mainly.'

Danko pulls the vehicle over to savour the magnificent view of the Dalmation Coast. 'Well, I'm glad you do, Sam. I'm really glad you do.' He smiles for the first time at the picturesque scenery in front of him. 'So do we have more of this happening now, here? In Croatia? Is that why you are here? Is it about to blow again?'

And his hand shakes on the stationary steering wheel as he asks his question.

'Perhaps, but unlikely in the way you have experienced. We work on establishing proof that could be admissible in court. Luka is helping me track down some bad people before it might get worse. But I don't think the danger will affect Croatia itself.' He pats Danko on the shoulder and then shakes the offered hand. 'Thank you for sharing some of your understanding with me. It is good to hear what it was like.'

Ivana's uncle appears pleased that he has been heard – the repeated nod, the intense eye contact of shared awareness, a moist eye at some memory.

Then he gives a resigned shrug. 'Well, Vukovar is a now divided city, Sam, physically and emotionally. I don't know if it will *ever* get over its past. Serbs and Croats don't mix like they did before. Too much pain.

'You see, is not like happened in Berlin. That was wall keeping apart people who wanted to be together. Vukovar is more like Jerusalem or Belfast or Nicosia in Cyprus – they even built dividing wall there too for a while, I'm told. Those peoples appear no longer to want to live together. Vukovar is divided by pain; by its inability to see what happened for what it really was – an aggressive invasion to annexe an area of Croatia, a country that had freely voted to be independent of Yugoslavia.

'Yes, you might think we all would know what happened at that time. But knowing the facts doesn't mean that everyone shares same understanding of truth. It depends whose eyes you are looking through. And I know Serbs who talk of Croat atrocities. Look, Sam, it was war. Bad things happened in heat of conflict and uncertainty … but it wasn't balanced ledger. We didn't invade anyone.

'I don't hide from the killing. We were fighting for survival. You know that, Sam, from Iraq and Afghanistan. It happens. But single truth that no-one can ignore is that it started from Serb aggression to settle our lands; to take them over and put their own people there.

'That might have worked in Roman times when people could flee to empty spaces but are no empty spaces any more. Look at Syria. Refugees are piling up in Turkey ... and Lebanon and Jordan, which already has had to deal with generations displaced from Palestine. Shared rule of one land, one country, does not work.'

'So, Danko.' Sam peers at the Croatian veteran. 'At some time, things have to become normal again. Not necessarily normal as before, but a new normal – for the future – not forgetting where we have been. Croatia is calling it *re-integration*, other places call it *normalisation* or *reconciliation*. To move on from the past.'

'Yes, Sam.' Danko nods slowly, reluctantly. 'Soldiers learn to move on; to carry their scars, inside. Though, we can never forget. We *should* never forget. It's the sacrifice of others. If they are forgotten, why did they die? Should we just have submitted to aggressors, to bullies? No, of course not. We have to stand for what we believe. But this *re-integration* is hard for people like me. I know that hatred is a curse, but memories and conscience are curses too.'

He stops and stares through the windscreen, out west towards the horizon and distant Italy. Without looking away from the view, he says quietly, 'I think I am getting too old for this world now, Sam. There are just too many people on planet and no space. Of course there will be fighting, like rats in trap, it will happen more and more. I don't know solution but I will never forget those who fought with me, those who died and those who lived – are still living – with pain. What we did was for cause greater than ourselves. We were right to do that. I will go to my grave believing we were right to resist.' He turns from the view and gives a wan smile to his passenger. 'You are good man, Sam, for listening. Nobody much listens to us veterans now. The world has moved on.'

'Yes, Danko. It has. But it needs to heal – for Ivana and the next generation. And you will be in the European Union in a little over a day. Who would have thought that, thirty years ago? And, in your way, you helped bring the peace and the progress that the country now enjoys. Live in the moment, Danko. Savour what you have earned for this place. It is beautiful and we will thank you from the boat tomorrow, down there on that sparkling blue sea.'

* * * *

Sam's mobile rings. It is Luka.

'The policeman has found the house at Kuna Konovska. He has just rung in. There are no Arabs there, women or men. But he found a man who said he was the advance caretaker for a group of hikers, expected soon.'

He pauses, before continuing with a cheeriness in his voice, 'Now guess. The man is in his fifties, heavy build, red hair starting to thin and whiten, and who spoke with … an Irish accent.'

Sam splutters. 'How would your policeman know an Irish accent?'

'It is a hiking centre. People come there from all countries … including Ireland. It's a pretty recognisable accent. Sam, he is sure. And the rest fits too.'

'Good then,' Sam concedes. 'Your policeman has done well – very well. Will he be able to keep a watch on him while I contact Rotterdam?'

'Oh, there's more. He took a photo of him on the back patio. It's quite good. It shows his head and face clearly. He's sent it to my phone.'

'Luka, I should never have doubted the Croatian police force. Can you beam it over to my phone, please? How did he manage to get the shot, unseen?'

'Sam, Sam. Surveillance 101 is taught in all our police training courses. He took it through a crack in a stone garden wall.'

'Well done. I've just been out with Danko, up on the ridge behind the town. He has some interesting tales to tell, your father.'

'Vukovar again?'

'But a good insight for me who only saw occasional news headlines. Now, back to our red-headed Irishman. Ivana and I had planned to take Danko's boat out to the islands tomorrow. Did your policeman indicate that the man showed any inclination to leave?

185

I'd really like to wait until I get clearance from head office before jumping into anything. They have the whole picture of what's going on in other places.'

'Sam, you go with Ivana. That's an opportunity that falls to few others, believe me. Going sailing to islands with her, I mean. We will keep tabs on the Irishman for you. And I will have another chat with Horvat tomorrow, just to break up my day-off. Some of us have to keep the wheels of justice turning.'

'Sainthood will come to you, Luka. Thanks.'

Chapter 34

June, 2013. Rotterdam, The Netherlands

'Bashir Dorda was Egyptian ... and an expert in water catchment engineering. I found out quite a lot about him,' Nils Houweling announces proudly. 'Although, I wouldn't have thought he would be a terrorist crawling along in green cams. He was born in Cairo in 1942. So he would be seventy-one this year.'

'Another old man,' exclaims the astonished Arthur Blair while Sven Gulbrandson lowers his head into hands in mock despair.

Nils continues, 'He graduated from Cairo University at the end of 1963 with an honours engineering degree. He was a bright man. And he did a specialist year in 1964 at Cambridge, researching aquifer technology.'

Sven's head lifts sharply. 'Say that last bit again. Slowly.'

'Aquifer technology?'

'That's what I thought you said.' His eyes are very attentive. 'Sorry. Go on.'

'In 1966, he was working on water projects in the Golan Heights areas of Tel Dan and She-ar Yashuv in present-day Israel but, in 1966 as you would be aware, they were still administered by Syria, albeit with disputes. She-ar Yashuv is a Jewish settlement founded at the start of World War II, despite the British having put restrictions on any influx of Zionist immigration at that time. Tel Dan goes back into Old Testament times.'

Arthur Blair rises to his feet and paces over to the window, slowly shaking his head. The view of the roofs and docks always help his sense of perspective. Without looking back into the room, he mutters, just audibly, 'I don't like where this is heading. But carry on, Nils.'

'My homework suggests that the Golan Heights were formed where a basalt flow overlies light-coloured limestones and marls, characterised by lots of faults and solution channels – generally, the features of a karst landscape; sinkholes, fissures and the like – especially in places where the volcanic cap has been breached. This is high country, with snows in winter.'

Blair turns to give a despairing, questioning look at his operations manager.

Houweling continues, undaunted; indeed almost excited to be sharing his knowledge. He reads from his notes. 'The Banias and Dan rivers flow into the Hula Valley and on into the Jordan. Waters gush down those river courses after winter with the snow-melt; standing ponds remain scattered on the non-porous rock throughout the year; chuckling springs – I like that description – appear out of the limestone where cracks release water out of a complexity of aquifers and underground channels.

'Although the water-bearing beds are not as substantive as in the Mountain Aquifer of the West Bank or perhaps the Coastal Aquifer of Palestine, there may be linkages back from them to the Golan systems at a deep level. That was the type of investigation that Dorda was working on, nearly half-a-century ago. Did you know that two-thirds of Israel's substantial demand for water is met from its aquifers?'

'Why didn't anyone mention his age?' Arthur completely ignores his operations manager's question.

'Maybe it was the shock of finding a man with his tongue cut out and his hands chopped off.'

'But he would still look like a seventy-year-old. Surely?'

Sven lifts his head with a wry nod. 'Why would the finders be interested in his age rather than his injuries? They didn't have our background intel. They were first-response people. And now, we have three old men. Suddenly, I feel quite sprightly in this case.

Nils, do you have any more on what Dorda could be doing with crawling men and holes in the ground?'

'Only the sort of speculation that I don't like to engage in. Suffice it to say that the limestone in the Golan area is heavily faulted, hence the many springs, I imagine. So, logically, the tracking of aquifers would not be from the top of the basalt, the volcanic relics. It would be accessible only on weathered or eroded valley sides – in the limestone. My best guess.'

'Right. What else?' the Swede demands. 'We have a geophysicist in Sean McSweeney and now an Egyptian aquifer specialist – that adds up to a potential threat against Israel. And, doubtless, *Mossad* knows all about this, as Bashir Dorda was their informant. So, what else?'

'Sam has sent through a photo of a man he believes might be Michael McSweeney.'

Sven leaps from his chair. '*Now* you tell us, Nils. Have you done a master's course in suspense building?'

'Just trying to be methodical. It has just come through on my screen as I have been speaking. Look.' He turns the laptop screen to face the directors. 'It was taken at a place called Kuna Konovoska – I'm just pulling up a map on my other screen – and it was taken by the local police on a tip-off from Sam.'

They stare at the image.

'Mmm … could well be,' Arthur Blair surmises. 'What else do we know about Mr Michael McSweeney in Croatia?'

'First, Kuna Konovoska is a village in the hills to the south of Dubrovnik and Cavtat – in the karst country, favoured by hikers. Apparently, McSweeney told the policeman that he is an advance party for a group of walkers due there in a few days.'

'The policeman approached him?' gasps an incredulous Sven. 'I hope this doesn't end badly. Surely, McSweeney would have the same highly-developed danger radar that his father and Hennessy would have honed in the bad days of Northern Ireland, don't you think?'

Houweling shrugs. 'Sam is not flagging that as an issue. His detective contact – the nephew of Goran Bikić that you both know – suggests that in a village like Kuna Konovoska with hikers passing through regularly, the police effectively carry out welcoming checks. It may well be accepted as non-threatening.'

'Mmm,' Arthur ponders. 'Don't discount that McSweeney may be lying about his intentions and heading for the hills already.'

'He's already in the hills.' Houweling smiles.

'Nils, you are stretching a friendship.' Sven sighs. 'Perhaps he is waiting for the Arab women and Maziq to arrive.'

'I doubt it,' Arthur argues. 'They could have travelled there at the same time as McSweeney, surely. My gut instinct suggests that they are already heading for somewhere else in Europe to carry out whatever they have been planning – maybe with Val McSweeney and others. Maybe Michael is waiting for Macan Granić to arrive with Padraic Hennessy, who have both disappeared in, or from, Cyprus.'

'And,' adds Sven, 'Sean McSweeney could be in Israel now with the crawling hole-diggers, to do … whatever. While it is making more sense, it is actually making less sense.'

Nils stays quiet, glancing from Arthur to Sven and back again.

'Anything on Val McSweeney's whereabouts?' Arthur asks eventually.

'Not yet. We have put the word out, but nothing as yet.'

'So the current action seems to have moved back towards Croatia, that's where Michael is.' Arthur speaks his thoughts aloud. 'Cyprus may have gone off the boil. What connections are you sensing, Sven?'

The Swede lifts his head from the thought pose, ruffles his lank whitening hair slowly, and stares briefly at the ceiling. 'First, limestone – the Kyrenia Range, this Kuna Konovoska, the Golan aquifer. They are all limestone. Second, the long-term impact of forced settlement – Northern Ireland with its four-hundred-year history of an implanted colony, Cyprus with its partition of Turk and Greek areas, Croatia with the attempted Serb invasion to annexe the country in the 1990s, and Israel with its homeland being dropped onto an area of Palestine. And all the human conflict and residual resentment that has been caused; carrying on for years, decades, centuries, even millennia. Those are the connections, I'm sensing at the moment. But they make little sense combined. And you, Arthur?'

Blair paces to his window and back again. 'Israel would argue its valid entitlement to the land, citing its displacement over the centuries – the *diaspora*. But I accept your general premise. It really depends on whose shoes you are standing in. My senses are more about the revolutionary activists involved; the gun-running Libyans of the Gaddafi years, the Provisional IRA breakaway mobs that spawned Hennessy and the McSweeneys, the German Red Army Faction's association with Val McSweeney, the Palestine Liberation Organisation and its spin-offs, the EOKA movement in Cyprus, and the Serb Tigers et cetera in the former Yugoslavia.

'So many dissident rebels fighting what they see as the abuses of power – from governments and their military, from the colonial presumption to dictate how people can live or die, from division by ethnicity or religious belief … the list goes on. It is guerrilla resistance to the attempts of others to rule over them or to marginalise them or to even enslave them, physically or economically or ideologically.'

Arthur sighs and shrugs with the effort of his intellectual struggle.

Nils Houweling has not spoken. He lowers his eyes to his screens again.

'Nils …' Sven smiles. 'Please give us your analysis.'

Houweling looks up. 'Our brief is to find court-admissible evidence of international crime stemming from network chatter that something big is about to happen, soon, and in several places. The implication is that it is related to Israel and perhaps to Padraic Hennessy. The latter is based on Arthur's experience of his modus operandi and the interview tapes with William Maclean around a range of British espionage activities from the seventies through to the end of the twentieth century.

'As I see it, Arthur's initial instinct is supported by our agent Emma Jazy's revelation that her father, Jacques – the widower-husband of Maeve Gallaher, the mother of Padraic Hennessy's only child to our knowledge – had received a phone call two years ago. In that conversation, Hennessy was seeking redemption in the form of forgiveness from the stepfather of his deceased daughter, if the Irishman could engineer a resolution to the problems of the Middle East. And if that all sounds crazy … it probably is.'

'Good that you could draw breath after all that.' Arthur grins.

'But there is more,' Houweling adds. 'Now, most of the players that we have been tracking have disappeared like melting snow. We have a potential terrorist catastrophe on several fronts and we are reduced to the level of unsubstantiated speculation. Not a place I like to be.'

'Oh …' The patient voice of Sven Gulbrandson calms Houweling's frustration. 'I think we are a lot closer than you are crediting, Nils. You have uncovered a fair bit of substantiation. I grant you that the pigeons have scattered for the moment, but their instinct will bring them back to their familiar roosts. We just need to think this through a bit.'

'That's why we pay him the big Euros.' Arthur laughs to a bewildered Nils, while nodding at Gulbrandson.

'So, where to now, my leaders?' Houweling asks.

'Find the missing people, please,' Sven requests. 'Particularly Val McSweeney.'

'Inform the intelligence agencies of our allies,' adds Arthur. 'We need many eyes looking out for Maziq, for Sean McSweeney and for old Padraic himself.'

At that Sven holds up his left hand while his right hand massages his brow. 'D'you know, Hennessy won't be seeking publicity.' His eyes widen with inspiration. 'This is definitely not for the mass media. The only way that he could get the Israelis to change their immigration policies would be if they didn't lose face. That is so critical – understanding the mindset. Indeed, his ultimatum would have to happen with no announcement. Whatever Hennessy is up to will be silent. The power of clandestine negotiations – an offer they can't refuse, delivered without fanfare.'

And he scans the faces of his amazed colleagues …

Chapter 35

June, 2013. Nicosia, Cyprus

All six are sitting round the huge kitchen table, its white wooden surface worn smooth by generations of eaters. They have just greeted Ari – the last arrival to the safe-house – with his much-anticipated briefing.

'They sailed out of Girne Harbour last night. Part of Kyrenia, on the north coast, Emma.' Ari speaks in Greek and he looks questioningly to the IIB agent to ensure she is understanding clearly. 'That is the word from our spotter. He lives in the Turkish sector. A two-masted black-hull, he said. Brown-coloured cabin above. Big enough to hold all of them, but they weren't all there.'

'How many boarded, Ari?' Thea asks.

'Definitely the old white-hair. He was assisted by the red-head. The old man walked alright, just a bit slowly. Then there were four others – younger people, fit.'

Emma nods her understanding as she matches the description with Padraic Hennessy, Sean McSweeney, Macan Granić and the crawling men.

'Only four others?' Cristof questions slowly. 'Was the pale-face amongst them?'

'The spotter believes so. Couldn't be sure. It was on dusk, and he was looking through binoculars.'

Cristof bangs his fist on the table. 'I should've killed him when I could.'

'No, Cristof.' Thea's eyes flash. 'There is a bigger picture. We don't want to lose a war over revenge too soon. We will have our justice, just not today.'

Cristof growls, which causes Thea to assert herself, again.

'Nikkos was my husband, Cristof. I feel his loss more than any of you. Believe me.' Her steely look freezes her group into a downcast silence, while Emma silently admires the strength of this tough Greek-Cypriot woman – to be able to control her emotions in such a way after the loss of her husband. 'I want our vengeance – for all our sakes – and mainly his.' She takes a few seconds of dominant staring to reinforce her leadership and then continues in a quiet yet powerful tone. 'But our struggle requires discipline and patience. Isn't that right, Emma?'

Emma Jazy absorbs the new information, without it appearing on her facial expression. She looks slowly round all the faces at the table, particularly Galen who had seen Nikkos being abducted, before she says, 'I understand pain; your pain too, Cristof – all of you. I thought we would get him when we went back the second time. But I promise you, we *will* get him. And if I get him alive and can bring him back to you here, I *will* – for your justice being seen to be done. If not, I will bring you back proof that he is gone.'

'His head?'

She ignores the taunt. 'Proof anyway. There is something big about to happen – something that Nikkos and Bashir Dorda gave their lives for. You know the fear that was caused after the old man met with the clan leaders. People are scared. And it has probably moved to the next stage now, given that they are on a boat. Ari, a two-masted black-hull? How big is that? Where could they sail?'

'Big fishing boat size.'

Jason offers, 'They are probably sailing out to meet a carrier at night in the open sea. I'd doubt they are still on the same boat that left Girne. It's *The Run* – the old smuggling system. It's been going on for decades, for centuries, really.'

'So you are saying,' Emma clarifies, 'that there's no point in spotter planes looking for them?'

'They are lost, escaped.' Jason shakes his head to reinforce his answer to the question while the surly Cristof bangs the table softly.

'Only for a while,' Emma encourages. 'We have some idea of their plans now. Are you sure your spotter said that only *three* others boarded the boat, apart from the old man, red-head and the pale-face? Six in total?'

Ari nods.

'Then we are missing at least three from what we observed in the clearing. And there may have been many more in the cave, those that we didn't see. And they have left from the Turkish sector not the Greek part.'

'Your point?' Thea asks.

'Not sure. It just seems odd. A few things seem odd to me. I'm just rolling the information through my mind.' She pauses before changing tack. 'So, apart from the Arab leaders coming to speak with the old man … and then Bashir Dorda being killed, was there anything else happening?'

'Why do you ask?'

'My colleague, Sam, met with Nikkos down at Ypsonas. You remember. He had the impression that there was a lot of fear around; things happening, like gangsters. Just wondering.'

'There were a lot burglaries and muggings but mainly over in the Turkish section – stealing valuables, driving licences, passports, credit cards – small stuff. There wasn't much on our Greek side, which is why the police were blaming us. Typical … and on *our* island. But yes, there were quite a few bashings – stabbings too – before Dorda died. Nikkos had good radar for what was going on. That was why he was our leader.'

'Well, the gangsters seem to have been the crawlers and drillers – and they have left now – or at least some of them have. Why didn't they all get on the boat?'

'But pale-face got on the boat, didn't he?' Cristof asks, with an expression that wonders whether his nemesis might still be on the island.

Ari nods again and Emma gives a *what can I do?* shrug to Thea.

'You'll stay in touch, then?' Nikkos's widow asks.

Emma nods. 'Definitely! Thank you … thanks to all of you. Your network has been a great help. I am sorry for your losses. These are hard times.'

'We appreciate getting the new comms and extra weapons,' Thea adds, clearly the new leader since Nikkos's demise. She eye-balls each of her team to ensure that they are showing their gratitude. 'We'll get you to Akrotiri now.'

She rises as Emma reaches for her backpack. And, as they reach the door, Emma turns and points, 'You will have your proof, Cristof … or you will have your man.'

Cristof nods thoughtfully. *'Taxidévoun me asfáleia.'* And then in his best accented English with just a semblance of a kind smile, 'Travel safely.'

'Ef charisto, Cristof; and all of you.'

* * * *

Emma Jazy leaves Akrotiri for the trip to Maasboulevard on the last day of the month, pondering where the crawling men are heading … and to do what?

Chapter 36

June, 2013. Dubrovnik, Croatia

'Tomorrow, we will be in the European Union. Today, we sail to the islands. Tonight, we will party under the fireworks and stars.' Ivana Bikić's hair blows back in the breeze as she guides her uncle's sailing boat, under power, out of the Dubrovnik marina.

She stares at the new-look Sam Hall who sits grinning at her expertise. On the previous night, she had dyed his hair back close to his natural blond. 'You can't have blond roots and dark hair. Looks terrible. Let me take charge,' she had said. And now he is blond ... and the bottled tan from Cyprus is fading also into his normal hue.

Dressed in boating shorts and short-sleeved check shirt, with a sailor's peaked cap, he is reclining on the bench in the well of the weather-deck at the rear of the boat ... looking at the delightful apparition of his companion, also in nautical shorts and short-sleeved cotton top, pushed against her by the breeze to accentuate her breasts. No cap, but she is the captain of the ship, nevertheless.

'You have sailed before,' he notes admiringly.

'I had my licence at eighteen and I get out here when I can. More often, when I'm not over-burdened by work.'

'Then I appreciate your sacrifice to be out with me today,' Sam says. 'And I will send your father home *tout de suite* when I get back to Rotterdam.'

His comment draws a happy laugh. They'd had another pleasant night together through the darkness ... with his bags dumped in their loneliness on the floor of the spare room.

'There, we are out on the beautiful Adriatic, now. Unfurl the sails, crewman,' she calls with a flourished wave. And he dutifully leaps from the well to the mast deck to obey.

* * * *

They move out past Lokrum Island, a relic peak of an old limestone mountain range, submerged by sea level rises millennia ago.

An enormous white cruise-liner – a floating city in itself – has slowed almost to a stop to allow its decks of guests to view Dubrovnik in all its glory – the old fortifications, the red roofs and white walls, and the high ridge rising behind to Mount Srgj, where Sam had sat in the Opel on the day before, with Danko, taking in this view in reverse.

Ivana nurses the sails to the wind and heads north towards the islands of Greben and Koločep; past the northern city, low rugged cliffs, a cruise-liner terminal and a rash of sailing boats doing precisely what Sam is doing. On to Lopud Island, where Ivana anchors in the shelter of a bay.

'We have a picnic to enjoy.'

With wine, crab meat and salad, they lie back on the deck and enjoy the beautiful scenery in a jewel of the Adriatic.

* * * *

'This is nice, Sam. But I suppose you will be leaving soon to go back to your life of adventure. Leaving this poor hard-working lawyer to survive as she might, under the burden of case files.'

'I told you that I would send your father home immediately, to meet his business responsibilities to his daughter. What more can I do?'

She laughs. 'You could stay. Keep me company.' She pauses to read his eyes, before, 'But seriously, I am so happy, here with you. *Is your business in Dubrovnik nearly finished?*'

'No, not yet. Luka is great. We might be helping each other with our respective cases. But, no … I'm not finished here yet. Tomorrow, Luka and I have one of your local gangsters to interview again. And one of my persons of interest has skipped out of Cavtat and headed up to a mountain village behind. So, beautiful one, let us enjoy the day and not worry about anything. Tomorrow is tomorrow. And tonight we have to dance under the fireworks. Remember.'

* * * *

The afternoon sun is heading down over the Adriatic sky to kiss Italy in the west, as Sam lowers and ties the sails. The motor putters the boat gently towards the marina when Sam's mobile rings.

In answer to Ivana's questioning look, 'It's Luka.'

'Macan Horvat,' the detective begins, 'has started to be quite co-operative. He identified another house rented by the Cougar group. It is in the north of Dubrovnik, over the bridge, in the coast suburbs along Road 8. They look out to Koločep Island.'

'That's where we have been sailing today.'

'Lucky you. Of course, while I have been working my fingers to the bone to help your cause.'

'You are a saint, Luka. I've told you that. So what now?'

'A colleague and I went out to the house, to scout around, to see if Horvat was telling the truth. There is no-one living there but real estate confirms that it is rented and paid for by a business, based in Switzerland. We suspect that it is a dummy name but there hasn't been time to check yet. So, we have taken the liberty of placing a listening device in the main room – under the anti-terrorist legislation – we are part of NATO after all; we have international responsibilities. The warrant was signed without any issue. We have also taken the trouble to rent a property opposite, to observe and to listen if required. So I *have* been working. And you?'

'We are just coming into the dock now. The skipper is going to need my help, Luka. I'll have to catch you in the morning. Thanks for your good work.'

'Already taking orders. You poor, down-trodden soul.'

'*Hvala*. Thanks, Luka. See you.'

Chapter 37

July, 2013. Rotterdam, The Netherlands

'The first of the month and Croatia is now in the EU. I bet Sam didn't get time to be part of their midnight celebrations,' announces Arthur with a disbelieving grin.

The triumvirate has assembled in Arthur's high office as they always do at the start of the week – and often, as recently, at the start of every day.

Sven Gulbrandson has the look of a man who has just received a vision. His eyes are almost transcendental over his quiet grin – but he just nods his agreement at whatever Arthur has chosen to say.

Nils Houweling is in business mode at the table, with his screens and notes arranged in perfect semi-circular symmetry.

'Is there any news, perhaps, Nils?' asks the serene Sven.

'As it happens, I might have a thing or two,' the operations manager replies. 'Emma Jazy has just landed, back from Cyprus. She has advised that the old man, the red-head, with probably the pale-face and three others fled on a masted boat out of Girne Harbour on the north coast at Kyrenia, on Saturday. Her best information from the network is that they probably met up with an ocean carrier during the night and left for locations unknown. She adds that there would still be quite a number of the crawling men group – minimum of two – who were not on that boat. Their location is unknown.'

'So sad,' Arthur acknowledges. 'Sounds like shades of Bill Maclean and Maureen on their old gun-smuggling *Mediterranean Run* back in the 70s.'

'Indeed,' answers Nils. 'That system is still apparently working as it always has, beneath the radar and in the darkness – presumably also, under new management.'

'Where are they going, Nils?'

'I choose not to speculate.'

'Syria? Israel? Croatia?'

'Any of the above … and indeed any of the other countries in the region – even Libya.'

Sven still has his peaceful grin. 'But probably not Egypt given the current excitement in Tahrir Square. That place could be heading for another coup. And Turkey's Taksim Square doesn't seem to be quietening down either. Too many unhappy people. Syria's strife appears to be approaching the 100,000 dead mark from both sides. Not a pleasant place to be – but a significant distraction on the Israeli borders, don't you think? So do you have anything else for us, Nils?'

'I do. Val McSweeney may have been seen in Heidelberg. One of the intelligence agencies reported that *Waltraud has returned* and was apparently having coffee with some women in a coffee shop.'

'Didn't I tell you?' Sven wears a self-satisfied grin, 'The pigeons come home to roost. Any more?'

'Not yet. No further information on Michael McSweeney in Kuna Konovska. Sam has reported in. He says that the Dubrovnik police may have located another *Cougar* gang safe house. It is empty at the moment but under police observation now.'

Sven still watches on and Arthur has a bemused patient expression.

'Oh,' continues Nils. 'Following on from our earlier queries of what is happening in July and, especially after Waltraud's return to her old haunts, Heidelberg will host an EU Commission in the middle of the month. The preliminaries are already starting.'

'Who attends that?' asks Arthur.

'Reps from most European countries. They are trying to get *big picture* solutions. Their website has a quote, *We can't continue trying to solve European problems just with national solutions*. So that gives the flavour.'

'No Israelis attending?'

'Not to my knowledge – unless they have invited some bureaucrat for technical advice. Unlikely though, I would have thought. Apart from that, the Israeli parliament – the Knesset – remains on vacation until August. That will let them all attend the Maccabiah Games, perhaps.'

Arthur responds, 'That is still my best bet for Hennessy's actions to influence the Israelis. Why do I know of those Games? Are they famous?'

'There was a bridge collapse in 1997, with athletes falling into a polluted canal. Several died. It was all through the news at the time. Other than that, Jewish athletes – all teenagers – travel from across the globe to compete. It only happens every four years. It's big.'

'Right. Okay. Sven, you look like the cat that has licked the cream. What are you thinking?'

'Nothing particularly new. You will remember what I said last time – that Hennessy will be planning something that will stay right out of the headlines. The Jewish people – in Israel and worldwide – would never agree to a change to *Aliyah*, if there could be any suggestion of loss of face. They would fight with backs to the wall, rather than let that happen. And they are well-renowned fighters. Immigrant Jews even have the date of their *Aliyah* stamped on all their official documentation. It is part of who they are – as important as a birth date. So, if Padraic Hennessy is actually trying to sort the Middle East into a peaceful accord like has been achieved in Ireland or Cyprus or the former Yugoslavia, it will have to ensure no loss of face for the Jews. That's an almost impossible ask.

'It will also have to appease a group of very alienated Palestinians who believe they have been the victims of generations of oppression. So, no-one – not Jews, nor Arabs – can lose face. Even given that the Irishman must be mad, his plan would have to be one of very quiet persuasion. The sort of offer they can't refuse.'

'Alright. You've been watching too many movies. So what type of persuasion?'

'I have no detail in my mind, yet,' Sven replies, 'But I am encouraged by the pigeons returning to their home roosts. Waltraud Muller has gone back to her university town. So, it begs the question, where will the McSweeneys go? What about Macan Granić?'

'Well, on that logic, Granić will head for Dubrovnik – where we have Sam Hall waiting for him.'

'Precisely. And where is Granić now? And who is he with?'

Arthur and Nils nod. 'On a boat headed to somewhere' … and the operations manager makes a couple of notes.

'Maziq. Who is he? Is he an old Libyan gun-runner or something else?' Sven asks. 'Where is he? Where are the women? Were two of them in Heidelberg yesterday talking to Val McSweeney?'

Arthur breaks the pattern. 'What about Bashir Dorda working in the Golan Heights in the sixties? Where does that fit?'

The Swede grins. 'At the risk of annoying Nils with speculation, I would guess that the crawling men might turn up in Israel at some stage – perhaps to influence the Maccabiah Games. It's just a guess.'

'The Israelis have been given our information.' Nils ticks off a box on his checklist. 'They will be ready for anyone.'

Sven chortles at his operations manager. 'Good for you, Nils. Were you speculating there?'

'Another thing,' adds Houweling, ignoring Sven's attempted jibe. 'You might have noticed in Sam's report from Cavtat that he mentioned finding a torn blank page of a Turkish-Cypriot passport in the cellar where the hiking brochure was also found. He and the policeman, Luka, both picked up on a chemical smell, like industrial spirit, paint or ink. And,' he pauses to catch the eyes of each, 'there were two earlier mentions from Sam, and from Emma, about passports. You may have missed them in your hypothesising. Allow me to refresh your memories with a couple of details.' He gives the slightest of meaningful grins towards the almost jolly Sven.

'The first was a Zagreb gang, perhaps linked to the *Cougars*, who were stealing money, jewellery, passports and credit cards – all through the north of Croatia. The second was from Emma. The Cypriots mentioned a gang operating mainly in the Turkish sector stealing money, valuables, driving licences, credit cards and passports.

'Using your speculative model, the drilling gang could presumably be the thieves in the Turkish sector while Granić and his gang could be the Zagreb connection.'

Sven's eyes gleam. 'Well done, Nils. We will have to pay you more. Maziq might well be a bloody passport forger – unless it is one of the Libyan women. But maybe they would be too young for such a craft. You won't have time to get bored chasing up these leads, eh?'

'But why?' persists Houweling. 'Croatia has just joined the EU. Cyprus is already in it. Who needs passports for anywhere in Europe?'

The silence is tangible until Sven whispers, 'So they are needed for somewhere that is not Europe … just maybe.'

'Right,' Arthur stands up and claps his hands gently. 'Much more progress than last week. Let's get Emma in here when she returns. We need her on-the-ground perspective. If I am following your line of thought, Sven, Dublin should be in the mix. And, from my perspective, I think Padraic Hennessy will want to be in close proximity to Jacques Jazy – so Switzerland becomes part of the equation.'

'And,' adds Nils, 'someone is paying for all of this. Even if it is South American or Arab money, wouldn't there be a good chance that Swiss banks are involved?'

Arthur clicks his fingers. 'Ah, the Gnomes of Zurich – not to mention Vaduz, in Liechtenstein. Didn't Bill Maclean mention Hennessy's PIRA Cat Pack money being in Swiss banks? I'll need to go back to those recordings and listen again. Right, work to be done. A new month. Excitement is high.'

Chapter 38

July, 2013. Dubrovnik, Croatia

'You're in the European Union, Luka. How does it feel?' Sam asks as they head for the interview room in the police building.

'My mind is on more pressing matters, Sam. The fireworks are for the party set and the politicians. I really believe something big is about to happen around this *Cougar* business. That's much closer to my discomfort zone. Horvat seems to sense it too. While he wouldn't be *Brain of Croatia*, he has the survival instinct of a street crim.'

'This rented house up the coast. What's it like?'

'Secure. A bit like the Cavtat place. Just back from the water's edge. Hard to observe inside – which is why we have the listening device installed. We will see who enters and leaves, from our place across the road.'

One police guard stands outside the interview room; a second, Sam knows, will be inside.

'What is your plan for today then, Luka?'

'I want to recruit Macan Horvat into working for us – an offer he would choose not to refuse.'

'Can you trust him?'

'We will have checks – controls. Police Strategy 102, in the training courses.' He laughs and shrugs as he passes the guard outside.

Inside, Macan Horvat sits folded over at the table, head, face down resting on his forearms. He looks up as Sam and Luka enter and his eyes widen as he takes in the appearance of the IIB agent, with the now-blond hair.

The inside guard leaves the room and Luka pulls up a chair, in front of the desk.

The Croatian language is spoken very quietly. Sam can only watch the changes of expression on Horvat's face to judge how the conversation is progressing – perhaps fifteen minutes pass as the agent recognises Horvat's puzzlement, fear, resignation, hope and then fear again. Eventually, with a loud sigh, the big gang member nods slowly.

'He has agreed.' Luka turns and whispers to Sam. 'I'll tell you more outside.'

He turns back again to Horvat, shakes his hand and appears to wish him well.

Horvat manages a faint smile and gives a nod.

The two guards enter the interview room to start the process of the prisoner's release, as Sam Hall and Luka Jusić leave.

* * * *

Back in the detective's office, with its view of blue sky and little birds darting swiftly to catch insects, Sam asks, 'Are you sure? You'd better explain this to me.'

The policeman takes a silver pen from the desk and signs an official form, as he indicates with a pointed finger. 'His conditional release.'

The IIB agent holds out his hands, palms up, to encourage the story. 'I need information.'

'Horvat has agreed to be our agent. We will set him up in the house opposite the Cougar gang's rented place; with food, telescope, camera and monitoring equipment for the listening device in our quarry's main room. He has agreed to advise us of arrivals, departures and what anyone in the house is planning.'

'You are very trusting.'

'This is another of our tests for Horvat. He is scared. I have made him even more fearful. Fear sells. So, we have sold our pitch to our man. We have negotiated his transfer of allegiance from the gangs to us – with a bonus of some form of pardon in the future for his sins. He could be very useful to us for a long time to come.'

'And if he lets you down, then we blow the whole thing?'

'Trust, Sam. We have checks and balances. Horvat does not know that we have also installed a camera and listening device in the main room of the *Cougar* house. It relays *here* – not to the rented house. *He* does not know that.'

'You cunning devil. Not a saint after all.'

'The mobile we have given him has only one specific police number on speed dial – and it goes to others in our team who are working on these gang cases. We can monitor any other calls he might decide to make, despite him being told not to. He also now has a tracking bug sown into the hem of his jacket, inserted while we repaired a tear in his sleeve. And, to cap it all off, there is a monitoring camera in the house he will live in. Fair surveillance, eh?'

'I dip my lid to the Dubrovnik police, once again,' Sam says as he bows in respect.

'We are working on it. It has been a hard road from the corruption of the war era to today. We are getting there slowly. But, to our gangland guest who nearly didn't recognise you,' Luka pauses with another smile at Sam's new appearance, 'I am actually pretty sure that Macan Horvat will not let us down. He has really been looking for a way out. I have offered him a path. I think he will take it.'

'I hope you are right.'

'Now, how was your sail to the islands yesterday with Ivana?'

Sam taps his nose with a grin. 'What happens on sailing trips, stays on sailing trips.'

'Okay. Have it your way. Let's get our newly recruited spy, Mr Horvat, installed. Who knows when the gang might return. We need to be ready.'

Chapter 39

'Do we have a Jewish expert on staff, Nils?' Arthur asks.

'Not an expert, maybe, but certainly someone of that faith. Sol Levin works in logistics.'

'What security clearance?'

'Not at an agent level, but secure nevertheless.'

'Can you call him in to the office, please?' asks Sven. 'Tell him we just want some background understanding about the faith.'

As Nils leaves, Sven turns to Emma Jazy. 'It's good to have you back, Emma. A fair bit of pain in Cyprus, eh?'

'Yes, they're very passionate people and one of their leaders was killed in a nasty way.'

Arthur takes over to update his agent. 'Some background on the pale-face you reported. As you know, he is a Croatian called Macan Granić. He has just turned twenty-one – been bullied in his early life because of his looks, the strange pale face, the dark hair, huge freckles and haunting eyes. So he has translated that pain into delivering significant cruelty to others, through the gang system, using a knife. And the old man. We got your description. It certainly fits Padraic Hennessy, the old Irish *Cougar*. He is possibly as cold a killer as Granić, but with much more experience – and probably quite mad if he thinks whatever he is doing will solve the Middle East challenges and gain him some redemption in the eyes of your father.'

Arthur pauses at the knock as Nils enters with a curious Sol Levin.

* * * *

After the introductions, Arthur explains that they are seeking some understanding of the Jewish faith as it might impact on Israel.

Sol nods his cheery acceptance. 'If I can be of assistance.'

'*Aliyah*, Sol, and the *Law of Return*. What would you think the chances could be that the Knesset might change that law?'

The logistics man can't suppress a surprised laugh. 'None. Absolutely none.'

Arthur's patient lawyer-voice asks, 'Without teaching us the whole religion, can you just explain why you say that?'

Levin pauses just to check that it is a serious question. 'Okay. Leaving aside the long history of the pogroms against our people ... and the Holocaust, a fundamental tenet of our religion is that Israel is the land promised to the Jewish people through scripture. Okay?

'*Aliyah* is a deeply held understanding that, after the *diaspora*, the promises of scripture have come to pass and that those who wish to return to the land of their roots *can* now return – and live in a Jewish community, safe in the bonds of history and family. Our people have been displaced since Roman times, even as far back as the reign of Nebachadnezzar, after all. That is a long and painful time to wait to be reunited with a spiritual home.'

Blair nods. 'So, with the Declaration of Independence of the State of Israel, the concept of *Aliyah* became the Law of Return, which is why there are so many settlements needing to be built.'

'Yes,' replies Levin. 'Technically, anyone of Jewish faith can migrate to Israel – although there is a process to go through. It is not as automatic as *get on a plane and you will be accepted at Tel Aviv airport*. A whole government ministry looks after it, as I understand.' He looks at Emma, Sven and Arthur and their intent faces ... and slowly shakes his head. 'You really are serious about these questions, aren't you?'

He pauses again for their confirming looks and continues. 'Well, clearly every Jew on the planet can't fit into Israel – nor would they want to. For example, I am quite content living here in Holland. Anyway, I think the age of mass *Aliyah* is probably over. You could understand the groundswell for a mass migration and safety, after the war with Germany. And a lot have fled the old Soviet Union too. But I am told that the immigration is slowing down. Israel really does place very heavy demands on its citizens – military service, loyalty, no weakening even in an often unsafe land. Israel is like all countries in the sense that there are fanatical patriots and there are others who just go with the flow. But *going with the flow* in Israel is not the casual easy lifestyle approach of Western countries. Many Jews – like me – are very happy to live away from Israel and its discipline. Most do, in fact.'

'Fine.' Arthur acknowledges. 'What is the solution then in the Middle East, to cater for *Aliyah*?'

'You want me to solve the Middle East?' Levin gasps.

'No.' Sven laughs. 'We are just after an opinion. Humour us.'

Levin shrugs, tolerantly. 'Okay. There needs to be two states, Israel and Palestine ... and the fighting has to stop. Simple enough? Now, let's see you make it happen.'

'Okay,' continues Arthur. 'This is helpful to us. There have been a number of wars now since 1948, where Israel has expanded its borders. What would the fanatics agree to give up, for peace? There would have to be some give and take – some bargaining. Surely?'

Sol Levin pauses and shakes his head that his employers appear to be taking those questions seriously. 'There are extremists who will never be pleased, on both sides. Too much hurt. Too much belief that they are right. Too much listening to anger and hate. That it is God's or Allah's will – the righteous argument. And you can't argue, by using logic, against such deeply held belief. But, there are many others in Israel who would trade some land for an end to conflict; for Arab acknowledgment of Israel's right to exist – and peaceful co-existence.

'The sticking points will be around Jerusalem because the area is important to so many faiths. Yes, and I think any who agree to an accord would have to be very wary of creating exclusive states – where Jews couldn't enter Palestine and Arabs couldn't enter Israel. That would be like the apartheid system of the old South Africa – more walls being erected; no shared understanding. That wouldn't work for long, especially if you have to share Jerusalem and water. And about twenty per cent of Israel's population was Arab at the last census – and still is, I imagine.'

'Interesting, Sol. We don't always get that impression about the number of Arabs living in Israel. It doesn't tend to make the news reports. Why do you mention water?'

'You would know that much of that land is desert. I have been there. It is hot and dry for much of the year. Water is the key to everything. Give credit to Israel. They are world leaders in recycling water, desalination, harvesting clouds – all sorts of research technology – while the Arabs have really contributed bugger all, in that area.'

Sven intervenes. 'Mind you, in fairness, the Arabs aren't seeking to flood the area with migrants either. Yes? They just want their traditional lifestyle.'

'Agreed. And realistically, population control will have to play some part in the strategy for the future. They are not making more land. But that's a worldwide problem; not just one for Israel.'

'Good, Sol. You have been very helpful. We would be grateful if you treat this conversation as confidential. We are wiser now for your help. Thank you.'

* * * *

After Sol leaves, Arthur looks at Emma. 'You have been very quiet. What do you think?'

'There is no easy solution. If there had been, it would have been found over the years with all the American presidents who have staked their reputations on it. Hennessy must really have lost the plot in his old age.'

'Maybe,' agrees Sven, provisionally. 'But there have been people dying because of Hennessy's plan. If he is mad, there is a strange logic to his madness. We can guess roughly at what he is up to … and, from a logistics point of view, it appears to be working. People are being trained for something and a lot of people are quite scared at the moment. Nils reports a chill about the unknown, in the web chatter. Embassies are on alert.'

The operations manager just smiles in acknowledgement.

'So, Nils?' Arthur chimes in. 'What is new? Bring us up-to-date.'

'Certainly.' He glances at his notes. 'Following up on what may be happening where the pigeons could come home to roost, Dublin has a Riverdance festival planned for July. That would be big. There is the Donegal Town Summer Festival, soon, on 4th July; and there is the Irish-Jewish Gathering on 21st July in Dublin.' Houweling pauses for effect. 'Plenty of scope there for the mischief makers. Then, in Geneva, the United Nations is holding its Economic and Social Council throughout most of this month. Lot of countries will have representatives flying in.'

'Any Israelis attending?'

'They might be, but there is no attendance list published as yet. I imagine all countries would have the right to attend if they chose.'

'Okay.' Blair makes some notes. 'That's a lot of advising, for people to be on alert without frightening the horses. *G-2* is the Republic of Ireland's Intelligence Service. Can you make sure they are carefully advised, please, Nils. They'll mobilise the *Garda*, the police, and the Defence Force where required.'

'Isn't it *the Gardai*, Arthur? Plural? I've seen that spelling somewhere.'

'Ah, you linguists, who love your dictionaries. But I'm on home ground as a Celt. No! *Garda* is really just like *police* in English – in colloquial speech, the plural is the same as the singular. A bit like *sheep*, eh?' Blair smiles gently. 'As an Irishman might say, *If you want to go there, I wouldn't start from here.* Leave it as *Garda*. What else do you have?'

Houweling gulps, tilts his head slightly in respect and goes back to his screens. 'Yes. The Knesset is on vacation until August and I've been checking to see if there are any ministers away, travelling. It's early days in the inquiry, and I haven't had very much co-operation from Tel Aviv. To speed things along, I homed in on the Minister for Water and Energy Resources – given what we have learned of Bashir Dorda's background – as well as the Minister for Immigration Absorption, whose department manages the Law of Return. And on the Minister for Defence because he, Eli Dahan, is responsible for protecting the homeland.

'The Defence Minister is in the country, Israel – busy with the Games – and overseeing the security, I would guess. But the Water Minister, Golda Neeman – a widow as it happens – is vacationing with her daughter, accompanied by the Immigration Minister, Chaim Tamir, and his daughter. They are on a climbing vacation for a week. Somewhere cool, I imagine. But, Israeli security won't tell me where they are.'

Sven sighs. 'Okay. Keep trying, Nils. You are doing well.' He looks at Emma. 'Now we have done a fair bit of hypothesising while you have been away in Cyprus. We might release Nils from the torture of listening to it all again. Arthur and I will take you through the bones of it. But I *do* think we have a fair general idea of what might be happening. And we need to get your perspectives on whether the bad guys really have left Cyprus for good.'

'Well,' replies Emma. 'If they have, there is a very angry group of five Greeks in Nicosia who really want Macan Granić brought to justice – specifically, their form of justice. He made a painful mess of two men, to our knowledge, with that knife of his. They would like to return the favour. At the very least, I have promised them that I would bring proof of his fate if he doesn't go back.'

'A bold promise,' replies Arthur. 'Remember, we are in the business of finding admissible evidence not becoming vigilantes for the wronged.'

'I understand. My preferred option would be for him to return to Cyprus under his own steam. There is a man called Cristof there, who might give the definition of justice a whole new interpretation.'

Chapter 40

July, 2013. Northern Israel

The motel room television is on cable CNN. The enthusiastic American reporter announces:

> A rocket has whistled over the Israeli border from Syria, landing close to an Israeli Defence Force base in the Golan Heights. The United Nations Disengagement Observation Force, UNDOP, heard the attack and have confirmed the rebel aggression. That whole area has been tense for several months, since twenty-one Filipino peacemakers were taken hostage by Syrian rebel forces in March of this year.
>
> And then in May, the Philippines announced the withdrawal of their troops because the risks had gone beyond tolerable limits. In June, Austria announced that it would withdraw its forces after a border crossing at the ruined city of Quneitra was attacked by Syrian rebels and a peace-keeper wounded.
>
> At the same time, another rocket has whizzed over the electrified boundary fence at Ouazzani on the Lebanese border. There, the UN Interim Force in Lebanon, UNIFIL, agrees with the Israeli interpretation that people from the Lebanese side initiated the...

Sean McSweeney chortles at the screen as he presses the mute button. It is just as old Padraic said it would be. He checks his watch. The first of the group will be arriving soon.

* * * *

A grey Mazda 3 rolls into the motel grounds and parks beside McSweeney's pale-green rented Chevrolet Spark. A tanned man emerges holding a soft bag – carry-on luggage only, but critical nevertheless, and with a Turkish-Cypriot passport. The flight from Larnaca in Cyprus to Tel Aviv's David Ben Gurion airport was only a short time in the air.

McSweeney himself had flown into TLV International on Alitalia from Rome, near where he and his Cyprus connection had been off-loaded from *The Run*. He is using his valid Republic of Ireland citizenship and was the picture of confidence as he took the short hop to Haifa, telling the immigration officials in both airports that he would be attending a conference in fluid mechanics at the Institute of Technology in Haifa. Universally, his story raised a welcoming smile and he was ushered on his way.

Over the next two days, two more will arrive on separate flights from Rome by Easyjet to Dubrovnik and then on to Pleso Airport in Zagreb and finally to Tel Aviv. And the last two members will come in on the evening and morning last legs from Larnaca via Athens to Tel Aviv.

By then, all the pieces of the specially-hardened plastic equipment would have arrived separately and have been assembled. Likewise, the separate innocent liquids would have been combined into the required lethal potion.

He has to admire his grandfather's old leader. Normally dry and sombre, Grandpa Donnie's grey eyes always lit up when he was asked to speak to the family about the old *Cat Pack* days, with the young *Cougar*. And now, it is Padraic who is the old man – but he can still plan a mission with military precision, with enough tactical deceit to put an enemy off the trail. And with more than enough focus, so that the end will be achieved – quietly, as he has instructed.

On the third day, they will travel east then north, possibly by different routes, in three hire cars. That is Plan A.

While the Israeli Defence Force look away over the border to the aggression from Lebanon and Syria, the three cars will make their way eventually up the Hula Valley, to the Dan and the Banios rivers. Their GPS will guide them to the exact grid point location which Bashir Dorda had revealed in agony – as his other hand was finally completely severed. And before they perpetrated their last act of necessary violence against him. To ensure perpetual silence, his tongue was cut out.

The Croat had done his job well.

Now this practised multi-ethnic team of Tunisian, Turk, Moroccan and Irish, will soon enter Israel without the need for visas, on doctored stolen Croatian and Cypriot passports. At last, they will put Hennessy's complicated plan into action.

Sean can sense why the old fellas in *The Troubles* could rise to the challenge. The adrenalin is pumping through his veins as never before in his life.

Chapter 41

July, 2013. Rotterdam, The Netherlands

'I know who this Maziq in Croatia is,' announces Nils Houweling to Arthur Blair. '*Mahmoud* Maziq is a Libyan, brother to Abdul Maziq who did indeed run a smuggling network under the auspices of Gaddafi for many years. In fact, it seems to have been a family tradition – the generation before were smugglers too, under Khamis Maziq.'

'Let me get Sven in here before you say more.' Arthur picks up the intercom. 'We both need to hear this.'

* * * *

The office door opens to the expectant face of Sven Gulbrandson. 'You have news, I hear, Nils?'

'Yes, Sven. The Maziq family, who we were assuming were gun runners, were indeed just that – for generations, it appears. They probably were the chiefs of the consortium managing the *Mediterranean Run* back in the time of Maureen Jazy and William Maclean.

'Khamis Maziq had been the patriarch of the clan in the 1930s through to the 1950s, when his eldest son Abdul took over. In 1969, after Gaddafi became leader in Libya, Abdul Maziq's influence and wealth grew exponentially – ships, oil and weapon smuggling to revolutionary causes around the world.

'But, not all the Maziqs were in weapons logistics. The fifth son, Mahmoud Maziq, was an artistic man. You can hypothesise

220

that he was unsuited to the lifestyle of his family and he moved to Paris to study painting – and art printing. He became very skilled as a duplicator of famous art works. Spent five years in a French prison for his efforts and, on release, returned to the bosom of his family, where no doubt his new skills were appreciated.

'Now, the French *DGSE*, that is the General Directorate for External Security – their military intelligence agency – have always taken an interest in their former prisoner of the State, because they suspected his involvement in illegal activity in Algeria, Chad and some countries of former French West Africa. They have supplied me with photographs of the old and new Mahmoud. See?' He turns his screen towards Arthur and Sven to show them a range of pictures of an Arab man ageing, right through to a recent shot of a tanned man with a ring of white hair above and behind the ears.

'Very good, Nils,' Sven says, very slowly, his tone indicating anticipation. 'You have more than this.'

'As it happens, Sven, yes.' Houweling grins. 'Mahmoud Maziq is apparently well-known in circles where, I confess, I don't travel. He is, as you postulated earlier, a renowned passport counterfeiter. The French have a whole dossier on him but they have never caught him returning to French territories.'

Sven and Arthur look at each other with raised eyebrows.

'But wait, there's more. Two years ago, the French operatives followed him on a visit to Dublin where – you are staying with the story, I trust – he met up with some unnamed former business associates of his eldest brother, Abdul. They were, in fact, former recipients of armaments and explosives destined for offshoots of the Provisional IRA. Should I speculate or leave that in your skilled hands?'

'Nils.' Sven smiles sardonically. 'Not only are you a very talented researcher of obscure information but you are also one of the most irritating taunters I have ever known.'

Nils chuckles his appreciation. 'I take that as a compliment from you, Sven. But wait, there is more. Again, two years ago, early 2011, a Michael McSweeney went to Libya, ostensibly to visit his son, Sean, who was a geophysicist in the oil fields – and he met with Mahmoud Maziq in Sirte. Da da!' He raises his hands in the triumph of the conjuror revealing his amazing finalé.

'You have done well,' Arthur acknowledges. 'You have the linkage between the McSweeneys and Maziq, which presumably ties in with the elusive Padraic Hennessy too. The recent photograph is a fair match for the description we have. And, with Sam Hall and his Dubrovnik detective smelling ink and finding a torn page of a Cypriot passport, I think we have the start of an admissible argument.'

'Don't forget the passport thefts noted in Croatia and Cyprus,' Nils says.

'No, I have remembered,' Arthur replies. 'The only catch is, my meticulous friend, with micro-chip technology and scanners at airports, the faces on the photograph would have to match whatever is stored on the chip.'

Sven shrugs with a grin. 'So close and yet so far, Nils. So sad. Never mind, you were going really well for a while.'

'No, I have thought of that. If I were a betting man – and thank the Lord I'm not – but if I were, I would bet that, of the many passports stolen, the thieves would be looking for old books, nearing renewal date – the ones that don't yet have chips implanted. Now if you were to go for passports from the States or UK or Israel, they would all have that fail-safe technology. But a new nation like Croatia, just entering the EU where passports are usually not a priority anyway … and Cyprus, battling to keep its head above water with financial bail-outs from the EU. Many of their passports would be the old style.'

'*Touché*, Nils.'

Arthur rises again to the picture window to ponder. 'What else has come in, Nils? Any more on Heidelberg or Dublin or Donegal or Geneva?'

'Each country has been advised. But, when you don't really know what you are looking for, it is hard. An IRA bomb? That's the problem with terrorism, if you shut down all activity, then the bad guys win. So, the security forces wait – trying to guess what might be happening.'

Sven lifts his head from his reflective pose. 'Let's assume your hypothesis about the passports is correct, Nils. Then Mahmoud Maziq has been ensconced in the cellar in Cavtat, amending stolen passports. To access where?'

'Israel would be my guess. You wouldn't need them for most of Europe. Bashir Dorda's link with aquifers, the Maccabiah Games ... Yes? And neither Croatia nor Cyprus need visas to enter Israel. I've checked.'

'How interesting. I didn't know that. You have done well. Then, let the Israelis know, Nils. *Mossad* is probably ahead of us anyway.'

Sven adds, 'Crawling men? You don't need to crawl if you have a passport. Maybe, the passport thing is another red herring and they are planning to enter by a different way. My problem is the country is surrounded by electrified fences – and walls, metres high – and armed guards and tanks of the fighting type.'

'Tunnels?'

'They would have sensors in the ground. That border is more secure than most high-security prisons.'

'So why are they practising crawling? They must be aiming to get under some infra-red beams.'

'You would think so,' Sven ponders, but his troubled expression suggests that he is unconvinced. 'I just can't see how a group of crawling men can get at the aquifers. I reckon we could well be off-track.' He fixes his colleagues with challenging eye contact. 'Let's work on the theory that Israel *is* impregnable – many have tried and failed; even national armies. Nils will advise Israel and they will handle any incursions. For us, rather than waste valuable thinking time on distractions, let's focus back on the main game.

'Hennessy has said that he wants to sort out the problems of the Middle East. We are assuming, just by his associates, that he is trying to get some Palestinian solution by putting pressure on the Israelis. On the other hand, to return to one of my earlier questions, isn't it just possible that he is doing the polar opposite, by backing the expansion of the Israeli enclave to secure a *larger* heartland...? Taking over more productive land? Lebanon? Syria? The latter, at least, is in a total mess at the moment. Ripe for a takeover, perhaps, with a consortium of rebellious Arab assistance? I don't buy that all Arabs are opposed to Israel's existence. Hennessy is showing that there is always a deal to be made. History has a catalogue of alliances in the Arab world, changing like the selling of camels.'

Sven is on a roll. 'Alternatively, perhaps, it is not about Israel at all – don't lose sight of that – but it could be about Arab peoples with old scores to settle. There are enough of them that don't like each other. We often fall into the trap of thinking that they are one homogenous group of peoples, but that is just the manufacture of geo-political commentators, looking to simplify the complex into a *them* and *us*. The rewards for any Arab tribal groups taking over could be substantial. The spoils of war redistributed amongst the supportive? Look to history again, even in that region.'

Arthur shakes his head slowly. 'On your first theory, if it was to be about Israeli expansion, that would be asking for the mother of all fights.' He lets the possible scenarios percolate through his mind. 'That really would have Iran shooting warheads at them. It would bring in lots of world players ... on both sides and no side. And for what? Why would Israel want that? A bigger border to defend? No buffer with potential enemies. Rockets from Iran can potentially reach Israel now, and vice versa. Occupying Syria would make no difference – it would just make them even closer to more conflict. And the Arabs looking to settle old scores? I don't know.' He shrugs with upturned hands at the fanciful suggestion. 'Are you suggesting that somehow that will produce peace in the Middle East? Isn't peace what this thing is all about?'

'But,' argues Nils, 'I have another proposal. The Arab chiefs are apparently signing up for *some* deal. That's what our evidence from Sam and Nikkos is suggesting. If it is not to be more land, why could it not be that the Palestinians just ask for the same *right of return* as the Israelis have used – their own version of *Aliyah*?'

His colleagues' eyebrows rise in an admiring concession to his proposal.

After a pause, Arthur says, 'For someone who doesn't like hypothesising, you can come up with some *doozies*.'

Nils grins but persists. 'Couldn't the Palestinians equally argue their *own* claim to their ancestral homeland, from which *they* have been displaced by a world power mandate and Jewish militant groups? Wasn't that Hennessy's argument in Ireland – to argue from the position of strength gained by his IRA breakaway groups? He must have *some* bargaining tool to get them all on board so quickly in Cyprus? They would need some really significant Israeli concessions – wouldn't you think? – if generations of displaced refugees were to concede peace, and Israel's right to exist, after more than sixty-five years of struggle against it. No?'

'Mmm. Mmm,' is Arthur's final response to the suggestion. 'Good to hear your theorising though, Nils.'

His operations chief purses his lips, never liking to be caught straying from his non-speculative position.

'Just reminding you both of the evidence,' he mutters.

'Point taken. And,' Blair continues, 'it's a good idea to keep in the mix, nevertheless. And, Sven, I can't see any reason why the Israelis would increase their vulnerability by expanding their land base, at this time.'

The Swede pauses, nods and concedes, 'Yes. I grant you that the expansion of an Israeli state is both unlikely and not supported by any evidence so far, not least by world opinion. Just thought I would float it anyway. Always good to stand in the shoes on both sides of the border. But, I have to say I can't see any guerrilla group of crawling men mounting any successful attack on Israel.'

'So,' Arthur summarises, 'that brings us back to something big happening in Europe or pressure being used to influence the decision makers. Any more word on where those Israeli cabinet ministers were going on their vacations, Nils?'

'Nothing yet.'

'Okay. You have done well again, Nils ... yet again. But we still have more loose spaghetti ends to follow.'

Nils shrugs. 'And another thing. There is no timeframe on this. We have made an assumption that it is to be in July. Where is the evidence for that?'

Arthur sagely notes the question. 'Let's try for starters: the crawling men have left Cyprus, the Cat women have left Cavtat, Hennessy has been in both Croatia and Cyprus ... and has now left both. Only Michael McSweeney is in a place where he can be watched. Whatever it is, it will happen soon.'

Chapter 42

July, 2013. Northern Israel

'Something has gone wrong.' Sean McSweeney glances anxiously at his watch. 'We can't wait any longer. Plan B. We leave now.'

The other four sprawl over the beds in the Haifa motel room. The red-haired Irishman, known to the team only as Puma, is the leader – the man in charge, the man who knows the answers and the strategy. He is talking again.

'All that we are missing are some plastic extension parts – and our man, Tiger, of course. But we have the main borer parts assembled here now. We can improvise. We move … now.

'Leopard, you take the Mazda, with Panther. Cheetah, you drive my Chev, with Lynx. I'll lead in the Hyundai on my own. Three kilometres between us – never closer – but on the same track, behind me. Use the GPS, the trackers and the comms. If any of us is stopped, flick the warning buzzer twice and then discard the gear. Okay?'

He watches the silent nods. 'You each have your separate stories. Panther, your cover?'

'Yes, Puma. Here to watch the Maccabiah Games.' Panther has a hint of a Turkish accent but there is another inflexion too. 'A dream of my friends from the old days in Tunisia. Taking the opportunity to be tourists before going to watch athletics. And we are travelling to Golan to see the ancient ruins at Katzerin. Love history and archaeology.'

'Old Tunisian days? You are travelling on a Cypriot passport. Why is that?'

'My father worked in Famagusta, in meteorology. He liked it. We stayed and took on Turkish-Cypriot nationality. I'm Cypriot now.'

'Okay. Let's hope they don't put us through the inquisition. We should get past superficial road blocks, if we appear confident and innocent. But we must assume that Tiger has been apprehended. If so, they will be grilling him … and they would have information from that traitor, Dorda. So, if we are asked about Tel Dan or She'ar Yahuv, what do we say?'

'We plead ignorance. Archaeology is our interest. Katzerin or Gamla. We have no interest in going anywhere near the current borders – too many rockets on the news.'

'Good. And absolutely, we go nowhere near Tel Dan or She'ar Yashuv. Not even turning in their direction. Follow the GPS to Site 1. If it looks compromised, beep us on the comms and we head for the high value of 2. The key site is number 3. That is where we will all assemble, if things go wrong. *The Cougar* always teaches that we must expect things to go wrong. It doesn't faze us. We just absorb, re-adjust and keep heading towards our goal.'

* * * *

McSweeney – Puma to his troops – pays the bills and the three cars move slowly east, up onto the plateau using Highway 781. Gradually, their pace adjusts to keep around three kilometres between them. They pass fertile fields, small villages, olive orchards and rocky outcrops as they head for Tiberias and the famous old Sea of Galilee. Tiberias itself is like a Lego town of white boxes – the architecture of fast settlement; expedient, efficient construction to cater for the steady return of the faithful.

And as Sean McSweeney eventually pushes his Hyundai north, up the path of the Jordan River, he mutters to his empty car, 'You have to give credit to the Jews. They have certainly transformed this land into a lush productive country.'

He watches the progress of the other two vehicles on his tracker and he wonders how Tiger would have been compromised. They have always known that a vigilant immigration official might stop them ... but *The Cougar* had explained that is why they are using old passports. The micro-chips would have exposed them in seconds, but the old ones rely on going past a human checker ... and Mahmoud's forgeries are very good.

All the team know they could be questioned. They have each practised their cover stories in front of the old man himself. And he always spoke quietly – almost a whisper – as he encouraged and suggested.

For Sean's part, he had been welcomed past the checkpoints as an esteemed attendee at the Haifa conferences. The others also had non-threatening explanations for their visit to Israel. They are tourists, about to link up with existing groups, wanting to understand the culture, wanting to see the sports at the Games.

In fairness, getting five out of six through the security checks is good. They would have settled for that when they were back in training in the Kyrenia Hills.

Yes, Sean is feeling relaxed, all things considered.

He wonders how his mother is faring.

She has a hard task. She and his father have to be the negotiators for *The Cougar*. They have to do the very quiet persuasion – on a plan which defies all intuitive logic.

No left-brained engineer would have come up with the strategy, which is probably why Grandpa Donnie always used to speak so highly of *The Cougar's* understanding of what works and what just gets you killed in the business of revolution against the *status quo*.

Chapter 43

July, 2013. Heidelberg, Germany

The urban regeneration of Zollhofgarten with its new international standard conference facilities is a subtle advertisement for an advancing city. The state-of the-art centre is designed to retain the industrial history of the precinct – built with the feel of nostalgic character inside the shell of the railway freight yards, beside the main station, the *Bahnhof*. Heidelberg clearly values its past – and its present – as a focal point for academic research and discussion on behalf of the European Union Commission.

The Zollhofgarten location is intended to meet most people's needs – hotels, transport, shops. It's one of the reasons why Britain's Right Honourable Chief Secretary to the Treasury, David Cowdrey, thought that he should attend the gathering in a beautiful city in the valley of the Neckar River.

His young wife, Daphne, has a similar view, if from a different motivation. Second families sometimes miss out on so much, with older politician husbands. Daphne insists that she and their six-year old son, Peter, be part of David's main life – and not some adjunct to parliamentary business – despite the demands of high office. This trip is, at least, a compromise – a concession to family life. And they are now in the historic city, just off the Rhine and in the fringes of the Black Forest. Travel, zoo animals, river cruises, shopping – the exotic nature of foreign language and culture. Something for a mother and son, while the husband/father prepares to strut his prestigious international stage.

Cowdrey's main reason for attending however – and his justification to the British Parliament – is the significant platform for discussions which will be held on the vexed questions of national insolvency across the Union. Prior to entering parliament, Cowdrey's widely acknowledged financial sector expertise could bring a sense of fiscal reality to the committee deliberations – as well as ensuring that Britain's interests are front and centre. Or so the Prime Minister has indicated, after some persuasion.

* * * *

'See the architecture,' Daphne Cowdrey says to her son. 'Buildings,' she adds, seeing his confused expression.

Peter's eyes obediently take in every image from the quaint houses, tree-clad slopes, turrets on the castle and sunshine sparkling on the river. And he is on holiday from school too, for a few weeks. His mother seems overjoyed at the adventure. How good it is to see her happy, laughing, unpacking their suitcases in the very plush hotel in Kysastassa. 'No, no, Peter. It is *Kaiserstrasse*,' she corrects.

No matter, they are going to the zoo. If only she would stop singing that damned nursery song, 'Mummy's taking you to the zoo, today … zoo today.'

He knows the right response – smile and look grateful – and they will get to see the flamingos; their incredible colours fascinate him. What else would be there? Maybe a giraffe or a hoppopitamus – he doesn't say the word; he knows that some words trip him up every time; he doesn't want to be corrected, again – big fat animals anyway.

So, having managed to persuade his mother to get a German bus over the river-bridge to the zoo, for the adventure – 'We are on *holiday*, Mummy' – he sets off with his mother, Daphne, from their hotel in Kaiserstrasse towards the Bahnhof where they will get a 32 or a 31 to the Tea Garden. 'No Peter, it is *Tiergarten*; where the Heidelberg Zoo is'.

His father stays in the room, dealing with phone business from London.

Excitedly, Peter is waving a brochure for the zoo, happily taking in all the sights and sounds, as he skips in front of his mother, heading along the old street for the *Bahnhof* station bus stop.

She isn't even telling him to behave properly – how good – when a big yellow open-topped vintage car rolls along the street behind them, driven by two women with long dark hair flowing over the streaming scarves wrapped round their necks.

'What a car, Mummy. Look at that. The ladies are laughing so much … and waving us to come over. Can I go over, Mummy, please?'

* * * *

Daphne has been concentrating on which shops she will visit after they have suffered the obligatory trip to the zoo. Perhaps today, and definitely tomorrow, would be the fashion houses of the *Hauptstrasse* – and maybe she would *have* to visit the castle with Peter. She should have thought to bring a nanny along, just to entertain her son with the things little boys like to do.

She is suddenly startled by her son's request and the spectacular car.

'Going to the zoo?' the lady in the driver's seat asks, noticing the brochure. 'So are we. Do you want a lift in this super car? You'd really enjoy it. Isn't it a super car?'

The ecstatic grin on Peter's face and the rush to collect her thoughts – 'Better than the bus, Mummy,' he calls, 'Can we?' – have left Daphne stammering.

'Alright. Thank you,' she manages, slightly bewildered by this new event, as she moves to catch up the few metres to Peter, who is already clambering into the back seat.

Even before her son has turned to hurry his mother along, Daphne feels the sharp jab into the back of her neck.

A male voice grunts behind her and a powerful arm tightens around her body, pinning her handbag and arm against her waist. A female voice at her side whispers forcefully, 'Shout to him to carry on. You'll catch him up. Say nothing else or you will both die. Do it now.'

She feels something hard dig into her back. The woman is standing beside her, smiling and waving to Peter while giving urgent orders from the side of her mouth, 'Wave, Daphne. Smile, Daphne … or he dies.' She even lifts Daphne's free hand to the waving position.

And Daphne manages to shout, 'You go on, Darling. I'll catch you up at the zoo.'

As soon as Peter hears her voice, his puzzled expression changes back to a joyous wave. He laughs at the happy women and the car disappears up the street.

'Well done, Daphne.' The man and woman usher her into the back seat of a parked saloon car, the man now with his hand over her mouth.

The woman – not a young woman – places her face very close and says, 'We will set you free in about two minutes. No harm will come to you or your son, if you do precisely what I say. Do you understand? Nod if you understand.'

Daphne nods … even though she doesn't understand anything that is happening.

The woman is speaking again.

'I am going to give you a letter to take back to your husband. This is not about him either … but it *is* about the British Government. The letter explains everything that Mr David Cowdrey has to do …. including, and most importantly, NOT going to the police or the press. If this letter or our meeting leaks out, Peter will die. Believe me. That is *not* a threat. It is just a statement of what will happen.

'If you follow my instructions exactly, neither Peter nor anyone else will be harmed and he will be back with you safe and happy, within two days. Nod if you understand.'

Daphne's eyes are wide and white … but she nods.

'We are about to put you back on the street. I have your mobile. See?' She holds it in front of Daphne's eyes. 'I will ring your husband from it as soon as you are back in the room. We are putting you out on the road now. Turn back towards your hotel with this letter in your hand and walk without looking back. Do you understand?'

She nods as a letter in a clear plastic bag is placed in her hand. She is shuffled out on to the pavement and pushed back along the Kaiserstrasse.

* * * *

Daphne Cowdrey does not look back.

She staggers somehow, in shock, along the hundred metres or so to the hotel ... through the lobby ... up in the lift.

She manages to find her swipe card in her pocket ... in through the door ... gasping towards her husband, who is talking as usual on his mobile.

David Cowdrey turns, sees the dishevelled stunned appearance of his wife, ends the call and stands up ... about to ask the obvious question ... when ...

'They've taken Peter. Yellow car. This letter. You must read ...' and her eyes roll towards the ceiling in response to the strain of her effort. Her legs collapse beneath her and she crumples in a faint to the carpet.

Her husband rushes to her side, shakes her ... to no response and places her in the recovery position.

Then he reaches out for the letter in the plastic bag ... ripping it open in bewildered fury ... and starts to read.

* * * *

The laughing lady has asked him to wave to his mother. She will catch up with them at the zoo, she says. She has flashing white teeth and a very tanned face ... and then Peter feels a prick ... and the laughing lady seems to disappear.

Chapter 44

'The Israelis have arrested five people in conjunction with a suspected attempted attack on their water resources.' Nils is looking at his smart phone screen as he relays the information to Arthur and Sven. 'One arrested on entry at TLV – that's Tel Aviv International – off a flight from Athens, but the journey originated in Larnaca, in Cyprus. Four others in two hire vehicles.'

He laughs. 'They even give the vehicle type. Aren't Israelis just sticklers for detail? A Chevrolet Spark and a Mazda 3, grey. Goodness, even giving the colour. The vehicles were apprehended, heading south towards the Sea of Galilee. The occupants claim to have been visiting historical sites on the Golan but the passports they are carrying – wait for it – are Croatian and Cypriot, without micro-chips. Well, well.'

Arthur rubs his hands. 'Good, that's one threat off the agenda. I told you the Israelis were very capable. What else do we have? Anything on Mahmoud Maziq's whereabouts or Macan Granić?'

Houweling shakes his head in the negative.

Sven mutters, 'Find Padraic Hennessy and we find Granić. Michael McSweeney doesn't appear to be looking out for him. Is he still in that Croatian village? What was its unpronounceable name again?'

'Kuna Konovoska,' Nils replies. 'No evidence to say he is not.'

'What about Sean McSweeney? Anything on him? Last seen on a slow boat from Girne.'

'No. I'll do a specific recent track on him … and his mother, Waltraud. The German domestic intelligence service – the *BfV* – is handling the surveillance of her. Of course, it may have nothing to do with Heidelberg. Val McSweeney could just have been back with old friends in her university town. I did find that she served prison time in Germany for her service with Red Army Faction. Three years, the record shows. In the 1980s, so her slate is clean now.'

'So who looked after the son, Sean, when she was in jail?'

'The grandparents in Donegal.'

'Donnie McSweeney?'

'Yes. And his partner of the time, whoever that was.'

'A nice little education that would have been for an impressionable young boy.'

'He went back to his mother after she was released.'

'Where was Michael?'

'Who knows? But I'm guessing at least that he was in Dubrovnik in early 1991, running guns with Padraic Hennessy and maybe Abdul Maziq.'

'And fathering Macan Granić – leaving the mother to rear him on her own, too.'

'That could be a fair explanation of the pale-face's strange colouring. The complexion of a red-head mixed with his Croatian mother, who is presumably dark-haired – and something happened in the DNA mix to have him look neither fish nor fowl, but odder than any of the others around.'

Sven whistles and speaks slowly. 'If that is true, then Sean McSweeney in his mid-thirties and Macan Granić, a twenty-one-year old, are stepbrothers.'

'I wonder how they each feel about that. Or even if they know.'

'They were together with the crawling men in Cyprus.'

'So back to them. That's five captured. Do you think they just went in on their own? Could Granić have been with him?'

'No. He's just a smart thug … and they'd be terrified of him. If anyone was with them, it would have been Sean. He was the trainer … but he wasn't mentioned as being picked up, was he? Can you check with the Israelis on that too, Nils?'

'So what is Hennessy up to? The more it makes sense, the less it makes sense.'

Chapter 45

July, 2013. Dubrovnik, Croatia

'The red-headed man has vanished from Kuna Konovoska.'

That is the advice that Luka is passing on to Sam, from the local policeman.

'Did his hiking party arrive?'

'Yes, apparently they did. A party of four but only two remain in the house.'

'McSweeney has probably gone with the other two, for a hike. Isn't that why they are there?'

'Perhaps. But my colleague on the mountain is a fair judge. He says the two left behind look really worried, a mature man and woman. When he knocked on the door to make them feel welcome, they couldn't get rid of him fast enough.'

'So, are they lost on a hike or have they just taken off in a huff?'

'I'm just passing on the intel … such as it is.'

'Okay. Thanks for the update. We could be in for a long wait,' Sam suggests. 'I'll get in touch with head-office. They have the overview. Perhaps there is something we could be doing.'

* * * *

It takes a few minutes for the secure link to be relayed from the Dubrovnik police station to Maasboulevard.

Luka watches Sam's face as the agent is briefed from the Netherlands.

Sam whistles in surprise and says, '*Mahmoud* Maziq.'

He listens to Arthur and Sven for another few seconds before replying, into the phone. 'Yes. We are told that Michael McSweeney's party has arrived. He seems to have gone off hiking with two of them. The two others have been left to worry apparently, around the house.'

He pauses to listen some more.

'Yes, we are monitoring the other rental house over the Dubrovnik Bridge. We'll stay in touch with you. Oh, and can you let Goran Bikić know that his daughter is complaining about carrying the practice on her own while her father parties with you in The Hague?'

As he breaks the connection, 'At least I have started to keep my promise to Ivana.'

Luka holds his patient questioning look. 'Mahmoud Maziq? Who is Mahmoud Maziq?'

'The speculators in head office think he might be a professional forger – the bald old man at Cavtat. They are chasing it up. Maybe he is the connection to the Zagreb thefts you mentioned.'

'Doctoring passports would fit with that ink smell. He must have been sitting at the table in the cellar for days, working away at his forging, then.'

'Probably for a lot of hours. It's no easy task to forge passports … what with their microchips and tamper-proofing.'

'But he didn't have to start from scratch. He was only amending genuine passports stolen up north.'

'True. But how many did he have to do … and for whom?'

'And to take people where? We are in the EU now. We don't need passports except for ID.'

'And where is Mahmoud Maziq now? Is his work finished or has he more tasks to complete?'

Chapter 46

'Sean Hennessy left Tel Aviv International for Zurich. It is confirmed that he disembarked at Zurich's Kloten Airport and left the terminal.'

Nils Houweling glances at Arthur, Sven and Emma Jazy ... before continuing. 'Israeli Intelligence advises that he entered their country on a valid Irish passport and flew on to Haifa to attend a conference on fluid mechanics. There is no record of him actually physically being at the conference and he flew out of TLV as advised.' He looks up. 'They have no other information on him.'

Arthur asks, 'And the people arrested in the cars and the airport?'

'They apparently only really know each other by cat names, like Tiger or Panther. Nicknames. They have a vague awareness of the names on the passports of their fellow passengers, but they are all false anyway. *Mossad* would have blown that apart very quickly. They say their tour organiser was called Puma but they haven't seen him recently. But they are sticking to their story – pleading ignorance of anything sinister. None of them has admitted to anything illegal, other than the method of their entry to Israel. They are being held for further enquiries. So far, there is no evidence that they have done anything other than visit tourist sites as illegal entrants. And I'm still chasing the Israeli Government for info on the ministers' vacation places.'

Nils's phone buzzes. 'It's Sam. He wants to speak. I'll text back. Okay?'

'Put him on speaker phone.'

* * * *

The distinctive sound of the scrambling relay from the secure call-centre precedes Sam's crisp voice, 'Are you hearing me?'

'Loud and clear, Sam. Arthur here,' he advises, more as a courtesy than for identification. 'I have Sven, Nils and Emma with me. What do you have?'

'Re-confirming that Michael McSweeney is no longer in the house in Kuna Konovoska but two adults are now there – a man and a woman. The local policeman says they appear worried. He says two others in the party left with McSweeney, presumably to hike. I'm really checking in for updates from your end, but I have some progress to report from here.'

Nils's mobile vibrates again with another message.

Sam Hall's voice continues. 'The local detective, Luka Jusić, – a good man – believes he may have turned a gang member to our advantage. He has the second Dubrovnik rental house under observation. But it's a waiting game …'

'Can I interrupt you all, please?' Nils voice sounds unusually agitated. 'The message I have just taken is from Israel. The Water Minister, the Immigration Minister and their respective daughters are vacationing on a hiking holiday in southern Croatia – at a place called Kuna Konovoska. Just match Sam's scenario to that.'

'Wow!' Hall is all business as he speaks again. 'That fits. I'll get moving on it here now. Keep me informed. The local police have risen to the challenge every time so far. No reason to doubt them now.'

'Just one more thing, Sam,' Sven adds. 'The Israeli police have picked up four tourists near the Sea of Galilee and another at the international airport. They all entered on forged passports from Cyprus and Croatia. No further evidence of wrong-doing at this stage. But Sean McSweeney was also there at the same time, travelling through Tel Aviv to Haifa for a business conference that he didn't attend. He has flown out now and is confirmed to have landed in Zurich.'

'Thanks. It's moving now. I must fly and find out what has happened up in the karst country.'

'Good. Check in regularly.'

As the call disconnects, Arthur turns to Emma. 'You'd better be ready to move at a moment's notice. Who knows where the next event will happen. I'll get a response team available on immediate scramble, just in case it is something outside the normal rules of engagement for local authorities.'

Then he turns to Nils and Sven. 'No sleep now, for a while.'

'What's new?' the operations man replies.

Chapter 47

July, 2013. Heidelberg, Germany

The letter is written in beautiful hand-drawn calligraphy – and in English. It reads:

> Peter Cowdrey is safely in the custody of our organisation. He will not be harmed if the following conditions are obeyed. He will be returned safe, well and happy *when* these conditions are fulfilled.
>
> 1. There is to be no contact with the police or emergency services of any country until this matter is resolved – probably in forty-eight hours.
>
> 2. If any mention of this matter is leaked to the press in any country in the world, the child will be killed.
>
> 3. We require David Cowdrey to contact his Prime Minister in Britain, with the strictest security, ***immediately***, to advise that we will make contact very soon with other instructions. They will require the PM's personal intervention with the President of Israel and the Prime Minister of the Government of Israel on an extremely confidential matter involving world peace.
>
> 4. We will contact the British Prime Minister via phone within twenty-four hours giving further instructions. He needs to be ready to receive the message and respond. He will know when the correct contact comes through.

The instructions will be placed in a secure location in the area of the British Isles and Ireland. We suggest that the Prime Minister puts immediate secure contingency plans in place to retrieve the further instructions, when given.

* * * *

Daphne Cowdrey is still unconscious but breathing evenly.

The Right Honourable Chief Secretary to the Treasury stares at the document in his hand. Bewildered – his wife … his son … the PM … and here he is in Heidelberg … not London.

No police, no house detective, no ambulance for his wife?

She stirs as the thought passes his mind.

Suddenly, his accustomed poise in the arena of debate on world issues has dissipated into a malaise of inadequacy, indecision … and fear.

And then his business phone rings … and rings. He pulls it out of his trouser pocket in dumb frustration and looks at the screen. It is from Daphne, who is still lying asleep on the floor beside him.

'Hello,' he answers tentatively.

'Mr Cowdrey, as you would now know, we have your son, Peter, in our care.' It is a female voice.

'You bastards. If you touch …'

'Mr Cowdrey, save that for the movies. You have read the note?'

Cowdrey grunts an affirmative response.

'Then contact your Prime Minister now. There is a deadline on this. If your PM gets it wrong – or even worse – does not listen to his Chief Secretary to the Treasury … Don't let that happen, Mr Cowdrey. We will be in touch.'

Chapter 48

July, 2013. Dubrovnik, Croatia

'I told you Macan Horvat would come good,' Luka announces with vindicated pride, on Sam's mobile. 'The bad guys have returned to the house. I'm just going to check the video tapes to see what has happened. How are you positioned?'

'Rather nicely,' Ivana's voice chirps in the background over Sam's cough. 'But I understand when duty calls. Shall I drive him over to the station?'

And Sam's voice comes on. 'What she said, Luka.'

After the embarrassed pause, 'Sorry, both of you. I should have realised. Yes, when you are ready, Ivana,' Luka adds sheepishly. 'Sorry, Cuz.'

'You'll keep.' She laughs over the phone.

* * * *

Twenty minutes later, a smiling Sam Hall strolls into reception at the police station and a very business-like Luka ushers him urgently downstairs to a video room.

'You need to see this tape from the *Cougar* house. I have just been over to check on Horvat – to give him encouragement. He has done well, flagging the arrival and not phoning anyone else. But, there's nothing to see over the road. Blinds down. All quiet. They came in a van, straight into the garage. All out of sight. He'll keep watching. We'll leave him be. We have a special response team on twenty-four hour stand-by for when they might be needed.'

Sam's eyebrows rise at this escalation as he settles in front of a huge *high definition* TV screen.

Luka gives his quick summary explanation as he stands by the recording machine.

'This red-headed Michael McSweeney, with an olive-skinned woman and another very tanned man, has two drugged young women on camp-cots in the main room. Where I have paused this, he is waking one up to speak on a mobile. Just watch and listen.'

And he presses play ...

Sam takes in the scene on the screen. It is a modern living area, light painted walls, carpeted floor, with a three-quarter wall-unit holding a television on the facing wall. The lounge chairs have been pushed aside to accommodate the two camp-cots in the centre of the floor.

Both women appear to be in their teens or early twenties and are each secured by what looks like a wide strap over their stomachs, pinning their arms to their sides and themselves to the cots. One of the tethered women is in the process of being woken by the powerfully-built tanned young man, with black hair and shadowed eyes, shaking her and lightly slapping her cheeks ... while Michael McSweeney watches on, with a mobile phone in his hand.

The strong-looking olive-skinned woman sits watching on a lounge chair, lazily smoking a cigarette, until with a frustrated shake of her head, she announces, 'Here. Let me.'

She passes her cigarette to the dark-haired man and picks up a bottle of water. Pouring drips onto the tethered woman's fore-head, she says in English, 'You can hear me. Open your eyes.'

Then she pours water on the lips and cheeks. The woman on the cot sparks into dazed life with a rolling of her head, to escape the water. It takes a minute before her wide eyes are taking in the scene and she starts speaking in one language before changing over to English.

At that point, Michael McSweeney takes over, crouching beside the cot. 'Your friend is still asleep. No harm will come to you if you do precisely what you are told.' He doesn't wait for a response from the staring wide-mouthed woman. 'You are our guests for a couple of days. You will be returned safely, unharmed, if you do what I say. Do you understand?'

The woman doesn't speak initially but wriggles against her bonds. Then she nods warily as she recognises his face. 'You are our guide.' Her brow wrinkles, confused, as she struggles to remember. 'Just a walk to the village shop for milk, you said.' She swivels her head around to see the others in the room. 'We stopped to say hello to these two. What is going on?'

'Your mother is the Minister for Water in the Knesset and she is with your friend's father, who is the Minister for Immigration Absorption. I called them on your phone an hour ago to let them know you were in our custody. I am going to call them again in a minute on your phone, now that you are awake … so that they can verify that you are safe, but in our custody. This is not about your parents. They will just have to relay my message.'

She looks at him bewildered.

'I repeat. You will not be harmed. When I pass the phone to you, you will tell your mother that the guide has you prisoner, that you and your friend are well. And ask them to do what I say. Got it?'

There is no reply.

'Got it?'

She nods.

McSweeney dials the mother's number on the daughter's speed dial and an anxious torrent of words can be heard on loud-speaker mode, from the other end.

'Golda Neeman, it is me again. I told you I would call back.' The voice at the other end is suddenly silent. 'Have you managed to stay away from police, the press and everyone else?'

'Yes. A policeman came round to welcome us but we sent him away. We have done what you asked. Everything. What do you want?'

'Listen to your daughter and then we speak.'

'Mum. Mum.' The daughter wails, tearfully. 'Yes, it's me, Rona, Mum. We are both here. Sarah is asleep. We are tied up. Do what they say. Then they will release us.'

At that, the smoking woman places her hand over the captive's mouth until the man ties a gag to muffle her voice.

Michael McSweeney puffs out his chest and struts the carpeted floor as he starts his speech.

'They are both alive and will be returned safe in two days if you follow my instructions. Is Chaim Tamir with you?'

'Yes. You are on loudspeaker,' she says and a male voice echoes in the background. 'I'm here.'

'Right, here it is. No police or press, not even leaked by accident or you have had your last conversations with your daughters. I need you both to contact your Prime Minister of Israel, confidentially and immediately. Impress on him your situation. Tell him that the Prime Minister of the United Kingdom will contact him and the President with vital information within twenty-four hours. He must respond positively to that call. Do you understand?'

The male voice comes on. 'Confirm. We contact our PM securely to tell him to await the British PM's call to him and the President. Is that it?'

'That is it. But if he doesn't take that call or you don't convince him how important it is, then our agreement is over. You won't

248

hear from me again until your PM has fulfilled his obligation. Call him now.'

McSweeney cuts the connection, turns and smiles at his companions, while removing the battery and SIM card from the mobile. He hands the parts to the man. 'One in the sea, another in a public garbage bin a dozen kilometres from here and the third on the back of a moving truck. Take the other girl's mobile too. Same process. Get *her* father's number written down too, just in case. And be back here as soon as you can. We want things kept tight.'

* * * *

Luka pauses the recording and turns in question to Sam. 'The man drove off with the mobile parts. How much can you tell me about this?'

'I'm not sure that I know much more than you have seen. I need to contact Rotterdam urgently. Did the parents contact the police?'

'No. As they said, they sent him away, politely.'

'So, apart from this surveillance, there is no tracking of phone calls or anything?'

'The first call was brief – before they reached this house, and now they have scattered the parts over the coast. Nothing to track.'

'Suddenly, your intuition with Macan Horvat is proving very, very astute; even if you do phone your cousin at inopportune times.'

'I was phoning *you*.'

'I think she said that *you'd keep*. Now I must phone Rotterdam. Then we'll know more about what is happening.'

Chapter 49

Sven, Nils, Arthur and Emma listen quietly to Sam's voice over the secure speaker phone, describing the video recording of the *Cougar* house.

'Make sure that tape is preserved, Sam,' Arthur instructs. 'We may well need it for a later trial. I'm just trying to digest it all.' He shakes his head, trying to make sense of the new development.

'Do I have it right? The Prime Minster of Britain is going to call the President and Prime Minister of Israel within twenty-four hours … and the latter has to respond positively for the daughters to be released. What has the bloody British Prime Minister got to do with this?'

'Can't help you there,' replies Sam. 'What do you want us to do at this end? Luka has a police response team here. The place is under constant video surveillance. We could take them out and free the women when you give the call.'

'Sven here, Sam. Given that the situation appears to be relatively stable there, under the circumstances … we don't want to frighten the horses. I think we hold off for a bit more information. This is bizarre. We need to know what the British PM is going to ask for. And presumably this is all to do with Padraic Hennessy's agenda for peace in the Middle East. The men that the Israelis have picked up are most likely five of the crawling men, Sam. Maybe, McSweeney and Hennessy think they have been successful in what they were trying to do in Israel ... and he will find probably that they have failed. What then? Does he get rid of the women?'

Arthur adds, 'I agree with Sven. Hold for the moment. We are here, on call, all the time. We will sleep in the office – if there is time for that luxury. Keep monitoring. I will check with British Intelligence to see what they know. Stay ready. It is moving, but in a strange direction.'

'Maybe you need to be mad to understand a madman,' offers Sam.

'Mad? Perhaps. I will reserve judgement. But maybe it is all moving too fast for his seventy-eight-year-old brain.'

* * * *

As the connection is broken, Arthur glances at the pensive Sven, whose head is lowered into his familiar pose ... and giving no response. Then Arthur looks to Emma. His wondering expression seeks a comment from her but she is quietly thinking through the options.

To the whole group, Arthur says, 'We need information. This British connection is new. Nils?'

'I have nothing, I'm afraid. Certainly not of a factual nature. I tend not to like speculating.'

'Okay. I'll contact Britain. Sven, will you get onto *Mossad* with this latest info? Maybe they can cast some light. Nils, anything on Mahmoud Maziq or the other McSweeneys?'

'Not yet.'

* * * *

'The Brits are in a spin.' Arthur gestures with open hands to Sven and Emma. 'The Prime Minister has been told to stand by for a set of instructions from a group who have kidnapped a cabinet minister's son in Heidelberg. And all of it to be secure from police or press. That's it, at this stage.'

Emma responds. 'Waltraud Muller/McSweeney? That's my best bet.'

'Undoubtedly. The minister was in town for the EU Conference. Took his family there for a holiday. The six-year-old boy was snatched. The Brits won't release any information, except that little part to us due to our security interests, until they know what the instructions contain. Sven?'

'The Israelis are quietly processing what we sent them. It has taken me an hour of cutting through their *neither confirming nor denying* to get through to the deputy head of *Mossad*. He confirmed at least that they were investigating a request made of their Prime Minister to stand by for a call from the Brits. But, apparently, the Israeli PM made a pre-emptive call to London anyway and was met with a perplexed British PM who only knows what you have just told us, Arthur.'

'Okay. Ears open. Ready to move. Any word from Nils?'

'He was chasing up something with the French?'

'God! Are they involved in this too? How much chaos can a geriatric Irishman cause?'

Chapter 50

July, 2013. Donegal, Republic of Ireland

G-2 – the Irish intelligence section – and an elite team of the *Garda* zones in from two directions on the global positioning co-ordinates.

The message had come through from Dublin an hour before, forwarded on from London. And all that the British have been given, apparently, is the location. No explanatory message ... but directed, as a matter of priority, to the Prime Minister's office.

The *open sesame* to get past the PM's gate-keepers had been 'Heidelberg. Peter. Listen carefully. It will be said once.'

The voice was Mediterranean-sounding and female. And the co-ordinates were given from a lonely public phone box in London – empty by the time the police arrived; one of the very few with no CCTV monitoring it.

Maghery Bay, Donegal. That is the location. A blue sky on a summer's day but still with a bite in the wind whipping off the Atlantic.

The vehicles converge at the head of a section of shingle beach. Elite troops form a perimeter. Two helicopters circle overhead.

A camera-guided robot rolls slowly forward towards the GPS location and an officer in bomb-disposal gear stands at the ready.

The robot controllers pick up the shape of a closed laptop computer lying on the shingle with a sheet of laminated paper, flapping gently underneath.

Carefully, yet quickly, the robot zones in. Its mechanical arm seems to scan the laptop and then, after about twenty seconds, it lifts the computer from the ground, without incident. Then the machine turns and carries its prey back to the temporary sandbagged obser-vation point, and the waiting police.

Only the shriek of the gulls slices the air, over the background noise of waves gently rattling the beach pebbles.

No talk.

Elite troops communicate by signs and whispers while watch-ing all around.

At the GPS site, a bomb-disposal man moves forward like an animated *Star Wars* character. He stoops clumsily to reach the weighted-down laminated paper and shouts, 'Oh shit!' to the others. 'Better come in here.'

Carefully, several men circle in, following the pointed hand of the armoured man.

There … there, in the shingle, is a woman's old shoe, battered by weather and time. But below, in a hole carved out through the small stones, dug recently by animals presumably, is the clear skel-etal shape of a human foot and part of a lower leg.

* * * *

Having retreated to the safety of the police vans and their explo-sives-scanning gear, the *G-2* men examine their prize.

The laptop fires up on battery. It holds a solitary file – a voice message with an Irish accent. The laminated page gives a summary. And it is written in neat calligraphy, by a skilled hand.

Given the high-security nature of the find, the file is relayed elec-tronically to London, with the note scanned and sent close behind.

Even as the helicopters leave with the *G-2* personnel, the police have called in a *scenes-of-crime* team with their own specialist pathologist to examine the site and the remains.

The grave is being treated with extreme urgency, care and secu-rity – in case there is some particular significance in the choosing of that place to leave a message for the British Prime Minister.

* * * *

'My best estimate?' The pathologist speaks quietly and carefully. 'The remains are human, female, perhaps in her thirties, killed by a single bullet to the back of the skull. How long ago? Judging by the deterioration and the location – best guess – about forty years ago. The early seventies.'

* * * *

The information is relayed through to *G-2*, then onto London … and to Arthur Blair at IIB in Rotterdam.

Chapter 51

July, 2013. Rotterdam, The Netherlands

'My office is being over-worked,' complains Arthur Blair, with a wry grin. 'Nils will join us shortly. Then I'll get a summary through to Sam.'

Around the table, with Arthur, are Sven and Emma, waiting with quiet anticipation, notepads and smart-phones at the ready.

'Right.' Arthur is in full business mode. 'London has received the instructions. It is a voice file on a laptop, which was left lying over the grave of an executed person, believed to be a woman from Derry who disappeared in 1973. It is suggested that she most probably had been killed for informing on Padraic Hennessy's *Cat Pack*. The symbolism should not be lost. Maghery Bay was also where Maureen Jazy came ashore back in 1973. For all we know, she might have been a witness to the filling of that grave.

'The instructions came in a whispering Irish accent. Three guesses, folks? You've got it.' The IIB lawyer grins at the tired smiles, which quickly become serious again. 'They were for the British Prime Minister to contact the Israeli Prime Minister with a series of demands to enable the release of the three kidnapped people – the boy in Heidelberg and the women in Dubrovnik.

'The conditions are along the lines of the Israelis stopping, or very significantly reducing, the immigration into Israel; discreetly, without public announcement or grandstanding which would bring in major world powers or the international media vultures. In

Padraic's own inimitable words – *to bugger up the play*. You were on the money, Sven, with your earlier assessment.

'This initial demand is to be coupled with serious negotiations at the discussion table with the Palestinians and named neighbouring countries, for a peace accord along the lines of the 1998 Irish agreement, and a two-state solution – but not to produce exclusive states.

'Rather, they would be countries where people of different racial or cultural backgrounds could live in either country with full citizenship rights in practice, not just on paper. As Sol Levin told us earlier, there are indeed many Arabs living in Israel today as part of the population and it would be a condition that they could (and should) still be citizens; able to move freely over the borders, although subject to the normal laws of each country.

'So, no more violence or intimidation – overt or insidious.' Arthur's tone is flippant, as if reading some fanciful manifesto. 'In the new arrangements of the future, thugs from either side would be treated as criminals, not freedom fighters. As long as the governments stick by the agreed new rules of fair treatment, all would be well.'

The lawyer shrugs his grudging, though cynical, acceptance. 'The rules would also be *laws* too, I trust. That's a really big concession from an old Northern Ireland revolutionary to accept the rule of law, but maybe Hennessy's memories of Derry can be a catalyst to setting workable standards for the new regimes – the *new normal*, instead of generations being brought up to hate and fight.'

Sven smiles weakly but says nothing. Nils just shakes his head in disbelief.

'And,' Arthur continues, 'for the two-state solution to be acceptable, a negotiated land handover would occur in exchange for peace. Access to shared territories would be agreed – such as for holy sites – and security of water would be required.'

'And in return?' queries Emma.

'In return,' Arthur responds, relaying his information, 'the voice indicates that he has locked in the promises of beys, sheiks and several appointed revolutionary leaders, as well as Arab presidents and prime ministers, who will all ensure that a seriously negoti-ated outcome will be honoured.' He pauses to acknowledge the wry expressions. 'They will be responsible for keeping the hotheads in line. That is their investment in both states being able to co-exist. But, clearly, the architect of this scheme has been taking his advice from those particular parties before formulating his solution because there is even more for the Israelis to agree to ...' He checks his notes to verify the next part. '... they will be required to have a part-financial investment in the successful business future of Palestine as in a guarantee of economic development ... and water sustainability ... and, fundamentally, proper access for all religions to sacred sites.'

Arthur sighs to collect his thoughts before giving a summarised update of his understanding.

'So, folks, as I read this, it is essentially a land deal, real estate – and some processes to make sure that everyone is committed to making it succeed. It has nothing to do with religious superiority or inferiority. It has nothing to do with who is right or wrong, nor who treated the others worse in the past. It is not a bi-national solu-tion in the same way that similar arrangements have failed in so many places in the past – Yugoslavia and Cyprus to name a couple. I agree with him there. In my view, there would never be equality in bi-nationalism, shared administration. It is a fantasy, especially where there has been such a brutal history and such entrenched fundamental beliefs. Rather, this is a clear two-nation solution to give negotiated personal and sovereign space to two groups who each have historical rights to this relatively small area of land, in their own ways. This separation, however, will have each committed to the success of the other or there will be serious consequences, as yet not clarified by our Irish matchmaker. But, he is definite about making sure that it can and will work ... or else.'

Sven's quiet Swedish accent interjects, 'And I was expecting something nice and simple from a revolutionary fighter – your stan-dard *surrender or be shot* scenario. And he wants to keep all these concessions *quiet*? Go on – how will he make this work?'

Arthur continues with a knowing look. 'After that – and I am making the assumption that it *was* Hennessy speaking – the voice gives a GPS location in the Hula Valley. British Intelligence has given me a sample of the voice, actually delivering its instructions. Listen to the cold chill in his whisper. It would terrify stone statues.'

Arthur plays the recording:

Go to that GPS location and you will find a box over a hole, drilled into the very limestone gryke. Inside the hole is a tube which extends through the fault, deep into the ground. In the box is a container with a phone-activated detonator. When fired, it will drop the liquid down the tube and it will reach to the very aquifer itself, below.

The liquid at that site is benign. But it makes the point that the Golan aquifer can be poisoned by a phone call. Be very aware. The tube is designed to hit an aquifer which actually links into the West Bank or Northern Aquifer. Half of Israel's water source out of action … and for a long time.

Now, I know you are thinking that's an idle threat from a madman. However, that is just your arrogance. There is a second drilled hole which also accesses the aquifer, and it does have a particularly lethal liquid above it. And I will not reveal that site's location until we get incontrovertible proof – within twenty-four hours – that you have accepted my peace terms.

And before you get so smart as to think that all you have to do is to turn off the mobile transmitting towers, let me point out the chaos and negative publicity that action would cause for the Maccabiah Games, with all the tourists who are in the country at the moment, unable to access their mobile phones. What spin would you put on that – to keep it out of the media?

But, more, that particular second detonator also has a timer on it, not activated by radio, but set for four days from the time our hostages were taken. So, let's not be silly. I am giving you a serious offer for Middle East peace which you cannot realistically refuse.

* * * *

'That's some ultimatum.' Sven moves his wise head in contemplation.

While Emma asks the practical question, 'How are the Israelis supposed to communicate their acceptance, without letting everyone know what it's about or Hennessy revealing his location?'

Arthur purses his lips before a reminding glance at his computer screen, 'The announcement is to come from the British. These instructions are in part of Hennessy's file. It is to be an announcement that Israeli hydrologists will conduct a study in Loch Ness to identify water patterns which could create the illusion or confirm the reality of a monster.'

Sven actually laughs. 'Well, that will light up the Twittersphere; and most of the TV info-entertainment channels.'

Emma shakes her head. 'Bizarre! Amazing! But not totally mad. It is as if he has thought about the issues, but he reckons he is the only one who can make it happen.'

Arthur nods. 'The old bully boy tactics, but he is out of his league with this. Back to reality. The only window we have into countering Hennessy's plan is Sam monitoring the *Cougar* house in Dubrovnik. We can't afford to move in before we have the other two variables tied up; the six-year-old boy and the unlocated drill hole.'

'It is possible,' says Sven, with a musing look, 'that Padraic is bluffing on the second drill hole. The five activists have been caught in Israel; the four in the cars and the one at the airport. Maybe the old man doesn't know that they didn't get to finish their mission?'

'Well, did they or didn't they? Do you want to take that chance?' asks Arthur. 'I'm sure the authorities in Tel Aviv will now be working very hard on the five to break their stories. *Mossad*, Sven? Anything?'

'Oh, not much,' Sven responds. 'The only useful snippet I got out of my *Mossad* contact is that the five activists only know the others by cat names. The boss man is Puma, and he is not captured. I'm betting that the real boss is *The Cougar*.'

They all pause to take in the symbolism.

'And the boy?' asks Emma. 'We have no links to where he might be?' There is a tap at the door and Nils Houweling enters as Emma finishes her question. 'Have they been tracking the mother's mobile phone?'

'Nils will know.' Sven smiles at the new arrival. 'Speak of the Devil. Hi, Nils. What have you uncovered from the French?'

'Possibly Mahmoud Maziq. But were you mentioning tracking mobile phones?'

'Yes, I was wondering about the mother's phone in Heidelberg. The boy's mother? Didn't they steal her phone?'

'The German Police tracked the phone to an empty rail carriage in Stuttgart station. The street where Peter Cowdrey was abducted was right beside the *Bahnhof* – an easy drop into a rail carriage heading in the wrong direction. However, our French friends with a penchant for tracking Mahmoud Maziq have observed him at Heidelberg rail station, boarding a train to Mannheim, where they changed for Basel in Switzerland.'

'They?'

'He was with three women, another man and a sleeping boy who was being carried by that man.'

'Basel? And from there?'

'Geneva. That's where they are at present, according to the French.'

'Not far from my father in Montreux,' observes Emma. 'Do you want me in Switzerland?' she continues. 'I do speak the languages.'

The agent's whole demeanour is poised in anticipation; wide eyes, tensed muscles and gritted smile.

'We do indeed want you in Switzerland, Emma,' agrees Arthur. 'It is time for you to move, I fancy. But we need a back-up squad of our specials in case something comes up that is outside the normal rules of engagement for the Swiss authorities. Gaston Mimoun would be my choice as that team leader – our Belgian special forces king. But they will answer to your assessment, Emma. We are up against quite a number, potentially. I'll get the approvals, internal and international. Liaise with the attack team and with Nils's French contacts. What else Nils?'

'That's it for the moment. I'll get up to speed on Hennessy's ultimatum. If we can get Emma and the team close to the little boy, then with Sam in Dubrovnik, we can retrieve all the hostages. That only leaves the threat to the aquifer.'

'Only! Such a simple word.' Sven lifts his head. 'This is always supposing the Israelis don't agree to Hennessy's solution anyway – why wouldn't they agree? Like putting the Loch Ness story out just to gain time; four days in effect. What's to stop them doing that within twenty-four hours as requested?'

'Perhaps Padraic has another way of checking,' Arthur suggests. 'We would have, wouldn't we, if we were organising this? We wouldn't leave it up to the media to pick up a story. He must have another way of checking that it is all on track. We really need to find Padraic Hennessy.'

Nils interrupts the thinking with, 'In terms of priorities, where do you want me to spend the critical time we have left? Finding Mahmoud Maziq and maybe the boy? Finding Sean McSweeney and maybe Hennessy, guarded by Macan Granić? It all seems to be heading towards Switzerland and Jacques Jazy – for the redemption speech. What happens if *he* doesn't accept it?'

Emma smiles despite the situation. 'And Dad probably *would* tell him to get lost. I'll have to check on his protection too. He would only have my brother, Martin, looking after him. Not much of a defence if all the potential forces of evil descend on him.'

Arthur Blair smiles. 'On the other hand ...'

Emma looks at him, questioning.

'So where is Padraic Hennessy?' Sven ponders. 'How can we locate him? He seems to have access to enough people who can train saboteurs, kidnappers and forgers ... as well as still having his Irish contacts who can place his instructions on an old grave, that just happens to be where Maureen came ashore all those years ago. Is he just a sentimental old fool?'

'Sentimental? Undoubtedly,' Nils agrees. 'Even in seeking redemption. What's that if not sentimentality? But Michael McSweeney must know where Hennessy and the others are. He is second in rank on that food chain. Wouldn't he expect to catch up with his son and wife? Why don't we get Sam and the Dubrovnik police to recapture the women and work over Michael.'

'For a researcher, Nils, you can have quite a hard-line operational approach.'

'Do we have a better idea?'

'Old IRA stalwarts don't give out information easily. And if we take him out, I'm guessing that Hennessy would know … and that could precipitate all kinds of nastiness.'

'So we have no real course of action?'

'Not necessarily …' And Arthur Blair smiles. 'Here's a plan. It's not pretty. It is not the ideal … but it *is* a plan.'

Chapter 52

July, 2013. Montreux, Switzerland

Gunnar Andersson knows that he is Jacques Jazy's last line of defence. A decorated IIB agent, Andersson leads a small Bureau section which has been deployed around Jazy's chalet for several days.

Jacques and Martin are aware … but no-one else.

As Arthur had said to Jazy, 'At the end of whatever Hennessy has schemed up, he will come limping through your door to seek something – whether it be praise, forgiveness or redemption – whatever he thinks he needs at the end of such a life. So Gunnar and his team will be a quiet spider trap waiting for a big fly (or flies) if that's the way it pans out. There is no time limit. They are former special forces men. When Hennessy was a young *Cat Pack* leader, the predecessors of these men hid in hedges, trees and lofts throughout the north of Ireland for days – just observing and waiting – not caring about jurisdictions but ready for whatever was needed. And they will wait patiently here too. It will come to a head in days; not weeks, and maybe even in hours.'

* * * *

Jazy's retirement home is a modern two-level villa, up the slope behind Montreux town. It is built in the traditional Swiss chalet style with the steep pitched roof reaching out to cover the verandahs and walkways – all accessible as living space in the days of heavy snows and places of quiet shade in the summer warmth of a Swiss July.

This home represents the fruits of a lifetime of labour and enterprise in the world of print and protest – a business sold, long before computer technology totally undermined its value.

Jacques and Martin live in the top floor. Traditionally, the ground floor would have kept animals safe through the winter. However, in July 2013, it houses Gunnar's team on rotation between their inside and outside surveillance hides.

* * * *

Martin Jazy picks up the phone on the second ring. 'Emma.'

Chapter 53

July, 2013. Dubrovnik, Croatia

'We've been given the go-ahead,' Sam advises quietly. 'Approvals from your Ministry of the Interior in Zagreb should be whizzing down your chain of command past the senior police directors to this station. But this is a very sensitive operation. They are leaving it to us as to how we develop our tactics.'

'Really? You certainly have some clout, Sam.' Luka's head shakes slowly in admiration.

The IIB agent ignores the comment, focused as he is on the daunting task ahead. 'It's more that they want us to produce a miracle. But it has to be a very discreet operation, not stun grenades and a frontal assault – but still releasing the abducted women into police protection, as well as taking out the male and female heavies. And me interrogating Michael McSweeney for information which needs to be extracted in minutes or hours but certainly not with the luxury of days. And there's a catch.'

Luka sighs. 'There is more?' His eyes roll to the ceiling.

'More catches? Yes. Many and varied. Rotterdam believes that, if McSweeney gets the chance, he will alert his network and a potential international crisis will move to a new level. But, they also suspect that there will be some pre-arranged regular check-ins with the network – and if those pass without the contact, the alarms will go off.'

The Dubrovnik detective's eyes widen and he runs both hands through his hair. 'Sam, you are operating in a different world from me. I just catch criminals, collect evidence for court cases and see them locked up. And we usually go in fast and hard. What is the information you need from McSweeney?'

Sam takes a moment to collect his thoughts. 'Luka, this is international terrorism, blackmail and a threat of mass murder. We believe that Michael McSweeney knows the location of his son, Sean, as well as his employer, an old Irishman called Padraic Hennessy ... our *Cougar*. This interrogation needs to get a hardened gun-running thug, who is also a seasoned mercenary, to reveal information that he would normally die for – rather than divulge. And to do it by yesterday. What thoughts do you have?'

'Not many. Let's start with my humble area of expertise – getting into the house and taking out the bad guys. Are you going to bring McSweeney back to the station for interrogation?'

'I don't think that would be wise. Is there a cellar in the *Cougar* house?'

'Yes. Most probably. All these new places have roughly the same design. Why wouldn't it be wise, Sam?'

'You are restricted by your police protocols. I am not. IIB is authorised by its clandestine contract to secure admissible evidence by ...'

'You are moving into illegal territory. Torture is forbidden.'

'Luka, we interrogate using deception, not thumb-screws. But it is best that you are not compromised in any way. Often an implied threat coupled to a bribe is the way to go. Isn't that exactly what you are doing with Macan Horvat? Our challenge with McSweeney is to find the key which will loosen his tongue – in minutes rather than hours. So you stay out of it, please, for the sake of your career.'

'Okay, Sam,' the detective replies slowly, thoughtfully. 'We'll see how it pans out. I'll make my own decisions. These criminals are on my territory. Now, to get in without raising the balloon. Our usual technique is that someone who is clearly innocent goes to the door. In the distraction, the team goes in. As a base concept, how does that sound?'

'Fine. Did you have someone in mind?'

Luka smiles. 'Horvat is looking for brownie points. But the red-head might remember him from the gang visit at Cavtat. It has to be someone really innocent … to put them off-guard.'

And his phone rings …

Chapter 54

July, 2013. Rotterdam, The Netherlands

'Nils, give us an update. Anything new from Geneva?'

'Maziq, the other man, three women and the boy are still there.'

'No ID on any of them? A pale face, for example?' Arthur persists.

'The French don't know the others. A startling pale face has not been mentioned. But they are not in that loop.'

'Well, thankfully, Nils, you are in *their* loop. We are still in the game. Emma is on her way, as is a small team headed by Gaston Mimoun.'

Sven lifts his head to agree with the comment. 'I like that choice, Arthur. The Belgian should be very good after all his experience in the African conflicts.'

'And we already have Gunnar Andersson in Montreux ...' adds Arthur.

'Do we?' Nils makes a note. 'So that's where he is. All I knew was he was on secret ops – and I paid his team accordingly. But good. That gives some rapid-response coverage of that area between Geneva and Jazy.'

Arthur smiles his acknowledgement. 'Any word on Sean McSweeney?'

'Negative. He disappeared after he walked out of the Zurich terminal. Maybe someone was there to pick him up.'

Sven adds, 'There is no official word on the Israeli interrogations. But they *did* find a drilled hole, as Padraic described, at the GPS location. So, the remaining four *did* get through alright.'

'Bummer! Okay. No idle threat, then. Hennessy is proving to be as good as we feared.' Arthur rarely allows himself to dwell on negatives when in attack mode. 'On the Dubrovnik situation – which is our only really firm lead – Sam has been given authority to proceed with recapturing the hostages and interrogating Michael McSweeney. We have top-level support from Zagreb, so there should be no police delays.'

Sven asks, 'Is British Intelligence talking with *Mossad*?'

'I believe so. But, I have to say, they appear to be relying on us to make the breakthrough. And there is another squillion going into the account, Nils, if we can pull this off in the timeframe.'

'And the Israeli attitude to the demand about Hennessy's demand about *Aliyah*?' Sven questions.

'The sense is that the Israeli PM is prepared to sacrifice the few for the greater good – the Ministers and children could be dispensable – but the aquifer is a different story.'

'That's a big moral call.'

'Aren't they all? That's what Hennessy is banking on. Let's hope we can save the aquifer *and* the captives.'

Chapter 55

July, 2013. Dubrovnik, Croatia

'I don't like this,' Sam mutters. 'I don't like this at all.'

'What?' replies Luka. 'That women take over control.'

'No. Not that. Just this particular woman.'

The plan has been set.

She couldn't be dissuaded. 'Croatians stand up for what is right,' she had said. 'Lawyers even more so. We need to be counted. How could I face Danko or my father if I squibbed on this?'

Ivana had phoned from the police station reception. She had been passing and thought it would be good to phone her cousin, Luka ... to see how *he* was positioned. And the man in her life was also there.

It had come up in conversation that Luka needed someone who looked innocent to knock on the door of a rented house – doing a survey, checking for a government department. And, before any of the danger could be explained, Ivana had volunteered – and prevailed – with all the persuasive wiles of her profession and personality. And the pressing time element was the critical factor in her winning the day.

* * * *

At that moment, with a flick of her long dark hair, clipboard clamped under her elbow, Ivana Bikić is walking up the path to the front door.

The special response team are in position. The video monitor is now in an unmarked police van around the corner.

Sam and Luka are only metres away, SIG and Glock at the ready.

But earlier Luka stressed to Sam that, 'This has to be a Dubrovnik police operation. You *don't* intervene. Our team will take out the bad guys and deliver Michael Hennessy to you in the cellar. That's when you can start your interrogation. And I have an idea for that. It might interest you, if you will let me be involved in a small way?'

And Sam has gratefully accepted the suggestion.

* * * *

Ivana rings the bell a second time, looking impatient. Then, as if to look for any movement in window curtains, she steps back; before, undaunted, she strides forward to ring again.

Suddenly, but slowly, the door opens a fraction and Ivana launches into her smiling Croatian patter.

The woman answering the door shakes her head, gesturing that she doesn't understand.

So, Ivana launches into several languages, as rehearsed back at the station, while Luka sidles unseen along the wall.

A noise at the rear of the house has the woman look back into the room. Ivana nods and Luka is in, wrestling the woman to the ground.

Ivana turns away from the open door, as she has been instructed, while several fast-moving police in dark assault-suits stride past the fallen Luka and his captive … and into the house. She has been told to take cover against the wall in case of shooting but, as she turns, it is into the arms of Sam Hall.

'Well done. You're one brave lady, Ivana Bikić. Thank you.'

* * * *

It takes less than two minutes.

From the street, if observers had missed the first twenty seconds of action, there would have been nothing to see.

272

Everyone is inside the house; the assault team, the unconscious captives, the male and female heavies, Sam, Luka and Ivana.

'They have McSweeney in the cellar,' Luka advises. 'All the bad guys accounted for.'

And Macan Horvat comes to the front door, as arranged.

* * * *

To minimise any street attention, a police medic checks the girls on-site ... and they are left where they sleep, with only the medic to monitor them until support personnel can arrive later.

The assault team melts away through the back door. Ivana leaves with them, having received praise from all. The two heavies – trussed and gagged – are carried amongst the assault team to the discreet van.

* * * *

Downstairs, Sam Hall walks into the cellar to find an angry red-headed Irishman tied securely to a solid chair, with a gag preventing his gargled oaths from being understood.

Sam pulls up a chair – backwards – in front of the clearly irate captive, whose face is almost matching the colour of his hair.

'Michael McSweeney, I presume?' he asks with a polite smile. 'Not so much fun on the receiving end, eh?'

The wriggling man kicks out and tries to topple the chair.

'That will hurt if you succeed. We need to have a civilised talk, Michael. Almost in a whisper, eh? *An cogar.*'

The struggling stops – replaced by a questioning look.

'Just tell me when you will be ready to have our quiet chat, Michael.' The IIB agent watches him with a pleasant smile. No reaction. 'A pity, Michael. I heard a story once about a man in Donegal ... his name was Donnie McSweeney. Would he have been a relative? No, probably not. They tell me he was a clever man ... but cold. Carried out many interrogations of informers and traitors. If they wouldn't speak, he brought in someone to beat the shit out of them ... and then they *always* talked.

273

'And do you know what old Donnie would say to them, then? He would say, *"Now here you are talking away – just like I asked you to, an hour ago – except now you have two broken shin bones and no knuckles on your right hand. So why didn't you just talk when I asked you? It would have been so much more pleasant."* A very clever man was Donnie McSweeney ... or so I'm told.

'Now would you like to speak with me, Michael? Should I remove that saliva-ridden rag from your mouth?'

McSweeney shakes his head and growls at the back of his throat.

So, Sam clicks his fingers and Macan Horvat walks to the door, filling the door-frame with his mass. Luka, as a translator, follows Horvat through, squeezing his way past the big man, to observe the whole room.

'Is this the man?' Sam asks Horvat. 'The one who stuck a gun in your face in Cavtat?'

Horvat nods at the translation.

'Now, Michael. We might have to leave you with this Croatian gentleman for a few minutes, if you don't want to talk. How long does it take to break a few shin bones or a knee cap? Do you want to speak with me yet? Your name is McSweeney, isn't it? Surely you would have inherited some of the wisdom of the great Donnie McSweeney. Or was he really on the other side of the family; the part that got the brains? Do you want to speak or will I leave for a few minutes?'

McSweeney's head lowers into a nod and he tries to speak through the gag.

Sam rises and unties the muffling cloth. 'There, that is better. Now say something nice to start our conversation.'

'Fuckin bastards. Fuckin bastards. Go fuck yourselves.'

'Not quite the response I was looking for, sadly,' Sam responds in a gentle tone. He nods towards Macan who takes three further steps into the room ... and produces a metal bar from behind his back.

'Alright. Alright.' McSweeney's voice sounds tired but not defeated. 'Ask your questions.'

At Sam's nod, Luka and Horvat leave the room.

'Donnie McSweeney would be proud of you.'

'Would he? Shit! He'd cream me for being caught. But I have nothing to tell you. I don't know anything. We just had to take these two girls so that their parents would pass on a message.'

'Who are their parents?'

'Government ministers in Israel, I'm told.'

'What was the message?'

'That they had to get their Prime Minister to expect a call from the Prime Minister of Britain ... and then respond positively.'

'How did you tell the parents?'

'The girls' phones.'

'And where are the phones now?'

'Far gone.'

'Who told you the parents were government ministers in Israel?'

Michael McSweeney suddenly stops and stares at his interrogator. 'You're not the fuckin police at all, are you? What you're doing is illegal.'

'No, I'm not the police; any more than Donnie McSweeney was, but he enforced the law of *the cause*, did he not?' Sam stares at the tied man and gives him a weak knowing smile.

Then the lights come on in Michael McSweeney's eyes. 'You're fuckin military. Secret Service. Fuckin James Bond. SAS.'

'I'm afraid not, Michael. James Bond was too much of a gentleman. And you were going *so* well.' He pauses to smile at his adversary. 'Now, are you going to co-operate or do we return to Donnie McSweeney's persuasive methods?'

'I want a lawyer. I know my rights. I'm telling you nothin.'

'You're right, Michael. You are the tough mercenary. You would die for *the cause*, wouldn't you?'

'Too fuckin right! You'd better believe.'

'Oh, I do, Michael. I do. And it is such a pity that I had trusted you to co-operate because I sent that big Croat with the iron bar away.'

McSweeney sneers. 'Don't have the bottle for the hard stuff, yourself, eh?'

'Indeed, Michael. I came across a tough lad down in Cyprus recently. A real bastard with the knife – carved a couple up big time. Came from here, I believe. Maybe you know him ... Macan Granić?'

'Why would I know a Croat?'

'Well, because his mother says that *you* are his father.'

The fifteen seconds of staring silence is broken by a visceral roar coming from deep in McSweeney's body.

'His mother was a whore, is a whore, always a whore. You wouldn't believe her if she swore she was lying.'

'So you *do* know Macan Granić? Twenty-one years old. Pale face ... but not unlike yours, Michael. Bigger freckles, though. They tell me he had joined your *Cougar* gang. Naw, he wouldn't want to be in a gang run by a father who couldn't even hang around to watch him grow up. Who pissed off and left him when he was needed most. What sort of father would that have been, Michael?'

The Irishman resumes his sullen silent expression.

'So why would he want to be in your gang? To kill you perhaps, for the way you treated his mother? For not being around when he was being brutally bullied because of his looks?'

'His mother was a whore. She poisoned his mind. That's why he ran to the family of the gang. My gang ... to be with *me*.'

'Does he *know* it is actually *you* who is his real father? Not just any Irish Sweeney that his mother might have mouthed off about.' Sam Hall waits patiently, but McSweeney only drops his eyes to the floor. 'Did you *not* even have the balls to tell him that, Michael? And what about Sean? They've both been working together in Cyprus? Do they even know they are brothers?'

McSweeney looks up, his eyes narrowed to slits. 'You can keep this up for days. I'm not saying anything to the fuckin SAS.'

'No longer with the regiment, Michael. Moved on to less disciplined pursuits. Now, I answer to no-one. A bit like old Donnie, eh? But ... you'll like *this* story. When I was up in the hills of

Afghanistan, some old fellows with turbans on their heads told me about their special way of getting prisoners to talk. Do you want to hear?'

The Irishman glares.

'There are women up in the high valleys who do elaborate embroidery with needles and little knives. So skilled they are, such delicate cuts to the threads to give their distinctive stitching style ... Well, the men in those valleys would hand the prisoner over to the women. He is staked out or tied up ... a bit like you are at the moment. Nowhere to go. And women come with their little sharp knives and gently, very carefully, they slice away the skin from the face – just muscle left showing. Then they cut away the clothes so that the whole skin can be flayed from the prisoner. They don't kill him, so that he can feel the whole sensation. You see, Michael, women are so much tougher than men. They can handle all that blood and moaning and ...'

McSweeney's eyes are bulging. 'Why are you fuckin telling me all this?'

'Only because you have to make a decision about when you are going to tell me what I need to know. Like old Donnie used to say, *Before you decide that you will always have to walk with a limp, you could tell me now.*'

'You're full of shit.'

Sam whistles ... and the door to the cellar opens. Luka walks in carrying two very small knives in his left hand. Then, he turns to wave another figure into the doorway.

'Well hello, *Gospodja* Granić,' Sam welcomes. 'The father of your child has just been calling you a whore who poisoned his son's mind.'

A torrent of Croatian invective flows from the angry woman's mouth, even as Luka translates, but her entry to the room is barred by the policeman's strong right arm.

'You shouldn't have raped her all those years ago and then left her with child, Michael. A woman scorned ... and with two little knives …? As Donnie would say, before the pain or after the pain? … your choice.'

The venom can be felt in the eye contact between the mother and father of Macan Granić.

Gospodja Granić lets fly with another volley of Croatian abuse and spittle roughly in McSweeney's direction, while the Irishman's eyeballs bulge even more, in horror.

Sam whispers, 'I believe she is saying she will start with your penis and your balls and gradually work up till she finishes at your eyes.'

Eventually, McSweeney turns away from the woman's hateful gaze. He gasps out, 'I'll talk.'

Luka removes the still-shouting woman from the doorway.

'So talk. I'll be the judge of whether or not we let her loose on you.'

'You are a callous bastard, even for a Brit.' His head slumps and then he mumbles, 'Old Padraic told me that the parents were Israeli ministers. He has some idea to bring a peace accord to the Middle East. I'm just to make sure that the parties talk.'

'Who else is involved?'

'No-one.'

'I'll count to ten … but I want to know at least about your wife, Val. Where is she?'

McSweeney snarls. 'I don't know. I've been here in Croatia … dodging any chance that I'd bump into that harridan outside.'

'Where is Sean?'

'Sean?'

'Your other son … Sean. Come on, Michael. I probably don't have the patience of the old *Cat Pack*.'

'He'll be with Padraic. Looking after him while I am here.'

'And Macan Granić?'

'The same, eventually. They were picking up another hostage somewhere. I don't know where … to make sure that the Brit PM danced to the right tune.'

'And Mahmoud Maziq?'

'Fuck! You've known this all along.'

'Like Donnie used to say. There's an easy way and a hard way, but it all comes out in the end.'

'They'll all be together.'

'Where?'

'In Switzerland. Near to Jacques Jazy. He is going to him with the peace accord delivered. He's fucking mad … but he is still *An Cogar* and deserving of that respect.'

'So where are they?'

'I don't have the bloody address. It's in Switzerland, for fuck's sake.'

'How do you get there?'

He gasps a huge sigh. 'Hold it. What happens from here?'

'You've been co-operative, Michael. I'm not the prosecution but I'll tell the police you have been co-operative … and you'll still have your own skin …' Sam smiles weakly again.

McSweeney shudders and speaks quietly. 'There's a town called Vevey on a lake. You get there by electric train. I know how to drive to their place from the station. It's one of those chalet things but I can't describe how to get there. I'm a doer, not a dreamer.'

'Draw a map.' And Sam produces a notepad from the corner of the room … and a pencil. 'Left or right handed?'

'Right.'

'I'm going to untie your right hand. Don't even think of doing anything stupid or I'll beat so many colours out of you, you'll wish you were with Mother Granić.'

McSweeney gives an evil sneer but can't hold it.

'You might be tough, Michael. But you're old, and out of condition. I'm young. Just saying …' He shrugs. 'How do you contact *An Cogar*, Michael?'

'I don't.'

'How does he know that everything is sweet here in Croatia?'

'Are you starting to worry, soldier boy?' McSweeney scribbles his map with his pencil while Sam stays out of attack range from any errant pencil. 'There's to be some advert in the media from the Brits. That'll confirm that the Israelis have accepted.'

'Then what?'

'We will release the hostages.'

'How will you know?'

'We will watch the news … a big red flare flying up over Switzerland. What the hell do you think? On the phone. That copper took my mobile. Padraic will ring or text. Fuck all this! You'd better be telling me it straight. Am I still right for the plea bargain? This map is the best I can do.'

'Drop it on the floor.'

'You're not very trusting, old SAS man, now are you?'

'That's why I'm standing here … and you're sitting there. We'll check that this is correct. And then I'll hand you over to the tender care of the Dubrovnik police.'

Chapter 56

July, 2013. Over the Mediterranean

It had been a hard *au revoir*.

For all Sam's pledges of *I'll be back* and *This is not goodbye*, it had been a difficult parting for both Ivana and him at Dubrovnik airport, after such a brilliant few days. But IIB had sent a private jet to fly him from Croatia to Geneva direct. That part wasn't a matter of argument.

En route over Italy, he is catching up on Nils's downloaded concise confidential IIB summary about the developments in Israel and Heidelberg – men attacking the aquifer, now caught and being interviewed by the Israeli Defence Force; a British cabinet minister's son kidnapped in a German town, as leverage to facilitate message sharing.

As well, linked in to the plane's wifi, Sam is tracking as much background as he can about the Lake Geneva area on his smart phone – tourist attractions, land use, even the bird life – and on through to the news in the rest of the world, scrolling through the websites of the print media. So much for phone signals interfering with a jet's navigation system.

A quirky anecdote catches his attention: *Israeli hydrologists will conduct a study of Loch Ness to solve at last the mystery of the famous monster.*

'Hardly bloody likely,' he shouts at his empty passenger cabin. 'They'll all be too busy chasing down the monster who was drilling holes into their aquifers.'

281

He is still pondering all the scenarios as the plane swoops over Lake Geneva – or Lac Leman as the people at IIB are always calling it – to land at the airport.

Still taxiing in, he feels a vibration in his pocket. It is Michael McSweeney's mobile – signed over to him by the Dubrovnik police so that IIB could do further analysis into tying up the loose ends of the Hennessy network.

He stares at the phone screen. It actually reads that it is a text message from *An Cogar*. Amazing! The message is: *Israel agrees. Free the women and return to base.*

* * * *

He is met by Emma Jazy, looking as efficient and professional as ever, while not losing anything in her ability to be attractive company.

'Electric train to Vevey. There's a Volkswagen hire car waiting in your name at the station. All the usual gear is in the trunk. Good luck!'

* * * *

July 2013. Geneva, Switzerland

The little boy looks at the browny-pink building.

The smiling lady stands with him in the entrance way. The other ladies have dropped him off from the car. Not the yellow car. Where is the pretty yellow car?

It has been a blur.

The train station … all these fast white electric trains with the red flashes … the park … Vermong, the lady called it. Now here … Shemong Looee Doonong. Why do they speak so funny?

Nanny used to read *Alice through the Looking Glass* to him. That made him see such weird and colourful images too. Dreams. Mad. This is the same.

'You go up to the third floor in the lift,' the smiling lady is saying. 'Here, I'll press the buttons for you.' And she does, in the lift with him. 'You just walk through the door and say, *I am Peter Cowdrey and I have lost my mother.* And you hand over this note.'

She is smiling again … such a nice person, beautiful olive-coloured skin, always happy … so much better than that grumpy older woman. That one reminded him of Granny Cowdrey. She is a real moaner … old, wrinkled and complaining … but Mother always insists that he be ever so polite to her. 'Manners', she would say. 'Manners, Peter.'

This is all so much like a whirling rainbow … so confusing. He doesn't even know if he wants to find his mother. She is just so picky … always correcting … always rushing him. It really is a relief to get away to school most times … just for the peace … to be left alone … without criticism.

The lady is nudging him out of the lift. 'Through that door. Just tell them that you are Peter Cowdrey. You need help to find your mother. It's been fun, Peter. Hasn't it?'

And he nods. It *has* been fun. The yellow car. The whizzing around.

The laughing lady kisses him and the lift door closes. Why is he so dizzy and befuddled? Alice was like that in the story.

He walks through the door, like another child going through her looking glass, and he announces in a voice to be heard, 'I am Peter Cowdrey and I need to find my mother.'

The people in the room just stare at him but he holds out his note … and, as they read, the puzzled expressions seem to change to hurrying. It makes them pick up phones.

Chapter 57

July, 2013. Rotterdam, The Netherlands

Arthur, Sven and Nils are huddled over Michael McSweeney's scanned map, while Nils tries to match it with Google Earth.

'It's hard to judge. It could be any one of five chalets – all reasonably isolated from each other, given that it is in fairly densely-populated Switzerland. He's not much of a cartographer.'

Sven smiles despite the tension, 'Try it some time, Nils – one handed, balancing a page on your knee while the rest of you is tied to a wooden chair. Would you like to test the theory? Happy to tie you up.'

The operations manager gives a conceding grin, 'Alright. I'm just trying to help you find the right place.'

'Sam is on his way there now. He heard the detail of what McSweeney said about the house; and the route. Let's leave him to establish the correct location. Now, update us on this developing Cowdrey story.'

'Yes.' Houweling scans over another screen. 'Yes, well. It was only an hour ago that a dazed-looking Peter Cowdrey walked into the Commonwealth Small States Office on Chemin Louis-Dunant in Geneva – the third floor, mind you. He had come up in the lift, said who he was and that he was looking for his mother. He carried a note – written again in brilliant calligraphy – which gave the names of his parents, their hotel in Heidelberg and even the German police number ... in Heidelberg. Someone certainly wanted him to be found quickly.'

Arthur nods thoughtfully. 'So, it seems. And Sam's update?'

'Yes. He was carrying Michael McSweeney's mobile back for us, on the plane, when he got a text from *An Cogar* himself authorising the release of the Dubrovnik women. He reads into the message that the Israelis have already agreed to Hennessy's terms. The Loch Ness story must have been correct, after all. Bizarre! And what does *agreeing* really mean? There must be a lot happening behind the scenes that we don't know about.'

'More than likely. Thanks, Nils. And you, Sven?' Arthur asks.

'*Mossad* is saying nothing; neither confirming nor denying. But Sam's hypothesis seems to fit what we know, so far.'

'And London. Nils? Anything out of there?'

'Yes, they confirm very quietly that Peter Cowdrey has been located. Consular officials are in the process of returning him to his parents. He appears to be unharmed physically – but he is rambling, almost hallucinating.'

'Drugged,' Arthur suggests. 'No use for ID. Just one confused boy who can't remember anything really useful at all. Certainly not admissible. They are cunning, this lot.'

The methodical Nils is working through his checklists. 'We have the hostages released. We don't know if the Israelis have found the second drill hole. Sam should have reached Vevey by now. Emma is on the trail of Mahmoud Maziq and that team. Gunnar and Gaston are on stand by. We have to be quite well positioned to close the net on Padraic Hennessy now. Don't you think?'

Arthur Blair gives the smile of a man who never counted his chickens before he actually has them. 'Except that Padraic Hennessy has survived nets that were tighter than ours ... and he is still here causing mischief after seventy-eight years on the planet.'

Chapter 58

July, 2013. Behind Vevey, Switzerland

The Volkswagon hire car has been waiting for Sam, just as Emma described. He straps on his familiar gear from the trunk – particularly the snug-fitting SIG pistol and the sheathed knife.

Carefully and slowly, he drives his way north up the slope, in the morning sunshine, ignoring the startlingly beautiful lake behind him.

McSweeney's map is spread out on the passenger seat but the Irishman's sense of scale matches little on the ground. Sam tries to fit any key features from the map – the scratchy pencilled river, rough road bends – with what he can see in front of him. The real view is tree-lined river courses, white-walled houses and red roofs, statues, churches, freeways, railways, terraced vineyards …

He is out of the main town, amongst intensely green fields, fir and pine trees … and crisp clean air.

He checks in with Emma on his mobile, giving his GPS location and general direction. For her part, she tells him she has just left a meeting with the French trackers in Geneva; and that Michael McSweeney's mobile is being securely couriered to Maasboulevard to start the forensic analysis of the gang's call chain.

It seems from the French information that, since the boy has been returned, the snatch group has split up. Val McSweeney is heading back to the Geneva railway station with the two other women. Maziq and the other man had apparently headed out the day before, in a car going generally east. Emma intends to follow the trail of those men, as were the French already.

They had placed a spotter in wait at Lausanne but the car has not arrived … or, at least, it has not been seen there. The trail of the two men appears to have been lost somewhere around that large city. Meanwhile, Gaston Mimoun's team has been delegated to cover the women's departure and to relay the information on, before following Emma and Sam.

All the strands of the chase are methodically moving into action, with nervous anticipation reaching high performance level.

* * * *

Sam checks his map and studies the chalet again. It looks as if it could, and should, be the one McSweeney described back in Dubrovnik, especially in the supplementary descriptions he had given Sam after the scanned map had been checked for general authenticity. This house fitted the colour and position – the fields, the trees – pretty much as he said.

It is set back, across a field.

He texts the GPS co-ordinates to Nils in Rotterdam and to Emma's mobile. Then, with the adrenalin starting to rise again, he checks his gear; ever careful; weapons, camera, mini-scope, GPS, secure phone on silent. No other identifying or incriminating evidence on him. To all intents and purposes, he is a wind-jacketed bushwalker out for a stroll.

He tucks the car key into the exhaust pipe and starts to circle through the trees, with the practice of years guiding his muscle memory.

* * * *

A peaceful morning. He scans the building through his mini-telescope from the security of the tree line. Dairy cattle graze peacefully on the thick green sward. The sun seems fresher with the altitude. A bird soars high in the blue sky. A black kite, if he remembers his research from the plane correctly.

It is then that a man walks out onto the verandah. He is in the shadows, moving around briskly. Sam's scope tracks him until he steps into a patch of sunlight.

He has red hair, well-built, in his thirties, at a guess. He has to be the elusive trainer of the crawling men from Cyprus, Michael and Val McSweeney's son, Sean.

Methodically, Sam crafts a text describing his find and the GPS location. He beams them to both Nils and Emma.

* * * *

It has taken an hour to crawl and sidle his way closer to the house; checking all the way for trip wires, signs of electronic surveillance and farm animals which might bark or honk away his presence.

But it has been quiet.

Only the one man has been seen. He seems to be getting on with his business, walking in and out of the chalet, doing chores – seemingly unsuspecting of anyone watching.

Sam has moved to within only a few metres from the house – closer into the shade which is cast by the sprawling chalet roof, when … a powerful force grips him from behind and, in the split-second of potential reaction time, a knife is digging into his neck.

He has been around enough Croatian speakers in the past few days to understand the gist of the growled command – which is that he should not resist or he will be dead.

His captor nudges him forward, the knife edge definitely breaking through the skin. He can sense his blood trickle. The voice from close behind his head shouts, 'Sean' … and the red-head turns to look.

* * * *

Sam sits in the heavy wooden chair, secured to its frame by velcro straps around his legs and with his arms pinioned separately and painfully behind the chair back. His neck feels wet where the blood from the cut is starting to congeal. He pretends to be dazed by his rough treatment. He can feel a bruise starting to develop at the back of his head where he had been hit with something heavy.

His captor with the pale distinctive face and Croatian language remains behind him, as the red-headed Sean methodically goes through all of his possessions on a card table to the front.

Sam looks slowly up into the high beams supporting the roof. The varnished timbers are lit by the ambient outside sunlight from the verandahs. It is an airy modern chalet, but in a style harking back to centuries ago.

Shaking his head to give the impression of clearing his thoughts, Sam protests. 'Hey, you! You, with all my gear. Let me go! I am an innocent birdwatcher. Why am I being manhandled, bashed, cut up and now tied up?'

A hard object thumps into the side of his head from behind.

There is no other response. Sam winces and sits quietly.

Sean McSweeney mutters as he holds the SIG pistol, turning it lovingly in his hand. He peers at the mobile with its disguised address book and phone list. It would pass muster for a routine glance, but there hadn't been time to set everything recent into dummy codes. Text messages would come up blank without a password. The phone log was cleared routinely to remote archive every couple of days. Sam thanked his foresight to clear the photo gallery before he left Dubrovnik or Sean McSweeney would now be looking at a photo of his father in Kuna Konovoska and the police mug shot of Macan Granić.

Nevertheless, the red-head is freezing at something. Has he seen a particular number – possibly a Dubrovnik one that Sam has missed? It may have been the hotel. Neither Ivana's nor Luka's direct numbers are there. They were memorised. But an area code – perhaps that is it? A code might be identifiable for someone who could recognise a Croatian area prefix. It would have been a routine call, checking on something – nothing critical. He remembers … a jeweller in the *Stari Grad*, just checking for a possible gift for a kind friend.

And McSweeney turns.

'Who *are* you?'

'I really must protest at this horrendous treatment. You cannot treat innocent people like this. It is against the law.'

'Innocent, eh? Who *are* you?'

'The name's Sam.'

'Who are you, Sam? Why are you here? Why do you carry weapons and scopes?'

'You can't be too careful these days. I'm a twitcher,' he answers, his brain trying to react as quickly as possible to the emerging situation. 'I am spotting birds.'

'Are you Swiss?'

'No, just a tourist from Britain, from Dorset actually – a little place called Swanage.' The adrenalin is freeing up his imagination – a little bit of truth mixed with distracting fantasy. 'Lovely chalk cliffs ... on the south coast ...'

Sam's prattle is interrupted by a soft Irish voice, almost a whisper, 'I think you are a liar, Sam.' It is coming from the shadows at the side; and the sound of the voice sends the adrenalin shooting through Sam's body.

An old man with floppy white hair limps slowly into his vision. He has entered very quietly, watching almost quizzically. He wears a loose dark jacket, open-necked checked shirt, baggy grey trousers and new running shoes. Sam is in no doubt as to the old man's identity. The reputed dark curls of his youth have certainly gone, perhaps along with a cherished spring in his step.

He whispers again in a soft Irish accent. 'You are as military as I have ever seen. And I've seen a few over the years. British military, I'm guessing. SAS? Eh?'

'No. You have me wrong.' Sam tries his best innocent English prattle. 'I did serve in my twenties. Devon and Dorsets actually – bloody amalgamated into The Rifles Regiment now. Is nothing sacred? But no, no! I'm in I.T. now. Live in Amsterdam. Technology solutions. Information. And bird watching. That's my bag here.'

The old man points to a bird that has just perched on the verandah rail, 'So what's that bird?'

'A nuthatch,' Sam answers in a flash, surprising himself with his rapid response. Danger can give an amazing jolt to quicken reaction time, he is thinking. 'Some people confuse it with a pale chaffinch but not the same genus. No, not at all.'

The old man gives a slow smile. 'Alright, Military Man. You and me, we are going to have a frank chat. And if I don't like your answers, I may well have to kill you. You see, I'm always honest and straight. You get no lies from me. I always say it as it is. So don't give me any bullshit. I don't have time for that. As you can see, I'm nearer the end of my days than the beginning. Don't insult my intelligence. You're no more a twitcher than I am. I know your Hereford SAS training. Hold out as long as you can. Feed them a little bit of information at a time. Well, Sam – what's your second name, by the way? – that lying stuff won't work with me. You'll be dead, if you try that on.'

'Hall. My second name is Hall.'

'And who am I?'

'I'm guessing you are a man known as *The Cougar*.'

'Well done. You've just gained a life. Honesty is always the best policy, you see. And why are you here?'

'Apart from being a genuine twitcher, looking for new birds' – never let all the cover story be taken away – 'I'm an investigator. There is something going on with the Israelis at the moment; something to do with the peace process.'

'And how do you know that, Mr Sam Hall?'

'Because there has been chatter – the bloggers. I deal in IT. I pick up the waves. There has been a fear around. I have a spotter in Tel Aviv who tells me four men were arrested near the Sea of Galilee and the Israeli Defence Force has been scouring the valley to the west of the Golan Heights.'

'And what are they looking for?'

'That I don't know. Not likely to be a bomb, I wouldn't think. But I don't know. My spy tells me that the captured ones all use cat names, like Panther and Tiger. That their boss is called Puma and the big boss is *Cougar*. That, I imagine, is *you*.'

The old man breaks into a weak grin, which morphs into a wheezy laugh. 'You would have to be one of the most fluent liars I've ever met, Sam Hall. They really did train you well. But perhaps not well enough. You'd almost have me believing that you are *Mossad*, with your insider intel, eh? So this spotter you have. Who is he?'

'A student of the Middle East. He's really there trying to get a handle on Syria; and now, in the last couple of days, Egypt. Aren't things changing there fast? Israel is usually just boring. The run-of-the-mill stuff – but a lot of rockets have been coming over from Syria and Lebanon in the past few days. That's not so usual. The journalist in him started looking for answers because it seemed like a distraction for something else. That's when he heard about the *cat people* being arrested.'

The old man smiles weakly again. 'Cat people, eh? But it doesn't explain how he found out this information from a secure Israeli interrogation. Now, does it?'

'There are moles everywhere. You don't want to believe the Israeli propaganda. Money. Disenchantment. I don't know his source. So, is it correct?'

The old man flicks back his white hair and laughs, almost loud, this time. He looks over to Sean McSweeney. 'Can you believe this man, Sean? And now he wants to be the interrogator. Mr Investigator, do you know my real name? And remember what I said about honesty.'

'I think you are Padraic Hennessy – a revered Provisional IRA commander from years ago and sometime mercenary for other revolutionary causes.'

'Wow! Wow! You're better than anything I ever saw out of Hereford. And bold too. Indeed, you are right. So, Sam Hall, how would you be knowing all of that?'

'My journalist contact in Israel. He's really based in Beirut, in the Lebanon.' Sam's brain is working overtime. His life depends on it. Recovering gems of information from his memory bank and fitting them into this conversation without any of it showing on his face – gaining time. 'He's a student of the history of that time – the revolution, the arms runs from Libya. He did a profile on people from that era, people that his father had known. And one of those was a Maureen Jazy, who also had been known as Gallaher. And the word was that she was the illegitimate daughter of an IRA commander called Padraic Hennessy or … *The Cougar.*'

Hennessy's recoils, his shoulders tense and his eyes drill through Sam, with a burning ferocity. He breathes in slowly and deeply. But Hall continues, trying to rattle the old man's composure, to give himself more seconds – and, for the others who know where he is.

'And there's more. That Maureen was killed by Hennessy.'

'Wha…at?' The eyes glare and a growl starts deep in the Irishman's chest.

'When she returned to fight for *the cause*. That he murdered her, his own daughter, and buried her in a shingle grave where she came ashore.'

The guttural rumble is intense at the back of Hennessy's throat. 'Lies. All fucken *Praatestant* lies. She was my dearest. The fruit of a love so dear, so precious …' The voice rises in a wheezy cadence to a harsh loud croak. 'She was murdered by a loyalist *bamb* in Dublin.' He wipes some sweat from his brow … and the voice returns to a slow whisper. 'But, for sure, you knew all that already, Sam Hall. And I'm wondering how you could know all these things – from a time before you were even born? Who is your source in Lebanon?'

'The son of Maureen Jazy and Bill Maclean. Maclean was a British agent and the partner of your daughter.'

'She had a son?' His shock takes several seconds to subside. 'It couldn't be. It couldn't be that Maeve's daughter had a son and she didn't tell me over those months in Ireland.'

'It's only what I heard.'

Hennessy suddenly looks startled – his eyes show that he is listening to peripheral sound. Chickens outside have changed from gentle clucking to a cacophony of loud agitated squawking. By reflex, his hand goes to his jacket pocket and the shape of gun strains against the material.

'Macan, get out and about again. What is spooking those birds?'

The big Croatian moves quickly onto the verandah and disappears, gun in his right hand, his left hand tapping the big knife in its sheath – as Hennessy starts into a slow limping pace; circling, head cocked.

'I do sense something.' The Irishman's voice seems different – distant, confused. He is talking distractedly, as if to some spirit in the room; he is glancing up into the rafters like a Shakespearean actor in soliloquy. 'Maybe it is just the way this Sam Hall has turned up like he has. Or,' he forces a chortle and the attention comes back into focus, 'maybe it's just the chicken birds coming to see the twitcher.'

And then he turns back to face Sam Hall …

Chapter 59

July, 2013. Rotterdam, The Netherlands

'The Swiss police have detained several women in Geneva,' Nils announces. 'That decision is based on information supplied by Gaston Mimoun and endorsed by the French state intelligence service. It's only a twenty-four-hour holding warrant, so that they can question them in relation to Peter Cowdrey's abduction.'

'Do we know who they are?' Sven asks.

'Two Arab-looking women, but travelling on Croatian passports, and one other older person, travelling on an Irish passport. That's what my briefing message reads.'

'That could be Val McSweeney with the Cavtat women,' suggests Arthur.

'Oh,' Nils adds. 'And Gaston has sent another note to say that the younger women are stunning lookers and fit too; like aerobics instructors.'

'Trust the Belgian to get fixated on their looks.' Sven shakes his head in mock despair. 'Any men detained?'

'No information about that.'

'Mmm. But what we have could tally with the women from Gaddafi's guard,' Arthur notes. 'What else? From you, Sven?'

The Swede returns to briefing mode. 'The Israelis say they are still interviewing five people in Tel Aviv. They are the four intercepted near the Sea of Galilee and the one detained trying to enter at TLV International … but they have no information that they want to share with us yet.'

'Alright. Nils? What about Sam?'

'Sam has sent in a GPS location for the possible chalet location outside Vevey. Emma is heading to that spot as we speak. Gaston and his team won't be far behind, by now.'

'And Hennessy? Is he located?'

'No information,' replies Nils.

'We might assume, however,' suggests Sven, 'that the old Irishman is at the Vevey chalet. That would be logical. And further, since no *men* were picked up by the Geneva police, that Maziq and Granić would be either there or heading there.'

'Pure speculation,' responds Houweling. 'There is no evidence to support that hypothesis.'

'Agreed,' replies Sven, 'and while we are at it, I would suggest that Sean Hennessy would also be there.'

Nils shrugs with open palms. 'I work only with evidence.'

Chapter 60

July 2013. Vevey, Switzerland

'Now, Mr Sam Hall, back to your lies about Maureen Gallaher and the British agent, Maclean, with the grandson we both know I never had.' The quiet Irish lilt continues. 'You're an interesting one, that's to be sure. To know about the grave on that Donegal beach ... as well as all the other bits. I think you might be higher up that secret service chain than even James Bond was. What do you think, Sean?'

He turns to look at the red-head, who still stands by the card table, trying to find useful links in Sam's smart phone.

'Maybe,' Sean replies. 'This is an interesting mobile for a twitcher. What's this Dutch number?'

'I told you,' Sam answers. 'I'm in Information Technology in Amsterdam. That's the business number – really just a messaging relay. You'd hardly ever get through to the company direct.'

Hennessy's eyes narrow at the comment. 'And why would that be?'

'We are all coders, program writers. You can't be interrupted in that sort of work. You'd lose the whole train of thought.'

At that point, another man enters the room, an older man, sleeves rolled up looking dishevelled and distracted. Dark tones to his skin, white hair circling over his ears and below his bald crown ... and he is staring down at a sheet of thick cream-coloured paper as he walks in the door, saying, 'What do you think of this, Mr Hennessy?'

Hennessy gives a quick glance at the newcomer and then looks back at the captive, Sam Hall. 'Now what were you saying about interruptions? I'll need to come back to you, the mystery IT man from Amsterdam and Dorset who knows Maclean and Maureen's son in the Lebanon.' He gives an evil grin before turning to command quietly, 'Maziq, bring it over here.'

Sam watches the elderly olive-skinned man continue his walk across the polished wooden floor. He can see the fingers stained with ink and that it is actually parchment that is being carried. It looks heavy duty, stiff ... like thin cardboard.

'Highest-quality vellum, this is, Mr Hall,' the old Irishman's eyes glow with pride, 'for a document to be treasured as *the* peace accord of the past thousand years.' Hennessy peers at the title and the first few lines, while nodding his satisfaction. 'Now, take Mr Maziq here,' and he flicks his glance from the old man and back at his prisoner again, just to check that he is being understood. 'He is the best calligrapher on the planet. Aren't you, Mr Maziq? One of Libya's finer exports. Just making some finishing artistic touches.'

Mr Maziq gives a tolerant smile and waits for further comment.

Hennessy stares again as he turns the parchment towards Sam, showing the lavishly-coloured title clearly, *Peace Agreement for Israel, Palestine and surrounding nations. 2013.* This is followed by, *We, the undersigned parties, solemnly agree and commit ...*

The Irishman's fingers shake gently as he speaks to his captive again. 'By tomorrow – in Geneva, July 2013, Mr Sam Hall. Mark the historic time. See?' He points to what appears to be Arabic writing – like signatures, perhaps a dozen of them – on the lower part of the scroll. 'Mark my words – there will be Hebrew writing here too; to make up the complete twenty signatures at the bottom of this document, guaranteeing a two-state solution to the arguments over the Middle East which have gone on for thousands of years; since as far back as stories have been passed down.

'I have the verbal agreement of the Israelis now, to join the Palestinians and most of the influential Arab leaders in these troubled lands.' Hennessy draws his old finger down the line of signed writing. 'The Prime Minister of Israel will be flying into Geneva tomorrow along with the British PM. Some friends of ours, and Mr Maziq with his particular expertise, will ensure that their signatures complete the deal. All the principles of the accord have been established, even if a little duress has had to be applied on occasion … and with only some minor details to be finally confirmed. Then, at last, the oppression of the disadvantaged will be over … and the quest of the two most important women in my life will be signed off. And do you know who they were, Mr Hall?'

Sam sits silent, as Maziq's face shows a tolerant patience.

Hennessy draws his head up, straightening himself from his old man stoop, and announces, 'Maeve Gallaher and Maureen Gallaher. The mother of my child … and the actual child that you have tried to accuse me of having murdered. You nearly had me believing some of your story, till that …'

A gunshot splits the air outside.

A male voice is shouting.

Sean McSweeney moves with speed to protect *An Cogar*, standing between him and any danger from the verandah.

'No time for that, Sean.' Even under such a threat, his voice is remarkably quiet. 'This place is compromised now. This twitcher … and now something or someone outside. Get the vehicles to the front. Maziq and me in the first one. Macan in the back-up – covering at a distance in case we are followed. Maziq, help me outside.' The two older men shuffle and limp to the door, the Libyan holding his parchment carefully and grabbing a picture folder as he leaves.

At the door, Hennessy turns to look at the still-trussed Sam Hall. 'You were good, Military Man. Better than most. And you have witnessed the start of history being made; but,' … he points back at the IIB agent's head … 'you should never tell lies, especially about my daughter. C'mon. Maziq.'

With the room empty, Sam starts sliding his chair towards the card table where all his gear still sits.

He hears a vehicle leave. It might even have been two vehicles. There is no more shouting from outside.

With his teeth, he grasps the sheathed knife from the table-top and tries to manoeuvre it to a position where he can extract the blade – when a voice interrupts.

'You might have amused the old man but you have not amused me.'

As Sam turns his head quickly, he can feel the blood flow freely from his neck-cut again … and he looks into the face of Sean McSweeney, who clearly didn't leave with others in their two cars.

'So now that the others are all gone, tell me what have you done with my father?'

Chapter 61

July, 2013. Vevey, Switzerland

Emma Jazy watches two vehicles leave – gone before she can get close to the chalet – the occupants spooked by a fox.

She had been heading for the GPS location to back up Sam Hall.

Approaching silently and observing from the tree line, it had all looked and sounded peaceful. She had watched the fox creep stealthily over an open green field towards the chicken coop, edging nearer to a few birds that were clucking and feeding outside the netting of their shelter.

She had smiled as she watched one hen dip low, strain to compress its feathers and force its way through the small flap door to get to the safety inside – a bolt hole from any danger. And the fox had crept closer and closer. Eventually the red-brown predator had sprung forward and grabbed a hen by the throat. The fox leapt towards the protection of a rhododendron bush, accompanied by a terrified squawking and screeching as the outside birds tried to force their way back through the tiny gate into the netted pen.

A large man had appeared on the verandah, a pistol in his right hand. Emma had watched him move, crouching in attack mode, looking for any source of danger. His pale face was jerking from side to side as he scanned the area around the rustling from the bush. The captured hen was making no sound. But a branch moved as the fox tried to escape with its prey.

The single shot from the pale-face's pistol sliced through the air – and nothing moved again in the rhododendron bush.

The large man shouted to those inside, in a language Emma couldn't follow. Then he stalked carefully down from the verandah, quietly covering the space to the pink flowers of the shrub.

Emma had watched, wary; ready.

A call came from inside the chalet. The sound of cars engines starting came from the other side of the house – the front where the driveway exits to the bitumen road.

The pale-face turned, apparently satisfied, and ran around the house towards the revving car sound.

Suddenly, vehicle engines roared.

Emma caught a quick glimpse of two vehicles on the drive as they headed out to the open road.

* * * *

The sounds gradually fade away. A frightened gentle clucking comes intermittently from the chicken coop.

Now, Emma moves stealthily towards the base of the verandah steps – pistol drawn – and she starts to climb.

Chapter 62

July, 2013. Vevey, Switzerland

Sean McSweeney's voice is as quiet as Hennessy's had been.

'You've been to Dubrovnik. There's a number on your mobile. You've probably come straight here from Dubrovnik. My father isn't answering his phone. What have you done with him?'

Caught as he is at the card table, struggling with the sheathed knife in his mouth, Sam drops the weapon to ask, 'Who is your father?'

McSweeney grabs the back of Sam's chair, slides it across the polished floor with force and then tips it heavily onto its back, pinning his victim's arms painfully under his own weight.

'Don't fuck with me, Sam Hall. I'm not the old man. My father is Michael McSweeney and he was in Dubrovnik. You have a Dubrovnik number in your mobile. Two and two usually make four. What have you done with my father?'

'Sorry. I phoned Croatia to talk to a friend of my employer ...'

McSweeney is kneeling over his captive. He drives a big fist into the side of Sam's jaw. 'Well? Try again.'

Sam can smell McSweeney's breath, he is so close. 'I don't know your father.'

The red-head rises, walks over to the card table and unsheathes the knife. 'I saw a man extract all sorts of information only a week or so ago. It's amazing what can be done with a knife.' He moves to stand over the fallen Sam Hall, knife in hand. 'I think we'll start with the blade into the knee joint ... and twisted around. There's lots back in my homeland from the old days, who will for evermore walk with a limp. They should just have spoken when given the chance. Don't be a hero, SAS man.'

As he draws the knife back to stab, a single pistol shot rings out.

McSweeney screams and grabs at his right shoulder. His knees buckle under him and the knife clangs to the wooden floor from his paralysed right arm.

Emma Jazy covers the metres from the verandah to the wounded man in seconds, to knock him unconscious with a hard blow from her pistol.

* * * *

Five minutes have passed. Sean McSweeney now sits, unconscious, trussed in the heavy wooden chair, a bloodied towel wound tightly around his damaged shoulder.

Sam Hall sits facing him on a reversed chair, rubbing his hands and forearms where they have been bruised from being pinned under his own weight, earlier.

Emma Jazy is texting furiously through to Nils Houweling and to Gaston Mimoun.

Sean McSweeney winces and moans as the pain from his shoulder and his head bring him slowly back to consciousness.

'Not much fun, back in the hot seat, eh?' Hall whispers at his quarry. 'Time for you to talk, Sean.'

'Fuck off!'

'You know that's just what your father said to me ... but he changed his mind pretty quickly. Oh, and he is alive and well in Croatia, helping the police with their enquiries, as you will be too, depending on whether I decide to stay within the law or just say ... bugger it, like you and Hennessy have been doing. What do you think, Sean? Are you going to talk?'

Emma Jazy walks over, takes a picture of the captive with the camera on her webbing. She points at the small lens. 'We are recording your conversation, Sean. It is your only chance for mitigation

– like your mother got after the Red Army Faction business. She got out of jail after a time and carried on with her life. You are young. Think about it.'

McSweeney sits grimacing.

'You need medical attention, Sean,' Emma continues. 'You won't get it from us. I'm afraid that my big blond colleague here is more than a little pissed off at the treatment he has received. He's just as likely to spend an hour or two squeezing that shoulder of yours.'

The Irishman glowers at his captors while failing to conceal the wincing pain he is feeling from the shock of the gunshot.

Sam Hall takes over. 'The Israeli Defence Force has captured five people that they suspect might have been trying to poison an aquifer. They tell them that a red-headed man known as *Puma* was their boss – but he got away. In my opinion, he bailed out and left them to their fate; that might be more like it.

'Sean, I think you are *Puma*. I want you to tell me the GPS location of the final drill site before the Israelis squeeze it out of your crawling men team. There will be no mitigation if they tell before *you* do? What's it to be?'

McSweeney continues to scowl as Emma returns to the questioning, 'The Geneva police have arrested your mother, Val McSweeney – formerly Waltraud Muller – and a couple of other women involved in abducting the son of a British cabinet minister.'

Sam adds, 'Your father, Michael, is under arrest – with others – for kidnapping the teenage daughters of two Israeli cabinet ministers. Your five men in Israel are in custody. It's over, Sean. Are you getting that message? The Israelis will find out the location of the second drill hole, eventually. You know they will. And if you haven't told us, you will be hung out to dry – no sympathy, no amnesty. The Israelis won't make concessions like the British did in Ireland. They will see you rot … and I mean, *rot*. In solitary. No communication. Just gone to the rest of the world – but not to you; you won't be gone; you will still be there, bored and lonely, in your solitary cell … just thinking and rotting.'

The prisoner glares some more.

Emma returns to the fray. 'Now Sean, you might think *the cause* has been worthwhile, that Padraic has achieved *peace in our time* for the Middle East. But that's not the case. He's delusional – you know that – an old man tortured by the guilt from his past. Do you really want to wake up in a prison cell – years from now – realising that it was all for nothing? That you held the line, but the line was just an illusion?

'And you might think that you can hold out for more time – that Padraic and the others are away free. They're not. They're being tracked by two teams of former special forces people. I'd say they might be free for another half hour or so, at best. And, in that time, I'm expecting the Swiss police to arrive here. When that happens, we just hand you over and the history books can write about what happened to the red-headed patriot – sorry, *idiot* – who thought it was better to hold out than tell what he knew.'

'I'm saying nothing.'

'Sean.' Sam's voice is as gentle as a whisper. 'There was a man in Cyprus called Bashir Dorda who had his hands sawn off by the sharp serrated edge of a big knife until he divulged the location of the aquifer access that your team has used. Another Greek resistance man, Nikkos, had his thighs and biceps sliced so that he bled to death in much the same position that you are in now – very, very painful. We have testimony that it was *you*, Sean McSweeney, who killed both of these men. You as much as admitted it to me earlier when you were going to give me a free knee cartilage removal. You are up for double murder, with malice.'

Suddenly, McSweeney's head rises. 'That was the fucking Croatian. He's mad. He did that.'

'Who is going to believe you, Sean? You give us nothing to help your case.'

'Fuck off!' And he sits sullen again.

'You know that Macan Granić is your stepbrother?' Sam queries. 'The man you have just called *the fucking Croatian*.'

'What? Fuck off!' He shakes his head in an effort to clear his mind.

'It's true, Sean. Your father was in Dubrovnik off and on from 1991 to 1993, running armaments to the Croatians in their Independence War, probably with Mr Maziq's elder brother, as it happens.

'Michael McSweeney had his way with an attractive Croatian woman while he was there. I'm guessing it was pretty brutal and without her consent. Sanja Granić gave birth, nine months later. The baby grew up into a young man who was bullied all his young life because he had strange eyes and a pale-face that wouldn't tan … and he just looked odd with those large brown freckles and his dark hair. It should have been red hair like yours. Eh, Sean? It's cruel how genetics can work some times.

'Anyway, your father bailed out on Sanja too. A family trait, eh? Macan joined the gangs and was recruited by the *Cougar* mob to help them in Croatia and Cyprus. He's your brother, Sean. Does your own mother even know? Did Michael tell Waltraud?'

'Aaargh!' Sean struggles with his bonds until the excruciating pain in his shoulder pulls him up short.

'We could take DNA to prove it to you – just a bit of your hair. But Michael has already confessed. We have his voice recorded, admitting it, rather than face the vengeance of the woman he wronged all those years ago. Sanja is a very fiery woman – still alive in Dubrovnik and hurting bad from her hard life trying to bring up the man you call *the fucking Croatian*. Well, Sean? I can only give you a couple of minutes more. Then it's out of our hands.'

Sean shakes his head; not in defiance this time, but in bewilderment. He takes a few seconds as the IIB agents watch him make the connections about what has been said – what is on offer – and what his prospects for the future might be.

'Granić was the killer of Dorda,' he whispers, 'and the Greek called Nikkos. We didn't condone that. *He* did that. It was too late to stop him when we arrived. I'll testify to that in a court of law.' He pauses. 'There were others too, around Nicosia. Granić's job was to stand over them, to get them to rob and stay quiet about us.' He gives out a long sigh … and pauses. 'And I'll give you the GPS location for the second drill hole. You just make sure that you keep *your* fucking side of this bargain, you bastards.' And his head slumps forward in defeat, slowly shaking as he mutters, 'He can't be my fucking brother. He's a total arsehole.'

Emma smiles at Sam. 'There's an irony in that.'

Chapter 63

'That's brilliant information. Thanks Nils,' Sven assures his operations manager. 'I'll get that second GPS location through to our *Mossad* contact as we speak.' His fingers key in the number. He puts the phone to one ear and his finger in the other as he turns away to concentrate.

Arthur gives an appreciative nod to both of them. 'The team is doing well. And that was great work by Sam and Emma in Vevey. So, to the next phase. Hennessy, Granić and Maziq are presumably on their way to Montreux to the home of Jacques Jazy. Would that be right, Nils?'

'That's what all our evidence should indicate. But, not to worry, we have Gunnar and his men waiting. They'll take them out as soon as they appear.'

'No! No, Nils.' Blair is vehement in his objection. 'Our job is to get the admissible evidence for the court cases which will follow. That is *justice* – not the law of jungle warfare. Please confirm my earlier instructions with Gunnar that they are to let Hennessy and the others through – perimeter defence only. Tell Jacques Jazy and Martin, too, that Padraic and his men are on their way. We have the recording gear set up all through the house. They just have to start it when Hennessy comes in the door to seek his redemption.'

Houweling looks stunned at this development. 'But Sam and Emma will be in close pursuit – and Gaston's team not far behind.'

Nils says as he tries to rationalise his need to accept the instruction. 'We will have them bottled up with nowhere to go.' He shakes his head as if to clear foreign thoughts, unsuccessfully. 'You aren't serious. This could end badly.'

'Nils,' Arthur replies in a very definite, precise tone. 'Reaffirm my instructions to Gunnar, Jacques Jazy and Martin. Hennessy is to be allowed into the chalet and the recording gear activated.'

Houweling hesitates, as if he was about to refuse the instruction. 'I'll do it. But this is *your* decision, Arthur. I am just relaying it. I don't like it. I put that on the record. I don't like it. I trust that nothing will go wrong for Jacques and Martin.'

'Of course things can go wrong, Nils,' the calm Scottish voice replies. 'But that is what has to happen sometimes in the reality of our business – that the good guys have to stand up, or the bad guys continue to flourish. This is not a thriller novel. This is the real thing. We have to get evidence that will convict him in a court of law. Padraic Hennessy has had his charmed life long enough.'

Sven disconnects his phone with a huge grin, turns and refocuses on the other two in the room. 'The Israelis are off checking the information. If it is right, we will have favours galore from them, that we can call in, whenever. Are you two alright?' He looks at the concerned expression on Houweling's face.

'I'm fine,' Nils replies to Sven, stiffly, with a pointed look at Arthur. 'About to relay instructions to our team to hold back and let an acknowledged terrorist and murderer, Hennessy, get access to Jacques Jazy.' He does not look at all comfortable.

'Admissible evidence. That is the business of IIB. Isn't that right, Sven?'

'Absolutely. We are very close.'

Chapter 64

July, 2013. Outside Montreux, Switzerland

'Very trusting, Jacques. Very trusting indeed.'

The wily Padraic Hennessy, on his soft shoes, limps with Mahmoud Maziq into Jacques Jazy's chalet outside Montreux. The distinctive sound of Louis Armstrong's horn is filtering gently through the house's speaker system. 'Good music too. How thoughtful. Nostalgia is a very pleasant sensation at our age.' He twists his head around to check out the scene. 'I expected a phalanx of the Swiss Guard to be waiting for us.'

'Ah,' Jazy responds. 'So you must be Padraic; and you are confusing us with the Vatican. All Swiss people can, and do, guard our nation. We are *all* warriors in a way – part of the nation's defence. Anyway, you come in peace, do you not? And who is your companion?'

'I introduce Mahmoud Maziq, calligrapher of the highest order, who has drawn up the Middle East Peace Treaty for us, on quality parchment.'

'For us, Padraic? I don't think so. This is all about *you*.'

'Oh, Jacques, I wouldn't deny you a piece of the glory. We have the solution to a problem which was foisted on innocent others, by the oppression of imperial powers. This is about making something good happen while politicians dither in their wallow of compromise. We have achieved this, Jacques, with no fuss, no fanfare, no media hype – because it has been done in the memory of two of the

312

finest women to have walked this Earth. And, you and I, Jacques, loved them both – each in our own way. I will not leave you out of this acknowledgement. Mr Maziq, the scroll please.'

Maziq steps forward and slides the parchment out from the large art folder he has carried in. He spreads the strong vellum out on the table-top and anchors the edges while Jacques and his middle-aged son, Martin, look on.

'*Voilà!* My best French for you, Jacques. Here.'

Hennessy holds his hands out, upturned, to emphasise the magnificence of the document. 'The Israelis have agreed to sign. I have all the Arab peoples committed. See? Their official marks of endorsement. What do you think? My people will have the remaining key Hebrew signature in place tomorrow. The Prime Minister of Israel will be flying into Geneva to complete this arrangement, in front of a very credible witness – the Prime Minister of Britain, no less. Isn't that poetic? It's all set up – pledges given – with significant consequences for anyone who would even think of reneging. Mr Maziq will take this parchment back to Geneva tonight and my people, on the ground there, will ensure that it is signed. They know I'm a man of my word ... and that I have them *all* over a barrel. They will do it – no question – however unpalatable, because they can't take the risk not to.' His chilling humourless smile erases any doubt that he has unknown sanctions in place. 'Negotiation and diplomacy only ever work properly when the peacemakers have a healthy dose of coercion and intimidation hitting them in the ribs; to keep them on track, as it were.' His whispering laugh matches the crazy confidence in his eyes. 'To the rest of the world, it will just appear to happen ... quietly. But we will know what was really behind it ... and why ... on behalf of ... '

The new voice cuts through the air from behind the old Irishman 'I think you are mad, *An Cogar.*' It interrupts the long-prepared flow of impassioned rhetoric, but Hennessy doesn't turn to look immediately.

'Ah, Military Man. You surprise us again. I hope you haven't caused harm to young Sean. He was supposed to keep *you* out of action. You made good time to catch up with us.' Hennessy eventually turns slowly to look at Sam Hall. 'And who is this Amazon you have with you?'

'She is *my* daughter,' Jacques Jazy announces. 'Meet Emma Jazy.'

'You are right, Jacques. All Swiss must be warriors.' He bows to Emma. 'Pleased to meet the sister of the same home as Maureen Gallaher/Jazy. I see now how you got here so quickly. You already knew the way home. Come in. Come in. Both of you, while we old men talk.' He turns back again to the parchment on the table. 'Jacques, this peace accord is, in a small way, my penance for the many years of, and for, abandoning the mother of my child all those decades ago. I thought that when Maureen arrived in Donegal, I could start to right some of the wrongs finally. But the enemy's bomb destroyed all that in Dublin in 1974.'

Jazy steps towards him. 'You owe me nothing, Padraic. In Paris, I found a lovely young woman and a baby girl in need of help – and we shared some fine years together before cancer took one and the need to fight for *the cause – your* cause – took the other. But I married again, Padraic. Emma and Martin here are two fine products of that relationship with my second wife, the late Simone. There is a third child also, William, but he is not here just now. And *you* never married again, did you?'

The Irishman shakes his head. 'How could I? I'd never even married once. And I wasn't able to stand up and be counted when my girl was sent away to France. We were young. I didn't understand … and I think old Seamus Gallaher would have killed me if I had argued. He threatened to hang me from a fucken tree, he did. To strangle me slowly; to humiliate me. And I believed him then.

'But I was wrong. I shouldn't have caved in. *You* picked up the pieces, Jacques, *my* pieces – and I am forever grateful. Sure, there were other flings. But they were the women you bed, not the women you wed – if you take my drift.

'So now I stand before you, a humble man, bearing the resolutions of one of the passions in Maeve's life, as she told it to Maureen, and as Maureen told it to me in Ireland. And you – with Martin

314

and Emma and the Military Man, Sam Hall – you can all bear witness that I have delivered, for *the cause*.'

Sam Hall's provocative voice cuts through Hennessy's emotional hyperbole again. 'Padraic Hennessy, you are a delusional murdering bastard who has used the notion of *the cause* to terrify, maim and kill innocent people for all of your miserable life.'

Hennessy turns quickly this time, his eyes blazing. 'I never killed anyone who didn't deserve to be killed.'

'Like the woman in the shingle grave in Maghery Bay ... like the soldiers sniped in Derry as they tried to keep the peace ... like the innocent mothers and children out shopping, who wore the shrapnel of your car bombs. None of them deserved what they got at your hands.'

'Liar! It was *the cause*. *You* weren't there! You don't understand what it is to be treated like shite, through no fault of your own, just because you were born to particular parents in a particular place. They had to be stopped. And we stopped them. It was groups like ours that brought the *Praatestants* and the Brits to the negotiating table. We won that freedom through our blood. And we have just now used our skills to bring the peace to the Middle East. If you have never had to live at the bottom of the cesspit, then you don't know what it's like. Or why we fought ... with brains ... with guile ... for a cause much bigger than ourselves.'

Sam Hall replies, 'Not with bravery or brains but with cowardice – and bombs and terror – always after the soft targets. You have just been fleeing from the likes of Seamus Gallaher – the man who first held you to account for making his seventeen-year-old daughter pregnant ... and out of wedlock too. You shamed him, his family and Maeve herself. You were just a Derry deadhead who couldn't control his emotions, couldn't keep his dick in his pants – and the planet has been suffering from your weak sense of inferiority ever since. And now you want fucking redemption from an honourable man like Jacques Jazy, who picked up the pieces after you headed for your dishonourable lair.'

Mahmoud Maziq's eyes are wide in disbelief, perhaps because no-one ever speaks to *An Cogar* with words like that – let alone with the derision in the tone.

Slowly, Hennessy's hand emerges from his pocket holding a hand gun.

To which, Sam Hall snorts contemptuously. 'Typical. When the going gets tough, the little man pulls a gun.' At that point, Sam pulls out his SIG automatic and, almost in sync, Emma draws her Glock from her waistband.

Sam's taunting voice continues, 'But you are up against people who can fight back now. We are not unarmed mothers, pushing their babies in prams. So, will you fire first? To be even more dishonourable?'

Padraic Hennessy shakes his seventy-eight-year-old head, making the soft white hair flop from side to side. The gun stays rock steady, despite his age. He glances – almost tearfully – towards Jacques and Martin Jazy still standing by the parchment at the table.

'Tell them, Jacques,' he wails in tense whisper. 'It's not supposed to be like this. I'm here to redeem the honour of two women who worked for *the cause*.' He turns back to Sam. '*You* weren't there. You don't understand. You weren't even a glint in your father's eye when we had to sort out a list of traitors, touts and assassins.'

Hall laughs sardonically, 'And I bet some of them said, *It's not supposed to be like this* … just before you coldly pulled the trigger.'

Hennessy's haunted expression suddenly changes as he looks beyond and behind Sam.

'About time,' his whispering voice seems to carry – even over Louis Armstrong's quiet trad jazz. And the distinctive grunt of Macan Granić comes from the doorway.

'Gun. Down,' the Croatian calls.

With a resigned sigh, Sam and Emma place their pistols carefully on the floor at their feet.

But Sam continues his quest for recording the admissible evidence. 'So Hennessy, is this the knifeman that tortured Bashir Dorda and Nikkos?'

Hennessy's dark eyes seem distant as he speaks. 'Dorda had the locations for the aquifer. We needed them for the peace. The accord wouldn't be agreed without the leverage of the aquifer and that was Sean McSweeney's good work.'

'But Granić amputated Dorda's hand, then slowly sawed off the other hand till he talked. Then he sliced out his victim's tongue.'

'He *had* to tell us. It was for the peace.'

'And Nikkos? He had no information.'

'He knew where we were training. He had to be silenced.'

'He was stabbed in the thighs and biceps, knife twisted into his knees. He was left, bleeding to death in agony.'

'Not my choice. That is Macan's way. There is a bigger cause at stake.'

Mahmoud Maziq crashes to the floor, in a faint, crumpling like a sack of potatoes. In the distraction, both Emma and Sam dive for their weapons on the floor at their feet.

Sam twists and fires at Granić, hitting him in the right shoulder just as the Croatian's gun fires at Emma. He hears his fellow agent give a wincing yelping cry as she fires at Hennessy, hitting him in the leg. The old Irishman's high-pitched scream puts paid to any notions of him always speaking *an cogar*. He collapses to the floor at the foot of the table, as his squealing morphs into a throaty growling moan.

As Sam turns to look at his fellow agent, he sees Emma clutching at a bullet wound in her left arm, her face fast draining of colour. Her pistol has fallen away from her right hand, with the shock. She falls heavily onto her right side on the polished floorboards.

In the blur of the noisy screaming action, Granić – large gleaming knife in his left hand – launches himself through the air at Sam. He is snarling and spitting like an attack dog and his first knife slice is at Sam's gun arm. The SIG falls uselessly away, released in reaction to a superficial cut across his forearm … and the backward fall under the attacker's weight.

From his superior position, despite his dead right shoulder and arm, the frenzied Croatian digs his knees into Sam's legs to get some purchase for his next knife lunge.

Sam prepares to parry again with his fast-bloodying right arm when the dark-clad body of Emma Jazy bursts between them, roaring with almost canine fury. Her attack dagger buries itself in the Croatian's throat, cutting off any grunts – and, with a last burst of her nervous energy, Emma's right hand pushes the dagger to the right, slicing through muscle and artery, before reburying in the throat.

With that final explosion of effort, Emma collapses scarcely conscious, over Sam's lower body, while the Croatian's heavy frame lies over his feet, his life-blood pulsing and spurting out of him.

Sam twists in time to see a shocked white-faced Padraic Hennessy slowly raise his gun in his right hand …

Chapter 65

July, 2013. Rotterdam, The Netherlands

'The Israelis have found the second drill hole into the aquifer,' Sven shouts, having read the message on his phone. 'It did have some toxic substance balanced on a timer over the drop. They are running tests on it now to see what the liquid is. That Irish bastard wasn't bluffing.'

'That's good news that they have it, Sven,' Arthur responds. 'Well done!' His eyes stay glued to his own phone and computer screens. 'Gunnar's team reports that Hennessy and Mahmoud Maziq have gone into the Jazy chalet, with the peace parchment. No sign of the second car that Emma saw leave the Vevey chalet. Martin has texted to confirm that the recording gear is running.'

'But the Israelis haven't signed the parchment, have they? How is that going to happen?' Nil asks. 'They're not at the chalet.'

'I don't know,' replies Arthur. 'I suspect he is trying for Jacques Jazy's endorsement first. Isn't that what this is all about?'

Sven's quiet tones interject, as he lifts his head from his continuing phone messages. 'This might clarify that point. *Mossad* have indicated that the Israeli and British prime ministers have each had to book private flights to Geneva for tomorrow – *bi-lateral trade negotiations* is the official line.'

'And?'

'There, apparently,' Gulbrandson summarises what he is reading. 'According to my *Mossad* contact, several women will produce a parchment to be signed or … I would imagine that Hennessy has some levers he is prepared to pull, if there is any resistance. He has thought this through, hasn't he?'

'*Akhawat?*' Nils asks. 'But *Mossad* will be there waiting for them. No?'

Sven purses his lips before saying, 'Presumably, the women will be untouched and will leave in peace, on pain of Padraic's threats being activated.' The Swede observes sagely, 'Women. Women … but maybe with men in the background?'

'My money would be that Val McSweeney is the main woman, being expected to pull those strings,' Arthur offers. 'She has that tough background. But the Swiss police have taken her into custody. Unless …'

'You expect the Swiss will release her to get the document signed. But how could that ever work … even under close supervision?' Nils asks. 'After the women leave the building, surely *Mossad* would track these people to the ends of the Earth.'

'It depends what these holds are that Padraic Hennessy has over all the parties. Who knows how many operatives Hennessy has? He has already produced people in surprising places.' He pauses. 'Assume for the moment that he can get the Israeli signature, witnessed by the British PM. Our task is still to get Hennessy and his team into a court of law. It will come back to admissible evidence in the end.' Arthur fixes Nils with an assured stare. 'Mark my words.'

Nils glances at his phone. 'Sam and Emma are there at the chalet as well, now,' he says, flatly. 'Just arrived, apparently, so hopefully the right words are being said for your court evidence. Call coming through now.'

'Sam will provoke them. That's one of his many talents. He'll get the story.'

'Oh shit!' Nils shouts, phone to his ear. 'Gunnar reports shooting. They're moving in from the close perimeter. They have a medic in their team. Gaston is still five minutes away.'

'Well, no-one will be escaping past Gunnar's outer defence. They won't get away,' Arthur adds.

Sven's head drops into his patient thinking mode.

'Are you okay, Sven?' Arthur asks.

The Swede answers, 'Just hoping that the price isn't greater than the recorded admissible evidence will be worth.'

And, silently, the three IIB masters of investigation wait out the tension till the next progress report.

Chapter 66

July, 2013. Outside Montreux, Switzerland.

Padraic Hennessy's scream has reverted into a grimacing strangled whisper. He squeezes his right leg with his left hand to dull the pain while he croaks a shout through his contorted mouth. 'Have I righted the wrongs, Jacques? Have I redeemed our women's work?'

Hennessy's gun still points steadily at the huddle of Sam, the unconscious Emma and the fast-dying Macan Granić, whose combined weight is trapping the defenceless Sam Hall's legs.

'You're just mad, Padraic.' Jazy's head quivers as speaks. 'Totally out of it. A fool – if this wasn't all so damned serious.'

The Irishman watches blankly, his mind on Jacques Jazy's words rather than on the IIB agent twisting furiously to free his legs from the unconscious bodies pinning him down. He gazes, with seeming disinterest, at Sam Hall desperately stretching for his fallen SIG pistol.

But the weapon is just beyond Sam's reach.

Louis Armstrong's throaty voice is incongruously chortling out the last few happy bars of *Wonderful World* through the speaker system in the rafters, while this insanely dangerous scene is playing out below.

'Mad, you say.' The old Irishman steadies himself, seated on the polished floor, his back propped against the table base; squealing briefly at a fresh burst of pain and clasping at his bleeding thigh. He looks from Jazy to Sam and back. '*You* weren't fucken there either,

322

Jacques. Don't be a judge when you weren't *fucken* there. Maureen understood. Maeve would have too if the bastards in her family hadn't denied us our happiness. I've given you *peace* – a lasting peace that no-one has *ever* achieved; and they've been trying for centuries. This accord won't fail. I have ensured it. They cannot renege. What greater gift could I have given?' He reaches up to the table-top and pulls his peace accord to his chest.

Jacques' son, Martin, moves between his father and any potential threat but it is immediately obvious that Hennessy only wants his parchment.

Jacques steps past his protective son to peer down at the wounded Hennessy. 'No, Padraic.' The Swiss man's hair falls loosely from side to side as he shakes his head with undoubted negativity – and his eyes drill right into the face of the injured Irishman. 'You and your fanatical cause were the reasons your Maureen died.'

'Lies. The fucken *Praatestants* killed her. In Dublin. They admitted setting off the *bamb*.' His face screws in an agonised silent scream as the pain lances through his wounded leg again.

Jacques Jazy ignores the Irishman's plight. 'Irrelevant. She wouldn't have been there but for you. Maureen went on that *Run* to Donegal to find her past, no matter what spin you put on it now. She might not have expected to find you waiting for her on the beach but she certainly wanted to find out about her mother – and about *you*. Because *you* had deserted her – and *you* were the one still alive. Her mother was gone, rest her soul.'

Jazy shakes his head in frustration at not getting his message understood, before trying his best English to explain, 'All her life, her natural father had deserted her. Don't you understand that? She wouldn't have been in Ireland taking those crazy risks if you had shown any of the normal human compassion of a parent. There. It is said, Padraic. Answer the charge.'

The Irishman's chin drops briefly and then he stares up over the table-top, towards the Swiss Frenchman. He winces again as he grabs at his thigh wound to ride out another sudden surge of pain. 'I always tell the truth, Jacques. I tell it as it is. I have come here seeking redemption – not from a God I don't believe in – but from a man I have always respected. You, Jacques Jazy. *You* are an honourable man. I bring you *peace in the Middle East*. What an achievement for mankind. Give me my redemption!'

'But at what price, Padraic Hennessy? At what price?'

'No, Jacques. No enormous price. It's just about free from price, for this to happen. You're not listening to me. Jacques. I've led a good life. I've achieved; dedicated to the revolutionary cause in Ireland – and in other places too.' His impassioned speech seems to be overriding the agony he is feeling in his wounded leg. 'I stood up for those who couldn't defend themselves – always putting *my* life in danger, being prepared to die for them – and getting resources to others who were being brutalised by the powerful. And the price at those times was always agreed to have been necessary – compared to the huge cost at the hands of the oppressors. The powerful can only abuse us when good men look away. Twas an Irishman who famously said that. Well, I haven't looked away. I'm a good man. I've stood up to be counted. I've risked the cost for the good causes.'

He sighs, almost tearfully, pleading, his eyes begging for Jacques Jazy's acknowledgement; and the pain is clearly returning to his leg after the euphoria of his rhetoric. His voice sounds tired as he continues, 'I lent my skills to seeing that the weak weren't downtrodden, bullied, conned … treated like shite; as my people were, in my youth. And now … now, it seems that you, Jacques Jazy, won't grant me what I most need – the recognition that I have achieved this peace in the name of Maeve and Maureen; that I have acknowledged the pain that needed to be caused by me in the past. Yes, I have killed – but never without a reason. It was a fight for survival or we would all have died. But I have shown – I *am* showing – remorse, regret for the suffering of others, and I was always honest with them. I never lied. They knew what was coming and why.'

He sighs and his face screws up again. His begging eyes look up at the impassive Swiss man, standing tall over him.

Another tired gasp. His strength is being sapped by the effort. He juts his chin and squeezes the bleeding leg again.

'Jacques, I can't change what's been – only what happens now. I've brought you *peace*. You can see that. They won't go back on this. None of them can. They are committed … compromised beyond argument on one hand, and with unrepeatable benefits on the other. This will work. I have set it up to succeed. You're a revolutionary. You've printed the protest flyers of resistance groups, for decades. We're on the same side.'

But the elderly Swiss calmly shakes his head, again. 'I don't want peace delivered by threats, intimidation, violence. I want peace through reasoned argument, not by the gun of the gangster. As you say, my life has been dedicated to protest. But not to killing innocents, blackmailing countries, seizing children from their parents. That's not my type of protest and I won't endorse it, now or ever. So take your thugs and your parchment and *get out* of my home. You have caused me too much pain over the years.'

Hennessy's head nods slowly in a new realisation. He has listened and attempted to persuade. 'I tried, Jacques. I have tried – but maybe I should have let Seamus Gallaher hang me all these years ago? Is that what you're saying?' He looks at the Swiss man who towers immovable above him. 'Yes. It probably fucken is.'

He drops the parchment to the floor at his side and nods at the Louis Armstrong music still floating through the room. As if acknowledging Satchmo growling about a shark bite and being rash, he gives a wry smile.

'Rash …?' Hennessy whispers, with another look upwards at the voice from the rafters. He snatches a glance at Sam Hall, writhing his legs almost free and stretching out hard to reach his pistol and then pauses briefly in thought. 'Well, t'ere's no love nor time for the old Padraic. It's over.'

Then, with surprising speed, Hennessy puts the gun barrel in his mouth and pulls the trigger. The shock of the shot echoes in the cavernous room. His blood and brains spatter thickly over the fine calligraphy on the parchment.

Jacques and Martin stand motionless at the table. Maziq still lies in his faint. Sam has finally kicked the dead Macan off his feet and is gently laying the exhausted Emma on the floor, to tend her wound – as Gunnar Andersson and his team enter the building with confidence and at pace.

'Good to see you,' says Sam. 'Took your time.'

'It's a few minutes from the perimeter.' Gunnar replies dryly. 'You've been handling it, anyway. Did you get the recording?'

'Yeh.' A wave of tiredness swamps him, as the adrenalin leaves his system. 'I think so.'

* * * *

Gunnar's medic treats Emma's arm as she lies on a stretcher.

She tugs weakly at Sam's arm and whispers urgently, 'I need you to take my camera from the webbing. Photograph Granić where he lies with my dagger still in his throat. There is a man in Cyprus that I promised … I would bring the killer of Nikkos back to face Greek justice or give proof of his death. Can you photograph Hennessy too? Sean McSweeney is already in the camera. The Cypriots know what all three looked like. They saw each of them with the crawling men in the Kyrenia Range.'

* * * *

'It's over now, Emma. You can rest.' Jacques Jazy stands with Martin beside Emma's stretcher as she is being ushered out to hospital. 'Maureen would have been so proud of you – as are we – Martin and I. And I'm sure that your brother William will be too, when he hears, named as he is after the William Maclean in that old saga with Maureen in the Lebanon.

He holds Emma's right hand in a fatherly grasp. A rare tear beads in the graceful old man's eye as he speaks on. 'Your mother, Simone, was always made of tough stuff and so was my first wife, Maeve. A chapter in the Jazy family may well have closed, although perhaps the rest of the book is yet to be written. And listen to old Louis giving us advice over the speakers. Love you, Emma.'

Old Satchmo is still singing away – but now on a new track. His gravelly tones echo through the polished wooden rafters. They all stop, feeling the ambience of the words – about the wonder of needing nothing more than love.

'Just like at Maureen's funeral,' Jazy says, with another tear just glistening in his left eye. 'Old Bill Maclean couldn't get over that song – nor our Maureen. *He* never found another love either – and that was the last song Louis ever recorded. He himself died a few weeks after.'

Jacques stands tall with his big son, Martin – a quiet caring gentle man – as Emma is wheeled away, just managing a faint encouraging smile to her family.

Sam Hall looks down at the bloody mess of Granić's body, the pale face swamped by the mass of blood, pooled and congealing under his dark hair, his distinctive eyes in a frozen stare.

Then Sam turns his gaze over to the broken form of the old Irish revolutionary, sprawled over the bloodied peace accord parchment. Its scribe – Mahmoud Maziq – is seated, sipping water, with a wet compress over his brow and the white fringe of hair.

'You can stop the recording now, I think, Jacques. We have all the evidence we need.'

Chapter 67

July, 2013. Nicosia, Cyprus

'She did the job on him alright,' Ari utters with horror and pride. 'A tough lady.'

Sam Hall sits with some of the same group who had helped him and Emma collect information, although their leader – Nikkos – whom he had met only once in the orange plantation is the very noticeable void in the meeting.

The sanded white kitchen table-top has not changed since Emma sat there, only a few days before, making her promise to Thea and her group that the death of Nikkos would be avenged.

The large colour photographs are graphic. One shows Macan Granić's bloodied corpse with its partially-severed neck and Emma's assault dagger still embedded to the hilt. Another shows the lifeless, drained face of the old man who had started the whole saga – Padraic Hennessy, the aged revolutionary fighter, with his brains splattered from the back of his head, over the parchment peace accord which had been intended to earn him redemption. A third shows a trussed Sean McSweeney, with a gory bandage on his shoulder, looking beaten and sore.

'Emma couldn't make it herself. The wound to her arm is very bad; the bullet broke the bone, chewed some nerves and muscle … but she will heal with time and luck. She wanted to be sure that Cristof knew that she had kept her promise.

'*Eennaion keeria*. Brave lady,' Cristof offers, his serious face lightened by the trace of vindication on his lips. 'Nikkos is avenged. What you think, Galen? She has done it – Cypriot way?'

Galen nods. 'Nikkos was a brave man. He didn't deserve the way he died.' He glances quickly across to Thea to make sure *she* is alright – but she is nodding solemnly with respect.

'Emma promised.' Thea Spyrou speaks the words with zeal. 'We trusted. She delivered. He is avenged. But the question is still *Why?* Why did Nikkos and the Egyptian, Dorda ... why did they have to die?'

Sam speaks quietly. 'It was a mad old revolutionary with a dream to forge peace in the Middle East. He thought he could get the Arabs and the Jews to agree to peace in the Palestine-Israel area – a two-state solution.'

Cristof spits the words out, 'Two-state is never solution. Just more anger, more pain. We want *enosis* here in Cyprus – a one-state solution, for us – not to be plaything of old empires. The British don't have empire either – nor do Greeks. The Turks no longer rule here. Why do they throw their settlements onto our island? How could that ever work?'

Jason joins in with, 'We could all just live together. It used to happen before the empire builders came in; with their armies, with their superior attitudes or their useless compromises which please no-one. And it will be no different over in Palestine or Syria or Iraq – or any of them. It needs respect.'

'*I* want to take over here,' grumbles Cristof. 'The only respect I want is theirs – for us.'

Sam smiles, perhaps too indulgently. 'Isn't that part of the problem?'

'How would *you* know?' Cristof snaps back. 'You aren't *here*, living it.'

'Okay. Fair point. Has the fear stopped? The people being bashed and stabbed?'

'It is quiet,' Galen replies, ignoring Cristof. 'I have spoken to some.'

'What was it about?'

'They were creating a base here; establishing who was – how you say it – *top dog*. Then the frightened ones stole for them or were bashed. Houses in the Turkish sector. Money, passports, credit cards. Small stuff. And blaming it on Greek-Cypriots.' He spits at the empty fireplace.

'And you want one state with these swine?' Cristof's spit follows Galen's into the grate.

'And the beys and sheiks who were brought in?' Sam persists. 'What did they want?'

'Nikkos thought they were being made offers by *The Cat*,' Ari suggests. 'If there was to be fighting on the mainland, they would stir uprising, the revolution ... in return for prizes, land, property, gang allegiances ... maybe overthrow of governments. It is happening all through here from Tunis to Basra. The ones in charge are really gangsters, after power over others or retaining hereditary rights – whatever justification they use. It is all lies. We know that; to let them control people. But not everyone sees through it. They feel too marginalised, on the outer, ignored. They fall for the dream, a promise, a mantra, hope ... but it is not there for them, for very long.'

'Could the old man have been threatening them too?'

'With what?'

'Stirring old hatreds. If they weren't to be in it, then they would be the ones receiving the attacks. Threats of terror. He seems to have been good at that.'

'Good, you say?' Cristof rises from his seat. 'What pale-face did to Nikkos was evil, bad ... never good.'

'Whoa! I meant that they caused fear. That's all,' Sam replies. 'Emma has rid you of that fear. The evil ones are dead.' And he flicks at the photographs on the table to remind them all.

At which point, Thea intervenes. 'Nikkos would have been honoured that you have come back, Sam, with proof that his murder has been avenged. Here, we will carry on our fight for *enosis* in our own way, remembering all the sacrifices. Please thank Emma, from all of us. We really are truly grateful. We hope she recovers. Maybe we will see her again, some day.'

'Yes. *Eennaion keeria*. Brave lady,' Cristof agrees, with a sheepish look at Thea and the faintest trace of a smile for Sam.

Chapter 68

July, 2013. Rotterdam, The Netherlands

'So what's the wrap up, Nils?' Sven asks, in their Maasboulevard headquarters. 'On the whole Hennessy business, from the *Mediterranean Run* to his ignominious exit from our world?'

The operations manager, Houweling, is back to his methodical evidence-cataloguing self as he checks the lists on his screens.

'On a human resources level, Emma Jazy is unfit for combat service and will be out of that role for some months until, or unless, her left arm rebuilds its strength. But she will be back with us soon, in an analyst role. That should bring a current field perspective to our deliberations.'

'Good,' Arthur notes. 'Good. A sensible resolution. And the McSweeneys? What of them?'

'They're all in custody for at least kidnapping and assault. In Sean's case, add conspiracy to commit mass murder – with the attempt on the aquifer. They are apparently plea bargaining like mad, giving up all sorts of stories, names of gun runners, terrorists, activists – anything to reduce the sentences.'

'Another good outcome.' Arthur seems a happy man as he ticks off his questions. 'Where are they? In whose jurisdictions?'

'Val McSweeney is in Germany again. Extradited back to Heidelberg. She will be processed quickly, along with her former Libyan assistants – more jail time for abduction, at least. Michael McSweeney is in Croatia with a couple of his assistants. Again, it appears he will do anything to avoid implied grief at the hands of *Gospodja* Sanja Granić. She apparently hates him with a ferocious passion, understandably. Years of pent-up dreams of revenge. That really is his *pigeons coming home to roost* – poetic. He knows she will testify against him, and do anything she can to make his life the misery that she has endured.

'Sean McSweeney is being held in Switzerland. The Israelis perhaps are not keen to try him in their country because it might expose a potential vulnerability that they'd rather not have publicised too much. Worst case, though, it will come here to The Hague and *we* will have to prosecute it. But it can still be done quietly. The press won't need to know how close they actually came to pulling off their intentions. Who would know what the Israeli response would have been, if it had actually come to the final decision making?'

'Okay. And Mahmoud Maziq?'

'Switzerland will deal with him too – leniently, I would expect – for forgery. He's an old man.'

'Old men can still be crooks. Wasn't he going to be there when the Israelis signed the accord?'

'Indeed,' Nils responds, thoughtfully. 'But he was more of a prisoner himself, I think, than an instigator. And the French are happy to leave him to the rehabilitation processes of the Swiss. They will at least know where he is and what he is up to.

'Now, a turn-up has been the last will and testament of one Padraic Hennessy. Back in the PIRA days, Padraic was a respected fundraiser for *the cause*. He travelled the world, soliciting funds.

'Perhaps that respect was misplaced because a lot of it was deposited in his own numbered accounts in Liechtenstein, not Switzerland where the IRA loot was. Through the will, he has disclosed account numbers, passwords and the location of the old deposit box keys. The will was lodged with a Republican lawyer in Dublin.

'You see, Padraic had no offspring other than Maureen. No wonder, his heart would have flipped to think that she might have had a son. So, in his redemptive sentimental state, he has left a bucket-load of money to lots of groups who will be wondering what they did to deserve it – and indeed, whether or not the money is legitimate.

'For example, there is money to go to Irish jazz clubs, to the Louis Armstrong Museum in Queens, New York, to Jacques Jazy and his family – accompanied by the notation, *With thanks for doing what I should have been doing*. And then there are others on a huge list of protest organisations – plus scholarships for young people in Derry and other named places. The McSweeneys are on the list – but the court will impound their shares, I would think. Then, it is just a catalogue of small philanthropic gestures – including to a Sanja Granić.'

'Well, well,' Arthur smiles. 'So he *did* know about Michael's indiscretion. Or much worse than a simple indiscretion, more than likely – from when they were in Dubrovnik. He could have shown that generosity to the mother when Macan was young. It might have made the difference as she struggled with the challenges of such a complex child. Still, better late than never – easing the wronged woman's pain just a little now, eh?

'Maybe old Padraic really *was* remorseful – eventually – as he wrote his final testament. And it's definitely better that the money goes to lots of good gestures than being in the hands of gun runners and smugglers on *The Runs*.'

Sven gives his provocative grin. 'And the bigger question of Middle East peace? Has it just been consigned to history?'

'Perhaps. Perhaps not.' Arthur volunteers his perspective. 'For all his insanity, Padraic Hennessy has at least shown one way forward. With ex-British PMs and US Presidents keen to assert their diplomacy skills anew, they might look at Hennessy's starting point – at least to the conditions he stipulated – to force each party to be responsible for the success of the other. That's a pretty good commitment to make sure it happens.

'They have to get beyond arguing about who has been victimised most. It has to be about co-existence – about peace. Really, they can have peace or they can try for justice – but justice in itself won't bring peace, only a revisiting of unappeasable pain. Even to start, they have to meet and listen to the other side's points of view, to walk in the other man's shoes – and then be prepared to draw a line, reconcile the past to what it was, and move forward together with a clean slate … or parchment even. Something has to break the cycle – a circuit breaker.'

'But,' Nils shakes his pragmatic head, 'that's a big ask. Hennessy left nothing signed. The peace accord parchment is left unreadable, covered with Hennessy's blood. There is nothing binding any of the parties, now.'

'Oooh! On the other hand …' Arthur smiles at his enigmatic best, 'they don't know if old Padraic hasn't left other time-bombs to be triggered by some means, as yet unidentified – as leverage – if the peace process doesn't go ahead. He was pretty clever with his first intimidators. He had enough clout to get two prime ministers to book urgent flights to Geneva – presumably for the Israeli one to sign the agreement and the other, the British one, to witness. And he released the hostages very quickly – in apparent good faith. Didn't that seem very strange to you all? It did to me.

'I would be pretty sure that he would have other tricks up his sleeve if any of the parties – Arabs included – were to renege on the deal, further down the track. He was very sure that the sheiks and beys would carry through on their commitment. Why do you think he was so sure? He has to have had something that we don't yet know about. He took his time to plan it all out.

'As for the Israelis, what if there was another drill hole – a third one, as yet undisclosed, for example? And he has left the trigger for that with someone else. Chew on that. It would be worth asking the Swiss to press Sean McSweeney very heavily on that before deciding on any plea bargain, with him. I'm sure *Mossad* will be working hard on the *cat people* in their care.'

Arthur has everyone's full attention, so he keeps on with his speculative scenario. 'You don't believe me? Think on this then. Emma always thought there were more people in the Kyrenia cave than turned up in Israel, didn't she? Who were they and where are they now? Perhaps there were also more women in *Akhawat* – if that group really existed – than turned up in Cavtat? Are they the Arab key? Are they the insurance that they will follow through on whatever was arranged, one on one, in Nicosia?'

'Arabs attacking fellow Arabs?' Nils queries.

'We've been down that path,' replies Sven. 'Arabs are not a homogenous group, all agreeing with each other. There's as much division there as in any cultural or revolutionary movement. There's a huge history of Arabs killing Arabs over family or tribal disputes, over religion or old caliphates, expansionist domination, rebel uprisings, just sheer power plays. Arthur is right. Look at the uprisings in the current Arab Spring. Just a thought.'

Blair chimes in to emphasise what he and Sven have already surmised, 'Look at the number of Palestinian resistance groups, as an example. It is not just one resistor. They all want their own way to fight back against oppression. They all want the kudos of fixing the problem … or dying for *the cause* in the process. And Hennessy lived that very same type of life with all the Irish breakaway gangs. There were dozens of them … on both sides of that conflict. He would understand that scenario so much better than most – playing one off against another; meeting with them one at a time, never all together.

'So, you never quite know, eh? Arab women might well be the ones to get under the guard of the chiefs and beys – to be part of an unknown threat; a hold over the Arabs clans if they don't comply with their pledges. That was Hennessy's business over the decades, his *modus operandi* – intimidation, stand-over tactics; cold manipulation backed up by maiming and killing. The third drill hole perhaps? What if something as lethal as that is still there, in place, just waiting … for the right moment? Was there nothing about this in his will, even written in a coded form?'

'Not that we've been told,' advises the operations manager.

'Okay. My best guess is that there would be other levers in place. Maybe the clue has been left elsewhere. Perhaps, whoever has it does not recognise the significance. But, in time …? So, if I were you, Nils, I would watch very carefully to see whether or not both the Palestinians and the Israelis don't sit down around a table very soon – albeit posturing for their interests – at least until they are very sure that another chill wind of fear won't take them by surprise. Look out for Palestinian prisoners to be released and gestures of concession all round. And, if my earlier premise of the third hole is right, it could come up much later, five years from now, ten … perhaps? But, if the threat is activated, it could bring them all to the table and settle a deal. Then, we who know what has happened, will give old Padraic a backhanded *thank you.*'

And Sven adds, 'My bet would be that the US Secretary of State would be the mediator, for the cameras, but the real progress will be happening very quietly behind the scenes, with no announcement, just subtle incremental changes – and no loss of face, for either party.'

'Well, I hope you're both right that it will be resolved in time.' Houweling smiles his support.

'So,' Sven pauses to change the focus. 'Emma will be in here working with us soon?' He looks positively cheery at the prospect.

'A few weeks away,' Nils endorses, checking something on his screens before glancing up at Arthur. 'She is looking for permission – from *you*, Arthur, I assume – to access Bill Maclean's tapes where they relate to her 'step-sister', Maureen, the Lebanon and *The Run*. She wants to write it up so that the context isn't lost. To capture the way people were thinking at the time – the mindset of that era. And a love story which has stretched on forty years after her passing.'

'A good thought.' Arthur looks unusually reflective as he mulls it over. 'It certainly was a different world back in the seventies, still with relic attitudes of the past. There were no computers nor electronic social media and memories of the hardships of world wars lingered on in family behaviours. But with the young ones feeling the need to struggle and protest, they challenged the imperialist attitudes of the powerful, in Vietnam, for example – which was shown daily in vivid colour on newscasts – feeling the release from community protocols by the freedom movements of the sixties.

'Old Bill Maclean would approve of Emma's idea, I think. He would never have been able to write the story himself – too painful to revisit that in his own hand – although he did talk eloquently and emotionally on the recordings. Growing older seems to play away at the consciences of those who had to make hard decisions in their youth and working lives. Maybe, in a perverse way, Maureen was spared that – to be forever young and valiant in old men's memories, eh?'

All three sit with their own thoughts for a few seconds before Sven asks (as if perhaps he shouldn't), 'And, Nils, the one you haven't mentioned – Sam Hall. Is he still in Cyprus?' He wears a quiet smile that seems to question whether or not he really does want the answer.

'At this moment, Sven, Sam Hall is en route to Dubrovnik with a promise to keep to a lady, as I understand it. And he has asked that we – that is *you* both, I imagine – have to tell Goran Bikić to go home very soon … and give his overworked daughter some leave from their family legal business.

'And when I asked Sam if he *was* really working very hard when he was in Croatia, he just replied, with his impish grin, *How could you understand? You weren't there!*'

About the Author

Jim Reay is a former high-school principal and senior public servant; now a writer of short stories and mysteries. Born a Scot, he brings a range of perspectives to his stories; from Europe – as well as his love of history, learning and culture.

www.jimreaywriter.net

Other titles by Jim Reay

Searching for Siobhan (2016)
ISBN 978-1-8758728-9-3 (paperback)
National Library of Australia Catalogue in Publication
Missing persons – Investigation – Queensland – Brisbane – History.
Detective and mystery stories.
Brisbane (Qld) – Fiction.

The Chess Board (2015)

ISBN 978-0-9943778-0-7

National Library of Australia Catalogue in Publication

Detective and Mystery Stories.

Suspense Fiction.

Stereotypes (Social Psychology) – Fiction.

Aboriginal Australians, Queensland – Fiction.

Queensland Fiction.

Catching Legends (Young Adult – 2015)

ISBN 978-1-8758728-8-6

National Library of Australia Catalogue in Publication

Official Secrets – Moral and Ethical Aspects – Fiction.

Available nationally and internationally on-line from: Rams Skull Press http://ramsskullpress.com/shop/; and in good bookshops on request.

Author's Note

If you want to know about the back story to William Maclean, then read *Catching Legends*. Details above.

www.ingramcontent.com/pod-product-compliance
Lightning Source LLC
Chambersburg PA
CBHW070802180626
46818CB00001B/70